Holly Hepburn is the much-loved author of commercial women's fiction. She lives near London with her grey tabby cat, Portia. They both have an unhealthy obsession with Marmite. Follow Holly on Twitter @HollyH_Author.

*Also by Holly Hepburn*

A Year at the Star and Sixpence
The Picture House by the Sea
A Year at Castle Court
Last Orders at the Star and Sixpence

# The Picture House By the Sea

**holly hepburn**

SIMON & SCHUSTER

London · New York · Sydney · Toronto · New Delhi

A CBS COMPANY

First published in Great Britain by Simon & Schuster UK Ltd, 2017

This paperback edition published 2020



3 5 7 9 10 8 6 4

Simon & Schuster UK Ltd
1st Floor
222 Gray's Inn Road
London WC1X 8HB

Simon & Schuster Australia, Sydney
Simon & Schuster India, New Delhi

www.simonandschuster.co.uk
www.simonandschuster.com.au
www.simonandschuster.co.in

A CIP catalogue record for this book is available from the British Library

Paperback ISBN: 978-1-4711-9259-3
eBook ISBN: 978-1-4711-6290-9
Audio ISBN: 978-1-4711-7105-5

This book is a work of fiction. Names, characters, places and incidents are either a product of the author's imagination or are used fictitiously. Any resemblance to actual people living or dead, events or locales is entirely coincidental.

Printed anc … , CR0 4YY

*For my grandmother, Agnes,*
*who introduced me to so many classic films*

# PART ONE

## Brief Encounter

# Chapter One

'Ladies and gentlemen, this train will shortly be arriving at Bodmin Parkway. If you are leaving the train at the station, please ensure you take all your personal belongings with you.'

Gina Callaway stretched, then reached for her coat. The journey from London had gone faster than she'd expected; a harassed-looking young mother had slid into the seat opposite just before they'd pulled out of Paddington, with a red-faced screaming baby clutched to her shoulder, and Gina had resigned herself to a noisy few hours. But the baby had settled down quickly, lulled by the motion of the train, and his mother started to look less harassed, especially after Gina surprised her with a tea from the buffet car just after Exeter St Davids. She'd murmured her thanks but hadn't felt obliged to talk; in fact, they'd travelled in companionable silence, both gazing out of the window as the tracks came so close to the sea that it seemed as though they were travelling by boat instead of a train. And now, as Gina stood up to leave, they exchanged a fleeting smile, two almost-strangers whose paths would never cross again.

The train stopped at the platform. Gina swung her case out of the door and onto the concrete below. A cloud of billowing steam drifted on the air, causing her to stop in confusion: admittedly it had been an age since she'd been to Bodmin station, but she was sure the Penzance-bound train usually stopped at Platform One. Yet here she was on Platform Two, right next to a crowd of day-trippers snapping pictures of the steam train that ran along the Bodmin and Wenford heritage line from Platform Three. It wasn't a major problem, just an inconvenience to have to carry her case up the stairs and down again on the other side before she could get into a cab to her grandparents' house in Polwhipple. If she made it through the throng of tourists clogging up the platform, that was.

She dodged out of one photograph and swerved around another cluster of cameras and smartphones just as the old-fashioned train let out a shrill whistle. A thick cloud of steam burst from its chimney and billowed across the adjoining platform, driven by a gust of wind. Gina blinked into the breeze and gasped at a sudden sharp pain in one eye.

She stopped mid-stride and let go of her suitcase, causing the man behind to mutter a curse as he was forced to change course. 'Ow,' Gina mumbled, as tears began to stream down one cheek. '*Ow*. Bloody hell, that stings.'

What she needed was a mirror, she decided, trying in vain not to blink as her eye burned. She rummaged in her bag with one hand, searching for a compact, but her eye was streaming so much that by the time she found it, she could barely focus and the other eye was swimming too.

'Excuse me, can I help?'

The voice was deep and male, with an unmistakably Cornish lilt. Gina swung towards the speaker. She got a jumbled impression of fair hair and height through her blurred vision. 'Oh no, I'm fine. It's just a piece of grit, I expect.'

'Here, take this.' A cool fold of cotton was pressed into her hand. 'Don't worry, it's clean.'

Gina's eyelid twitched, causing another needle of pain. 'Thank you,' she said, raising her tiny mirror once again and squinting as she dabbed at her watery eye with the thick white handkerchief. 'You're very kind.'

'It's no trouble,' he replied.

Gina twisted the corner of the handkerchief into a point and eased the black speck from the edge of her lower lashes. She blinked, causing another stream of tears, and the stinging lessened. 'I think I've got it.'

Now that her eyeball didn't feel as though it was under attack, she could see the owner of the handkerchief better. He was tall – perhaps a little over six feet – and tanned, with short, sun-streaked hair that suggested plenty of time spent outdoors. His eyes were blue, like the Cornish seas on a sunny day. He was very easy to look at, Gina decided; if her sight hadn't been compromised, she might even have kept on looking.

'Agony, isn't it? Even a grain of sand feels like a razor blade,' he said, sounding sympathetic. 'Are you sure you don't want me to take a look?'

In London, Gina would have taken his persistence as a chat-up attempt, but there was nothing more than friendly concern on his face. His accent was disarming too, Gina thought, all softness and warmth and long vowels. It had been a while since she'd been to Cornwall, and hearing that unmistakable burr again now summoned up memories of sun-drenched summers spent on Polwhipple beach and endless ice-cream cornets from her grandfather's ice-cream stall on the seafront. It was almost like being fifteen again.

Gina gave herself a mental shake. She might be back in Cornwall but she was very different from her teenage self. 'I'll be okay,' she said, pushing the handkerchief towards him. 'Thanks, though.'

The man shrugged. 'Why don't you hang on to it? There are toilets a bit further along the platform in case you want to splash some water into your eye but the tissue they use disintegrates as soon as you look at it.' He offered her a lop-sided smile, that faded into a thoughtful frown, as though there was something he wanted to say but wasn't sure how. Then he seemed to realise he was staring and gave her a brisk nod instead. 'All the best then.'

With a final flash of summer blue, he turned and vanished

into another burst of steam. 'Bye,' Gina called after him. 'Thanks again.'

She stared into the wispy white clouds for a second or two, half expecting him to rematerialise, then tucked the hankie into her handbag and started along the platform once more. It was like something out of an old film, she mused, as her case bumped along behind her: a handsome stranger helps a woman to remove some grit from her eye amid clouds of steam from a nearby train. Except that if this had been a movie, they'd have gone for coffee and begun a torrid love affair that could only end in disaster. Gina shook her head wryly as she walked; all those Saturday mornings she'd spent at the Palace, the old picture house in Polwhipple, while visiting her grandparents each summer had given her a love of the dramatic that had never quite let her go. Even now, she liked nothing more than settling back in front of a giant screen with a tub of popcorn and letting a film roll over her. Unfortunately, it was a pleasure her boyfriend, Max, did not share, meaning that the cinema was somewhere she went with her friends, not him. And girls' nights out were becoming more and more infrequent as her friends settled down and started families. I'll end up going on my own soon, Gina thought wryly. It'll be just like old times . . .

The station toilets smelled faintly of citrus-scented air-freshener and coal smoke. Gina gave her eye a careful rinse, flushing the last few specks of dust from her lash-line. Satisfied that it was all gone, she restored the cat flick eyeliner and black mascara her tears had displaced, and smoothed her long black hair before heading to the ticket hall. Beyond it, there would be a line of taxis; one of them would be more than happy to transport her to Polwhipple. Unless—

She glanced across at Platform Three, just as the piercing whistle of the steam train split the air. Gina hesitated. She *could* take the heritage line to Boscarne Junction, the way she had when she was younger, and ask her grandmother to pick her up from the much-nearer station. It was only a short drive from Polwhipple and the whole journey might even be quicker, given how snarled up the roads between Bodmin and the coast could become, even in March; all it took was a tractor trundling along a narrow country road to slow traffic to a crawl. And there was another, less practical reason to take the steam train; what if her chivalrous stranger was on board? It had been good of him to stop, unlike the commuters she travelled with every day in London, who were so intent on getting to and from work that they barely took the time to look around. She could thank him properly for his kindness.

She peered into the ticket office, wondering how much a one-way ticket to Boscarne might cost nowadays. But then a burst of steam wafted across the train tracks and the whistle screeched again, followed by the *chug-chug-chug* of a bygone time as the train at Platform Three began to move along the tracks.

The guard behind the glass window of the ticket office leaned forwards. 'There's another one at 16:20, if that helps.'

Gina shook her head. 'Don't worry,' she said, forcing away her memories of the rich velvet-covered seats and walnut-panelled doors inside each compartment of the old train. 'I'll take a taxi.'

'Where to?' the driver asked, once he'd hoisted her case into the boot and settled back behind the wheel.

'Polwhipple, please,' Gina told him, picturing her grandparents' immaculate grey-stoned farmhouse with its sturdy outbuildings tucked away behind. 'The Old Dairy on Tregarran Street. No, wait—'

If she checked into her hotel first there was less chance Nonna would insist that she stayed with them. As much as Gina loved her grandparents and treasured her memories of the summers she'd spent with them, they could be a little bit overpowering and she was thirty-one, not fifteen; she needed her own space.

'Could you take me to the Scarlet Hotel, in Mawgan Porth, please?'

Nodding, the driver pulled away and Gina settled back into the seat, wondering what she'd find when she eventually did get to her grandparents' house. Neither of them were frail – until recently they'd both been in perfect health – but Gina knew she'd begun to take their vigour for granted. Had it really been more than a year since she'd been down to see them? Even that had only been a fleeting weekend visit; she'd meant to go again but work had kept her busy – there always seemed to be one more client to accept, one more event to manage. Being freelance meant it was harder to justify time off and Cornwall seemed so far away, even though it didn't take that long by train. But as soon as she'd heard her grandfather had broken his leg she'd known she would go. Ferdie Ferrelli himself would never have asked for help – he was from proud Italian stock – but his wife, Gina's Nonna, was nothing if not practical. She knew that she couldn't run the dairy and produce enough ice-cream to satisfy customer demand, so she'd put out an SOS. And given that Gina was the only member of her family still living in the UK, she'd known there was only one answer, even though it meant taking a three-month break from her own work. She'd forgotten more than she ever knew about ice-cream, other than which flavours she liked to eat, and she had even less experience of running a food concession in a seaside cinema. But still she hadn't had the heart to say no. Not to her much-loved Nonna and Nonno, who'd given her so many perfect Polwhipple memories years ago.

All of which meant there was a small niggling knot of worry in Gina's stomach about how the coming hours, days and weeks were going to pan out. Ferdie would be overjoyed to see her, until he found out why she was there; he was famous for refusing to accept help, even from his own flesh and blood. He'd built his business up from scratch after arriving from Italy in the 1950s, and he'd run it single-handedly ever since, although Gina suspected her grandmother did far more behind the scenes than Ferdie was prepared to admit. If Gina was going to win her grandfather round, she'd have to convince him she could do the job. Ferdie Ferrelli had never been easy to convince about anything, but he was especially set in his ways where his beloved gelato was concerned. Gina was going to need all her charm and determination to persuade him to let her help.

# Chapter Two

'Gina! *Bella mia*!'

Elena Ferrelli wrapped Gina in a generous hug on the doorstep of the pretty grey house they'd lived in for more than fifty years. 'It is so good to see you. Have you grown?'

Gina smiled into her grandmother's jet-black hair, enjoying the sensation of being in her arms again. No one said her name in quite the same way as Nonna – the accent she'd never lost turned it into something elegant and exotic. 'It's good to see you too, Nonna. And I think I've finished growing, unless you mean my waistline.'

Elena stepped back to survey Gina from head to toe and plucked at her coat. 'Of course not, there is nothing of you. Do you even take the time to eat in that city of yours?' She sniffed and shook her head. 'But it doesn't matter – you are here now and I can take proper care of you. We'll soon have some meat on those bones.'

Gina laughed; for all Nonna's proclamations, she herself

was a trim seventy-something who thought nothing of donning her Lycra to join the surfers for beach yoga in the summer months. But she also loved to cook and expected the ultimate mark of respect from those she fed – an empty plate. 'Don't get any ideas, Nonna,' Gina said, patting her arm affectionately. 'I'm here to work, remember?'

'But you still have to eat,' Elena said, unperturbed. 'Now, come in and see Nonno. He is rude and bad-tempered but you will put a smile on his sour old face.'

A flutter of nerves flapped in Gina's stomach. How was her grandfather going to take the news that she was here essentially to take over his business?

Elena was frowning. 'Where are your cases? Surely you can't have everything you need for three months in that tiny handbag?'

Gina took a deep breath. Before she faced Ferdie, she had another minefield to negotiate. 'I've checked into a hotel,' she said, bracing herself. 'I know the plan was to stay here, but you've got enough to do taking care of Nonno and it seemed like the sensible thing to do. This way, we all get a bit of space and won't get under each other's feet.'

And I have somewhere to escape to when your well-meaning interference is driving me crazy, she thought but didn't say. It didn't matter, though; Elena was still looking at her as though she'd just been insulted. 'A hotel? How could you do such a thing? My own granddaughter staying in a hotel when there is a perfectly good bed here – people will think there is bad blood between us when they find out.'

Gina smothered a groan; she might have known Nonna would be predominantly concerned by what her friends and neighbours would think. 'Of course they won't.'

'And how can I look after you when you are not here?' Elena went on indignantly. 'You might as well have stayed in London.'

'It's just for a few days,' Gina said, doing her best to soothe her grandmother's ruffled feathers. 'Besides, it's a treat for me – a little present to myself. There's a spa and a pool and hot tubs on the clifftop overlooking the sea.'

Elena let out a ladylike snort. 'Sounds dangerous to me.' She threw Gina a hard look and then sighed. 'But I suppose it won't hurt, as long as you come home to us in time.'

Gina hesitated; once she'd found her feet, she planned to start looking for a reasonable holiday home to rent. But there was no need to mention that now. 'Thank you, Nonna.'

'Hmmm,' Elena said, leading her inside. 'Goodness knows what your grandfather will say.'

Ferdie Ferrelli was sitting in his favourite armchair, one leg encased in plaster and raised on a footstool as he studied *La Gazzetta dello Sport*. He looked up as she entered and his lined, olive-skinned face became wreathed in smiles. 'Gina! This is a surprise.'

He reached for his crutches. Gina hurried forwards. 'No need to get up, Nonno,' she said, bending down to hug him. 'I hear you've been in the wars.'

'Nothing so heroic,' Ferdie growled, looking disgusted. 'I slipped off a ladder while painting the windowsills. My fault.'

Gina shook her head. There was no point in suggesting he shouldn't have been climbing a ladder in the first place; Ferdie was seventy-eight on the outside but twenty-eight in his head and he liked to take care of things himself. Paying someone else to paint the house would never have entered into his thoughts. 'It was an accident,' she said, smiling. 'Even you have those sometimes.'

He grunted, as though unconvinced. 'It was stupid. But enough about me – what brings you here? Your nonna and I thought you had forgotten where we lived.'

Elena stepped forwards. 'Why don't I make us some coffee? Gina has come straight here from the train and you know what dishwater they serve aboard those.'

Gina smiled. Her grandmother's cappuccino was the stuff of dreams; strong and creamy with the perfect amount of froth, and her espresso could power the national grid. 'That would be lovely, thank you.'

'It's no trouble,' Elena said. 'And perhaps I can tempt you with some fresh biscotti. We may as well start as we mean to go on.'

'Nonna plans to fatten me up,' Gina said, settling onto the butter-soft leather sofa as her grandmother left the room.

'So she should,' Ferdie replied. 'You'll never get that young man of yours to propose when you look like a stick insect.'

And so it begins, Gina thought, half in amusement and half in resignation. If anyone wondered why she'd booked into a hotel, here was at least part of the reason. She took a deep breath. 'I don't want him to propose, Nonno. I like things the way they are.'

Ferdie gazed at her with unhidden reproach. 'Of course, I forget that you modern couples don't agree with the sanctity of marriage. It's all speed-dating and bed-hopping these days.'

She raised her eyebrows. 'Hardly that – Max and I have been together for more than two years now. We just don't see the need to get married.'

'So you don't love each other.'

'We do,' Gina insisted, then heard the defensiveness in her voice and softened her tone. She didn't want to have the same well-worn argument she'd had the last time she'd visited her grandparents, and the time before that. Not when she knew there was another, more important battle looming in the very near future. 'We *do* love each other,' she repeated, as an image of her razor-sharp, immaculately groomed boyfriend popped into her mind. 'But we don't need to prove it.'

He gave her a searching look. 'And yet here you are alone.'

She hesitated. Max was a very driven, highly successful property developer who'd invested in some of the most iconic new buildings that were flying up along London's waterfront; he wasn't a freelancer like Gina, so he couldn't simply fly away to Cornwall at a moment's notice. Especially not for three long months. But Nonno had no idea she'd be staying that long. 'Max is busy,' she said carefully. 'He sends his love.'

'Huh,' Ferdie grumbled. 'I don't suppose he even

remembers what we look like. How long is it since he came – a year?'

It was nearer two, Gina thought, but she didn't say so. She'd brought Max for a visit a few months after they'd started seeing each other, wanting the approval of her grandparents, and of course he'd charmed them the same way he'd charmed her. And then he'd never come back, despite frequent invitations, and Gina had ended up travelling down without him. It was another reason she'd found it so hard to get back to Cornwall since – there always seemed to be an important party to attend with Max or dinner with his business associates. Between her relationship and her work commitments, she'd barely had any time to call her own for months.

'Something like that,' she agreed. 'But I'm sure he'll come to visit me once I'm—'

She stopped, feeling colour creep up her cheeks. It wasn't the right time to tell Nonno why she was there – she needed her grandmother to back her up. But a glance at Ferdie told her it was too late.

'Visit you?' he said, frowning. 'Why would he visit you when you live on each other's doorsteps?'

Gina gathered herself together and sat up straight. 'I'm going to be staying in Polwhipple for a few months.'

Her grandfather stared at her, his bushy white eyebrows beetling together above his deep brown eyes. 'Why? Is there something wrong? You've lost your job, is that it?'

'No, nothing like that.' Gina shifted uncomfortably. She

was going to have to come right out with it. 'Nonna and I thought—'

She broke off as the living-room door swung open. 'Here we go,' Elena said, walking through it with a tray of steaming coffee and a plate piled high with biscotti.

'Gina says she's staying in Polwhipple for a few months,' Ferdie said, as Elena placed the tray on the low coffee table.

'I know,' she said, passing him a cup. 'It will do her good. In fact, it will do us all good.'

Ferdie glanced back and forth between his wife and granddaughter. 'What does that mean?'

Elena nudged the plate towards Gina with a significant look. 'Come now, Ferdie, isn't it obvious? She's come to help you with the business.'

Gina managed a smile. 'That's right. We thought I could do some of the running around, take some of the pressure off you until your leg is better.'

'I don't need any help,' Ferdie said, his expression growing thunderous. 'And I especially don't need people conspiring behind my back to organise it.'

'Nobody is conspiring, you old fool,' Elena said, taking a measured sip of her coffee. 'In case you have forgotten, your leg has six metal pins holding it together. It needs time to heal. Didn't they tell you in the hospital to get some rest?'

Ferdie snorted in derision. 'Doctors – what do they know? I have work to do. I can't laze around all day. Gelato doesn't make itself, you know.'

'So let me help,' Gina said, leaning forwards. 'The way you used to when I was little.'

Not that he'd allowed her to do much more than dip a spoon into the creamy mixture before it went into the freezer, Gina thought, but every little helped.

'Your stocks are running low,' Elena said. 'It will be Easter soon and the weather will start to get better – what then? Are you going to disappoint the restaurants – your customers – because your pride won't allow you to accept some help from your own family?'

'There's plenty of stock,' Ferdie said, glaring at his wife. 'Enough to see us through several weeks, at least.'

Elena's eyes flashed. 'I know exactly how much there is – twelve tubs of raspberry ripple, ten vanilla, eleven chocolate and eight honeycomb. You have no strawberry, salted caramel or mint choc chip left and they're the ones the restaurants are crying out for, not to mention the biggest sellers at the ice-cream stand.' She sat back and took another sip of her coffee. 'You need Gina's help, whether you like it or not, and you'd better accept it before she changes her mind and goes back to London, thinking you don't want her here.'

It was the last sentence that did the trick, Gina thought, admiring her grandmother's almost Machiavellian genius. Nonno still looked furious but she could see he was wavering. 'It would be a lovely way to spend some time together,' she said, widening her eyes in unspoken appeal. 'I've cleared my diary until June.'

There was a long silence. Gina's instinct was to continue

to persuade him but she followed Nonna's example, drinking her coffee and waiting. Eventually, Ferdie let out a short, irritable sigh. 'I suppose I could use some help.'

Gina resisted the urge to cheer as Elena nodded. 'Of course you could.'

'You'd have to do exactly as I say,' he went on, firing a meaningful look at Gina. 'My recipes have stood the test of time for sixty years; they need to be followed to the letter. A Ferrelli's gelato is like a Puccini aria – it needs no tinkering or improvement, it's perfect as it is.'

This time she did smile – Ferrelli's had served the same flavours of ice-cream for as long as she could remember, although the caramel had become salted caramel after a clandestine campaign by Elena the previous Christmas. Gina had sent a box as a gift and Elena had promptly asked her to get five more so that she could persuade Ferdie to change his recipe. It had instantly become their best-selling flavour.

'No tinkering,' she promised, relieved that the war seemed to have been won.

Elena leaned towards her with the plate of biscotti. 'Maybe just a bit of tinkering,' she whispered, a mischievous smile on her face. 'I've been trying to get him to make a tiramisu flavour gelato for years but he's always refused. Now you can do it for me!'

Gina glanced at her grandfather's determined expression, then back at her grandmother and her heart sank. She'd been wrong to think the war was over – from what she could tell, it was just about to begin. And she was caught right in the middle.

# Chapter Three

Gina finally got back to the hotel just after eight o'clock, stuffed full of Nonna's porcini mushroom risotto. She spent a few moments on the balcony, listening to the crash of the Atlantic against the rocks on the beach below and letting the wind whip through her long dark hair. The air was cold and biting; it almost took her breath away, but at the same time it felt so clean that she couldn't get enough of it, gulping down deep lungfuls even though it made her shiver. Gazing upwards, she saw the moon glimmering through the clouds above; it danced across the tips of the waves as they rolled in. Gina let out a long, heartfelt sigh; she felt a long way from London in more ways than one.

The buzz of her mobile interrupted her musing. She glanced down and saw Max's name on the screen. Pulling open the sliding glass door, she slipped back inside the spacious bedroom.

'Hello, Max, everything okay?'

'Of course, I just thought I'd give you a call and make sure Ferocious Ferdie hadn't eaten you alive.'

Gina laughed. 'He's not ferocious. Well, maybe a little bit, but his bark is definitely worse than his bite.'

'I know,' Max replied, a wry note behind the words. 'I've met him, remember? I think I've just about recovered now, although I still have nightmares about him sometimes.'

His voice was warm as he teased and Gina knew he'd be smiling.

'So how's the hotel? Is it as gorgeous as it sounded?'

Gina gazed around her luxurious room, with its king-sized bed, velvet chaise longue and blissfully subdued lighting. 'It's perfect,' she said. 'I haven't explored the hot tubs yet but I have a feeling I'm going to need them after today's conversation.'

She filled him in on most of Ferdie's reaction to her offer of help. Max let out an incredulous laugh when she'd finished.

'You'd think you were launching a hostile takeover, not getting him out of a potentially disastrous hole,' he said. 'Honestly, you need a degree in United Nations peacekeeping negotiations to deal with your family.'

'That's not true,' Gina objected, although she knew he had a point. One of the reasons she'd known she couldn't refuse Nonna's plea for help was that Gina's own mother had disagreed so violently with Nonno that she and Gina's father had moved to an entirely different continent to avoid him. 'All families fall out.'

'Hmmm,' he said. 'So what's the plan?'

Gina reached for her glass of Prosecco. 'First thing tomorrow, I need to contact the restaurants we supply, to smooth over any issues Nonno's accident might have caused. I also need to visit the Ferrelli's concession at the Palace Picture House and speak to Gorran Dew, the owner, to see what he thinks he's going to need in terms of stock over the next few weeks—'

'That can't be a real name,' Max interrupted. 'It sounds more like an exotic fruit.'

She summoned up an image of the cinema owner, who'd always reminded her of a ruddy-cheeked version of Doc Brown from *Back to the Future*. 'They're both traditional Cornish names – the Dew family tree goes back centuries in Polwhipple – but there's nothing exotic about Gorran. Eccentric is a better word.'

She shook her head and smiled, picturing Gorran presiding over the lobby of the Art Deco cinema, with its plush ruby and gold carpet and gilt-laden décor. 'I'm looking forward to seeing the old place, actually, it'll be a real blast from the past. I wonder if you can still sneak in through the fire exit to watch the film for free.'

'How long is it since you've been there?' Max asked.

'Years,' she answered. 'I spent half my summers there when I was a teenager. There was this surfer kid I used to hang out with and Nonno used to give us free ice-cream to make sure we stayed out of trouble.'

'Did it work?'

She laughed. 'Not really. I was Bonnie to Ben's Clyde – he was the one who taught me how to sneak in through the fire door.'

Gina paused, a sudden image of fifteen-year-old Ben Pascoe popping unbidden into her mind, all tangled blond hair and sunscreen as he stood grinning on the beach. He'd been her best friend for summer after summer; during her last visit there'd been a moment or two when she'd idly wondered if he might be more but nothing had ever come of it. She felt her cheeks grow warm at the memory. 'Wow, I haven't thought about him for ages.'

'Does he still live in Polwhipple?' Max sounded curious now.

'No idea,' Gina said, pushing the image away. 'I don't think he can. My grandparents would have mentioned it. Nothing so much as breathes in this town without one or both of them knowing about it. But enough about my mildly criminal past, how was your day?'

She listened as Max told her about the meetings he'd had, and the new contract he'd signed for twenty-five new luxury apartments overlooking the Thames at Battersea. 'It sounds like you're busy.'

'I am,' he said. 'But not busy enough to stop me missing you.'

'Ha, I bet you hardly even noticed I was gone.'

'I noticed,' Max said quietly.

Gina imagined him perched on the edge of his pristine double bed and felt a sudden wave of homesickness. 'It's only three months – honestly, I'll be back before you know it.'

'I know.' His sigh sounded deep. 'But that doesn't mean I won't miss you.'

His words filled her with bittersweet warmth; it was rare for Max to acknowledge how much he cared about her, although she had never doubted that he did. It would be hard being away from him and her life in London but at least she had plenty to stop her from pining. Max did too, although she had to admit she'd found a measure of comfort in knowing he was missing her.

He stayed in her thoughts for the rest of the evening; throughout her dip in the free-standing bath, as she towel-dried her hair and when she flicked mindlessly through the television channels in search of entertainment. When it became clear that the only thing worth watching was *An Affair to Remember*, she slipped between the cool cotton sheets and lay there trying not to cry as Cary Grant realised why Deborah Kerr had stood him up. Eventually, she gave in and sobbed out loud, not caring that her nose must be red or her eyes puffy. Once the film had finished, she dried her tears and settled down for the night. *I wish Max was here*, she thought, staring into the darkness as the sound of the sea lulled her to sleep. And then, just as her eyes drifted shut, another name popped into her mind: Ben Pascoe. A faint smile curved her lips as unconsciousness came to claim her; now there's another blast from the past. I must remember to ask Nonna if he's still around.

It was just over a mile and a half from Gina's hotel to the seafront at Polwhipple. Back in London, she was used to hopping on the Underground for much shorter distances, but her transport options were much more limited in Cornwall. It seemed wrong to call a taxi for a four-minute journey, especially on such a glorious spring day, and there wasn't a bus from Mawgan Porth to Polwhipple. It was, however, walkable – Google told her she could take the South West Coast Path along the cliffs. Determined to enjoy the sunshine and scenery, Gina pulled on her waterproof coat and brand-new walking boots and set off.

The breeze was stronger than she'd anticipated as she reached the clifftops but the view was worth the wind-chill. The sea sparkled in the mid-morning sunlight, an even deeper blue than she remembered, and the sky seemed to be trying to compete. Gulls whirled overhead, shrieking into the wind. Gina stopped, letting the wind whip her hair across her face. 'I've a feeling we're not in Kansas any more,' she murmured to herself with a contented smile.

Gina snapped photo after photo on her phone as she walked, making a mental note to upload the best ones to her work Instagram account later; being away from London didn't mean she had to be off the grid, and she needed to have some clients to return to once Nonno was back on his feet.

Polwhipple itself was exactly as she remembered; nestled in a rocky cove, with a golden beach and a seafront full of quaint shops, it was a sleepy seaside town that had never quite lived up to its gorgeous location. The jewel in Polwhipple's crown had always been the Palace, its gracious Art Deco curves towering above the other seafront businesses. Gina could see it long before she reached the promenade that ran along the length of the beach, and shining like a rainbow-coloured gem beneath the giant red-lettered sign was the window of Ferrelli's ice-cream concession. It was almost as though time had stood still.

But a frown creased Gina's forehead as she got nearer and realised the Palace wasn't quite as she remembered it. Up close, she could see the white paint of the building was yellowed and peeling, and several of the many lightbulbs that lit up the sign at night were either missing or smashed. The row of rectangular casing that used to hold enticing movie posters was empty; in fact, there was no way to see which films were showing at all. Gina's heart began to sink – it didn't appear that the last few years had been kind to the Palace; what was Gorran Dew playing at? The only bright spot was Ferrelli's – the push-pull window beneath the faded gilt cornices held a mouth-watering mix of pastel-coloured ice-cream waves. A tower of crisp-looking golden cornets leaned drunkenly from one side and bottles of sticky chocolate syrup stood beside jars of multi-coloured sprinkles on the other. And presiding over the sea of tasty treats was Manda, who'd worked for Gina's grandfather for as long as she could remember.

'Gina!' the older woman cried, sliding back the window and straightening her blue and white Ferrelli's apron. 'I didn't know you were in town.'

Gina smiled. Manda must be in her late fifties and was one

of several stalwart employees whose chief passion in life seemed to be serving Ferrelli's to Polwhipple's public. 'They came for a job and stayed for the ice-cream,' Ferdie told Gina, when she'd asked how he had kept the same staff for years on end.

'I only arrived yesterday,' she said to Manda. 'I'm here to help out for a few months, while Nonno recovers.'

Manda raised her eyebrows. 'Oh really? And what does Ferdie think of this plan?'

'He's come round to it,' Gina replied, glancing meaningfully at the glistening tubs beneath the sloping glass display case. 'Even he can't argue with an empty freezer.'

The older woman reached for a scoop. 'So what can I get you? Strawberry? Chocolate? Both?'

Gina's mouth watered at the thought, but she shook her head. 'It's a bit early for me. I actually came to see Gorran. Is he here yet?'

'He's here,' Manda said, pursing her lips into a thin line of disapproval. 'For what it's worth.'

'Oh?' Gina replied, her sense of disquiet growing. 'Is there a problem, then?'

'You'll see,' Manda said enigmatically. 'The door's open.'

She flicked her head towards the silver and glass double doors to her left. With an awkward nod of farewell, Gina went into the lobby.

If anything, the air of neglect was worse inside. The white walls looked drab and tired. The gilt swirls that adorned the columns and ceiling were flaking. One of the silver double doors that led through to the cinema itself seemed to be hanging off its hinges and was covered in *Do Not Use* tape. The glorious red and gold carpet that Gina had always loved still covered the floor but it was grubby and thin in places. Some of the lightbulbs in the chandelier needed to be replaced, giving the place a gloomy air. And the bar, which took up all of one wall and had once served the kind of elegant alcoholic cocktails the teenaged Gina could only dream about sampling, was empty and abandoned. The whole place felt deserted and unloved. It made Gina want to cry.

'Sad, isn't it?'

Manda was leaning in the doorframe at the back of Ferrelli's. There was a counter here too, although it was empty of ice-cream now. Gina assumed it was only filled when there was a screening, which, judging from the empty poster casings, might be infrequent these days.

'How has this happened?' Gina asked, shaking her head in bewilderment. 'This place used to be a proper goldmine. How has it gone downhill so fast?'

'You'll have to ask Mr Dew,' Manda said, folding her arms. 'The ice-cream sells just fine – we don't need a film to boost our trade. Which is just as well, really.'

Gina gazed around her again. 'How often is there a screening? Is there anything showing tonight?'

Manda squinted at the ceiling thoughtfully. 'Not on a Thursday, no. He usually puts something on at the weekend but you'll have to ask him what tomorrow's film is. Or you could wait until he puts the poster up outside.'

'So he does do some advertising,' Gina said in relief. 'That's something at least.'

'Well, I say poster,' Manda went on. 'It's really just a sheet of A4 paper with the name of the film and the start time printed on it in capital letters. It's been a long time since we had proper glossy posters.'

Gina's shoulders slumped. Why hadn't Nonna and Nonno told her how bad things were at the Palace? This was no way to run a business, especially not one that relied on public awareness to pull the punters in; it needed a regular audience and word of mouth recommendations, not an erratic schedule and cheap A4 paper. She'd be out of business in a week if she operated her own events this way. Gina narrowed her gaze. But hadn't Manda said that Ferrelli's sales were still good? Perhaps that was why her grandparents hadn't thought to mention the cinema's change in fortunes – technically, none of it was their problem. All Gina needed to worry about was how much ice-cream the concession might sell. 'Where can I find Gorran?'

'Maybe in the office, or the projection room,' Manda said, pointing to a single door off to one side. 'Good luck.'

The door led to a short corridor and a small flight of stairs. 'Gorran?' Gina called as she climbed the staircase. 'Mr Dew? Are you here?'

At the top of the stairs there were more doors, although these were plain white rather than the ornate silver style Gina had seen in the foyer. She tapped at the first one she came to, listening for sounds of movement inside. 'Hello? Is anyone here?'

No reply. She moved on to the next door and knocked harder. 'Hello?'

There was a rustling sound, followed by the thud of feet and the door was pulled open. Gorran Dew stood on the other side, his shock of white hair even wilder than Gina remembered. 'Yes? How can I help?'

His checked shirt was crumpled, with one wing of the collar tucked inside, and he clearly hadn't shaved in days. Gina had to force herself not to step backwards. 'I don't suppose you remember me, Mr Dew. I'm Gina Callaway, Ferdie Ferrelli's granddaughter.'

Gorran's pale blue eyes flickered with recognition. He held out a hand and began pumping Gina's arm enthusiastically. 'Of course! You've changed a bit since I last saw you.' He let go of her hand and stepped back, sweeping into an invitation instead. 'Won't you come in?'

Gina gazed past him into the room beyond. It looked like an office, with a desk piled high with papers and several brown boxes cluttering the floor. She did her best to smile. 'Thank you.'

There was only one seat that wasn't covered with paperwork: a leather desk chair on wheels. Gorran ushered her into it and set about shifting a teetering pile of what looked like invoices and receipts from a low sofa and onto the floor. The papers slithered into another pile. Gina tried not to wince.

'So,' Gorran said, fixing her with a beaming smile. 'What can I do for you?'

Gina cleared her throat. 'As I'm sure you know, my grandfather's broken leg means he's going to be unable to work for at least the next month, so I'll be taking over the reins until he's better.'

Gorran nodded. 'Great idea. Ferdie ought to be taking things easy at his time of life, not working every hour God sends.' He licked his lips nervously. 'Not that I'd tell him that to his face, obviously.'

'No,' Gina said, keeping her expression as straight as she could. 'Very wise. Anyway, I thought it might be good for us to have a chat about your screenings schedule, so that I can get a sense of how much ice-cream we might need to supply over the coming months.'

'Another good idea,' Gorran said, looking impressed. 'What do you need to know?'

'Perhaps we could start with this weekend. Manda tells me you're showing a film tomorrow.'

'That's right,' he replied. 'Fridays and Saturdays are our busiest nights. Sometimes we get upwards of – I dunno – maybe twenty customers.'

Gina almost groaned. It was even worse than she'd imagined. 'What film are you showing tomorrow night?'

He rubbed his hands together in obvious anticipation. 'Oh, it's a classic – a little-known Swedish gem about a pigeon's reflections on existence.'

'A . . . a pigeon?' Gina repeated, unable to believe what she'd just heard. 'Did you say a pigeon's reflections on existence?'

'That's right,' Gorran said. 'And it's all told through a series of tableaux, so you really get to appreciate each scene.'

Gina blinked. 'So no one moves?'

'And the voice-over is in Swedish, but obviously we'll have subtitles.' Gorran chuckled. 'Honestly, it's brilliant. Should pull in a good crowd.'

She stared at him. 'Right,' she said, hoping her voice wasn't as faint as it sounded. 'And what are you showing on Saturday?'

Gorran sighed. 'I couldn't get hold of another indie film so I've had to pick an old one from the archives. Have you ever heard of *Footloose*?'

Gina sat up a little straighter. This was more promising. 'Of course I have, it's a great film. Kevin Bacon lights up the screen.'

He pursed his lips doubtfully. 'It's not what I'd call a classic but I expect a few people will turn up to see it.'

He shrugged, as if to say: 'What can you do?' Unable to think of a reply that wasn't sarcastic, Gina let her gaze travel around the chaotic office, taking in the curling yellowed papers stuck to the noticeboard and the half-empty curdled mugs on the desk. 'Does anyone else work here, Mr Dew?'

'Call me Gorran, please,' he told her. 'Yes, there's Tash, who runs the projector room, and Bruno who mans the box office. You'll have seen that the bar is closed – we couldn't justify the costs, unfortunately. Alcohol is expensive and no one seemed to want it.'

Gina thought back to the bright, busy bar she remembered

and swallowed a sigh; if she had to sit through two hours of Swedish pigeon drama she'd need a stiff drink afterwards. But the cinema wasn't her business, she reminded herself. All that mattered was the ice-cream. 'It would be helpful to have a schedule of screenings for the next month – is that possible?'

Gorran rubbed his patchy stubble. 'I suppose I could draw up a schedule. The films might be subject to change, if I can't get hold of them, though. Would that be a problem?'

One of the things running her own business had taught Gina was the ability to know when to step back. 'Let's take things one weekend at a time,' she suggested, forcing herself to smile. 'And maybe I should come along and see how things work for myself. What time does *Footloose* start on Saturday?'

'It depends what time Tash says she wants to start,' Gorran said, with an encouraging smile. 'I'll tell you what, why don't you check the door for a poster on Saturday afternoon?'

# Chapter Four

Manda insisted on giving Gina a double scoop of Strawberry Sensation.

'You look like you need the sugar,' she said, shaking her head in concern. 'People often look that way after talking to Gorran.'

'Thanks,' Gina said, watching as Manda piled the ice-cream high with sprinkles and wedged a stick of fudge into one side.

'And don't even think about paying,' Manda warned, seeing Gina's hand move automatically towards her handbag. 'Think of it as on-the-job training. You can't sell the product if you don't know what it tastes like.' She patted her ample stomach. 'At least, that's what I tell my husband.'

Gina smiled. 'Point taken.'

She licked at the sprinkles and sweetness exploded on her tongue but the strawberry flavour beneath the sugary strands was less sweet, almost tart. Her taste buds reacted in delight.

She took another mouthful, then smiled. 'I'd forgotten how good this was.'

Manda nodded. 'That's why we don't have to worry too much about what Gorran Dew does, as long as he does enough to keep this place open. Your grandfather is a genius where ice-cream is concerned and everyone in this part of the world knows it.'

The sun was high in the sky now, shimmering on the wet sand left behind by the receding tide, and Gina had the sudden urge to walk along the shoreline. She smiled her thanks at Manda. 'It's lovely to see you again. I'm sure we'll be seeing a lot more of each other over the next few months.'

There was a slope that led down to the beach at the far end of the promenade but Gina opted for the set of narrow stone steps not far from the picture house. The short walk took her towards the Mermaid's Tail inn, its bunting-strewn beer garden empty for the moment, and past the Ocean Pearl bookshop, another of teenage Gina's favourite places. There was an unfamiliar shop next door, though, and its colourful window display made Gina pause for a moment; the mannequins looked like they'd stepped straight from the screen of the Palace. One was dressed in a 1960s mini-dress and thigh-length boots, another was draped in a fur coat and hat that Gina fervently hoped weren't real and a third wore a tea dress and chic cloche hat that wouldn't have looked out of place amongst the steam on the platform at Bodmin Parkway. She glanced up at the grey and hot pink sign over the window: *Carrie's Attic.* It made her smile. Who'd have thought that a vintage boutique would open in sleepy Polwhipple?

Dragging herself away, Gina crossed the road and made her way down the steps. The beach was almost deserted, apart from a dog-walker splashing along in the shallows with an enthusiastic Labrador. Further out to sea, Gina spotted a surfer riding along the crest of the waves. She found a patch of dry sand and sat down to watch for a moment, envious of the surfer's obvious skill as they flipped the board into the air; she'd always wanted to learn to surf, ever since she'd sat on the beach watching Ben ride the waves years earlier. She'd thought it was cool then and it looked every bit as cool now.

Her ice-cream was almost finished. Lifting the cornet up, she nibbled away the end and sucked the remaining slush through it. Then she crunched through the strawberry-drizzled cone and popped the very last bit into her mouth with a satisfied sigh. She'd have to watch how much she ate, Gina decided, licking her lips – if she wasn't careful she'd go back to London a stone heavier than she'd left it, especially if Nonna had anything to do with it.

The surfer was wading through the shallows now, his board in his arms. He stopped to make a fuss of the Labrador and exchanged a few words with its owner. A local, Gina decided, maybe even someone who surfed at Polwhipple every day. It was much quieter than the better-known surf spots just along the coast in Newquay and less showy than the famous Fistral beach. She watched as he shook the salt-water from his board and made his way up the beach. He was tall, with a typical surfer's physique, she noticed; hardly a surprise, given that his skill suggested he must be a regular. His wet hair glistened brown but she thought it would be blond when it was dry. He was good-looking too, with a chiselled jaw and good cheekbones. And then her eyes met his and she felt a jolt of recognition: the surfer was the same man who'd helped remove the grit from her eye the day before.

He stopped walking, his gaze fixed on her, and Gina knew he'd recognised her too. Then he began to move, heading her way. She stood up.

'We meet again,' she called, as soon as she judged he was within earshot.

'How's the eye?' he asked. 'It looks better.'

She smiled. 'Fully recovered – thanks for taking pity on me. I never expected to see you again, so I'm afraid I don't have your handkerchief. Sorry.'

He waved her apology away. 'Don't worry. I don't actually have anywhere to put it right now, to be honest.'

Automatically, Gina's gaze slid down his tight wetsuit and across some well-defined muscles. She dragged her eyes hurriedly back to his face, feeling a blush creep up her cheeks. 'No, I can see that.'

A brief silence grew before the surfer spoke again. 'So, are you here on holiday?'

Gina tipped her head to one side, a small frown creasing her forehead. Now that he was close, there was something familiar about him, something more than she could have gleaned from their brief meeting the day before. 'No,' she said slowly. 'I'm visiting my family. I used to come here a lot when I was younger and—'

His blue eyes widened. '*Gina?* It is you, isn't it?'

She stared at him warily. 'Yes. Do we know each other?'

His face lit up as he dug his board into the sand. 'I thought I recognised you yesterday. It's me, Ben. Ben Pascoe. We used to be friends ages ago. Don't you remember?'

And suddenly, she could see the ghost of the boy she'd known. 'Oh my God, I had no idea you'd still live here!'

He wiped his hand on his wetsuit and held it out for her to shake. 'I left to go travelling and worked in Australia for a while but came back this year to start my own business.'

His fingers were warm and damp and slightly gritty but Gina was so amazed that she almost forgot to notice. Ben Pascoe. They'd been inseparable all those summers ago. What were the chances that she'd run into him again, on the platform at Bodmin Parkway, no less? Her gaze roved across his face once more – he was so obviously the Ben that she'd known; how could she have failed to recognise him? Then again, there'd been the small matter of the coal dust in her eye . . .

'How are your grandparents?' Ben asked, releasing her hand. 'I see Ferrelli's is still doing a roaring trade.'

He nodded at the Palace as he spoke. Gina smiled. 'That's sort of why I'm here. Nonno broke his leg and I'm helping out while he gets some rest.'

Ben's eyes gleamed. 'So you're here for a few weeks?'

'A few months,' she corrected. 'I'm going to learn how to make ice-cream and soak up some of the famous Cornish sunshine. And then I need to get back to the real world in London.'

'Right,' he said. 'I tried the real world once. Didn't like it much.'

Gina laughed, thinking of her previously packed diary. 'Yeah, it can be a bit full-on, especially compared to Polwhipple.'

There was another silence but this one felt comfortable, even companionable. Ben adjusted his surfboard in the sand. 'We should get together for a drink sometime and catch up properly.'

'I'd like that,' Gina said, feeling a strange, fuzzy warmth flood through her. Had he always had this effect? 'Oh, I know! We should go and watch a film at the Palace – there's a screening of *Footloose* on Saturday evening if you're up for it?'

He laughed. 'That really would be a blast from the past. Although maybe we'll buy tickets this time instead of sneaking in for free.'

Gina thought back to Gorran in his disorganised office – there was no guarantee the film would even run, but she supposed they could always head to the Mermaid's Tail for a drink if it didn't. 'Okay. Do you want to give me your number?'

'Sure.' He gestured at his wetsuit again. 'I don't have my phone on me so you'll have to do the calling.'

This time, Gina managed to keep her eyes firmly fixed on his face. 'No problem.' She tapped his number into her phone and then pressed call. 'All done. Have you – er – been to see anything at the picture house lately?'

Ben shook his head. 'Not since I was a teenager. Why?'

Gina allowed herself a secret smile as a pigeon pecked at the sand not far away. 'No reason. Let's just say it's a bit hit and miss when it comes to film choices. I'm glad we're going on Saturday instead of Friday.'

'So, what do you know about making gelato?'

The old dairy building was tucked away behind her grandparents' house, a stainless-steel temple to ice-cream, and Gina was perched at the centre island. It had a multi-burner gas hob and behind her there was a floor-to-ceiling fridge, a walk-in freezer filled with the silver pans she'd seen full of ice-cream in the window of Ferrelli's and several chrome-coloured machines, none of which Gina could fathom. 'It takes a lot of skill?' she guessed.

He slammed one hand down on the shiny work surface, creating a mini thunderclap. 'Of course it does, otherwise everyone would be doing it. What are the core ingredients?'

She glanced back at the fridge. It was filled with full-fat milk, cream and eggs from a nearby farm and she didn't need a degree in catering to understand why. There was a bowl of something white on the counter that she assumed was sugar. But surely it couldn't be so simple? 'Uh – milk, sugar, eggs and cream?'

'Exactly so,' Nonno said, looking satisfied. 'No artificial ingredients. Just perfect fresh gelato, made to my mother's recipe.'

Gina knew the story – Ferdie had arrived in Britain in 1957 from Italy with no money and no plan, other than a burning determination to make a better life for himself. He'd fallen into a job working for the London Brick company in Bedford but secretly longed to become a chef. Then he met Elena, the daughter of another Italian immigrant, and it had been love at first sight. Ferdie had learned how to cook, adapting recipes from a notebook he'd been given by his mother, and saved all of his wages until he had earned enough to open a small business of his own. Then he'd proposed to Elena. Eventually, they'd moved to Cornwall, where Ferdie insisted the milk quality was the best in the whole country, and had never looked back.

'What about the flavours?' Gina thought back to the tangy strawberry ice-cream she'd enjoyed earlier. Where did Nonno get strawberries juicy enough to turn into delicious ice-cream at this time of year?

'Again, all fresh ingredients – there's a fruit farm near Padstow that delivers whatever we need, all year round.' Ferdie noticed Gina eyeing the equipment nervously. 'Don't worry, I'm not expecting you to understand the pasteuriser or the batch freezers yet. You're going to be starting much smaller. Take a saucepan from underneath the counter.'

Gina did as he instructed, lifting a heavy, copper-bottomed

pan from the shelf and placing it onto one of the hob burners.

'Today, you're going to learn how to make your own ice-cream from start to finish, just like generations of Italians before you,' Ferdie explained. 'Although I am not going to insist you beat it by hand with a wooden spoon like they did – I am not a monster, after all.'

He sat back on a stool and pointed to the fridge. 'You'll find most of what you need in there, and the sugar is in front of you.'

Once Gina had gathered her ingredients, Ferdie set about instructing her. She heated the milk and a much smaller amount of cream in the pan, then split the egg yolks from the whites and beat the yolks with the sugar in a shiny red mixer until it was thick and creamy.

'Now comes the tricky part,' Ferdie told her. 'You need to add the hot milk to the eggs to make a custard. Do it too fast and you will end up with scrambled egg.'

Under his watchful eye, Gina added spoonful after spoonful to the eggs and sugar, stirring constantly. Once both mixtures were combined, she poured it back into the saucepan and set it to gently heat again.

Ferdie unscrewed a nearby jar and pulled out what looked like a dried-up twig. He handed it to Gina. 'This is a vanilla pod. Split it along the middle and drop it into the pan. Then stir until the mixture makes a coat for your spoon. Be careful it does not stick – then it will burn and taste like the inside of a shoe.'

She smiled and concentrated on stirring the custard. There was something soothing about focusing entirely on cooking, Gina thought, as she watched the mixture slowly thicken, aware that Nonno's critical eye was fixed on her. She really couldn't afford to mess this up – he'd never let her back into the dairy if she did.

'And now it needs to chill down,' Ferdie announced. 'Pour it into a bowl and leave it to cool at room temperature, then it needs to go into the fridge for several hours or even overnight.'

Gina started at him in disappointment. 'So I won't get to taste it until tomorrow?'

He glared at her. 'You cannot rush gelato. But it is a good idea to try the custard, so that you know what it should be like at each stage.'

She dipped a spoon into the mix and blew to cool it down. It tasted delicious, reminding her of the apple pie and custard her mother used to make. 'Wow.'

'So now you know how it should taste.' Ferdie nodded in satisfaction. 'But I know that you are impatient, so if you look in the fridge, you will see an identical mix that I made this morning, ready for you to make into ice-cream.'

Sure enough, there was a covered bowl of custard there. Gina carried it to the work surface. Ferdie made her remove the vanilla pod and sieve the mixture. 'And now the magic happens,' he said, pointing to a much smaller ice-cream machine that sat on the worktop against one wall. 'I use this one when I am testing a recipe and only need a small batch.

The bowl has been in the freezer for hours – once you add the custard to it, the machine churns it and the mix becomes colder and colder until it is almost frozen too.'

'Can't I just put it in the freezer as it is?' Gina asked, frowning.

'No!' Ferdie looked as though she had slapped him. 'Ice crystals will form and your ice-cream will taste like water.'

The machine got to work. Gina watched in fascination as the custard thickened to something much closer to the ice-cream she'd seen at Ferrelli's.

'So now you begin to see how gelato is made,' Ferdie said. 'The hard work starts here. This time, you will make a custard with no help from me.'

He made his way to the door. 'The quantities are on the wall over there – you will need to convert them to make a smaller batch. The ingredients are all here too. You have thirty minutes.'

With a final nod, he turned and left. The door banged shut. Gina stared after him for a moment, then squared her shoulders. This was a test. All she had to do was repeat exactly what she'd just done, and not even that because she didn't need to churn the gelato, just make the custard. She could do it; it was only ice-cream, after all. Compared to managing a large corporate event it would be a walk in the park.

Checking the wall for the quantities, Gina gathered the ingredients again. The bowl that had held the sugar was empty so she searched through the cupboards until she found a large container and carried it over to the scales. Then she set about making her mixture.

It was all going well until she broke an egg yolk. Taking a deep breath, she rinsed her hands and tried again, passing each yolk between her fingers until all the white had slipped into the spare bowl below. She stirred in the sugar and started the mixer. Remembering Nonno's warning about scrambled egg, she took her time while adding the hot milk, then transferred everything to the saucepan and snapped in another vanilla pod.

The mixture had just started to thicken when Nonno came back.

'Let's see how you did,' he said, peering into the pan. He lifted the spoon and examined the back. 'The thickness isn't bad, although it isn't sticking as well as it should.'

Gina felt a needle of anxiety. She'd followed his instructions to the letter. 'Maybe it needs more time. Didn't you say you can't rush gelato?'

Ferdie gave her an even look. 'So I did. The true test will be in the tasting.' He lifted the spoon to his lips and took the tiniest of tastes.

The spoon didn't move as his mouth twisted in disgust. He glanced at Gina. 'You used the same ingredients as before?'

She nodded, feeling more needles in her stomach. 'Except for the sugar – I found some more in one of the cupboards by the oven.'

Ferdie lowered the spoon and dabbed at his mouth with a tissue. 'Show me.'

She led him over to the wall and found the container.

'And you assumed this was sugar? You didn't check?'

Gina stared at him in confusion. 'What else could it be?'

Ferdie shook his head. 'I don't know – salt, maybe?'

She felt her cheeks begin to burn as she glanced at the white crystals. They looked like sugar and poured like sugar so it hadn't even occurred to her that it might be anything else. Why would Nonno have an unlabelled container of salt in his kitchen anyway? Surely it was an accident waiting to—

Her eyes narrowed. 'You set me up!' she said indignantly. 'You deliberately left the salt where I would find it and you knew I wouldn't check.'

Ferdie seemed unperturbed by her accusation. 'The first rule of the kitchen – check your ingredients.'

'You just made that up,' Gina said. 'You wanted me to fail and so you made sure that I would.'

He shrugged. 'But you won't ever make a mistake like that again, right? You will always check you have the right ingredients in the future.'

She opened her mouth to argue, then closed it again. Because he was right – she would check. But surely there were easier ways to teach her?

'Class is dismissed for today,' Ferdie announced. 'Come back at seven o'clock tomorrow morning.'

Gina felt her shoulders droop. 'Okay, Nonno.'

Ferdie's expression softened a little. 'You did well today. Apart from the salt.'

Sighing, Gina poured her salty custard away and washed everything up. She wished Nonno hadn't set her up to fail on her very first day, but she supposed things could only get better. Couldn't they?

# Chapter Five

At dinner, Nonna was furious with Ferdie when she found out what he'd done and sent a volley of Italian across the dining table that Gina was fairly sure contained a number of unsavoury insults. Ferdie refused to be bowed, insisting it was a lesson Gina needed to learn.

'That is the most ridiculous thing I have ever heard!' Nonna cried, throwing her hands up into the air. 'Only an *idiota* would keep salt and sugar in a kitchen with no labels. It would teach *you* a lesson if Gina went back to London right now!'

'Nonna, it's okay,' Gina said. 'No harm done.'

Elena threw her husband a dark look. 'If I find out you are trying to drive Gina away—'

'Of course not,' Ferdie said. 'Gina understands, don't you? It was a rite of passage – something to be experienced and learned from.'

'The girl can read,' Elena said in a withering tone. 'I doubt it is likely she will mix up the salt and the sugar if they are properly labelled.'

'Enough,' Ferdie growled. 'It is finished, anyway. Done. Tomorrow, I will teach her all my secrets, okay?'

'You had better,' Elena warned him. 'Or else maybe I will start to mix up the salt and the sugar in your coffee.'

Early the next morning, Gina arrived at the dairy to find Nonno waiting for her. He spent several hours showing her how to add flavours to the basic custard she'd made the day before, encouraging her to taste and experiment with the ingredients so that she understood the balance of flavours. In the afternoon, he taught her what each of the large machines did: one pasteurised the ingredients so that they passed food safety requirements, and the other heated and churned the mixture in turn, so that it could be poured into the traditional stainless-steel Napoli pans used by ice-cream makers all over the world. By the end of the day, Gina's head was spinning but she had a much better understanding of what the business of making gelato actually involved.

'Have you ever thought about trying some different flavours?' she asked Ferdie as she wiped down the work surfaces. 'There's a place in London that sells—'

'No,' Ferdie interrupted her. 'It took me years to perfect these recipes and they sell very well. We don't need to complicate things with new, experimental flavours.'

Gina thought back to Nonna's plan to tinker with Ferdie's existing recipes. 'But what if there was a traditional Italian recipe that might work well as an ice-cream – like, I don't know, tiramisu maybe? I bet your customers would love a new flavour.'

Ferdie's eyes glittered. 'They like the ones we already have.'

'But how do you know? Have you ever asked them?'

'No. People are idiots – they don't know what they want. Before you know it, they will be suggesting bacon flavour ice-cream called Piggy McPigface.' He snorted. 'Like I said – idiots.'

Gina took a deep breath and tried a different tack. 'Wouldn't you like a fresh challenge, Nonno?'

His face darkened. 'No.'

Gina had learned when she could push her luck with Nonno's temper and when she should quit; this was definitely time to leave it. Besides, he looked tired, and spending a day teaching her how to make gelato wasn't exactly restful.

'Why don't you leave me to clean up?' she suggested, smiling. 'Go and get some rest.'

He eyed her suspiciously. 'Do you promise not to whip up a curry-flavoured gelato once my back is turned?'

She laughed. 'I know I still have a lot to learn. I won't even try to whip up a batch of salted vanilla.'

Gina spent most of Saturday morning looking at apartments. She finally plumped for one in a luxury holiday let complex on the edge of Mawgan Porth, which was near enough for her to be able to get to Polwhipple easily without being on her grandparents' doorstep. She signed the three-month agreement, trying not to wince at the cost, but at least her new home had the benefit of being furnished for holiday makers; it had everything she might need, right down to a Nespresso machine she knew she'd never use. Nonna never used anything other than freshly ground beans and Gina would have felt like she was cheating to slip one of the aluminium pods into the machine.

But it was the view that had really sold the apartment to Gina. She'd grown used to waking up to the sound of the ocean outside her hotel room over the past few mornings and wanted to stay as close as she could to the water. And this apartment had a view of the beach, with a set of steep stairs that led down the side of the cliff, so she could watch the tide crash onto the shore and see the surfers dip in and out of the waves from the comfort of her balcony or head down to the sands. She didn't expect to recognise Ben if he came to surf but that didn't stop her watching.

She found her mind straying back to him often since their meeting on the beach. Seeing him again had jogged her memory and she found herself remembering snippets of conversations and more of the mischief they'd got up to. There'd been the time she'd snuck some of Nonna's limoncello down to the beach so that they could get drunk, a plan that had ended the moment they'd tasted it. And there'd been the time he'd assured her he knew how to roller-skate and had borrowed her boots; that had ended with a trip to A&E. Most of all, she remembered laughing with him; big, helpless laughter that had them both doubled over and gasping. She was fairly sure it had got them thrown out of the Palace on more than one occasion, when their fellow cinema-goers had complained. If she was honest, Ben had been the reason she'd been so keen to spend every summer in Polwhipple, right up until her parents had moved to Los Angeles, taking her out of Cornwall's reach. It had been harder to stay in touch at a distance back then, before Facebook and smartphones, and gradually, she'd forgotten about their friendship.

After a quick trip to Newquay in Nonna's little powder-blue Fiat to stock up on essentials, Gina strolled into Polwhipple. The sun was shining just enough to take the edge off the chilly March breeze, and the beach had several hardy families populating it with sandcastles. She spotted a number of people enjoying ice-creams from Ferrelli's and smiled; soon they might even be eating a batch she had made.

Carrie's Attic was open for business. Once again, Gina lingered at the window, admiring a vintage leather handbag and watching the customers browsing within. She knew it was only a matter of time before she joined them but today she had a different mission.

Manda wasn't working when Gina reached the Palace to check for details of that night's screening. Instead, it was Heather, a forty-something single mum who brought her son along with her. Gina could see him now, sat in the corner of the concession, glued to an iPad. She waved to Heather over the heads of the queue; Manda would doubtless have filled her in and there'd be plenty of time to catch up with all of Nonno's employees over the weeks to come.

There was a sheet of A4 paper stuck to the door of the Palace, exactly as Manda had described. It contained the bare minimum of information – the film name, the age rating and the start time. Gina pulled a face; it did the job, just about, but it wasn't what she'd call enticing.

She tapped a message into her phone and sent it to Ben.

> **Footloose starts at 8:30 p.m. Meet outside at 8:15? Gina**

A few minutes later her screen flashed.

> **See you then. Shall I bring the limoncello or will you? Ben**

Gina swiped Reply.

> **Huh, I still remember what it tasted like. How about we stick to ice-cream?**

> **Deal! See you later.**

Smiling, Gina put her phone away and set off home. She was looking forward to the film, in spite of her misgivings about the state of the cinema. It might just be a night to remember.

The first thing Gina noticed when she approached the Palace that evening was that she'd been right about the sign; it was missing several bulbs. The second was Ben himself, wrapped up against the chilly evening in a black woollen coat and scarf. He smiled when he saw her. 'Is it me or does this feel a bit weird?'

Gina started to return the smile until it occurred to her for the first time to wonder whether Ben might have a girlfriend. Surely someone who looked like he did couldn't be single? But it also hadn't occurred to her to think of going to the cinema with an old friend as weird either; it definitely wasn't a date. 'In what way?'

'As in slipping-back-in-time weird, like one of those dreams you have when everything is the same but different. Do you know what I mean?' He paused and gave his head a shake. 'Sorry, I'm rambling. It's been a long day.'

So he didn't think of it as a date either, Gina realised with relief. Phew.

'No, I get it,' she replied slowly. 'I suppose in a way that's exactly what's happened. Here we are doing something we used to do all the time but we're not the same people any more.'

Ben considered her words. 'And there's the evidence that we've changed – I'm pretty sure our teen versions were never this deep. Do you remember the time we had a competition to see who could blow a Malteser into the air for the longest?'

Gina grinned. 'I swallowed one whole and thought I was going to die.'

'And some greaser from Newquay offered to give you the kiss of life.'

'Ugh,' Gina said, with a slight shudder. 'I'm not sure that's a memory I want to relive.'

Now it was Ben's turn to grin. 'Good times.'

His smile was infectious and they stood grinning at each other for a moment, until Gina realised that Manda was watching them with avid curiosity from behind the counter at Ferrelli's. 'Fancy an ice-cream?' she asked Ben.

'Of course,' he replied. 'It would be rude not to, right?'

Manda didn't ask any awkward questions but Gina could see her gaze sliding back and forth between her and Ben.

'I'd forgotten you two used to be friends,' the older woman said as she piled glistening ice-cream into two small paper tubs.

'We bumped into each other on the beach,' Gina explained. 'And I thought it might be nice to watch the film together, for old times' sake.'

'Uh huh,' Manda said, nodding. 'I can see how that might be more fun than sitting in an empty cinema on your own.'

Gina stared at her. 'Surely we're not going to be on our own?'

Manda shrugged. 'I haven't seen anyone else go in yet. Heather said there wasn't anyone at last night's screening. Mind you, it did start an hour and a half late.'

Gina tried not to groan. 'Honestly, how does Gorran expect to make any money when the business is so badly run? I've been to a gorgeous little independent cinema in London just like this one and it was a gold mine.'

'But that's London,' Manda pointed out. 'People in

Polwhipple see the Palace as a bit of a joke, especially when you can get most of the films on the TV at home these days, all at the click of a button. That's why Gorran puts on these confusing art house things – he says people are more likely to get off the sofa for something they can't get at home.'

Gina had to admit she could see his point, but she was fairly sure Swedish pigeons weren't the box office draw he needed. 'Well, his film choice last night was certainly unusual. What he needs to do is give people a night out – make more of an event out of it. Take tonight's film – *Footloose.* He could have made it a fancy dress night, with pre-drinks in the foyer and an Eighties playlist.'

Manda looked doubtful. 'Except that the bar is closed.'

Gina ignored the objection. 'And maybe Ferrelli's could sell a themed ice-cream flavour – something that totally screams 1980s.' She narrowed her eyes thoughtfully. 'I bet Nonna would have some great ideas.'

Ben tilted his head. 'That's not a bad idea.'

'It's a great idea,' Manda agreed, 'but you're forgetting one thing – Gorran couldn't organise a Pina Colada in a pineapple factory.'

Gina snapped her fingers. 'Pina Colada flavour ice-cream. Perfect.' Her eyes widened. 'It would be brilliant – I bet people would come.'

'I bet they would, too. I'd come,' Ben said, looking impressed. 'You're good at this.'

Gina felt herself start to blush. 'Well, it is my job. I'm a freelance events planner, when I'm not taking a sabbatical as an ice-cream assistant, that is.'

'You should speak to Gorran about it,' Manda said. 'I'm not saying he'll go for it and I can't see how he'd be able to pull it off, but he might just surprise us all.'

'Seconded,' Ben said, then checked his watch. 'We should probably go in now. Unless Gorran's running ninety minutes late again, in which case we should go to the pub.'

'Let's go and find out,' Gina said. 'Thanks, Manda. See you later.'

They bought tickets at the box office, where a lanky teen with the improbable name of Bruno assured them the film was due to start on time. 'Well, after the adverts,' he said. 'You could probably skip them if you wanted to, unless you're in the market for a mobility scooter from the shop in Padstow?'

Ben's lips quirked as he glanced at Gina. 'No, I think mine's got a few years left.'

'Have you sold many tickets?' Gina asked. 'Had any online orders?'

Bruno frowned. 'We don't do online tickets; you can only get them on the door, and we've sold a grand total of –' He made a big show of consulting the notebook on the desk in front of him. '– Two. To you, just now.'

'Right,' Gina said, not daring to look at Ben. 'Good. So we'll make our way into the screen then, shall we?'

'Please do,' Bruno said, nodding. 'Seats A1 and A2, although I expect you could sit somewhere else if you wanted to. Just be prepared to move if a crowd shows up and you're in someone else's seat.'

Ben's shoulders were shaking as he and Gina pushed through the double doors to the screen. 'Ever get the feeling you're in a sitcom?' he said. 'I kept expecting Ricky Gervais to appear.'

'Don't,' Gina replied. 'It's too tragic to be funny. In fact—'

She stopped and gazed around her, taking in the ugly woodchip-covered walls, the threadbare red curtain covering the screen and row after row of faded velvet seats. 'What the hell has happened in here? Where's all the Art Deco gone?'

Ben walked over to one of the walls and tapped it. 'Plywood,' he said. 'Or maybe MDF. I imagine all the decoration is behind it, anyway. If it hasn't been pulled down.'

Gina gasped. 'But why? I know I didn't really appreciate it as a teenager but from what I remember, the décor in here was pretty special.' She glanced up at the ceiling and saw that the ornate golden swirls had been painted over in dull white. 'Why would they hide it away?'

'You'd be surprised at what people do,' Ben said, running a hand over the gloss-painted woodchip. 'Gilt paint needs to be maintained in order to look good and it doesn't come cheap – maybe they were trying to save money.'

She frowned. 'How do you know how much gilt paint costs?'

He smiled. 'I'm a builder. Renovations of listed buildings, mostly, but I do a bit of painting and decorating from time to time. So I know exactly how much things like gilt paint cost.'

*A builder?* Gina thought, trying to remember if they'd ever talked about what they wanted to be when they grew up. All Ben had ever wanted to do was surf – maybe he'd given it a go and it hadn't worked out? Then again, she doubted she'd ever mentioned wanting to become an events planner when she was a teenager, so maybe Ben's career wasn't such a surprise. 'What kind of listed buildings?' she asked. 'Anything famous?'

'I've done a fair bit for the National Trust,' he said. 'I'm actually working on the abandoned station building in Polwhipple right now, although it's more of a hobby than a paying job.'

There was a loud hum and the curtain began to open. Ben nodded towards the seats. 'Looks like the show's about to start. We should take our seats.'

They'd always sat at the back in the old days, Gina recalled, underneath the projectionist's booth so that they had more freedom to chatter and laugh without annoying the people around them. But now they took seats in the dead centre of the rows.

Gina shuffled uncomfortably. 'Is it me or do these cushions have rocks in them?'

'I think it's the springs,' Ben said, shifting around. 'They look like the original seats – who knows how many bottoms they've supported before us?'

Gina glanced down at the lopsided popcorn holder on her

right. 'And that's another thing that's missing – there's no popcorn for sale! What kind of cinema doesn't sell popcorn?'

Ben gave her an amused look. 'I think your expectations are too high, Gina. We've already established that this place has had quite a fall from grace.'

The speakers crackled and Gorran's broad accent echoed over their heads. 'Welcome to the Polwhipple Palace, Cornwall's premier picture house by the sea. We hope you enjoy tonight's film.'

Gina inched sideways, wincing as a spring pinged against the thin fabric of her chair. '*Enjoy* isn't the word I'd choose,' she grumbled.

'Oh, it's not that bad,' Ben said, his eyes dancing. 'At least the company is good.'

She gazed at him and felt the corners of her mouth start to lift. He always had been able to make her smile. 'You're right. I'll stop moaning.'

The film, when it finally started after a torrent of terrible local adverts, was actually good. The picture was a little fuzzy and there was a slight sound delay which meant the characters' lips were a fraction behind their voices, but Gina was able to lose herself in the story all the same and her toes were definitely tapping along to the tunes. If she'd been alone, she might even have got up and danced. As the final credits rolled, Ben sighed and stretched. 'That wasn't half bad.'

Gina nodded. 'Kevin Bacon can show me some moves any time.'

Ferrelli's was closed and in darkness by the time they made their way out of the screen. Bruno was waiting by the double doors; he wished them a goodnight as he ushered them out and locked up behind them.

'Well, in spite of everything, I actually enjoyed myself,' Ben said. 'Next time I'd probably bring my own cushion—'

'And some popcorn,' Gina put in.

'And some popcorn,' he agreed. He raised an enquiring eyebrow. 'Want to do it again sometime?'

She did want to, Gina realised; it was fun having someone who enjoyed going to the cinema as much as she did, although obviously the Palace had tried its hardest to make their visit a dismal night out. But again, she found herself wondering why Ben didn't have better things to do with his Saturday nights. She could understand why he might not want to bring a girlfriend to the Palace, but there were other places to go in Polwhipple. Unless he didn't have a girlfriend . . . not that it was any of her business anyway.

'Yes, that would be great,' she said, pushing the thought of his relationship status firmly out of her head. 'We should probably wait and see what Gorran plans to show next week before we make concrete plans, though. I'm not spending two and a half hours watching some unintelligible dirge about the washing lines of Prague.'

'Are you kidding?' Ben gave her a scandalised look. 'I love the washing lines of Prague.'

Gina felt her forehead crease. 'Really?'

'No. You should talk to Gorran; pitch him your idea about

a special screening. I'd be happy to spread the word if it goes ahead.'

She hesitated. Her trip to Polwhipple was meant to be a break from her events management work; she really ought to be focusing on helping Nonno. Then again, a successful event at the Palace would increase ice-cream sales. 'Okay, maybe I will. Thanks.'

Ben smiled. 'How are you getting back? Want me to walk you to your grandparents' place?'

She shook her head. 'Then we really would have gone back sixteen years. No, I'm staying at the Tawny holiday complex, in Mawgan Porth, so I've borrowed Nonna's car for the night.'

Recognition flashed in his eyes. 'The one overlooking the beach? I know it. Great view.'

'That's pretty much what sold it to me,' Gina admitted. 'So . . . I'll drop you a message, shall I? Once Gorran reveals what films he's screening?'

He tilted his head. 'Or any time you feel like saying hello,' he said, gazing down at her. 'It's good to see you again, Gina. Really good.'

'You too,' she said, returning his gaze.

They stood smiling at each other for a few more seconds. How could he look the same as he always had, and yet so different at the same time? she wondered, gazing at him. Suddenly aware that she was staring once again, Gina pulled herself together and reached into her coat for the car keys. 'I'd better go. Take care, Ben, and thanks for tonight.'

She gave him a little wave and turned away, walking fast to the car. Must not look back, she told herself. Must not look back . . .

When she reached Nonna's Fiat, she did allow herself to glance over one shoulder: he was gone. She climbed into the car and started the engine, glancing quickly at her phone as she did so. Two missed calls, both from Max. A pang of guilt hit her when she saw his name; never mind Ben's relationship status, she was suddenly aware that she hadn't mentioned Max during the evening, mostly because the opportunity hadn't arisen. But surely if she was wondering whether Ben was single, he'd be asking the same question about her? He hadn't shown anything other than friendly interest but it made sense to clear things up as soon as possible, Gina decided, to head off any potential misunderstandings later.

Her gaze flickered to her phone again and her hand twitched on the steering wheel; should she turn the engine off and call Max now? Then again, it was late – Max might be out on the town and she was tired after her early start with Nonno.

Putting the car into gear, Gina set off for home. She had nothing to tell him that couldn't wait until the morning.

# Chapter Six

Gina gave herself the luxury of a lie-in on Sunday morning. There was no point in hurrying over to Nonna and Nonno's – they'd be attending Mass at St Peter's until gone midday – and there was nothing else to get up for, other than her overdue conversation with Max. She was sure he'd mentioned a party last time they'd spoken, so he probably wouldn't be in the mood to talk yet, anyway. Instead, she made herself a coffee and drank it on the balcony, watching the leaden clouds roll over the moody blue-grey sea. The waves were quite high, meaning the surfers were out; Gina squinted at them for a moment but she couldn't tell if Ben was among them. After a few minutes, she gave up trying and went inside for a shower.

Max called as she was drying her hair. 'You're a hard person to get hold of,' he observed when she answered. 'Been tearing up the night life in Polwhipple?'

Gina laughed. 'Sorry, I ran into an old friend.' She paused, suddenly aware of a reluctance to mention Ben's name. It was ridiculous; there was no reason not to tell Max the truth, but instead she skirted around it. 'We watched a film in the old cinema here – you wouldn't believe how awful the place is now.'

When she'd finished describing the Palace to Max, he gave a thoughtful whistle. 'Sounds like the place is on its last legs. I know it's got sentimental value but maybe it's time to call it a day.'

Gina frowned. 'What do you mean?'

'I mean close it down,' Max said, his tone tactful. 'Art Deco is really popular and this Gorran bloke could make a mint by selling it on for redevelopment. Enough to compensate your grandfather for the inconvenience and open a brand-new Ferrelli's somewhere else.'

Gina felt her jaw drop. 'Nonno would be devastated if the Palace closed down. He wouldn't want a new shop.'

'Then you'd just make sure any redevelopment agreed to keep the concession on as a going concern,' Max said reasonably. 'It's old, it might even be a listed building, so whoever bought it would need to bear that in mind. Sympathetically converted seafront apartments would be the most financially viable option, with Ferrelli's downstairs.'

'Maybe,' Gina said, trying to imagine Polwhipple seafront without its iconic picture house. 'Anyway, it's still open for the moment. I was going to suggest organising an event there, to see if I can whip up a bit of interest and bring in some trade.'

Max sighed. 'Sounds like a waste of time to me, but if anyone can pull something like that off, it's you. How's the ice-cream business going, anyway? Have you revolutionised your grandfather's business yet?'

'Not exactly,' she said wryly. She opened her mouth to tell him about Nonno's trick with the salt and sugar and then closed it again. Max had a bad enough opinion of her family already, she didn't want to make things worse. 'I've got a few ideas, you know how it is – one step at a time. What have you been up to?'

She listened as Max described a mutual friend's birthday celebrations in Mayfair the night before. 'Sounds like it got messy,' she commented once he'd finished. 'I'm amazed you don't have a hangover.'

'I was the sensible one,' he said, which made Gina smile. Max was *always* the sensible one – in the three years that she'd known him, she'd never seen him out of control, although she knew he could drink like a rugby player if the circumstances were right.

'I did wish you were there, though,' he went on. 'It wasn't the same without you.'

'Mmm,' Gina murmured, thinking how unappealing the night sounded. She'd been much happier tapping her toes to *Footloose* at the Palace. 'The pace is quite different down here, as you can imagine,' she said, gazing out at the gulls wheeling across the sky. 'But I have found somewhere to live.'

'Great,' Max said, and she heard the smile in his voice. 'So when can I come and have a nose around? I can't wait to experience Polwhipple's delights again.'

Was he being sarcastic or serious? Gina wondered. It was so hard to tell over the phone. 'Really?' she asked. 'It's beautiful here at the moment. I think you'll like it.'

'You're beautiful,' he said. 'I bet you fit right in.'

It was a cheesy line but Gina couldn't help smiling. 'Very smooth, Max. Why don't you come down for a weekend and see for yourself?'

'I'll make some space in my diary,' Max assured her. 'But not next weekend – it's the launch party for that new restaurant on the South Bank. Maybe the weekend after?'

'You could come for the cinema event. If I decide to pitch it, that is.'

'Ha – I think we both know you're going to pitch it.'

Gina smiled again – he knew her too well. 'Okay. Listen, I have to finish drying my hair. I'll call you soon and we can confirm the date for your visit.'

'Can't wait,' Max said, his voice warm and full of anticipation. 'I'll even turn on the famous Max Hardy charm, see if I can make Ferocious Ferdie like me.'

Gina laughed and ended the call. But something was niggling at her: should she have told Max exactly who she'd been to see the film with last night? Ben was just a friend and she was fairly sure Max wouldn't be able to name Sarah or Tori or any of the other friends she hung out with when she wasn't with him – why should she start naming names now, simply because she was a few hundred miles away? And Max had nothing to fear from Ben in any case – he was someone she used to know, that was all. Max wouldn't expect her to stay in every night, anyway – he'd understand she'd need friends in Polwhipple too.

Even so, Gina felt the tiniest bit guilty. If Max really had nothing to fear from Ben, then why hadn't she told Max his name when she'd mentioned her trip to the cinema? And why couldn't she stop glancing towards the beach?

Gina headed to the picture house just before midday on Monday, hoping to see Gorran. She was in luck; she found him tucked away in the little office, wearing what looked suspiciously like the same shirt as the week before, although she couldn't be absolutely sure.

'I came to see *Footloose* on Saturday,' she told him, once she was sitting in the leather swivel chair again. 'It was a lot of fun.'

Gorran nodded gloomily. 'Good. I suppose you know that no one showed up for the pigeon film. Such a shame – it really is an amazing story.'

Gina leaned forwards. 'It doesn't matter how good the film is if no one knows it's on, Gorran. Surely you understand that?'

'We put a poster on the door,' he said, firing a defensive look her way. 'That usually does the trick.'

'For the people who know where to look,' she argued. 'You don't have a website, there are no online tickets and screenings are erratic. I'm amazed this place is still running at all – you can't be making any profit.'

'We're not,' he admitted. 'I'm doing my best, Gina, but it doesn't seem to be enough.'

He looked so dejected that she felt sorry for him. 'Look, why don't you let me help you? I'd be happy to organise an event for you, try some new ideas to see if we can bring in more punters.'

'Oh?' Gorran said, his eyes wary. 'What kind of new ideas?'

Gina ran through the thoughts she'd had about *Footloose* the night before; everything from fancy dress suggestions to her idea for a bespoke ice-cream flavour. By the time she'd finished, Gorran was staring at her as though she'd just thrown him a lifeline. 'You'd do all that?'

'Of course,' Gina replied, crossing her fingers that she could convince Nonno to let her try her hand at some new flavours. 'You might need to invest a little upfront, although I'm confident the increased revenue will repay your investment. Why don't we start thinking of a few films that might attract a crowd?'

Gorran's face lit up and Gina knew – just knew – he was going to suggest some obscure art house flick. 'Something well-known,' she said, lightning fast. 'A classic movie that also has broad event appeal.'

His expression fell. 'Oh. I don't think I even know what event appeal means.'

She smiled. 'Think of it as added value – so the film itself is at the heart of the screening but I can add extra details to tempt people to come along. Things like a themed cocktail, maybe?'

'We are allowed to serve alcohol on the premises,' Gorran said. 'I still have my licence.'

'Okay, that's good,' Gina said encouragingly. 'All we need to do is find the right film. Do you have a mailing list?'

'Not as such, no.'

Gina couldn't say she was surprised. 'Any advertising space anywhere, like the local paper? Or the shops along the seafront? There's a vintage clothes boutique that could be the perfect partner for the Palace.'

He sighed, as though he knew she would be disappointed. 'No.'

'So we'll need to get some flyers and posters printed.' She took a deep breath. 'Which brings me onto the budget. You're going to need to spend some money if you want to make this a success.'

'Of course.' Gorran threw her an apprehensive look. 'How much money?'

Gina did a few quick sums in her head and named a conservative figure. He blanched. 'Really?'

'If you want to get bums on seats. And speaking of seats, you should look at getting those replaced – they're not what I'd call comfortable.'

'New seats would cost a fortune,' Gorran said morosely. 'Everything is so expensive these days. Tash wants a new projector – or at least one that doesn't break down once a week – and she keeps leaving brochures for digital projection systems around, although she's got no hope there. I'm not selling my soul to the digital devil – no way.'

His lip curled as he finished speaking. Gina paused, wondering whether to ask what he meant; digital sounded good – better picture and sound quality, and the films were probably easier to get hold of, although she wasn't naïve enough to assume any of that translated into cheaper. 'Sorry, I'm not sure—'

'We show analogue film here,' Gorran interrupted, the fire of the zealot burning in his eyes. 'The old school, traditional 35mm celluloid that the entire movie industry was built on. It comes in reels from the distributor and it runs through our admittedly creaky projector, the way film was meant to be shown. But a lot of the chain cinemas have moved over to digital projectors, so the movies don't come in big reels and they don't suffer from wear and tear. And some of the studios aren't even releasing movies on film any more, but that doesn't mean digital is somehow better.' He angled his chin stubbornly. 'Look at how people rushed to embrace music on CDs – now they're realising that vinyl has more soul and record players bring something to the table that digital can't.'

He stopped abruptly as he noticed Gina's raised eyebrows and his already rosy cheeks turned redder. 'Sorry. I got a bit carried away. What were you saying?'

'The seats,' she said, checking her notes. 'Maybe we could tell people to bring a cushion, or find a way to make the bad seats part of the experience. It might be better to choose a short film, so they don't have to sit for as long.'

'The older the better, in that case,' he replied. 'A lot of the classic black-and-white films are less than ninety minutes long.'

Gina thought for a moment. 'Okay, why don't you draw up a list of possible choices and get them over to me? Then I can have a look and see which one has the most potential.' She smiled. 'And then we decide on a date and the hard work will really begin. But I think it will be worth it. Imagine a full house for once.'

'Okay,' Gorran said, his gaze far away. 'We'll give it a go.'

'I can't believe you persuaded Gorran Dew to part with some money,' Nonna said, when Gina told her about the meeting. 'He's famous for having the tightest pockets this side of the River Tamar.'

They were in Nonna's kitchen, going over ideas for new gelato flavours while Nonno had lunch with his local Rotary club cronies.

'I think Gorran realised that the more tickets he sells, the more chance there is that the Palace will be able to stay open,' Gina said. 'And I don't plan to spend a fortune, either. It should pay for itself eventually.'

'It all sounds marvellous – you will work magic over the place,' Elena said, her eyes twinkling. 'So, what flavours do you want to start with – biscotti? Tiramisu?'

'I don't know. Such a lot depends on the film we choose . . .' Gina hesitated. 'You don't think Nonno will be angry, do you? I mean, I've only been here a few days and already I'm sneaking about behind his back, meddling with his recipes.'

Elena gave an elegant shrug. 'We are only experimenting – you haven't meddled with anything. Besides, you need to understand how to combine flavours. This is simply part of your gelato education.' She lowered her voice to a whisper. 'And Nonno doesn't need to know. Not yet.'

Gina couldn't help smiling. 'When you put it like that . . .' she said, tilting her head. 'All right. I love your tiramisu. Let's try that one first.'

Elena stretched up to pull a thick, old-looking notebook stuffed with extra pages and faded clippings from the high shelf over her head. 'This belonged to my mother, and her mother before that. It has every family recipe in it, including our legendary tiramisu.'

She pushed it towards Gina so that she could read the spidery handwriting. There was plenty of detail – all Gina and Elena had to do was work out how best to recreate the flavour of the dessert in an ice-cream. Chocolate, cream, sugar, mascarpone cheese . . . to get the flavour exactly right would involve a considerable amount of tasting, Gina thought with a suspicious sideways glance – maybe this was all part of Nonna's plan to fatten her up. Her jeans were already feeling a little tighter and she'd only been in Polwhipple for a few days. She'd have to start taking more walks along the cliffs, or join a gym.

'So I heard you and Ben Pascoe are getting on well,' Elena said, as she made an espresso to add to the recipe. 'I always thought he was such a nice boy. Hard-working, polite and very pleasing to look at. Proper handsome, Manda calls him.'

Her tone was neutral but she sent a mischievous glance sideways that made Gina laugh. 'Don't get any ideas, Nonna. I'm sure Ben has his pick of the girls and I've got Max, remember?'

The older woman sniffed. 'Barely. I have only met him once. What does he do again?'

'He's a property developer,' Gina replied. 'He's worked on a lot of very important buildings in London – he was involved in the Shard and several of the other new properties along the Thames.'

'So he takes old things and breaks them apart to make way for new ones, yes?' Elena handed her the golden caster sugar to measure. 'I'm not sure I like the sound of that.'

Gina checked the recipe and concentrated on tipping the sugar into the scales. 'Not always. If there's an older building that needs some TLC then he'll buy that and redevelop it as sympathetically as he can.' She tried not to think of the Palace as she gave her grandmother a pointed glance. 'He is also hard-working, polite and very pleasing to look at.'

'But does he make you happy, Gina?' Elena persisted. 'It breaks my heart to see you so thin and pale—'

'I'm not—' Gina began but her grandmother ignored her.

'You need some sunshine and laughter and joy in your life,' she went on. 'Why isn't Max giving you these things?'

Gina stared at the golden sugar crystals in the bowl beneath her. Max did make her laugh but it was true that most of their dates seemed to revolve around business these days. And she couldn't remember the last time they'd spent a day sitting in the sun – some corporate event or another in the summer, probably, schmoozing his clients. But they both worked hard and she knew Max loved her, the same way that she loved him. They weren't unhappy. Nonna didn't understand, that was all.

'We're not the same as you and Nonno,' she explained in a quiet voice. 'You met and fell in love in a different era, when you had time to really focus on each other – modern relationships aren't like that. Max and I don't spend every waking moment having fun but that doesn't mean we're not happy.'

Elena was silent for a long moment. 'I don't want to interfere, *bella mia*. You know your own heart and if you say Max makes it whirl and sing then I must believe you.' She squared her shoulders and smiled. 'Perhaps when you go home and cook for him he will appreciate you more, yes?'

Gina laughed – her grandmother's belief that food could fix everything was unwavering. 'I'm sure he won't have a problem with that, Nonna.'

'Good,' Elena said, with some satisfaction. She flexed her fingers and reached for the Marsala wine. 'Now, let me teach you the secret of the perfect tiramisu.'

# Chapter Seven

Gina spent the rest of the afternoon in the dairy, creating batches of gelato using Ferdie's traditional recipes. She was getting the hang of the process now and her mind wandered as she combined the ingredients and set the machines to do the hard work. What film should they choose for the Palace screening? *Star Wars* was popular and topical but she didn't feel it was different enough – she needed something that would appeal to Polwhipple's older generations as well as tempting the younger ones with cosplay; if there was one thing she'd learned, it was that people loved an opportunity to dress up. An Eighties classic, maybe? Or perhaps they should look even further back – *Gone with the Wind*? Or was that too much too soon?

She was mulling it over as she walked home after another waistline-busting supper with her grandparents. Gina had watched nervously as Nonno had tucked into his tiramisu, wondering whether he'd be able to tell that she had made it rather than Nonna, but he seemed to enjoy it in the same way that he always did and didn't appear to have made the connection between that and her comments about new ice-cream flavours. Elena had given her a tiny wink and had whispered as Gina left that they should meet again soon to decide how to make their ice-cream. The trouble was that Gina couldn't think of a classic film set in Italy that would have the impact she wanted – there was *Roman Holiday*, of course, starring Audrey Hepburn and Gregory Peck, but it didn't really have the wow factor she wanted for the Palace's first event. So although the tiramisu ice-cream might make an appearance at some point at Ferrelli's, it wasn't the flavour she needed first. She had no idea what that might be.

The next morning, she woke up early and sought inspiration on the beach at Mawgan Porth. She had the place to herself; the sun was just peeping over the clifftops as she unfurled her rug on the pale sand and settled down to watch the sky change from navy blue to pink and gold, her hands wrapped around a steaming mug of coffee. The breeze off the sea was chilly – she was glad of her warm coat – but there was also a hint of spring amid the salty fresh air and she didn't think the day itself would be cold. March was often drizzly and dull in London, although it had its fair share of spectacular sunrises, but in Cornwall it seemed as though someone had applied an Instagram filter to the view; everything looked brighter and prettier. Gina remembered Nonna's comment about needing some sunshine and smiled; she was sure her grandmother would approve of her early morning excursion.

The surfers began to arrive, only two or three, but enough to tell Gina it was time to climb the stairs that led to the top of the cliffs. She stood up, shaking the sand from her rug.

'Gina!'

The shout made her look up and she saw Ben coming towards her, a surfboard in his arms. Once again, her thoughts flitted back to Nonna the day before and she couldn't argue – Ben *was* very pleasing to look at. Had he been this good-looking as a teen? Surely she would have remembered; when she thought back to the summers they'd spent together, all she could picture was his untidy blond hair and freckles. But there had been a hint of attraction during that last summer, hadn't there? There'd been a moment one day on the beach when she'd been sure he was about to kiss her but something had interrupted them – she couldn't remember what – and the moment had vanished. She'd forgotten all about it until now . . .

'Good morning,' she called, burying the memory once more. 'Another day, another wetsuit.'

He grinned. 'Yeah, I sometimes feel as though I live in these things. Although you should see me the rest of the time – I'm mostly covered in dust and paint. And sometimes coal dust, if I've been working on the trains.'

'The trains?' Gina echoed, blinking. 'How many jobs do you have?'

'The steam trains,' he explained. 'The ones that run between Bodmin and Boscarne. They've been a passion of mine for years and I'm a volunteer driver, although there's a lot of competition so I don't do it as often as I'd like.'

So he was a steam enthusiast as well as everything else, Gina thought, with an incredulous shake of her head. But hadn't he mentioned something about restoring Polwhipple's old station building? That made a lot more sense now. 'Were you always a train spotter?' she teased.

Ben shook his head. 'I'm not a train spotter – they take their hobby very seriously. I just love the elegance and history of steam trains. Did you know that the Bodmin and Wenford railway used to come to Polwhipple after Boscarne Junction? British Rail closed the passenger line back in the Sixties but it carried on as a freight route for years. And then the Bodmin Railway Preservation Society restored the track to run steam trains in the 1990s but decided not to run it all the way to Polwhipple.'

Understanding dawned on Gina. 'Is that why you're restoring the building? So that the steam train can come back here?'

'That's the idea,' Ben said. 'Although there's no guarantee – I think it would be great for the town, but the preservation society doesn't agree and they own the trains and the track. I'm hoping they'll change their mind once they see how good the restored station looks, but in the meantime it's really a labour of love.'

Gina frowned. Business alarm bells were starting to ring at the back of her head. 'But they know you're doing it?'

He pulled a face. 'Sort of. My dad was a driver on the

freight line, carrying china clay, and he bought the station not long after the Great Western Railway closed it, hoping to turn the building into a house for us to live in. But he died before he could put his plan into action and it's been sitting there ever since, growing more and more derelict.'

Ben's dad had died long before Gina had known him, back when he was seven or eight, and his mother had raised him on her own. Teenage Ben hadn't talked about his father much and Gina hadn't wanted to pry. 'And now you're restoring it yourself,' she said slowly. 'How are you funding it? Have you got a grant?'

'No,' Ben said. 'I'm paying for it myself. Like I said, it's a labour of love. A nod to my dad's memory, if you like.'

'But—' Gina stopped as sensible objections crowded into her brain. Max would never embark on a project like this, not without having a clear idea of the outcome at the other end. But then, Max was a businessman through and through – he didn't have a sentimental bone in his body. Which wasn't to say that Ben wasn't good at what he did too; from the sounds of things he'd worked on some very prestigious restorations. But pouring his time and money into a project that had no guarantee of achieving his ambition at the end . . . that sounded foolhardy to Gina.

'Why don't you come over and I'll show you round?' Ben said. 'I know it sounds crazy but I think you'll understand once you stand inside the building.'

He looked so earnest and enthusiastic that Gina couldn't

say no. 'Okay,' she said, letting out a little laugh. 'When did you have in mind?'

He smiled at her. 'What are you doing this afternoon?'

The road to Polwhipple station was closed off with ornate iron gates. A heavy padlock had been threaded through the black metal, and sturdy wire fencing ran off to either side. Ben was waiting in front of them; his wetsuit had been traded for a pair of jeans and a warm woollen coat. Nonna would approve, Gina thought wryly as she got nearer.

'Ready?' he said, holding up a bunch of keys.

She gazed beyond the gates at the low sandstone building a short distance away. There was a white combi van parked in front of it, next to a yellow skip that seemed to be half-full of rubble. 'I think so.'

As Gina got nearer, she could see that some of the windows had been boarded up.

'Local yobs,' Ben explained, waving a hand. 'They love sneaking in to throw stones at the glass so I boarded the windows up. Some of these windows date back to the Victorian era and I'd like to preserve as many as I can.'

He unlocked the solid wooden door. 'This chocolate colour scheme was standard across the whole Great Western Railway network,' he went on. 'I've had a bit of trouble finding the exact shade of brown, although the blokes at Bodmin Parkway have been very helpful. Can you imagine if I used the wrong colour?'

Gina could. She didn't know any train enthusiasts but they

were famous for being sticklers over details and the exact shade of paint was something that they would probably be aware of; the last thing Ben needed was for his pet project to be historically inaccurate.

He flicked on a light switch as they stepped inside and Gina almost gasped. It was like travelling back in time. The ticket hall gleamed beneath hanging brass light fittings, its chocolate and cream walls immaculate and the high coved ceiling smooth. Facing them was a double door, complete with frosted glass arches halfway up and small stained-glass windows above, and at their feet the floor was inlaid with black and white tiles. There was a ticket window in one wall, picked out in the same rich brown as the main door and all the other woodwork. On the opposite wall there hung a wooden station clock with Roman numerals and golden hands and a space for a key to wind the mechanism. And beneath that, there was an ornate coat of arms emblazoned with the words *Great Western Railway Company.* Hanging signs pointed the way to the trains and the waiting room.

'Wow,' Gina said, gazing around her. 'This is incredible.'

Ben smiled. 'Thank you. I haven't done the ticket office yet, but the waiting room and the toilets are finished.'

'And you've done all this in your spare time?' Gina said, stepping forward to admire the intricate blues and greens in the stained-glass panels over the door to the platform. 'How long has it taken you?'

'About eighteen months, so far,' he replied. 'Obviously, I

get more done in the summer months but living on site helps—'

'Wait,' Gina interrupted, staring at him. 'You live here too?'

He shifted slightly. 'Not in here, obviously. But in the grounds.'

She frowned. 'In a house?'

'Not exactly,' he said. 'Look, it's probably easier if I show you.'

Mystified, Gina watched as he unlocked the door that led to the train tracks and disappeared through it. She followed him all the way along the platform, through a low white gate and down some steps, towards a side track where a chocolate and cream painted railway compartment stood.

'Here?' Gina said, trying not to gape. 'This is where you live?'

Ben smiled. 'It's actually quite cosy inside.'

Gina summoned up a mental image of the train carriages she'd travelled in before. 'If you say so.'

'Come inside and see for yourself.'

He climbed a set of metal stairs outside the middle of the compartment and opened the door. 'After you,' he said, stepping back down and waving her inside.

If walking into the ticket hall had been like being whirled back to a bygone era then the room Gina found herself in after she'd climbed the stairs was even more unexpected. It was compact like a train carriage, with a rounded ceiling and standard train windows but that was where the comparison ended. There were no rows of tables and seats, no luggage racks; the room had been fitted with comfortable-looking winged-back leather armchairs pointed towards a coffee table piled high with books in front of a wood-burner. The floor was a gleaming dark wood, contrasting with the honey-coloured panelling along the walls and the rounded ceiling, and was dotted with thick rugs. A door in the middle of the end wall suggested there was more to explore.

'Do you mind?' Gina said, pointing.

'Not at all,' Ben replied. 'I tidied up before you came, just in case this happened.'

Gina laughed. 'I did think it was suspiciously neat.'

She turned the door handle and found herself in a galley kitchen. Another door led her to a bedroom, with a large brass double bed at one end, luggage racks at head height along either side and a glimpse of what looked very much like an en-suite bathroom through a final door. Gina turned back towards Ben. 'I'm impressed.'

He shrugged modestly. 'It's not a bad place to live. Handy for the station, at any rate.'

Gina peeked into the en-suite, admiring the modern fittings and custom-built shower cubicle. 'And you did all this yourself?'

He nodded. 'I did tell you I liked trains.'

'You did,' Gina conceded. 'But there's liking trains, Ben, and then there's this – restoring your own station and living in a converted railway carriage. Didn't your mum ever buy you a train track?'

Ben laughed. 'I suppose it does look a bit like a second childhood. But I enjoy restoring old things, mending their broken bits and giving them a second lease of life.' He raised his hands in a shrug. 'People are too quick to move on these days – if something breaks, they throw it away and get a newer, shinier version. Sometimes they don't even wait until it's broken. But I prefer things that have a bit of history to them.'

He gazed at her then, his blue eyes unreadable and Gina wondered if he meant her too. But she knew what he was getting at; there was something comforting and warm about spending time with someone she had known for more than half her life, someone she shared a history with. She took a deep breath. 'Do you live here alone?'

His expression was steady. 'Yes, just me.'

She glanced discreetly around, looking for any signs that a woman might visit regularly. 'I suppose it's a bit small for two people.'

Ben tipped his head. 'You'd be surprised. The bed's big enough for two.'

Gina swallowed. Was he flirting with her or suggesting that the bed saw a lot of action? She couldn't tell. Except that she found herself hoping it was the former, if only because she didn't want to believe that Ben was the type to pull a different girl every night.

She shook the thought away. 'It's a lovely place. Really nice. When do you think the station will be finished?'

He turned and led the way back into the living room. 'It

depends on how good the weather is over the next few months, and how busy my real job gets. It could be as early as June, or as late as September.'

'Great – I'm here until June but I can always come back down to see it if things overrun.'

Ben nodded. 'That would be nice. But don't feel you have to – I know you have plenty to get back to in the real world.'

He meant London, and Max, although she'd never actually mentioned the fact that she had a boyfriend; wasn't *the real world* the exact phrase she'd used to describe her life when she'd met him on the beach? The trouble was that the longer Gina spent in Polwhipple, the more distant the real world was starting to feel – it had been that way when she'd been younger too. 'Yes,' she said simply.

They watched each other for a moment, then Ben reached for the door that led outside.

'Did you have any more thoughts about arranging an event at the Palace?' Ben asked, once they'd reached the station platform again. 'Or did Gorran run screaming when you mentioned it?'

'He didn't,' Gina said, grateful for the change of subject. 'In fact, he's totally on board. We just need to find the right film to show – something that will really capture people's imaginations.'

'*Brief Encounter*,' Ben said instantly. 'It's a classic, everyone loves it and the characters even go to the cinema.'

Gina laughed. 'And it's got nothing to do with the fact that most of the action happens at a station?'

He grinned. 'Pure coincidence. So what do you think? The film is set in the late 1930s – I could do a bit of work on the bar, make it look like the station café from that era?'

She nibbled her lip thoughtfully, casting her mind over what she remembered from the film. 'That might work. Costumes wouldn't be too hard or expensive for people to find and I'm sure I can find a few cocktail recipes to encourage people who don't know the story to come along. And I'm sure Gorran will be able to get hold of a copy.' She smiled at Ben. 'I think it's a really clever idea. Thank you.'

'If you build it, they will come,' he said. 'Just let me know what I can do to help,'

Gina smiled, recognising the famous misquote from *Field of Dreams*. 'Oh, I will,' she said. 'If this goes well it could be just what the Palace needs.'

She took out her phone. 'I hope Gorran knows what he's let himself in for.'

'I don't think he has any idea,' Ben said, looking cheerful. 'But don't let that hold you back.'

'Believe me, I won't,' Gina said as she dialled Gorran's number. 'I'm going to make him an offer he can't refuse.'

# Chapter Eight

Things started to move very fast over the next few days. Gorran confirmed he could get the film and they agreed on a Friday evening screening in two weeks' time. He seemed happy with the choice, which surprised Gina; she'd been expecting a battle. Even more surprisingly, Tash the projectionist was enthusiastic too.

'Top film,' she said, twiddling her eyebrow piercing. 'I love a bit of repressed emotion and stiff upper lip.'

In fact, it seemed to Gina that everyone was excited, especially when she explained the theme.

'Brilliant,' Manda said, rubbing her hands. 'I've got just the costume. I saw it in the window of the vintage shop a few months ago and couldn't resist buying it. You should see if they've got anything for you.'

'Great idea,' Gina said, feeling a surge of anticipation at the thought of stepping inside the gorgeous-looking boutique. 'I'll check it out right now.'

It was early afternoon and the promenade was quiet. Gina glanced into the window of Carrie's Attic, the way she usually did when she walked by, and then pushed open the door.

A bell tinkled as she entered, causing the dark-haired woman behind the counter to look up. She was around Gina's age, in her early thirties, with a friendly smile and an inquisitive expression. 'Hello. Do you need any help or are you just browsing?'

Gina gazed around; inside the shop was even more tantalising than it had appeared from the window and everywhere she looked something screamed for her attention. She reached out to touch a silky soft kaftan hanging from the nearest rail. 'I think I probably need some help.'

The woman eased around the counter. 'No problem. I'm Carrie and, contrary to popular belief, all the things you see here didn't really come from my attic.'

Gina laughed. 'No, you'd need to have some pretty eclectic tastes to own all of this.'

'So what can I tempt you with today?' Carrie said, her green eyes sparkling. 'Something everyday or have you got a special occasion coming up?'

'Definitely a special occasion,' Gina replied. 'I'm organising a *Brief Encounter* screening at the Palace a few doors up and I need an outfit that screams 1930s glamour.'

Carrie's eyes widened. 'Really? That sounds like my kind of thing. When is it?'

Gina filled her in, then took a deep breath. 'Actually, we're hoping to work with some local businesses to promote the event. Do you think you might be interested? Maybe put a poster in the window?'

The other woman nodded. 'Are you kidding? I'd be more than happy to get involved – do you need any help with the organisation?'

Her enthusiasm made Gina smile. 'I think I've got everything covered for now but I'll definitely keep you in mind if anything else comes up. What we need most is help spreading the word.'

'Count me in,' Carrie said. She steered Gina towards a rail at the back of the shop. 'The Thirties and Forties gear is all over here. Let's start by finding you a knockout costume.'

Forty-five minutes and a lot of laughter later, Gina left Carrie's Attic with two bulging bags and a promise to send Gorran down for a fitting soon.

'And make sure you let me know if you're planning any more events,' Carrie said as Gina waved goodbye. 'I've got an amazing gold bikini that would be perfect for a *Star Wars* marathon.'

Gina grinned; she couldn't imagine the look on Gorran's face if she turned up in that outfit. But the idea of working with Carrie on future events was appealing and it made good business sense. She'd taken a handful of Carrie's business cards too, intending to leave them at the Palace box office – with a bit of luck, sales for the *Brief Encounter* event would lead to some extra customers for Carrie too.

*

When Gina wasn't at the dairy, mixing up batches of gelato, she was busy scouring Nonna's recipe book for the perfect *Brief Encounter* ice-cream flavour. The rest of her time was consumed by planning. She commissioned a local website developer to put together a basic page so that people could find out more. Once that was done, she ordered flyers and posters. Together with Gorran, she set about distributing them around the local shops and businesses. Carrie was even more enthusiastic, taking a thick wedge of flyers and promising to promote the event to everyone on her mailing list as well as her walk-in customers. The owners of the Scarlet Hotel offered to loan the Palace their head bartender and cocktail expert for the night, and the nearby Pendragon restaurant gave Gina an excellent deal on canapés and snacks. She also pulled some strings with her journalist friends and arranged for the local paper to run a last-minute feature; the reporter and photographer surprised her by ordering tickets at the end of the interview. Everywhere she turned, she found people who were both helpful and keen to help where they could. Everywhere except in her grandparents' living room.

'No,' Ferdie said, when she'd tentatively suggested she might try her hand at a themed ice-cream flavour. 'We don't need gimmicks.'

Gina pulled out her iPad and brought up the website. 'But look, Nonno, it could be so good. All we need to do is find the right—'

He pushed the screen away. 'I said no. Gelato is a serious business – you don't mess with time-honoured Ferrelli family recipes. Before you know it we'll be serving Blue Bubblegum and other rubbish.'

Elena looked up from her book. 'But they do not all belong to the Ferrellis. You forget that you learned some of those recipes from my mother. She wasn't afraid to experiment.'

'Won't you let me try, Nonno?' Gina asked. 'I promise that if you don't like the flavour I come up with, I won't ask you again.'

Ferdie scowled at her. 'And what is this flavour, may I ask? Some cocktail or another, I suppose.'

Gina shook her head. 'No, nothing like that. I don't want to spoil the surprise, though. You'll just have to trust me.'

'I suppose you put her up to this, didn't you?' Ferdie growled, glaring at Elena. 'You've been desperate to meddle with my recipes for years.'

Elena arched an eyebrow. 'Not at all. But now that you come to mention it, those recipes are in need of a – what do they call it now – a makeover. Why don't you let Gina see what she can do?'

Ferdie glowered first at Elena and then at Gina. 'I suppose it can't hurt.' He wagged his finger in warning. 'But I want to taste it first. And it had better be good.'

Gina exchanged a triumphant glance with Elena. 'Oh, it will be, Nonno,' she said. 'Trust me.'

Gina took Nonna's car to Truro the following Saturday morning and bought herself an ice-cream maker. The machinery in Nonno's dairy was much faster and more efficient but she wanted the time and the space to experiment, which she couldn't do with Nonno breathing down her neck. Besides, the recipe she'd found called for some caramelised ingredients and she couldn't create those as easily in the dairy. And with only a week to go until *Brief Encounter* at the picture house by the sea, she really wanted to nail the flavour.

By the end of Sunday afternoon, she'd perfected her recipe, or at least she thought she had. What she needed was an impartial taste tester – someone who would give her an honest response . . .

She messaged Ben, who promised to come over in an hour and was as good as his word.

'So this is the irresistible view you mentioned,' he said, gazing out across the clifftops. 'I see what you mean.'

Gina smiled. 'I know. I could get used to it, actually.'

'That's the thing about Cornwall; it gets under your skin,' he said, with a meaningful nod. 'And then when you go away, it calls to you.'

'Is that why you came back?' Gina asked.

'Partly,' Ben said. He looked out at the sea once again, his shoulders hunched. 'That and getting my heart broken in Australia. I just wanted to go home after that.'

'Oh,' Gina said softly. 'I'm sorry.'

'Don't be,' he replied, sending her a swift smile. 'It was a long time ago now and everything worked out for the best. I'm where I ought to be.'

There was a lot she didn't know about Ben, Gina realised;

how he'd come to his career as a builder instead of pursuing his dream of being a professional surfer, why he was apparently single – although between his job and his surfing and his hobby, she couldn't see that he had much time for a girlfriend. Or a boyfriend, come to that, but then she remembered the way he'd looked at her when they'd stood in his bedroom and she knew he wasn't gay.

'Did you mention something about ice-cream?' he said, cutting into her thoughts. He held out one hand and she saw it contained a DVD of *Brief Encounter.* 'I wondered whether you fancied watching this?'

Gina grinned in delight. 'Perfect. I'll open some wine.'

They settled on the sofa as the opening credits rolled and Laura Jesson began to tell her story. But moments later, Gina was staring open-mouthed at the screen. 'Oh my God, that's us,' she said, pointing at the image of Trevor Howard helping Celia Johnson to get some grit out of her eye as steam billowed around them. 'I can't believe it!'

Ben shook his head. 'I can't believe I didn't think of it either. I must have seen this film five or six times over the years.'

'I've seen it too,' Gina said. 'It's one of my mum's favourites – we used to watch a lot of black-and-white movies together before I moved back to England. I even remember thinking that you rescuing me was like something out of a film. How funny!'

'I hardly rescued you,' he said, adopting a mock-injured expression. 'In fact, I think you insisted you didn't need my help.'

She batted him on the arm. 'I thought you were very kind. Now shhh – things are about to get interesting.'

They only talked once more before the end, to discuss some of the things Ben might do to make the derelict bar at the Palace look like the one on the screen. Eventually, the film rolled on to its bittersweet conclusion and Gina's heart ached for poor Laura as she watched her lover walk out of her life for ever.

'Do you think she did the right thing in staying with Fred?' Gina asked, gazing at the final credits.

Ben pursed his lips. 'I don't know. Fred didn't seem like a terrible husband and I assume she loved him at some point. I like to think they made a go of things.'

Gina took a thoughtful swig of her wine. 'So you disapprove of her affair?'

'I didn't say that,' Ben said mildly. 'You asked me if I thought she should have stayed with Fred and I answered. You didn't ask me whether she should have followed her heart – the answer to that question would have been yes.'

His eyes rested on hers for a fraction of a second too long, before flicking towards the kitchen. 'Anyway, I hate to suggest that you're a bad hostess, but I still haven't had the ice-cream I was promised. Unless you lured me here under false pretences?'

'Oh!' Gina squeaked, jumping to her feet. She crossed the open-plan living room to the kitchen area and reached into the freezer. 'This is the new flavour I'm thinking of suggesting but I need another opinion first.'

She scooped some of the golden-brown ice-cream from the tub and placed it in a bowl, which she handed to Ben. 'What do you think?'

He took a mouthful and his expression changed almost immediately. 'It tastes amazing! What is it?'

'Brown bread ice-cream,' she said. 'It's just a basic vanilla ice-cream with caramelised bread crumbs drizzled through it. Do you think it suits the theme?'

Ben took another mouthful. 'Are you kidding? It's perfect. Have you given any to your grandfather yet?'

'No, I thought—'

Gina's phone sprang into life on the kitchen counter, making her jump. She glanced at the screen and her heart jolted: Max. They'd been playing phone tennis for a few days, missing each other's calls. 'I should take this,' she said to Ben apologetically. 'Sorry.'

'No problem,' he said, checking the time. 'I should probably head home, anyway. No, don't come to the door – I'll see myself out.'

'Thanks,' she said, her hand hovering over the answer button. 'And thanks for coming over. I really appreciate it.'

His eyes crinkled as he headed for the door. 'No problem. You had me at ice-cream, to be honest.'

Gina hit answer, just as Ben turned back. 'Oh, and we should probably talk about how you want the bar to look at some point, but that can wait. See you soon, Gina.'

Smiling and waving, she closed the door after him and held her phone up to her ear. 'Hi Max, sorry about that.'

'Who was that?' he asked curiously.

'Just Ben,' Gina replied. 'He's the one I told you about – the one I used to hang about with when I was younger.'

There was a brief silence on the phone. 'So what were you doing together at ten thirty on a Sunday evening? Reminiscing about old times?'

Gina frowned. It wasn't like Max to be like this. 'No, we were working through some things for the event at the Palace,' she said, crossing her fingers even though it wasn't exactly a lie. 'Ben is a builder and he's going to make the bar look like the one from the film.'

There was another brief pause and then Max sighed. 'Sorry, I didn't mean to sound like an idiot. You don't owe me any explanations.'

He sounded tired again and Gina wondered whether he'd spent the weekend working. 'Don't worry about it. You've got every right to be curious. How are you, anyway?'

It didn't take long for Gina to work out that his tiredness was due to another late night, this time due to a stag do. She smiled as he described the antics the best man had got up to with the poor groom. 'It sounds like you need a rest,' she said when he'd finished. 'How about a weekend in Cornwall?'

'When?' he said. 'Just tell me the date and I'll be there.'

She frowned. 'I sent you the date, Max – it's next weekend. We talked about it last Sunday and you said you'd come, remember?'

'Did I?' His voice was suddenly muffled, as though he was

running his hand over his face. 'Bloody hell, I can hardly remember what I did yesterday, never mind a week ago.'

There was a silence, during which Gina imagined him checking through his calendar. Then he let out an irritated huff. 'I can't make next weekend. Can you rearrange?'

Gina almost dropped her phone. 'No, I can't! Flyers have gone out and it's been in the local paper – people have bought tickets. I can't just change the date because my boyfriend has double-booked himself.'

'Then I can't come,' Max said flatly. 'Brilliant.'

'What's got into you?' Gina said, frowning even more deeply. 'You've known this event was happening for a couple of weeks. Can't you cancel the other thing you have in your diary?'

'I don't think I can. Sorry,' he said and this time his tone was apologetic. 'I suppose I'll just have to come down another weekend. When works for you?'

Trying not to feel second-best, Gina flicked through her diary and gave him a couple of possible dates. Once she'd finished, the two of them fell silent.

'I really miss you,' Gina ventured, after a while.

'Yeah, me too,' Max said wearily. 'Look, Gina, why don't I call you back? I'm not in the best shape today.'

'Of course,' she said. 'Look after yourself. I love you.'

'Yeah, speak soon. Bye.'

He hung up, leaving Gina staring at her mobile, wondering what she'd done wrong. He's just tired, she reminded herself. And it was a shame he wouldn't be around for the *Brief*

*Encounter* evening but he hated the cinema anyway; she'd be too busy to worry about whether he was having fun or be able to spend much time with him. She closed her eyes briefly and lowered her phone to the kitchen counter. Maybe it was for the best that he couldn't make it, she decided, scooping the last of the half-melted ice-cream into her mouth.

The problem with having no precedent of customers buying tickets online or even much in advance was that Gina had no real idea how many people might be coming to the *Brief Encounter* screening. She'd set up a Facebook page for the Palace and linked it to the event she'd created, both of which had plenty of likes but none seemed to be translating into ticket sales; when she'd checked in with Bruno, he told her that he had ten pre-orders in his little notebook. With three days to go until the event . . .

'Have any of those pre-ordered tickets paid already?' Gina asked, trying to ignore the flutter of butterflies in her stomach.

'Around half of them have,' Bruno told her. 'Carrie from the vintage shop has paid and she's bringing a few mates. The others assure me they'll pay on the door.'

'It's not enough,' Gina said, sighing. 'Unless more people book, it won't be worth running.'

Bruno raised his shoulders. 'What can I say? They're used to just turning up. Or not, as the case may be.'

Gina glanced at the half-finished bar repairs – Ben was charging them very little to fix the uneven floor behind the counter and to turn it into the café they'd seen in *Brief Encounter.* 'I expect some more of that gorgeous ice-cream and a tub of popcorn, though,' he told Gina.

She'd just have to hope ticket sales picked up in the run up to Friday night or she was going to feel very embarrassed and Gorran was going to be considerably out of pocket.

She didn't dare tell Nonno. She'd stayed as vague as she could when answering his questions – he hadn't even tasted her Brown Bread flavour. And by the time Thursday morning rolled around, she couldn't bear it any longer and asked her grandfather to meet her in the dairy.

'Close your eyes,' she instructed him, placing a bowl of ice-cream on the work surface in front of him. She put a spoon into his hand. 'Now you can look.'

He stared at the golden ice-cream for a moment, then dipped his spoon in. Moments passed as he ate, closing his eyes and taking his time over each mouthful. When the bowl was empty, he turned to Gina. 'Very nice. What's that crunchy ingredient? It wasn't nuts, I know that, or praline.'

'Brown bread,' Gina said and she held her breath. 'So is it a yes? Does it get the Ferrelli's seal of approval for Friday?'

Nonno scraped his spoon around the edge of the bowl. 'Of course. I think it is the perfect choice.'

Gina felt her heart swell with a mixture of happiness and relief. 'Thanks, Nonno.'

'So it should,' he said, firing a fierce look her way. 'I knew gelato was in your blood, Gina, just like your mother. You're a true Ferrelli – I'm proud of you.'

He looked so sad when he mentioned her mother that Gina walked over to wrap him in a hug. She knew her mother was saddened by the rift between them too – in the past, she'd often asked the kind of indirect questions that made Gina suspect she wanted to know how Ferdie was doing. It gave her hope that one day they might resolve their differences; Ferdie had mellowed as he'd grown older and years of living in another country had softened the hurt Gina's mother had felt when Ferdie had accused her of neglecting a young Gina in favour of her career. The trouble was that they were both stubborn and hot-tempered, Gina thought as she hugged her grandfather. The trouble was that they were too alike.

She stepped back with a smile. 'That means a lot, Nonno. I'm proud to be a Ferrelli too.'

# Chapter Nine

The lights that spelled out 'The Palace' had finally had their missing bulbs replaced. Gina stood outside the picture house at just after seven o'clock, admiring the light that spilled from the building. It looked amazing, inside and out. Gorran had finally managed to rustle up some genuine film posters, which were on display in the casings outside. Manda was dressed as a 1940s usherette as she served behind the counter of Ferrelli's, and Bruno seemed to have found an old hotel bellboy's outfit that was perfect for his role at the box office. The bar had been restocked and transformed into an astonishing replica of the station café from *Brief Encounter* and their bartender was standing by to serve elegant Steaming Passion cocktails, while a 1930s playlist warbled away in the background. Even Gorran had made an effort and had dressed up in an almost uncrumpled suit and a trilby. Thanks to Carrie's genius, Gina had modelled her outfit on Laura Jesson, with a jaunty baker boy hat and a fake fur stole, although she couldn't resist a splash of red lipstick, which Laura would never have dared to wear. All they needed now were the guests.

Ticket sales had picked up throughout Thursday and Friday so that they now had a respectable number and the cinema wouldn't feel embarrassingly empty. Ben had appeared with a roll of old train tickets from Polwhipple station and Gina had instructed to give one to each guest as they arrived, so that they could be clipped by Gorran as people went in to take their seats.

Gina had laughed when she'd seen Ben's costume; he'd slicked his hair back underneath his hat and was obviously Alec Harvey to her Laura.

'You look like you should be on the screen,' he'd murmured as she'd greeted him. 'Let me know if you get any more grit in your eye.'

By seven thirty, the guests had started to arrive and Gina's stomach was in knots. What if something went wrong? 'Relax,' Ben said, when he caught sight of her tense expression. 'We've done all the hard work – this is the fun part.'

He was right, Gina knew, but that didn't mean her brain would stop racing at a hundred miles an hour; she knew from experience that she wouldn't start to feel comfortable until she was sure the event was a success, and that wouldn't happen here until the guests were seated in front of the film. But it also wouldn't do for her to look visibly anxious, so she took a deep breath and willed herself to calm down. At least I'm staying in character, she thought, picturing fretful Laura.

Time ticked on and more people began to arrive, a real

mixture of young, old and everything in between. Many of them had made a real effort with their costumes – no doubt helped with some inspiration from Carrie's Attic – and Gina thought the foyer looked like the set of a film. Carrie herself looked perfect – her costume was an almost exact replica of Dolly Messiter's, the gossipy woman who prevented the on-screen lovers from saying a proper goodbye.

'Wow,' Gina laughed when she saw her. 'You look like you've just stepped off the screen.'

Carrie adopted a snooty voice. 'Do you really think so, Laura, darling? How awfully kind of you to say so.' She glanced around the lobby with obvious satisfaction. 'This is a roaring success – well done.'

Gina raised her eyebrows. 'Due in no small part to all the amazing outfits. Did everyone in Polwhipple visit your shop?'

'Pretty much,' Carrie admitted. 'I've spent most of the last week glued to eBay, searching out costumes. It's been fun though and I think Ben makes an especially dashing Dr Harvey, don't you?'

'Does he?' Gina forced herself to sound disinterested. 'I've hardly seen him.'

'There he is,' Carrie said, pointing across the foyer. 'Over there, talking to Rose.'

Gina followed her finger and saw Ben talking to a glamorous blonde-haired woman. As she watched, the woman reached up and stroked Ben's face. Gina felt her stomach clench. 'I don't think I know her. Who is she?'

Carrie groaned. 'Rose Arundell – local It Girl and

practically Cornish royalty. Rumour has it she and Ben had a fling a while ago and she's been trying to get her claws into him again ever since.' She cast a sideways look at Gina. 'Poor Ben – shall we rescue him?'

Ben's voice echoed in Gina's head: *The bed's big enough for two . . .* 'You go,' she told Carrie, with a quick shake of her head. 'I need to check on the ice-cream sales.'

Trying her best not to look at Ben and Rose, Gina made her way over to Ferrelli's. There was a long queue, on both sides of the concession, and Gina was very glad she'd asked Heather to work too. Nonno and Nonna couldn't believe their eyes when they arrived and saw the hall filled with laughing, chattering guests.

'This is astonishing,' Nonno said, staring around him with the air of a man who thinks he is dreaming. 'You've worked miracles.'

A woman nearby lifted up her little round tub of ice-cream with an expression of pure bliss. 'Delicious gelato, Ferdie. You've outdone yourself.'

Her companion nodded. 'It's about time you introduced some new flavours. I hope we can expect more!'

'See?' Elena said, nudging Ferdie in the ribs. 'Now will you listen?'

Gina was just starting to breathe normally when she saw Tash peering furtively around the door beside the ticket office. 'Psssst!' the girl hissed, beckoning Gina closer.

She hurried over, a sinking feeling in her stomach. 'Is everything okay, Tash?'

The projectionist shook her head. 'No. I don't have all the film reels – there's one missing.'

Gina gaped at her, only partly understanding. 'So that means . . . ?'

'I don't have the whole film,' Tash said grimly. 'There'll be a large, very noticeable hole about 44 minutes in.'

'Oh no,' Gina said, feeling the blood drain from her face. 'Where is it likely to be?'

Tash shrugged. 'I've looked in all the obvious places. It's not in the archive, or in the projection booth. Gorran might know, but he's not answering his phone.'

'Leave it with me,' she said. 'And don't panic – it must be here somewhere.'

Doing her best to look untroubled, Gina wove her way through the crowd until she reached Gorran. He frowned at the news. 'But it can't be missing – I counted them myself just this morning.'

'So they were definitely all there then?' Gina asked.

He nodded. 'Yes. Nine reels, all present and correct.'

'Well, they're not all present now. Could anyone else have got to them?'

Gorran looked doubtful. 'I don't see how.'

'Problem?' Ben said, appearing at Gina's elbow.

'Just a small one,' Gina said, checking to see if Rose was still with him. Once she was certain he was alone, she explained.

Ben checked his watch. 'We've got twenty minutes. Do you reckon we can search this place from top to bottom in that time, Gorran?'

The cinema owner let out a long stream of air. 'We can try. I'll check my office, Tash can check the staffroom and you two can split the archive and the projection room between you.'

Gina took the archive, which was a dim room at the very back of the building, filled with floor to ceiling shelves. Each film was clearly labelled, and some had more reels than she had time to count. She pulled over a stepladder on wheels and started at the very top, pulling out each reel in turn and checking the label. She was very aware of the passing minutes – a short delay wouldn't matter but the guests would get restless if they were kept waiting too long. But they couldn't start until the missing reel was found.

She was starting to give up hope by the time she reached *V for Vendetta*. The bottom shelf wasn't completely full – it finished halfway along. With a groan of despair, Gina pulled out the last reel and saw it wasn't the one she was looking for. *Now what?* she asked herself, getting to her feet and dusting off her knees. They had precious minutes before the film was due to start: where else could she look?

She pushed her hair out of her eyes and turned around to hurry for the door. Her eye was caught by the edge of a reel poking out from beneath a pile of *Brief Encounter* posters on the floor. Darting forwards, she pulled at the silver circle.

'Yes!' she cried, when she saw the label. Gorran must have accidentally left it here when he was getting the posters.

Tucking it carefully under her arm, Gina yanked open the

door. 'I've found it,' she called as she ran for the projection room. 'Gorran, Tash, I've found it!'

Gorran burst out of his office, a sheaf of papers in his hand. Tash appeared through another door, relief pouring from her. She took the reel from Gina and hurried away.

Ben was standing in the middle of the projection booth, looking dejected, when they arrived. 'Got it!' Tash said triumphantly. 'Give me a few minutes and we'll be ready to roll.'

Gina sagged against the doorframe, unsure whether to laugh or cry.

'Come on,' Ben said, squeezing past Tash. 'Let's leave her to work her magic in peace.'

Gorran was still in the corridor, looking as though his life had flashed before his eyes. 'Imagine if we hadn't found it,' he said. 'All those people would have been disappointed.'

'But we did find it,' Gina said, patting his arm kindly. 'Disaster averted. Now, hadn't we better go and let them find their seats?'

He blinked. 'Yes, of course. Leave it to me.'

Gina watched him scurry away. 'That was close,' she said to Ben.

'It was,' he agreed. 'Where did you find it?'

'Buried under a pile of posters,' she said. 'It's lucky I spotted it.'

'Speaking of spotting things . . .' Ben stepped forwards to cup her face. 'You've got some dust on your cheek.'

Gina stayed perfectly still and he gently rubbed her skin.

His eyes seemed bluer than ever as he concentrated on removing the mark and she could see the faint outline of the freckles he'd had when he was younger. They could only have been stood like that for a second or two, but it felt to Gina as though she was gazing at him for ages. It's just like the film, she thought dreamily: I'm Laura and he's Alec.

Then he looked into her eyes and the breath caught in Gina's throat. He's going to kiss me, she thought, feeling herself grow even more still. And I don't think I'd mind if he does.

For a moment, he simply stared into her eyes, as though he was debating what to do. Then his head dipped towards hers. She didn't close her eyes as his lips brushed hers, even though part of her wanted to; she wanted to be aware of what she was doing. There were so many reasons why it ought to feel wrong, but it didn't. It felt warm and natural and soothing. It felt like home.

When the kiss ended, Gina's heart was thudding in her chest and she realised she had closed her eyes after all. Ben was staring at her, stricken. 'Look, Gina, I—'

The door to the foyer opened and Gorran stuck his head around it. 'It's show time! Come on.'

Ben started to speak but Gina cut him off. 'Later,' she said, reaching up to rub lipstick from his mouth. 'We can't sort this out now.'

On the other side of the door, the guests were starting to make their way into the screen. Hoping she didn't look as guilty as she felt, Gina found her grandparents.

'You don't need to babysit us,' Nonna scolded, when Gina said she would sit with them. 'We've been going to the movies for a long time. Go and sit with Ben.'

Gina felt her cheeks flush as she glanced over at Ben, who was watching her from beside the entrance to the screen. Rose was stood beside him, one arm linked possessively through his. 'No, I don't think—'

A shout rang out across the foyer. 'Gina!'

She spun around to see Max framed in the doorway, a trilby in one hand and a carnation tucked into the buttonhole of his old-fashioned suit. For a moment, she froze, then hurried towards him. 'Max!' she gasped. 'What are you doing here?'

'I wanted to see you,' he said, pulling her into his arms for a kiss.

Acutely aware of her audience, Gina stepped backwards as soon as she could. She didn't dare look at her grandparents. Or at Ben.

'I thought you were busy,' she said.

Max shrugged. 'I cleared my diary, skipped a couple of parties. I can only stay tonight but I know how important this was to you.' He glanced around, taking everything in. 'So this is what the inside of a cinema looks like. You were right – it's a great building.'

Gina swallowed hard, forcing herself to smile as he put his arm around her shoulders. 'Come on. Let's go and say hello to the grandparents.'

Apprehensively, she glanced up at the doors to the screen

as she led Max towards Nonna and Nonno. There was no sign of Ben. Giving herself a mental shake, she pushed him from her mind. She couldn't think about him, or what their kiss had meant, or even the way Rose had draped herself all over him. Ben was going to have to wait.

# Chapter Ten

The audience broke out into spontaneous cheering as the end credits rolled and Gina knew it wasn't because Laura had chosen to stay with her husband. The evening had been a triumph, in spite of the scare over the missing film reel. She watched people stop to congratulate Gorran and he generously waved them away and pointed them towards her. By the time she'd finished shaking hands, her arm ached almost as much as her cheeks did; she didn't think she'd ever smiled quite so much.

She spotted Ben once or twice over the heads of the crowd as they streamed out but he was never looking her way, and by the time the numbers had thinned, there was no sign of him, although she did see Rose standing alone at the bar looking furious. Max, on the other hand, seemed to be on a charm offensive. He was with her grandparents and a group of their friends, making them laugh with some outrageous stories of London property disasters. She stood for a moment, watching him; it was good of him to clear his diary for her and travel all this way to be here. And he was clearly making an effort with her grandparents. From the look on Nonna's face, his charm was working wonders.

'And here she is, the woman of the hour,' Max said, stepping back as she approached to place his hand solicitously at the small of her back. 'This was an amazing night, Gina. I hope you had the press here?'

Gina nodded. 'The local paper sent a journalist and a photographer so we should get some good coverage.' She glanced at him curiously. 'Did you enjoy the film?'

He didn't quite meet her eyes. 'Of course. It felt a tiny bit old-fashioned and dull but that's kind of the point, isn't it? To make us all feel as though we'd stepped back in time?'

Gina stared at him. 'Dull? How can you call it dull?'

Max raised an eyebrow. 'Oh, come on, all that long-suffering guilt and bottled-up emotion? It wouldn't happen nowadays – people don't behave like that any more.'

An image of Ben's face, close enough to kiss, popped into Gina's mind. She felt her cheeks grow warm. 'You don't think so?'

He laughed. 'No, I don't. Now, are you going to give me a tour of this wonderful apartment I've heard so much about? I'm looking forward to waking up to the sound of the sea tomorrow.'

Gina smiled at her grandparents. 'I hope you had a good time?'

Elena squeezed her hand. 'The best. And Nonno here wants to talk about some new flavour ideas.'

'No rush,' Ferdie said gruffly. 'When you've had time for a rest.'

Gina's smile widened. 'I can't wait.'

She leaned down to kiss her grandmother's cheek. 'Ben said to tell you goodnight,' the older woman whispered, so that only Gina could hear. 'He said he didn't want to trouble you but personally, I think he just wanted to escape that awful Rose Arundell.'

Gina felt a needle-sharp stab in her stomach. She drew back fast and gazed into Elena's knowing eyes. 'Goodnight, Nonna.'

'I could definitely get used to this,' Max said the next morning, as Gina brought him a mug of coffee in bed. 'I see what you mean about the sound of the waves too. Very soothing.'

Gina stifled a yawn. She hadn't slept well and had lain awake for what felt like hours as her mind raced. And then, when she'd finally dozed off, her sleep had been punctuated by jumbled dreams in which she was searching the Palace for something that changed every time she thought she'd found it. It had been a relief to wake up.

'We can go for a walk along the cliffs if you like,' she said, wrapping her hands around her own mug. 'Grab some breakfast in Polwhipple.'

Max gazed at her through heavy-lidded eyes. 'I'd rather stay here.'

Gina glanced out of the window at the clear blue skies. Last night, he'd shown her how much he'd missed her; they'd barely been through the front door when he'd started kissing her and it hadn't taken long for Gina to forget about Ben. But this morning felt different; she wasn't sure what she wanted. Having Max here seemed all wrong – he belonged in London, back in the real world. She swallowed a sigh. How could things have become so complicated?

'I want you to come home,' Max said, breaking into her thoughts. 'I miss you.'

Gina turned back to him. 'And I will, just as soon as Nonno is back on his feet.'

'He looked fairly steady last night.'

She frowned. 'He's able to get around, if that's what you mean. But there's a big difference between that and keeping Ferrelli's stocked with enough ice-cream. It will be Easter soon and trade will really start to pick up. Besides, you heard Nonna – he's finally accepted that it's time to try some new flavours.'

Max gave a good-natured sigh. 'Okay. I knew it was a long shot, especially after things went so well last night. I suppose I'll just have to come and visit you more often, that's all.'

Gina smiled. It really was sweet of him to come – she couldn't remember him ever cancelling his plans to spend time with her before, not even when they'd first met. 'It's a deal. Now, get up and put some clothes on. I want to show you the town.'

*

Gina spent most of Monday with her grandparents, tossing around ideas for new Ferrelli's flavours. On Tuesday morning, she met with Gorran, who was overwhelmed by how successful the *Brief Encounter* screening had been and wanted to know when they could do something like it again. Tuesday afternoon was taken up with recipe testing so it wasn't until Wednesday that Gina had the time to go in search of Ben. He hadn't messaged her, had been entirely silent, and she couldn't say she blamed him; she felt guilty and awkward too. But they needed to clear the air so she squared her shoulders and went to the station.

The gates were closed but unlocked. Gina followed the loud whine of a drill into the ticket hall. The noise was coming from the office on the right. She cleared her throat and called loudly. 'Ben? Ben, it's me. We need to talk.'

The whine stopped abruptly and Ben materialised in the doorway of the ticket office. He lowered his dust mask. 'Hello.'

'Hi,' Gina said, ignoring the butterflies his appearance had caused. 'How are you?'

'I'm fine. You?'

She managed a strained smile. 'I'm okay. Listen, about the other night—'

He held up his hands. 'You don't need to say anything, Gina. It was wrong of me and I'm sorry. I know you're not single – can you forgive me?'

It was all Gina could do not to gape at him open-mouthed. 'I was going to apologise to you. I knew what was going to happen and I should have stopped it. I'm sorry too.'

Ben studied her. 'I think we both got carried away by the romance of the film.'

She nodded. 'You're right. It was a mistake. But I hope it's not going to get in the way of us being friends?'

Now he smiled. 'No. It'll take more than a silly kiss to come between us, right?'

Relief washed over Gina like a wave. 'Right.'

Ben was silent for a moment. 'So apart from that, the evening was a smash hit. The whole town is talking about it.'

'It went really well,' Gina said. She almost made a comment about him being a smash hit too, with Rose Arundell, but stopped herself just in time. What he and Rose did or didn't do was none of her business. 'Much better than I hoped, to be honest. Gorran is already asking when we can do the next one but I think we really need to do something about those seats first. That's something I wanted to ask you about, actually.'

'Oh?'

She took a deep breath. 'I want to refurbish the Palace.' He started to speak and she held up her hands to stall him. 'I know it's a massive job and will cost a fortune, but I think it's got real potential. So I wondered whether you could help me to put together a funding application for the town council. Obviously, I know how to pull in a crowd, but you know all about how much a project like this might cost.'

She sent him a beseeching look. 'So what do you say? Will you help me, Ben?'

He stared at her for what felt like an age, his forehead crinkled into a frown that was made all the more serious by the dust that settled in the lines. 'On one condition,' he said eventually.

'Yes?' Gina said, wondering what he was going to say next.

'That you help me persuade the Railway Preservation Society to re-open the branch line to Polwhipple. I think we make a pretty good business team – if we work together, we should both be able to get what we want.'

Gina hesitated. It was true; she and Ben had made a good team on the *Brief Encounter* screening. But working on two big projects would mean spending a lot of time together; they'd have to make sure they established proper boundaries and ensured their relationship stayed platonic. Because now that Gina had found Ben as a friend again, she didn't want to risk losing him.

Making a decision, she stepped across the tiled ticket hall floor and held out her hand. 'Ben Pascoe, you've got yourself a partner. And all the ice-cream you can eat.'

# PART TWO

## Singing in the Rain

# Chapter Eleven

It had been the wettest Easter anyone could remember.

Gina Callaway shifted in her battered leather armchair beside the flickering fireplace in the Mermaid's Tail Inn, gazing out of the picture window that overlooked Polwhipple's sodden beach. Raindrops spattered against the glass, racing in rivulets to the dark wooden frame below. Beyond the thickened bull's-eye panes, the clouds were a sullen, gun-metal grey, driven across the sky by gusting winds that also whipped the waves into a white-tipped frenzy and whistled around the old pub. No one was braving the blustery sands, not even the hardiest of dog-walkers, and there was certainly no sign of the surfers who usually rode the waves. The beach was deserted, apart from the occasional seagull.

Gina cradled her half-drunk cup of coffee and sighed. The Easter weekend had been a wash-out as far as the weather was concerned and she'd spent a restless few days cooped up in her apartment, watching the relentless rain and venturing out only on Easter Sunday for a hearty roast dinner at her grandparents' house. Unable to bear the thought of a long Bank Holiday Monday on her own, but equally reluctant to impose herself on Nonna and Nonno again, Gina had packed up her laptop and headed for the cosy Mermaid's Tail, where she'd been greeted with a smile by the landlord, Jory.

'All right, Gina,' he'd called across the bar, with a welcoming nod as she'd entered the low-ceilinged snug. 'What can I get you?'

'Just an Americano, please,' she'd replied, shaking the rain from her coat.

He'd gestured towards the coat rack on her right. 'Hang your things up there and warm your bones by the fire. I'll be over with your coffee dreckly.'

Gina had settled into the armchair nearest the flames with a grateful smile. It had been over a month since she'd arrived in Polwhipple and she'd mostly stopped noticing the Cornish lilt that coloured the words of almost everyone she met. But every now and then, a word or phrase caught her ear and reminded her where she was – *dreckly*, meaning 'sometime soon', or *my 'ansum*, which was a common term of endearment whether you were male or female – and Jory's speech seemed to be more peppered with distinctly Cornish phrases than most people she encountered. It had taken her a few seconds to mentally adjust, the first time she'd heard Jory hail one of his regulars with 'All right, *shag*,' and then she'd remembered that it was another friendly greeting rather than an instruction.

'Still pizen down, then,' Jory commented now, appearing with an insulated silver jug to top up her coffee.

Gina held out her cup, nodding. It was hard to believe it right then but the forecast for the next few days was better; blue skies and unseasonal highs of fourteen degrees, if the Met Office was to be believed. And if Polwhipple *was* to be blessed with sunshine, the demand for Ferrelli's ice-cream would increase too. Gina planned to spend the rest of the week in her grandfather's converted dairy, whisking and churning and freezing so that the restaurants and paying public of Polwhipple were not disappointed when the sun finally showed its face and they felt a craving for gelato.

'Thanks,' she said to Jory, adding a splash of milk from the little jug on the table beside her. 'I imagine rain is bad for your business too.'

The landlord shrugged. 'It takes more than a downpour to keep our regulars away. But we're only proper busy during the summer. Even then, Polwhipple ent as heaving as Newquay or Padstow.' He stared out at the rain-lashed beach. 'There's not much to come here for, save the scenery, and there's plenty of that elsewhere.'

Gina opened her mouth to argue; as a teenager, she'd spent several idyllic summers in Polwhipple and, from what she could remember, the beach had always been packed with families. There was a small surfing contest in August, nothing like the international tournaments held elsewhere on the

Cornish coast, but well regarded enough to draw a good crowd of visitors to the town. But she knew what Jory meant – in the warmer months, there were parts of Cornwall where it felt as though you couldn't move for tourists. Unfortunately for the local businesses, Polwhipple wasn't one of those parts. What they needed was an irresistible attraction – something that would draw visitors in and encourage them to see what the sleepy seaside town had to offer. Gina glanced down at her laptop and the funding application that sat on the screen; what they needed was money.

The door creaked open and a petite brown-haired woman stepped into the snug. She glanced around and beamed when she saw Gina.

'You're a sight for sore eyes,' she said, hurrying over. She glanced up at Jory. 'A pot of tea, please. Got any warm pasties left? I'm starving.'

Jory smiled. 'Afternoon, Carrie. I'll see what I can do.'

He threaded his way behind the narrow bar and disappeared into the door that Gina imagined led to the kitchens. Carrie tugged off her coat and hung it next to Gina's, then pulled up a chair at her table.

'Thanks for giving me an excuse to escape,' she said, warming her hands against the fire. 'The shop is so dead this morning that I thought I might actually die of boredom. There are only so many times I can pretend I'm Elizabeth Taylor winning an Oscar.'

Gina grinned, picturing her friend standing among the silk- and satin-covered clothes rails of her vintage boutique further along the promenade, graciously accepting an award from an imaginary host. 'I know what you mean. I needed a change of scene too and Jory makes a mean cup of coffee.'

'Not to mention the food,' Carrie said, patting her stomach. She nodded at the open laptop resting on Gina's knees. 'What are you working on? Please tell me it's another awesome movie extravaganza.'

'Not exactly,' Gina told Carrie, pulling a face. 'But it is to do with the Palace. I'm due to meet Ben tomorrow night to go through a few things and I want to make sure I've got most of the details worked out before then.'

Carrie gave her a sideways look. 'And has he got you doing the paperwork for the train line too?'

'No,' Gina said thankfully. 'He's doing that himself, which is a good thing because you could fit what I know about steam trains and heritage lines on a very small Post-it note.'

'You and me both,' Carrie observed. 'Although I could probably find him a very fetching station master's outfit if he needs one.'

Gina tried to picture sandy-haired, surf-loving Ben in a smart uniform and failed. 'I'll be sure to mention it to him,' she promised, as Jory appeared with a Cornish pasty that was bigger than the plate on which it rested. The smell was amazing, and breakfast suddenly seemed like a long time ago; Gina felt her mouth begin to water. 'I don't suppose—'

Jory grinned. 'Had a feeling 'ee might say that. Hang on, I'll go and fetch another.'

Carrie glanced at her own pasty and hesitated, as though she wasn't sure whether she should wait. Gina waved her on. 'Get started before it gets cold. Mine won't be long.'

The other woman bit into the golden pastry and the scent of beef and vegetables with a tantalising hint of pepper wafted towards Gina. 'Sorry,' she said indistinctly, round a mouthful. 'Skipped breakfast.'

Jory was as good as his word and Gina soon had a crisp pasty of her own to tuck into. It was every bit as mouth-watering as she'd anticipated. Carrie finished first. 'I needed that,' she said, sitting back with a satisfied sigh. 'So, what else have you been up to?'

Gina popped the last piece of curved crust into her mouth and crunched. 'Arguing with Gorran over the film choice for our next event, mostly,' she said, once she'd washed the pastry down with some water. 'He's determined we should show *The Shining*.'

Carrie tipped her head. 'It is a great movie.'

'But not a timeless romantic classic,' Gina countered. 'And I can't see it having quite the same appeal as *Brief Encounter*. I'm not sure the cosplay would be quite as classy either.'

'Good point,' Carrie said, who'd supplied half the town with costumes to match the chic 1930s theme at the last event. 'Maybe save the horror for Halloween. So, what's your preference?'

That was half the problem, Gina thought ruefully; she didn't really have one. Unfortunately, it wasn't just Gorran who had strong views about what the next film should be – Ferrelli's had produced a themed ice-cream flavour last time and it had proved extremely popular. That meant Ferdie thought he had a say in choosing the theme for the next event, and Gina's nonna, Elena, had her own ideas. And none of them agreed.

'I was wondering whether we should do a musical,' she told Carrie, who looked instantly enthused.

'Brilliant idea – what about *The Rocky Horror Picture Show*? Plenty of cosplay opportunities there.'

Gina smiled as she pictured the basque and suspenders outfit Dr Frank-N-Furter wore in the film. 'I'm not sure Polwhipple is ready for that yet. I was thinking more *High Society* or *My Fair Lady*.'

Carrie pursed her lips. 'Both great movies, but not what I'd call true classics. Have you thought about *Singin' in the Rain*? That's definitely one of the greats.'

It was, Gina thought, wondering why she hadn't thought of it herself. It also contained one of the most iconic scenes in movie history, where Gene Kelly danced through raindrops and puddles, which seemed even more apt considering how wet Polwhipple had been over the last few days. It was a movie about making movies too, meaning the glamour of cinema was at the heart of the story, and gave plenty of opportunities for dressing up. Gina felt a shiver of excitement as she considered the possibilities; it was the perfect choice for an event. They might even sell out.

'You are a genius,' she told Carrie, beaming at her. 'I can't think of anything better.'

Carrie grinned back. 'Let me know if Gorran agrees and I'll start looking for props. Did you know that Debbie Reynolds kept a lot of the costumes from the film? She sold them at auction years later so they're out there somewhere.' Her expression became wistful. 'Imagine wearing the actual dress she danced in for *Good Morning.*'

'I'm not sure I'd be a good Kathy Selden,' Gina said, thinking of Debbie Reynolds' short brown hair and luminous on-screen beauty.

Carrie eyed Gina's long black hair thoughtfully. 'I think you'd make a fantastic Cyd Charisse.'

Gina laughed as she pictured the lithe, beautiful dancer who'd run rings around Gene Kelly in one of the scenes. 'As long as no one expects me to dance like her, then we won't have a problem.'

The rain hadn't abated by the time Gina left the Mermaid's Tail and made her way back to the car park at the end of the promenade. The Palace was in darkness as she passed and the shutters were down on the window of the Ferrelli's concession: no one was buying ice-cream today. She glanced at the glossy *Brief Encounter* posters in the holders on the wall – Gorran really should update them but there hadn't been any posters at all previously, and something was definitely better than nothing. Some *Singin' in the Rain* posters would look great – bright and eye-catching; she made a mental note to suggest to Gorran that he order some. Assuming he agreed to the film choice, that was . . .

She was so deep in thought as she crossed the almost-empty car park, that she wasn't really paying attention, just dodging the puddles absent-mindedly as she headed for her grandmother's little Fiat. She needed to buy a car of her own, except that she would only be in Cornwall for another two months and neither she nor her boyfriend, Max, had need of a car to get around London. Elena's powder-blue Fiat was doing a very good job at getting her from A to B, especially when the rain seemed to be never-ending.

Gina only became aware that there was a car speeding across the tarmac at the very last second. She heard the engine first and glanced up, startled, to see a red Audi TT heading towards her. With a yelp of alarm, she leapt for a nearby kerb, avoiding a deep puddle as she did so. The car seemed to slow a fraction, then continued onwards through the puddle. The spinning wheels sent a wave of cold, dirty water washing over Gina, drenching her from head to toe. She gasped and turned her dripping face to stare after the car, which had zoomed through the exit and turned left to vanish along the high street.

Gina stared after it for a few shocked seconds, then shook herself down and wiped her face. Whoever had been behind the wheel of that car needed a lesson in driving skills, not to mention good manners, she decided irritably, resuming her journey towards Nonna's car. There was no need to drive through the puddle – it could only have been done on purpose. A kid, Gina thought, as she got into the Fiat and rummaged in her bag for something to dry herself with.

Someone who thought it was funny to soak other people for fun.

If she ever found out who it had been, there would be serious trouble.

# Chapter Twelve

The sun was starting to burn off the rain clouds on Tuesday morning as Gina dropped by the Palace. She found Gorran in his cluttered, chaotic office, looking as though he might drown in paperwork as usual. His shock of white hair almost quivered with anticipation when Gina passed on Carrie's suggestion for the film. 'Marvellous!' he said, his ruddy cheeks glowing. 'When can we do it?'

'We'll need a few weeks to get the word out but I can use the mailing list I built from our last event to do that,' Gina replied. 'How soon can you get the film?'

The Palace's projection room ran on old-fashioned reels, which Gorran staunchly insisted were more authentic than newer digital projectors. Gina assumed the cinema owner would need to arrange for the film to be delivered, but he surprised her. 'I've already got it – it's in our archive.'

'Of course it is,' Gina said, snapping her fingers. 'I saw it there when I was looking for the lost *Brief Encounter* reel.'

The lost reel that had almost snatched disaster from the jaws of triumph, she added to herself but didn't say. 'Actually, it's been a few years since I watched *Singin' in the Rain*. Do you think you'd be able to run it for me one afternoon?'

'Of course,' Gorran replied. 'Let me know which day suits you and I'll arrange for Tash to be here.'

Tash was the Palace's part-time projectionist and arguably the most important person on the picture house payroll – without her to coax the aged projection system into cooperation, there would be no screenings. The trouble in the past had been that both Tash and Gorran had taken a relaxed attitude to movie start times, which had meant customers had sometimes faced a lengthy delay before their film began. Gina couldn't help wondering whether the erratic screen times had something to do with the usually woeful ticket sales, although Gorran's enthusiasm for showing obscure foreign language films probably didn't help.

'Do you think there's a chance you'll be able to persuade Ferdie to dream up another themed ice-cream flavour?' Gorran asked, looking hopeful. 'I gather people are still asking for the one he made for *Brief Encounter* and they get very disappointed when they discover it was a one-night-only flavour.'

Gina tried not to smile. She'd been the one who'd found the perfect recipe and, together with Elena, had persuaded a reluctant Ferdie to add it to the Ferrelli's menu. He'd spent most of the event accepting compliments about it. 'I'll see what I can do,' she promised Gorran.

They agreed on the last Saturday in April for their screening. On her way out, Gina stopped at the Ferrelli's concession. The window in the foyer was closed but the one that looked out onto the promenade was open and Manda, one of Ferrelli's longest-serving employees was there, stocking up for the day ahead.

'Morning,' she called, as Gina approached. 'Can I tempt you with a cornet?'

The freezer below the glass screen was already full of pastel-coloured goodies – strawberry, honeycomb, salted caramel – but Gina shook her head. The trouble with working in her grandfather's dairy was that she tasted so much ice-cream that it had lost its appeal as a special treat. 'It's a bit early for me,' she told Manda, smiling.

'It's never too early for gelato.' Manda pointed to the Napoli tin half-filled with soft chocolate waves. 'See? The sunshine has given some people the hunger already.'

Gina smiled. 'So I see. Any messages for Nonno? I'm heading over to the dairy now.'

Manda looked thoughtful. 'We need some more Strawberry Sensation, if you don't mind – I'm down to my last two tins and I reckon that'll go today.'

'Strawberry,' Gina echoed. 'Got it. Anything else?'

The other woman sighed. 'Another pair of hands for later, when it gets busy?'

'Oh,' Gina said, startled. 'Of course, I didn't realise you needed help—'

'Relax,' Manda said, throwing her an amused look, 'I've

got it covered. You just concentrate on planning our next event. Do you know what film you're likely to be showing?'

Gina looked quickly around, as though she expected to find Gorran listening in. 'We've got an idea but it's top secret for now. I think you're going to love it, though.'

She said goodbye to Manda and headed for the car. Parking outside Nonna and Nonno's house, she tapped lightly at the door. Elena answered almost immediately and gave Gina a warm hug. 'Come in, come in!' she said, planting a warm kiss on each of Gina's cheeks. She stepped back to let Gina inside. 'Nonno is in the dairy already – he says he's got a surprise for you.'

Gina accepted Elena's offer of a cappuccino, although she declined the biscotti that were offered, and took it, plus a green tea for Ferdie, out to the dairy. He much preferred coffee too, the stronger the better, but he was under doctor's orders to reduce the amount of caffeine he drank and Elena was insisting on drastic measures to ensure he cut down.

Ferdie was leaning against a stool in the dairy, his plaster-encased leg resting lightly on the ground and his crutches beside him as he stirred a large saucepan. As Gina pushed open the door, she saw him lift a spoonful of thin creamy liquid and examine it, his bushy grey eyebrows knotted in concentration.

'Good morning, Nonno,' she said, lowering his cup of green tea to the steel work surface. 'I thought we agreed that making the custard was my job?'

Dropping the spoon back into the mixture and adjusting the gas, Ferdie grunted. 'That doesn't mean I can't help, does it?'

Gina took a sip of her cappuccino, savouring the rich bitterness beneath the milk: no one made coffee like Nonna. 'Of course it doesn't,' she told him equably. 'As long as you take things easy. So, what's the plan today?'

Ferdie reached for his cup, glanced at the contents in disgust and put it back down without drinking. He eyed Gina's coffee with obvious envy. 'Is that a cappuccino?'

She wrapped her hands around it. 'Yes, and you're not allowed it.'

'Not even if I tell you I am thinking of introducing a coffee-flavoured gelato?' he said, throwing Gina an innocent look that didn't fool her for a second.

'Not even then,' she said firmly. 'Although speaking of new flavours . . .'

She told him about the proposed screening at the Palace. Ferdie frowned. 'I still think you should persuade that old goat Gorran to show *La Dolce Vita*. That scene at the Trevi Fountain is a classic.'

Gina hid a smile; the scene he referred to starred the voluptuous Anita Ekberg frolicking in the waters of the fountain in a dress that clung to every curve. No wonder Ferdie liked it. Elena, on the other hand, favoured *Roman Holiday* which featured a charmingly chiselled Gregory Peck. Apart from the sex appeal of the respective leads, it didn't take a genius to work out why Gina's grandparents had chosen their favourites; both films were set in Rome.

'We've been over this,' Gina said to Ferdie. '*La Dolce Vita* isn't well-known enough – I don't think it's as big a box-office draw as *Singin' in the Rain*. Why don't you let me find it on Netflix?'

Ferdie regarded her scornfully. 'Netflix. A film like that was made to be watched on the big screen, not a laptop or a tablet.' He stirred the vanilla custard. 'And I suppose you want Ferrelli's to serve another themed ice-cream.'

Gina took a deep breath. 'Yes. It went down so well last time and I can make it a feature of the event – an exclusive, one-night-only new gelato from Ferrelli's.' She hesitated and then plunged on. 'I wouldn't be surprised if some people are more interested in the ice-cream than the film.'

She stopped. Ferdie liked to arrive at a decision in his own time and she'd learned from her grandmother's example that it was best to be patient. But she had one last thing to add. 'The trouble is, I can't think of a flavour that suits the film.'

He looked intrigued in spite of himself. 'Something bright,' he said. 'An explosion of colour on the taste buds. Lemon, perhaps, or orange.'

'The *Good Morning* song is pretty famous,' Gina suggested. 'Oranges might remind people of that – maybe we could try a sorbet.'

She knew as soon as she'd spoken that it was the wrong thing to say. Nonno's eyebrows bristled. 'We make gelato, not sorbet. There's no skill in freezing water and sugar.'

Gina swallowed a sigh. 'No, of course not. It was just a thought.'

Apparently mollified, Ferdie continued to stir the custard and stared into space. 'There's no harm in testing a new recipe. But we won't be able to get citrus fruits from our usual supplier – they don't grow them.'

Whenever he could, Ferdie bought strawberries and any other fruit he needed from a local fruit farm. Gina pursed her lips. 'The Scarlet Hotel might be able to help – I could speak to their chef, see if they could spare an orange or two?'

'See if they'll give you a few lemons and limes too,' Ferdie said, nodding. 'Just in case the oranges need a bit of oomph.'

Putting down her coffee, Gina pulled out her phone and tapped out a quick email, certain the Scarlet wouldn't mind helping out again.

'This custard is ready,' Ferdie announced, peering at the back of the spoon in satisfaction. 'Why don't you begin chopping the strawberries?'

Gina washed her hands and retrieved two large punnets of strawberries from the fridge. As she returned, she noticed her coffee cup was now at her grandfather's elbow. And it was empty.

She stared at him in disbelief, unsure whether to tell him off or laugh. 'Did you—?'

Ferdie did not seem in the least perturbed by the unspoken accusation. He shrugged. 'I regret nothing.'

Gina shook her head. 'I can't believe you just—'

'Desperate times mean desperate measures,' he cut in, switching off the gas hob and fixing her with a glare. 'Now, are we making gelato or are we talking?'

'Making gelato, Nonno,' Gina said, deciding that discretion was the better part of valour on this particular occasion; Ferdie's stubbornness was a force of nature, after all, and she had no doubt there would be plenty of other battles that mattered more than a few swigs of stolen coffee.

She threw herself into making ice-cream, consulting the spreadsheet she'd created to keep track of orders to make sure they would have enough of each flavour. As well as keeping supplies up at the concession in the cinema, they also needed sufficient stock to fulfil orders for local restaurants and cafés. And if the weather continued to improve, she had no doubt demand for Ferrelli's would soar.

By lunchtime they had a freezer full of gelato, each glistening creamy-waved pan ready to go wherever it was needed. Gina cleared up then collected her empty cappuccino cup, along with Ferdie's half-drunk green tea, to take back to Elena.

'No need to mention the coffee incident,' Ferdie told her, as they crossed the yard to the house. 'Nonna will only become cross.'

'With good reason,' Gina said, sending him a stern look. 'The doctor says you need to lower your blood pressure.'

'*Che palle*!' Ferdie growled, stomping along on his crutches. 'I feel fine. Or I would, if the lack of coffee wasn't making me so grumpy.'

'It's for your own good,' Gina said but she wasn't without sympathy. Ferdie had begun each day with a double espresso for as long as she could remember – she wasn't surprised he was irritated by its sudden absence. She'd be grumpy if she had to give up her morning caffeine hit. 'But I won't tell Nonna about the cappuccino, as long as you promise you'll cut down.'

Ferdie was silent until they reached the back door. 'I hate being old.'

'Nonno!' Gina exclaimed, her heart aching at the suddenly defeated look on his lined face. For seventy-eight, he was actually in very good health, although it wouldn't do him any harm to be reminded that he was not in his twenties any more. She squeezed his arm. 'No one is trying to make you feel old. You need to take a little better care of yourself, that's all.'

'No dancing through the puddles for me, is that what you're saying?' he said, lifting one eyebrow.

Gina pulled open the kitchen door and smiled at the Gene Kelly reference. 'Not unless you can persuade Nonna to dance with you.'

Gina tried to squeeze in a hurried phone call with Max that evening but the call went straight to voicemail. She left a short message, asking him to phone her when he got the chance; she'd only wanted to share her excitement about the *Singin' in the Rain* event with him – it would keep.

Ben arrived at seven-thirty sharp, an untidy sheaf of papers in one hand and a bottle of Merlot in the other. 'Happy Tuesday,' he said grinning at her when she opened her door. 'I thought we might need this tonight.'

'Oh?' Gina said, stepping aside to let him in. 'It's that bad?'

He placed the bottle on the worktop in the open-plan kitchen and rubbed his lightly tanned cheek. 'I've been tying myself in knots,' he admitted. 'I'm okay with the figures but making an irresistible case for restoring the train line to Polwhipple is a bit beyond me. No matter what I write, it sounds boring and rubbish.'

Gina had a sudden flash of memory, taking her back to the summers she'd spent in Polwhipple as a teenager, when she and Ben had been practically inseparable. Surf-obsessed Ben had never been especially academic and hated school, although Gina knew he was bright and quick-witted. During her last summer in Polwhipple, the year her family had moved to Los Angeles and she'd lost contact with Ben completely, he'd confided in her that he'd been diagnosed as dyslexic. She'd forgotten all about it until now.

'I'm sure it's neither of those things,' Gina said, her voice warm. 'But we're a team, remember? So, you help me with the numbers on my application and I'll help you with the words for yours.'

His look of gratitude warmed her. 'Thanks, Gina,' he said. 'But I still think we're going to need the wine.'

She reached for two glasses. 'You'll get no argument from me.'

They settled around the small kitchen table. Gina opened up her laptop and turned the screen towards Ben. 'As you can see, I've made a start on the funding application for the restoration. I've explained that the structure itself is sound, but the interior is in need of significant refurbishment.' She pointed to the relevant part of the document. 'I've broken it down into four main areas – the foyer, theatre, toilets and the exterior – and then listed what needs to be done in each.'

Ben scanned the screen. 'I see you're suggesting that we replace the seats. The bottoms of Polwhipple will thank you.'

'That was first on the list, believe me,' Gina said, shuddering. 'How anyone can relax and enjoy the film when it feels as though a thousand evil springs are having a fight underneath them is a mystery to me.'

'And you want to remove the chipboard from the walls.'

She nodded. 'Didn't you say you thought the original Art Deco features might still be behind it?'

'It could be,' Ben said. 'But it might not be in a fit state to restore. A lot depends on how the chipboard was put up – you'll only know what the damage is once it comes down. And it goes without saying that you'll need someone who knows about historical property restoration to do it.'

Gina took a long sip of her wine. 'Actually, I was hoping you'd be up for doing it. But I have no idea what your costs would be, or even whether you've got time.'

He was silent for a few moments, as though he was thinking something through. 'I might be able to fit it in. But it's a big job, especially on top of the station restoration. I've still got the ticket office to finish there.'

She pictured the immaculately restored station, upon which Ben had spent months and months of his spare time and attention. He'd do an amazing job at the Palace too, if she could persuade him to say yes.

'Could we budget for someone to help you?' she asked. 'Obviously, it depends how much Polwhipple town council is prepared to donate.'

*If* they're prepared to donate, she added silently. She had no experience of putting together funding bids, and much less of dealing with town councils, but she hoped that the success of the first event that she'd arranged proved how much potential the Palace had to enhance life for everyone in Polwhipple. The meeting next Monday was going to be critical – they'd only get one chance to impress the funding committee.

'Maybe,' Ben said, his expression still thoughtful. 'What does Gorran think of all this? Apart from not being able to believe his luck, I mean.'

Gina laughed. 'I haven't run the detailed plans by him yet but in principle he's happy. All he has to do is nod in the right places and sound enthusiastic at the meeting.'

'I bet he's like a dog with two tails,' Ben said, grinning. 'Especially since he doesn't have to dig into his own pockets to pay for any of the work.'

'So, what do you think?' Gina pointed at the laptop again. 'Does this all sound achievable? How much should I put down for each area?'

'It's certainly doable,' Ben said. 'But the costs are going to be harder to pin down.'

They spent the next forty minutes working through the

gaps in Gina's application. Ben told her the best websites to check for the costs of supplies and materials. 'Prices will fluctuate a bit but this should give you a rough idea of how much money you'll need. But whoever you eventually employ to do the work should give you a quote that incorporates all that.'

Gina nodded, trying not to look disappointed. From the way Ben was talking, it didn't sound as though he wanted the job of restoring the Palace. And she supposed she should have expected him to say no; she knew how busy he was, after all.

'If you give me a couple of days, I'll put something together and send a detailed quote,' Ben went on. 'But a word of warning – knowing how town councils work, they might want you to have a couple of quotes in the application so that you demonstrate best value.'

'Okay, I'll ask Nonno if he knows any other builders who might be interested, although we need someone who really knows what they're doing, rather than a standard builder. Which is why I wanted—' She glanced across at him as the implication of his words sank in. 'So, you're up for the job?'

'Yeah, I am,' he said, with a decisive nod. 'The station is almost finished and the Palace is important to me too. I'll do whatever I can to help.'

Gina could have hugged him. 'Thank you,' she said, elated. 'I can't think of anyone else I'd rather have on board.'

He glanced across at her and there was something she couldn't quite decipher in his eyes. 'You're welcome,' he said, reaching for his own paperwork. 'Now, can you work your magic over the mangled wreck of my application forms, please?'

It took Gina an hour and a half, plus two more glasses of wine and several slices of Pepperoni Passion pizza, to unravel Ben's words and rearrange them into something resembling a halfway decent proposal. He'd approached the Bodmin and Wenford Railway Preservation Society once before, informally, to ask them to restore the steam line back to Polwhipple, the way it had been in the railway's heyday. They'd said no and, reading between the lines, Gina suspected Ben's feelings had been hurt by the refusal.

'There,' she said, typing the last few words into another document. 'How's that?'

Ben skimmed what she'd written. 'Wow,' he said, looking at her with admiration. 'That's really good – exactly what I had in mind. You could do this for a living.'

She felt the beginnings of a pleasurable blush creep up her cheeks. 'Oh shush,' she told him. 'It was all there – it just needed teasing out, that's all.'

He raised his glass to hers. 'To good partnerships and future successes.'

'To the Palace and Polwhipple station,' Gina said, chinking her own glass against his. 'And old friends.'

When her phone rang not long after Ben had gone, Gina assumed it was Max returning her call. But the name that flashed up was Sarah's, one of her friends from London.

'Hello, stranger,' Sarah said, almost as soon as Gina answered the call. 'Long time no speak.'

'Hi, Sarah,' Gina replied, smiling. 'How are you?'

'Better now I know you haven't fallen over a treacherous Cornish cliff,' Sarah said in a dry tone. 'What's been keeping you so busy?'

Gina filled her friend in on what she'd been doing, keeping any reference to Ben carefully neutral; Sarah had known her for several years and Gina was well aware of her sharply-honed instinct for emotional drama.

'I saw Max yesterday,' Sarah said, once Gina had finished talking.

'Oh? How is he?' Gina asked. 'We seem to keep missing each other on the phone.'

There was a pause. 'You know Max,' Sarah said, and Gina got the sense she was choosing her words with care. 'His energy is always ramped up to eleven.'

Gina frowned. 'That sounds like him. But—'

'I'll be honest, Gee, I don't think he's coping all that well,' Sarah interrupted. 'He seems fine on the surface – all business and good cheer – but underneath . . . well, I think he's missing you. *Really* missing you.'

'I miss him too,' Gina said, trying not to sound defensive. 'But it's not like this is forever—'

'You're not listening,' Sarah said impatiently. 'He's lonely. And with you all the way down there, he's also a target. I'm sure I don't need to spell it out.'

Gina felt her face flush. 'Max would never cheat on me.'

Her friend sighed down the phone. 'No, I'm not suggesting he would. Not deliberately. But you know how these things go – sometimes a situation *escalates*.'

Ben flashed into Gina's mind and her cheeks flamed even more. She knew exactly how fast things could get out of hand.

'Just keep the home fires burning,' Sarah went on, her tone softer. 'Pay him some attention. Max loves you but he's not made of stone – don't take any chances, okay?'

It took Gina a long time to get to sleep once she'd said goodbye to Sarah; her friend's words whirled around her head and kept her eyes fixed on the ceiling. Max hadn't called her back, which probably meant nothing but even so, Sarah's advice struck a chord; she needed to try harder with Max – distance made him vulnerable. It made them both vulnerable.

# Chapter Thirteen

Gina awoke the next morning to a message from Ben.

> **Thanks again for all your help last night. Fancy a day out? I want to show you some of my handiwork.**

She'd already seen some of his work; the station restoration was a shining testament to his skill and ability. She'd also seen how much time and effort had gone into his home – a converted railway carriage that stood in one of the sidings beside the station itself. Her conversation with Sarah the night before resurfaced – *keep the home fires burning* – but work was work and she couldn't avoid spending time with Ben; they were partners after all. Besides, she hadn't seen much of Cornwall since she'd arrived, and it might be nice to give him the chance to show off a little.

> **Love to! When?**

His reply took less than a minute.

**Tomorrow too soon?**

Gina shook her head; he was nothing if not keen. But she wanted to talk to him about her ideas for transforming the foyer of the Palace into a silent movie lot for the *Singin' in the Rain* event and this gave her the perfect opportunity. She pushed Sarah's insistent voice out of her mind.

**Sounds perfect,** she replied. **Shall I drive?**

**No, I will. Pick you up around 10:30?**

**It's a date,** she typed, then hastily deleted the words and replaced them with, **See you then!** What would Sarah have made of that?

Feeling a sudden surge of guilt, Gina picked up her phone again and tried to call Max. It rang for a while and then his voicemail kicked in. She ended it without leaving a message, gnawing at her lip and hoping he'd call her back soon. Maybe she'd invite him down from London for another visit.

Focusing on work to help clear her head, she spent a little while designing flyers for *Singin' in the Rain* and sent them over to the printers she'd used for the last event. Then she fired off a few emails, inviting the local press and Polwhipple's mayor to attend, and announcing the screening to the people who'd come along to *Brief Encounter.* As an afterthought, she sent the flyer to Carrie too, asking her to forward it to the people on her mailing list. But she couldn't shake her feeling of restlessness. Her gaze came to rest on the view beyond her balcony; the weather was as different as it was possible to be from the rainy, windswept Easter weekend. The sun was beaming from the summery blue sky, which in turn was making the sea sparkle and shimmer. What she needed was some fresh air to clear her head, Gina decided, getting up and heading purposefully towards the bathroom for a shower. If a walk along the cliffs to Polwhipple couldn't do the job, nothing would.

She was familiar with the South West Coast Path by now, but the view never failed to take her breath away. The Atlantic was a perfect turquoise, flecked with white as the waves ebbed and flowed. Over her head, a few lazy gulls floated on warm air currents, occasionally calling out. Once or twice, she encountered other walkers and they exchanged a pleasant, 'Good morning!' but for the most part she was alone to enjoy the spectacular scenery. Slowly, she felt the tension in her shoulders drain away; walking in London never did this for her. There, it was often a constant battle to avoid others, all hell-bent on getting to their destination as quickly as possible. Unless they were tourists, of course, in which case they moved at a snail's pace. There were plenty of tourists in Cornwall too but not here; the cliffs felt deliciously empty.

Gina called in to see Gorran first, to let him know she'd be sending some builders his way to quote for the refurbishment funding application, then walked through the town to her grandparents' house.

Elena greeted her warmly when she arrived at the Old Dairy. 'Look at you, with such roses in your cheeks!' she cried, standing back to observe Gina with evident satisfaction. 'Our fresh Cornish air agrees with you.'

Gina smiled. 'I did have a lovely walk across the cliffs today.'

'Of course you did,' Elena said. 'Maybe the land is casting a spell on you – next you will be telling us you don't ever want to leave.'

Gina thought about Max again; Sarah was right, he seemed further away with every day that passed. She'd put everything on hold to come and help Ferdie run his ice-cream business, including Max. When she'd first arrived in Polwhipple, she'd referred to London as her real life but now she wasn't so sure; the city and its relentless stream of busyness seemed like a dream she'd once had, distant and hard to fathom. Life in Polwhipple felt more tangible; obviously, it was quieter and less pressured – although it still had its moments – and the things she'd disliked about the town when she'd been a teenager, such as the friendly interest she had interpreted as nosiness back then, she appreciated now. She supposed she'd just adjusted to living outside the capital – it was going to be a shock when she went back. Perhaps it was time to try and integrate her two lives sooner rather than later . . .

'Mmm,' she said as she took off her coat. 'Maybe.'

Elena led her into the kitchen. 'Ferdie has gone to meet a friend for brunch, although if you ask me it is just an excuse to drink coffee where I can't tell him off.'

Gina thought of her stolen cappuccino and kept her face as straight as she could.

'But it means we have the place to ourselves at least,' Elena went on, firing a mischievous glance Gina's way. 'Shall we do some experimenting?'

She meant with gelato flavours, Gina realised instantly; her grandmother had been trying to persuade Ferdie to update the range of flavours Ferrelli's sold for years, without much success. But now that Gina was helping out in the dairy, Elena had seen an indirect route to achieving her goal and had recruited Gina to help her create some new recipes. They'd already perfected a tiramisu-flavoured gelato, which Gina was waiting for the perfect opportunity to test on Ferdie, and Elena was now keen to find another recipe to challenge them. Gina was enjoying their experiments – it was fun to spend time with Elena and to hear her stories about her family back in Italy – but she couldn't help feeling a niggle of guilt about sneaking around behind Ferdie's back.

'What did you have in mind?' she asked her grandmother.

Elena waved a hand at the recipe books she had laid out on the kitchen table. 'How about something typically English? Do you suppose we could create an Afternoon Cream Tea gelato?'

Gina narrowed her eyes thoughtfully. 'We could add some clotted cream to the custard base, although strictly speaking it's too heavy for traditional gelato, and drizzle strawberry puree over the top. But that's just strawberries and cream.'

'How about crumbling plain scones through the mixture?' Elena suggested. 'That way, we'd have all the elements of a traditional cream tea.'

'That could work,' Gina said, picturing a tin of glistening red and white ice-cream dotted with tiny morsels of sweet scones. 'In fact, it could be delicious.'

Elena whisked two aprons from the back of the kitchen door and handed one to Gina. 'Then what are we waiting for? Let's begin!'

Using a recipe from a Mary Berry book, Gina and Elena whipped up a batch of scones. The smell of baking filled the kitchen as Gina told her grandmother all about her plans for the *Singin' in the Rain* event at the Palace.

'Ah, I loved that film,' Elena said, sighing. 'Gene Kelly was so very handsome. I'm sure this event will be even more successful than the last one – who could resist all those magical dance routines?'

'I hope you're right,' Gina said. 'A big audience will help to persuade the town council that the Palace is worth investing in.'

'And has my stubborn husband agreed to let you serve a special gelato at the event?'

'He has,' Gina said, smiling. 'In fact, he wants to develop it himself.'

Elena threw her hands up in the air in mock astonishment. 'Praise be to God, it is a miracle! Call the Pope immediately – Ferdie Ferrelli has agreed to try a new recipe!'

Gina laughed. 'I suppose it is kind of a breakthrough. It sounded delicious, anyway – I can't wait to try it.'

Which reminded her, she needed to call in at the Scarlet Hotel and collect the Spanish oranges they'd kindly agreed to supply. And it wouldn't hurt to increase her publicity efforts too; if the meeting with the town council went well, this could be the last event the Palace ran for a while. It seemed more important than ever to make it a success.

'And how are you and Ben getting along?' Elena asked. 'It must be nice to be spending time together again after all these years. He was very upset when you stopped coming to visit, you know, back when you were younger.'

'Was he?' Gina said, blinking. She didn't think Elena had ever told her that before.

'Oh yes. He was quite heartbroken and pestered the life out of Nonno, asking when you'd be back and whether we had an address for you.' Elena paused. 'But of course we had to say no, because we had no idea where you had moved to.'

Her tone was neutral but Gina sensed the undercurrents beneath the last sentence: this was less about Ben and more about her parents' sudden decision to move to Los Angeles, not long after Gina's sixteenth birthday. There'd been an almighty argument, mostly between Ferdie and Gina's mother, and terrible things had been said on both sides. Sophia Callaway had been so angry and hurt that she'd immediately taken a job across the Atlantic, where she and Gina's father had stayed ever since. Gina had left them there shortly after her twenty-fifth birthday, taking a job in a London-based events company, and although they'd visited her from time to time, she doubted her parents would ever come back to the land of their birth.

But Elena's revelation about Ben stunned Gina. Had he really been heartbroken when she'd vanished from his life, she wondered, or was Nonna exaggerating? They'd been close friends, it was true, but that was all they'd ever been. Apart from one night on the beach, just before she was due to leave Polwhipple, when she and Ben had been sat around a fire with a small gang of his surfer mates, watching the sun dip below the horizon. Gina and Ben were side by side and there'd been a moment when their eyes had met; their heads had been so close together that it seemed to Gina like the most natural thing in the world to close the distance and brush his lips with hers. But something had happened – a shout from one of the surfers or perhaps a friendly scuffle – she couldn't remember what it had been but it had broken the spell. Neither of them had mentioned it and Gina was never sure that she hadn't imagined the whole thing. Elena's comment suggested that she hadn't.

'I wish Mum and Nonno weren't so stubborn,' Gina said aloud, pushing the thought of kissing teenage Ben out of her mind. 'I know they were both hurt, but it's been fifteen years.'

And time might be running out, she thought but didn't say. Nonna and Nonno were generally in excellent health for their age but they were both well into their seventies. There was a very real danger that they might succumb to a sudden illness and then it would be too late to resolve the feud that had ripped the family apart.

Elena sighed. 'The trouble is they are too alike – both strong-willed and headstrong. There were faults on both sides – your grandfather handled things badly but what he did was only born out of love and concern for you – he was worried that your mother's obsession with her career was causing her to neglect you. She felt that he was interfering in her life, not for the first time. And now neither of them wants to admit that they were wrong.' The older woman's mouth turned down at the edges. 'It breaks my heart sometimes.'

Gina lowered the strawberry she'd been hulling and gave her grandmother a fierce hug. 'We have to make them see sense,' she said. 'There must be a way.'

After a few seconds, Elena pulled away and dabbed her eyes. 'I've tried many times. But perhaps between the two of us, we can think of something.' She smiled at Gina. 'We are a good team, after all.'

'We are,' Gina replied, thinking of the last time she'd spoken to her mother on the phone. Sophia hadn't directly asked about her parents but she had wanted to know how the business was going, whether Gina was coping okay as she learned the ropes at the dairy and how she was enjoying life back in Polwhipple. And Gina had answered carefully, dotting in little references to Nonna and Nonno that told her mother they were fine without her ever needing to ask. Maybe – just maybe – there was hope for reconciliation.

The conversation turned back to the recipe. Gina left her grandmother to finish the strawberries and crossed the courtyard to the dairy, where she borrowed some of the vanilla-based custard Nonno had made the day before. He'd be sure to notice it had gone, so she'd have to whip up another batch before he returned, but it meant she and Elena wouldn't need to wait for their own custard to cool before they combined it into their Afternoon Tea gelato.

The scones – golden-brown and smelling divine – were out of the oven when she returned. Elena was wafting a baking tray back and forth over the top, trying to cool them, and she'd opened the window so that a spring breeze was drifting into the warm kitchen. Adding clotted cream to the chilled custard, Gina whisked it hard before putting the mixture to one side. She took one of Elena's heavy copper-bottomed pans and began to create the strawberry drizzle.

Once the scones were cool, Elena crumbled them into small chunks and filled a bowl. Gina sieved her strawberry puree and set it aside to cool.

'Ready?' Elena asked, lifting the lid of the ice-cream maker she'd bought so that she could test the tiramisu recipe she and Gina had worked on before. The machine was usually kept hidden in one of the kitchen cupboards, where Ferdie never looked; the kitchen was Elena's domain, just as the dairy was his.

'Ready,' Gina replied.

She folded the crumbled scones into the cold custard and tipped it into the ice-cream maker. Elena switched it on and the machine began to churn. 'And now it is time for coffee and a freshly baked scone,' she announced.

Gina smiled; Elena was convinced her granddaughter was

too thin and was on a mission to fatten her up, something Gina was combating by long walks along the cliffs and membership of a gym in Mawgan Porth. 'Let me make a batch of custard to replace the one we used first. Nonno will know what we've been up to if I don't.'

Elena nodded in approval. 'Of course. First rule of subterfuge: always cover your tracks.'

Forty minutes later, the replacement for the missing custard was chilling and the kitchen was immaculate. Once the machine had finished churning, Gina had scooped some of the resulting ice-cream into two bowls and drizzled the strawberry sauce over the top. She held her breath as Elena took a mouthful.

'*Delizioso*,' she announced, digging her spoon into the bowl for another mouthful. 'Perfect first time – we are getting better at this.'

Gina took a spoonful of her own and savoured the sweet, crumbly texture of the ice-cream. It really was like eating a strawberry and cream scone. 'Do you think Nonno will like it?' she asked, once her bowl was empty.

Elena's gaze narrowed in thought. 'He'll need some convincing. Let's see how he gets on with the recipe for your picture house event. Maybe we can find a way to make him think it was all his idea.'

Gina couldn't help laughing. When it came to handling Ferdie Ferrelli, no one was better than Nonna.

# Chapter Fourteen

Max called Gina as she was walking along the cliffs back to Mawgan Porth.

'Where are you?' he asked once she'd said hello. 'It sounds like it's blowing a gale.'

'I'm on the South West Coast Path,' she told him. 'It's not actually very windy – maybe it sounds worse than it is. Shall I call you back?'

'No,' Max said immediately. 'I've got back-to-back meetings and it feels like ages since we've spoken.'

Gina mentally spooled back over the last few days. She'd last talked to Max just before the Easter weekend – six days ago. Back in London, that had been unheard of but there hadn't been such a distance between them then. 'It has been ages,' she told him, thinking of Sarah's comments the night before. 'So, what have you been up to?'

He started to describe the party he'd been to the night before. Gina knew most of the people he mentioned – they had a wide circle of mutual friends – but she had to interrupt more than once to ask about an unfamiliar name.

'Oh, didn't I tell you? Dexter split up with his wife – Izzy is his new girlfriend,' Max said. 'He asked after you, by the way.'

He went on, filling her in with titbits of gossip along the way until her head started to spin with the names of the people he'd seen and the glamorous places he'd been to. It wasn't that she missed the parties and dinners, exactly; more that she missed being at them with him. And at the back of her mind, Sarah's suggestion that underneath it all Max was lonely . . . The last thing she wanted was for him to sit moping around at home but the sense that his life could reform itself without her was unsettling.

'Come down,' she burst out, cutting into his story about lunch at the Oxo Tower with a new business associate. 'And not just for a weekend – come for a week.'

Max laughed. 'I'd love to but you know it's impossible – my diary is booked solid for months. Why don't you come up here? Surely your grandparents can spare you for a few days? You must be bored silly down there in the arse end of nowhere – come up to London and let me remind you what you're missing.'

She probably could, Gina thought; no one would begrudge her a weekend away. But the funding application needed to be completed by Friday and there was a lot to do for the Palace screening. She couldn't get away for at least two weeks.

'I'm not bored,' she said, doing her best to keep her tone level. 'It's actually good to be out of the city. I don't miss London especially – I miss you, Max.'

He was silent for a moment and she pictured him half-dressed, standing beside the window of his riverside apartment, running a hand over his morning stubble. 'I miss you too. Look, leave it with me; maybe I can shift a few things around. I'll see what I can do, okay?'

Gina felt her eyes fill with tears. 'Okay. Thank you.'

The call ended shortly after that, with Max promising to call her in a few days, once he'd had a chance to look at his diary. Gina put her phone away and walked slowly, trying to ignore the heavy feeling in the pit of her stomach. When she'd agreed to come to Cornwall, she had been sure that her relationship with Max was solid enough to survive the three-month break. But now it felt as though the ground was shifting underneath them; she'd be happy to be reunited with Max, of course, but the thought of going back to her frenetic, whirling lifestyle filled Gina with a strange reluctance. The trouble was, there was nothing long-term to keep her in Polwhipple, apart from Nonna and Nonno; Ferdie wouldn't need her once his leg was mended and providing they got the funding to go ahead, the refurbishment of the Palace would be finished by the summer. She'd made friends she'd be sorry to leave – Carrie and Ben – but she'd still be able to see them when she visited, which she suspected might happen more often now she'd tasted life in Polwhipple again. And she had friends in London – Sarah and Tori and plenty of others – although they all had young families now, plus there was her career as an events planner; her clients were waiting for her to come back. Gina shook her head – maybe it would do her good to go up to London for a weekend, as Max had suggested, to remind herself of everything she loved about life in the capital. It wouldn't do her any good to get too comfortable in Cornwall. Her future was in London. Her future was with Max.

**Up for walking today?**

The text message from Ben arrived at 7:23 a.m. Gina stared blearily at her phone and it took her a few seconds to remember that they were due to visit one of the properties he'd worked on restoring, although she had no idea which one.

Blinking the last vestiges of sleep away, she tapped out a reply.

**Of course. What time did we say?**

**Will be there at 10:30 – wear boots and bring a change of clothes.**

Frowning, Gina got out of bed and padded across to the window. The sun was bright as she twitched the blind aside, forcing her to shade her eyes. Where exactly was Ben taking her?

He pulled up in his van exactly on time. Gina was waiting

outside the entrance to the small block of holiday apartments she called home, and waved as he drove up.

'Morning,' Ben said, smiling as she climbed into the passenger seat. 'How are you?'

'Intrigued,' Gina said, stowing her rucksack in the foot well and glancing around the immaculate interior of the van. For some reason she'd expected it to be cluttered and untidy. 'I thought we were going to visit an old building – why do I need a change of clothes?'

'Because I'm of the opinion that the best way to arrive at this particular property is on foot,' Ben said. 'And it's a lovely walk but it might be a bit muddy after all the rain. The change of clothes is for disaster management.'

The penny dropped. 'In case I fall head first into the mud, you mean?'

Ben glanced swiftly sideways, his blue eyes dancing. 'Or in case you have to come and rescue me. Remember that time I got stuck in sinking sand over at Watergate Bay? You had to come and pull me out.'

Gina laughed; he hadn't really been in any danger but the pair of them had ended up covered in dark sand. 'Fair enough. So, are you going to tell me where we're going?'

'Ever been to Lanhydrock House?'

She shook her head. She'd heard of the grand old stately home, of course; situated above the River Fowey, it was a popular tourist spot. Elena had called her up in great excitement one Sunday evening years ago, instructing her to switch on *Antiques Roadshow* because it had been filmed at

Lanhydrock, so she knew it was an impressive building. 'You worked on the restoration?' she asked Ben.

'Some of it,' he said. 'I'll show you which bits, if you like? Consider it a reference.'

'I don't need a reference,' Gina replied, smiling. 'I've seen the quality of your work already, remember, at the station. I already know you're the best.'

He didn't answer but Gina thought he looked pleased with the compliment. 'There's something else, too. We'll walk from Bodmin Parkway station but I thought it might be nice to travel there in style.'

'The steam train,' Gina guessed, feeling a little burst of delight. 'We're going on the Bodmin and Wenford Railway, right?'

Ben nodded. 'If we catch the eleven-thirty from Boscarne Junction, I can show you the rest of the line. It might help with the funding application and it's a lovely journey.' He glanced at her. 'But we don't have to if you don't fancy it. We can drive straight to Bodmin if you're pushed for time.'

Gina thought back to the day she'd arrived in Cornwall, when she'd stepped off the train from London to be enveloped by a cloud of coal-scented steam from the old-fashioned engine at the next platform. She'd felt a strange impulse to take the steam train instead of the taxi she'd planned. The impulse had faded but now the desire to while away half an hour on the velvet seats, gazing out of the window and swaying with the gentle motion of the chugging train, was back. 'It's a great idea, Ben. I'd love to.'

They left the van at the Camel Trail car park, named after the river that flowed nearby, and walked the short distance to Boscarne Junction station.

'There's no ticket office,' Gina observed, frowning at the small waiting room and empty platforms. 'Did there use to be?'

'No, there's never been a ticket office here,' Ben said. 'You need to get tickets from Bodmin General. I popped in there yesterday and got yours – volunteers travel for free so I don't actually need a ticket.'

A puff of steam became visible in the distance. He checked his watch. 'Looks like they're running on time today.'

Stepping on board the almost-empty carriage was like a mini trip down memory lane for Gina. She was instantly transported back to her teenage days when she'd travelled from London and caught the steam train from Bodmin Parkway to be met by Nonna or Nonno at Boscarne Junction. She'd forgotten how much the smell of coal and oil and age permeated the seats.

'It hasn't changed at all,' she said, as the whistle blew and the train jolted into life.

'No, but that's kind of the point,' Ben said from the seat straight across from her. 'Imagine the uproar if train enthusiasts didn't get the authentic experience they came for.'

She took in the look of boyish enthusiasm on his tanned face. 'So, what do volunteers do?'

'Pretty much everything,' he said. 'The Preservation Society is staffed by volunteers who run the whole line and maintain the engines. Almost everyone you'll see is a volunteer – on the weekdays, it's usually retired people but at the weekends there's a real mixture.'

'And what's your job?'

He shrugged. 'It varies. Obviously, I like driving the trains the best but so does everyone else. Most of the time I'm doing odd jobs around the station buildings, keeping everything neat.'

'And even though you do all that, they still won't listen to your idea about extending the train line to Polwhipple?'

Ben looked uncomfortable. 'It's not that they won't listen, although some of the senior members are a bit stuck in their ways. It's more that they can't really afford the outlay, which is why our funding application is so important. If I can show them that they won't have to spend a lot of money making it happen, the society might be more open to running trains to Polwhipple again.'

Gina was about to ask who the senior members were when the train braked suddenly and she was thrown forwards. Ben steadied her, and for a heartbeat, she found herself almost in his arms. She glanced up, feeling her cheeks grow warm as his eyes met hers; the last time she'd been this close to him he'd kissed her.

She pushed herself back into her seat, clearing her throat and brushing her hair from her face. 'Sorry.'

'No problem,' he said, watching her closely. 'Are you okay? You didn't hurt yourself?'

Gina shook her head. 'No, I'm fine.'

Apparently satisfied, Ben turned and peered out of the window towards the front of the train. 'I bet they've got a rookie at the helm today. It's not usually such a bumpy ride.'

Staring out of the window, Gina waited for her jangling nerves to settle down. Her shoulders were tense and her stomach was still fizzing with adrenaline from the shock of the jolt. But that wasn't what was troubling her the most; the thought that was racing round and round her head was the uncomfortable knowledge that in the split-second Ben had held her, she'd felt the strongest urge to lean forwards into his arms and kiss him. And worse than that was the unwavering certainty that Ben would have kissed her back. What was it Sarah had said – sometimes a situation could escalate . . .

They didn't talk much for the rest of the journey. Both kept their eyes fixed on the picturesque scenery rolling by the window, breaking the silence only to observe a particularly pretty aspect of the view. Gina stole glances at Ben when she knew he wouldn't notice, feeling guilty each time she did so. They'd agreed after the last time that they'd got caught up in the romance of *Brief Encounter* – their costumes had even inadvertently reflected the lovelorn Laura and Alec from the film – and that the kiss had been a mistake. So why was Gina allowing herself to fantasise about kissing Ben again? And what did it mean for her relationship with Max?

Her stormy thoughts continued as they left the train at Bodmin Parkway and followed the signs for the footpath to Lanhydrock.

'You're quiet,' Ben observed as they took the bridge that crossed the River Fowey. 'Everything all right?'

Gina dredged up a smile; clearly Ben had forgotten the fleeting moment on the train and that was exactly what she needed to do. 'Miles away, sorry.' She waved a hand at the wooded path ahead, where the trees were slowly unfurling glossy spring leaves. 'This is lovely.'

'It's a nice walk, especially at this time of year,' he agreed. 'The path doesn't look too muddy, either. Maybe you won't have to rescue me after all.'

She managed another smile. 'Good.'

She forced herself to take deep, slow breaths as they walked, concentrating on putting one foot in front of another and focusing on the swirling patterns of the tree bark to either side, the fresh smell of new leaves and the gentle rushing of the river as it ran alongside the path. Sunshine filtered through the trees, dappling the ground, and slowly, Gina felt herself start to relax. Ben seemed to sense her change in mood because he began to talk, describing the work he'd been involved in at Lanhydrock. Gina kept her eyes on the path and listened, finding his descriptions of breathing new life into the worn building fascinating; his obvious enthusiasm for his work shone through and although she knew he'd never say as much, he was quite clearly a master of his craft. But she knew how much he loved restoring old things already; the attention to detail he'd lavished on the converted railway carriage he called home told her that, to say nothing of the care he'd taken with the station.

There were one or two muddy stretches of path to negotiate but after about twenty minutes they reached a break in the trees, through which Gina thought she saw the glimmer of parked cars.

'Respryn Bridge is just up ahead,' Ben explained. 'It's a popular spot with ramblers so there's a car park there. Just beyond that is the Avenue, which leads to Lanhydrock House.'

The Avenue turned out to be a long carriageway that led to an impressively gothic-looking gatehouse. Gina bought herself a ticket – she was not surprised to see that Ben had National Trust membership – and they passed beneath the arches towards the imposing grey-brick house. It presided over gravel paths and formal gardens with a majestic air, its leaded windows surrounded by thick-leaved ivy. To the right, Gina could see a church steeple standing proud above the rooftop of the sprawling house.

'Wow,' she said.

Ben grinned at her. 'It's even more incredible inside.' He nodded towards the arched front door. 'Shall we?'

'Go ahead,' Gina said, grinning back. 'Show me the money.'

# Chapter Fifteen

Ben had not been wrong, Gina thought, as they strolled through room after sumptuous room inside Lanhydrock; the house was filled with breathtaking delights. One corridor had a pristine Art Deco design stretching overhead, but her favourite was the long, wood-panelled gallery with its ornate plaster ceiling, which Ben told her he'd worked on restoring.

'They filmed a version of *Twelfth Night* here,' he told her as they passed beneath the curved ceiling. 'The one with Helena Bonham-Carter and Ben Kingsley in it.'

Gina raised her eyebrows. She knew Ben loved films but she'd never had him down as a fan of Shakespeare.

'We watched it at school,' he said, noticing her unspoken query. 'Don't ask me what happens, though. I was too busy admiring the architecture.'

The below-stairs rooms were impressive too, Gina decided as they roamed the kitchens and servants' quarters; she liked imagining the staff working there, gossiping and grumbling about their employers in the grand rooms upstairs.

They rounded off the visit with tea and sandwiches and then set off back to the station. The sun was warm and the scenery even prettier in the glow of the afternoon; Gina wasn't sure whether it was due to the buzz from the exercise or Ben's company but she found herself enjoying the walk immensely and she was sorry when they reached Bodmin Parkway. Ben introduced her to some of the volunteers, who gave her a tour of the signal room and ticket office.

'I'm hoping some of them will want to come and work at Polwhipple station, if we get the funding,' Ben murmured, as they listened to an enthusiastic white-haired man explain the inner workings of the ticket machine. 'They're a good bunch.'

Gina was even sorrier when Ben parked the van outside the door of her apartment. 'Thanks for today, Ben. I had a really lovely time.'

'No problem,' he said, his eyes crinkling at the edges as he smiled. 'I did too.'

A small, natural silence grew, during which Gina knew she should simply turn and get out of the van. 'Gorran is arranging a private viewing of *Singin' in the Rain* for me one afternoon at the Palace. Want to share some popcorn and join me?'

His face lit up. 'That sounds great. Let me know when and I'll be there.'

'Are you busy on Saturday?'

Ben pulled a face. 'I've got something on. But Sunday is okay.'

'I'll have to ask Gorran,' Gina said doubtfully. 'Tash has to be there to run the projector and she might not want to work on her day off.'

'I've got it on DVD,' Ben said. 'It was one of Mum's favourites and I couldn't face getting rid of it after she died. You could come over to my place instead?'

Gina pictured the living room of Ben's cosy railway carriage with its wing-backed armchairs facing a small flat-screen TV. 'Okay,' she said, nodding. 'Nonno might even have some samples of his new gelato flavour by then too.'

'Great – I'll be around all day,' Ben said. He reached into the back of the van and pulled out an A4 envelope, which he passed to Gina. 'Before I forget, here's my quote for the Palace refurbishment. Want me to email it over as well?'

'Yes, please,' Gina said. 'Thanks, Ben.'

She opened the passenger door and climbed out. 'See you on Sunday.'

After dropping her rucksack into her apartment, Gina decided to call into Carrie's Attic. Polwhipple's beach glimmered in the sunshine and the *Singin' in the Rain* posters that had appeared outside the Palace were bright and cheery. Gina paused for a moment to admire them as she passed by on her way to the vintage boutique.

Word was clearly spreading about Carrie's talent for finding amazing outfits; there were several shoppers browsing the rails when Gina pushed open the grey and pink door.

'Hi Gina,' Carrie said, standing beside the changing room, her arms full of clothes. 'Just give me a minute.'

'No rush,' Gina called, more than happy to browse. She'd need Carrie's expert help to source her *Singin' in the Rain* costume but the shop had plenty of other temptations. Pulling out a little black dress that reminded her of Audrey Hepburn in *Breakfast at Tiffany's*, she held it up against herself and studied her reflection in one of the full-length mirrors on the wall.

'Now that would look amazing on you,' Carrie said to her, passing a silky Grace Kelly-style dress through the curtain to the unseen customer in the changing room. She sighed and studied Gina's slender figure with undisguised envy. 'But then *anything* would look good on you.'

Gina laughed. 'That's not true. Believe me, there are plenty of fashion disasters hiding in my wardrobe back in London. Just ask Max next time you see him.'

The curtain was pulled abruptly back and a vision of cool blonde elegance stepped out. Gina frowned for a moment, unable to place the twenty-something woman and then it clicked: it was Rose Arundell, the woman who'd draped herself possessively around Ben at the *Brief Encounter* screening as though he was her personal property.

The look Rose gave Gina was icy. 'I don't think you've quite got the waist for that dress.'

There was a busy silence, the kind that reminded Gina of a scene from a Spaghetti Western, when a fight was brewing and all the locals scattered. The other customers became deeply engrossed in the clothes on the rails and one of them hurried for the door. Gina took a deep breath and plastered a bland smile on her face. 'You're probably right.'

Unsmiling, Rose turned to Carrie. 'I'll take this, thanks. And you'll source the other dress I asked for?'

Carrie gave an awkward smile. 'Of course. I'll let you know once I've found what you're looking for.'

Without so much as a glance at Gina, Rose swept back into the changing room. Carrie threw Gina an agonised look and began returning the outfits she was holding to the rails. A few minutes later, Rose was holding out a platinum credit card. Gina kept her gaze firmly on a blue dress that reminded her of Jackie Kennedy until she heard the bell above the door tinkle, suggesting that Rose was gone.

Carrie scurried over. 'I'm so sorry,' she said, in a low voice. 'Rose can be a bit of a cow but she's also one of my best customers.'

'Don't worry,' Gina replied, brushing Carrie's concerns away. 'I'm a big girl, I can take an insult or two.'

'She was wrong, anyway,' Carrie said, pulling the black dress from the rail and pushing it towards Gina. 'Go and try it on.'

Gina shook her head. 'Maybe another day. I only came in to talk to you about an outfit for *Singin' in the Rain*. I haven't watched it again yet but time is slipping by – how long do you need to find the Cyd Charisse dress for me?'

Carrie flourished a hand. 'Already done. But I should warn

you, I think Rose is coming to the screening too. She's asked me to source a Lina Lamont outfit for her.'

Gina frowned. Lina Lamont was the leading lady who thought Gene Kelly was in love with her, a nasty piece of work who tried to take over the whole film studio. 'Sounds like the perfect role for her,' she said, and a muffled snigger from one of the women browsing immediately made her feel bad. She pulled a face at Carrie. 'Sorry, I know she's a customer. I'm not normally so bitchy.'

'Trust me, Rose Arundell is cold enough to bring out the bitch in all of us,' Carrie sympathised. 'Your dress is due to arrive on Monday – want to pop in and try it on?'

'Can't wait,' Gina said, forcing an image of Rose's sneering expression from her mind.

She left Carrie to her customers and set off for home. As she rounded the Palace, she caught sight of a red Audi TT zooming across the car park. This time, however, she had a clear view of the driver: Rose Arundell.

Gina gasped. 'I might have known!'

Manda was watching from the window of Ferrelli's. 'Huh,' she called to Gina. 'Apparently, things like speed limits don't apply to Rose. Her mum's on the town council and she thinks that makes her a VIP around these parts.'

'I'm pretty sure she drove through a puddle on purpose to give me a soaking the other night,' Gina said, glaring after the disappearing Audi.

Manda seemed unsurprised. 'Like I said, she thinks she's a cut above. I dare say she's annoyed about you being so friendly with Ben Pascoe – he's another thing she thinks is hers by right.'

Gina thought back to the frosty look of dislike Rose had given her in the shop. 'You know, I think you're right, Manda. That explains a lot.'

'Shame Ben's got no time for her,' Manda said, her tone cheerful. She winked at Gina. 'He's got better taste, thank goodness.'

It was meant as a compliment, Gina knew, but she couldn't help feeling uncomfortable. She changed the subject. 'Got your costume for *Singin' in the Rain*?' she asked, waving towards the bright posters Gorran had mounted in the rectangular casings on the Palace walls.

Manda gave her a self-satisfied grin. 'Of course – I'm coming as one of those pink-frocked dancers with the swimming caps on their heads.' She pointed at the Strawberry Sensation gelato in the display case. 'I'll look just like a cornet.'

Gina laughed. 'Perfect. I wonder what Gorran is wearing.'

'I know the answer to that too – he's—'

'No, don't tell me,' Gina said quickly, holding up her hands. 'I want it to be a surprise.'

'That's not always a good thing where Gorran is concerned,' Manda said doubtfully. 'But I think this time you're on safe ground.'

Bidding Manda goodbye, Gina headed over to her grandparents' house, hoping to borrow the Fiat and go to the

Scarlet to pick up the oranges for Ferdie. But when she arrived, Elena told her he already had them.

'He made me drive him over there first thing this morning,' she grumbled. 'I almost missed my yoga class. And he's been locked away in the dairy ever since, experimenting.'

Gina's eyes widened. 'He sounds keen.'

'Obsessed, more like,' Elena said. 'But if it means he opens his mind to new flavours, who are we to complain?'

By the end of Friday, Gina was relieved to see that ticket orders were starting to come in. With only a week to go, she'd started to wonder whether she'd left enough time to generate enough word-of-mouth support for the event but it looked as though her fears had been unfounded. A positive mention in the local paper had helped, and businesses around Polwhipple were supporting the Palace too, placing posters in their windows. The bartender at the Scarlet had emailed Gina his cocktail suggestion – a vodka, orange juice and Galliano concoction he'd called the 'Moses Supposes' that was the exact colour of the raincoats from the movie poster – and Gina couldn't wait to see it, much less drink it.

The quotes had come in from the builders who'd visited the Palace and Gina was both relieved and pleased to see Ben's was the lowest. She added them to her application pack, hoping that Monday night's meeting would be just a formality.

She was halfway through a Chinese takeaway and *Pretty Woman* when her mobile rang. Glancing at the screen, she was amazed to see Max's name there.

'Hello,' she said, trying not to sound as surprised as she felt. 'Everything okay?'

'Fine,' he replied. She heard a jumble of voices in the background and guessed he was in a bar somewhere. 'I meant to ring earlier but you know how it is. How are you?'

Gina's forehead wrinkled. She'd never known Max to call her from a bar before. 'I'm fine. How are you?'

'Good, thanks. Listen, I was thinking about our conversation the other day and I was just wondering . . . how do you fancy a house-mate for a few days?'

'That would depend on who it was,' she said cautiously, unsure where the conversation was going. What if Max was trying to wangle a free holiday for a client in the hope that it might swing a business deal his way?

He laughed. 'I meant me, Gina. I've managed to clear a few days' mid-week and thought I could head down on Tuesday. What do you think?'

Unbidden, an image of Ben popped into her head, sat opposite her on the train. 'I think that sounds great,' she said, pushing the image away. 'But between Ferrelli's and the Palace, I might be a bit tied up. I've got another eve—'

'I'm sure I can find something to do while you're busy,' Max cut in as the noise level in the background increased. 'Let's have dinner one of the nights too – what about the Scarlet? I hear the food there is good.'

'Sure,' Gina said, a little taken aback. 'I'll book a table for Wednesday evening. But how—'

'Great,' he said, almost shouting now. 'Listen, I've got to go. See you soon, okay?'

'Okay,' Gina said. 'And thanks for this, Max. It means a lot.'

'Yeah, to me too. Bye, Gina.'

The line went dead. Lowering it to the sofa, Gina pressed Play on the remote control and Julia Roberts continued shopping. But Gina was so deep in thought that she barely registered the action on screen. It was very out of character for Max to cancel business meetings, although it wouldn't be the first time he'd driven down to Polwhipple to see her. Maybe her plea had hit home the last time they'd spoken, or maybe he was just missing her, she thought, taking an absent-minded mouthful of chicken chow mein. She'd ask him when he arrived. Just like she'd ask who had recommended the food at the Scarlet.

# Chapter Sixteen

Gina arrived at Polwhipple station just before midday on Sunday, a large bag of popcorn tucked under one arm and a tub of her grandfather's brand new gelato flavour in her hand. The gates were wide open and parked outside the station itself was a red Audi TT. Gina's heart sank. What possible reason could Rose Arundell have for being at Ben's on a Sunday? What possible reason could she have for being at Ben's *any* day of the week?

Gina thought about turning back, but then she remembered Manda's comment about Rose disliking her friendship with Ben and she squared her shoulders. She wouldn't be intimidated by Rose – Ben was one of her oldest friends, after all, and they had plans.

Pushing open the door of the station, she peered inside the ticket hall. 'Hello? Ben?'

Silence. Feeling a little like a trespasser, Gina crossed the tiled floor to the door leading out to the platform. There was no sign of anyone. Swallowing her misgivings, she made her way along the platform to the white fence at the end. Beyond it, she could see Ben's home, the converted railway carriage parked in one of the sidings. Gina's guts twisted unpleasantly; was Rose inside with Ben?

The question was answered a few seconds later, just as Gina reached the bottom of the steps that led up to the carriage entrance. The door sprang open and Rose stood there, a triumphant smile on her face. Beyond her, Gina could see Ben, half-dressed in a pair of jeans and nothing else.

Rose glanced backwards. 'Thanks, Ben,' she said, her voice low and husky. 'For *everything*.'

She swept down the steps, pushing past Gina with just enough calculated force to make her stumble. Gina's cheeks burned with fury and she longed to push the other woman back but she clenched her fists instead and counted to a long and uneven ten.

Ben appeared in the doorway, his jaw shadowed with blond stubble, and saw her for the first time. His eyes widened. 'Gina! Is that the time? Bloody hell, it's not—' He seemed to realise he was semi-naked and stepped back hurriedly. 'Sorry, can you give me a minute?'

Gina averted her gaze from his six-pack and stared at the gravel beneath her feet. 'Of course,' she said in a voice that sounded tight and angry even to her. 'Take your time.'

Still looking dazed, Ben stepped back and closed the door. Gina heard muffled thumps and curses and she guessed he was either trying to get dressed or tidying up – possibly both. A few minutes later, the door opened again. This time, he was wearing a Rip Curl T-shirt and a pair of mismatched socks to go with his jeans.

'Sorry about that,' he said, giving her a look of sheepish embarrassment. 'Come in.'

Taking a deep breath, Gina climbed the steps. Once inside, she handed him the popcorn and ice-cream. 'That will need to go in the freezer.' She looked at him, trying to conceal her bewilderment and hurt at the same time as wondering why she felt as though she'd been kicked in the stomach. 'You've got lipstick on your cheek, by the way.'

His hand flew to his cheek and he rubbed hard, smearing the peach mark and making it bigger. 'Sorry,' he said again, moving towards the door that led to the galley kitchen.

Gina made an effort to pull herself together. 'You don't have to apologise, Ben. What you and Rose do is nothing to do with me.'

He turned around. 'But that's just it – we haven't been doing anything.' His fingers touched his cheek. 'At least, I haven't done anything. Rose turned up around half an hour ago, ringing the bell on the door of the station. It rings in here too so I raced over there, thinking there was some kind of emergency, and she demanded I let her in so she could talk to me. I brought her over here because it was a bit nippy to hang around in the ticket office.'

She stared at him, trying to decide whether or not she believed him. But why would he lie? He didn't owe her an explanation. 'You weren't dressed? At eleven-thirty in the morning?'

His cheeks turned rosy. 'I was out with some mates in Newquay last night. It turned into a bit of a late one.' He threw her a shame-faced look. 'I'd probably still be in bed now if Rose hadn't turned up, so in some ways I suppose it's a good thing she did.'

A whoosh of relief washed over Gina: Ben hadn't spent the night with Rose, which was clearly what she'd wanted Gina to think. 'But why was she here in the first place? What was so important?'

He raised his hands in a helpless shrug. 'That's the weirdest thing – all she wanted to know was whether I was going to the *Singin' in the Rain* screening as Gene Kelly's character, Don Lockwood. Then she saw the DVD next to the TV and I explained you were coming over to watch it with me. After that, I couldn't get rid of her, until you arrived.'

He looked so confused that Gina took pity on him. 'Are you hungover?'

'A bit,' he admitted. 'Nothing that a decent breakfast won't fix.'

Gina smiled. 'Have you got bacon? And eggs?'

He nodded. 'In the kitchen. But—'

'Put the ice-cream away and go and get in the shower,' she ordered him kindly. 'I'll make you a fry up.'

By the time he reappeared, fully clothed and clean-shaven, she'd placed two plates of bacon, eggs and beans at the small dining table at the far end of the living room, along with a mug of steaming hot tea for him and a coffee for herself.

'Thanks,' he said, his tone grateful as he sat down. 'And sorry again.'

She held up a hand. 'Stop saying you're sorry.'

He opened his mouth, as though he was going to say something, then closed it again fast. They ate in silence for a few moments, then Gina asked curiously, 'So what exactly is your history with Rose? Carrie said she thought you'd been an item.'

She stopped, suddenly aware that he might think it was strange for her to be discussing his love-life with Carrie, but Ben merely shrugged. 'We went on a couple of dates, about a year ago. It didn't go anywhere – she's not really my type – and I assumed she thought the same about me.'

Rose Arundell was young, beautiful and wealthy, Gina thought to herself. What exactly did Ben mean when he said she wasn't his type?

'But then she started coming on to me whenever I saw her,' Ben went on, looking more embarrassed than ever. 'My surfer mates started to take the mick, called me her bit of rough. So I started to avoid going anywhere I thought I might run into her, which is part of the reason I was in Newquay last night. The *Brief Encounter* screening was the first time I'd seen her in ages.'

It all made sense, Gina mused, finishing her breakfast and reaching for her coffee. Poor spoiled Rose wasn't used to rejection and couldn't believe Ben wasn't interested. So she'd pursued him and then Gina had materialised, apparently very close to Ben, and Rose had become jealous. She obviously had no idea Gina was with Max. Although, a sly little voice whispered in Gina's head, the truth was that Rose did have good reason to be jealous. Maybe she saw what Gina was trying so hard to ignore: that there was something there between her and Ben . . .

She pushed her plate away and the cutlery clattered to the table. 'Shall we watch the film, then?'

Ben swallowed his last mouthful and washed it down with a mouthful of tea. 'Yeah. Sounds like the perfect way to get rid of a hangover.'

He got up and slotted the disc into the DVD player. Gina carried her coffee towards the seats and paused. Last time she'd been in the living room, there'd been two wing-backed armchairs. There was no sign of them now – they'd been replaced by a small two-seater sofa which faced the television. Ben sat down and propped his feet up on a low wooden coffee table. 'Come on,' he said, patting the cushion next to him. 'And bring that popcorn over too. I'm still hungry.'

Gina did as he asked, settling on the sofa and trying not to notice the way their bodies leaned into each other. If they'd been a couple, it would have been the most natural thing in the world for Ben to slip his arm around Gina's shoulders and for her to snuggle into him as they watched the film. But they weren't a couple – couldn't be – and it was dangerous for her to even think such things. So Gina sat stiffly for the first fifteen minutes of the film, hardly registering what was happening on screen, acutely aware of Ben's closeness.

'So, what have you got in mind for the foyer?' he asked, as a pink-clad Debbie Reynolds leapt out of a cake. 'Want to turn it into a film set?'

Gina felt him looking at her and kept her gaze fixed on the television. 'I was thinking that a red carpet might be simpler – like the one at the start of the film.'

She felt him nod. 'Okay. Do you need me to do anything special with the bar? I'm working over Penzance way next week but I'm sure I can fit something in if you need me to.'

She did look at him then, and wished she hadn't, because he was closer than he'd been on the train. 'Thanks, but I think it will be fine.' She cleared her throat. 'Shall I get the ice-cream?'

Ben pushed himself off the sofa. 'I'm not much of a host, am I? All you've done since you got here is run around after me.'

Gina didn't mind if she went to the kitchen or he did, as long as she got some space. By the time he returned with two bowls of Ferdie's new creation, she'd moved onto the floor.

'Bad back,' she lied when he studied her quizzically. 'I'm better off down here.'

The gelato distracted both of them; it summoned up warm summer mornings and every mouthful was bursting with flavour. How had Ferdie done it? Gina wondered, savouring each taste. How had he captured so much exquisite, mouth-watering taste? It was sheer perfection and, unless she was totally mistaken, it was going to bring the house down.

'Your grandfather is a genius,' Ben said, scraping the last dregs of melted gelato from the bottom of his bowl. 'That was amazing.'

Gina smiled, basking in the glow of reflected pride. 'I think Debbie and Gene are in real danger of being upstaged by an ice-cream.'

From her much safer vantage point on the floor, Gina could finally relax and enjoy the film. She couldn't help a tiny snort of amusement when Lina got her comeuppance; was it too much to hope that something similar might happen to Rose?

As the final credits rolled, Gina turned to Ben. 'You know, I don't think you said what you're wearing to the screening.'

'That's right, I didn't,' Ben said, his tone teasing. 'You'll just have to wait and see.'

He had to be coming as Don Lockwood, Gina decided; maybe he'd gone for the period costume from *The Dancing Cavalier.* The thought almost made her smile. Almost.

Checking the time, she got to her feet. 'I'd better get going. I want to go over the paperwork for the council meeting tomorrow evening, to make sure we haven't missed anything. Want me to check the station application too?'

'Would you mind?' Ben asked. 'Tell me if it's too much work. Or maybe we could go through it together now?'

Gina wasn't sure she could bear another half an hour of sitting on the floor and she definitely wasn't going to risk joining him on the sofa again. 'No, don't worry, I'll look at it all together later. It's no trouble.'

Ben didn't seem convinced. 'Are you sure?'

'Totally,' Gina assured him, gathering up her bag and coat. 'I'll let you know if I spot any problems, but if you don't hear from me, I'll meet you and Gorran outside the council offices at six-thirty tomorrow evening.'

'Okay,' he said, with a smile that made Gina's stomach fizz. 'Thanks for the ice-cream and for breakfast.'

'See you tomorrow,' she said, heading for the door.

The town council meetings were held in the grey-bricked town hall, just behind the war memorial in the heart of Polwhipple. Gorran was already waiting, looking nervous, in a suit that was considerably less crumpled than his usual clothes. He'd made an effort to tame his crazy white hair too, not altogether successfully, but Gina decided he'd do. She'd also dressed formally for the occasion, in a cream dress with matching heels that made walking on the cobbled street difficult. Ben arrived a few minutes after her and she was pleased to see he'd aimed to impress; his charcoal suit was well cut and flattering, and Gina thought he wouldn't have looked out of place in the pages of a men's magazine. She sat on the thought and managed a brisk, business-like smile. 'Hello. All set?'

He nodded in greeting, first at her, then at Gorran. 'I think so. You?'

She handed him a plastic wallet that was full of neatly bundled papers. 'Yes. Shall we go in?'

Inside the town hall, the floor was tiled in a faded claret

and white mosaic. The walls were wood-panelled with dark wood that Gina felt had been in place for a long time. A brass chandelier hung in the centre of the reception area and a wide wooden staircase curved upwards and split into two as it reached the first floor.

Gina approached the receptionist. 'Gina Callaway, Gorran Dew and Ben Pascoe, to address the Fiscal Planning committee.'

The receptionist made them sign in and issued them with visitors' badges. 'Up to the first floor and round to the right,' she said, in a way that made Gina think she said the same words over and over each day. 'Through the double doors and take a seat until you're called.'

'It's like being back at school,' Ben said, after they'd been waiting for a short while. 'I feel like I've been summoned to the head teacher's office again.'

'Speak for yourself,' Gina replied in a low tone, as Gorran nodded his agreement. 'I never got summoned to the head teacher's office.'

Ben raised a disbelieving eyebrow. 'Oh really? Whose idea was it to steal cigarettes to smoke on the beach after the sun had gone down?'

Gina smiled in spite of her nerves. 'All right, it was mine. But that was down to your bad influence – I was a good girl at school.'

'My bad influence?' Ben said, sounding half-shocked, half-amused. 'I seem to remember *you* teaching *me* how to blow the perfect smoke ring.'

This time, Gina grinned. 'And I remember you turning so pale you outshone the moon. Then you threw up.'

Gorran looked back and forth between them, as though working something out, while Ben let out a quiet laugh. 'Good times.'

The dark wood door opposite opened and a smartly dressed woman appeared. 'Callaway, Dew and Pascoe?' she said, after consulting her clipboard. 'Come with me, please.'

'We sound like a bunch of bleddy solicitors,' Gorran mumbled, running a finger around the inside of his collar.

She led them into a high-ceilinged room surrounded by wood-panelled walls, lit by another chandelier. This one had a long, highly polished table running through the centre, with five council committee members sitting along the far side: three men and two women. The men nodded in greeting as Gorran, Gina and Ben approached the table, and the elder of the two women smiled. The other woman, who was blonde, in her fifties and looked very much as though she had a terrible smell under her nose, did not smile.

'Your names?' she snapped, glancing down at a sheet of paper on the table in front of her.

Gorran stammered as he introduced himself, making Gina want to squeeze his hand in solidarity. She concentrated on her own introduction, then listened to Ben, who sounded cool and calm in spite of the nerves she knew he was feeling. The woman did not look impressed at anything she had heard. 'According to this, you're requesting tax-payers' money to invest in two privately owned businesses, is that correct?'

Gina glanced at Ben and cleared her throat. 'That is true, however—'

'I'm afraid we don't invest in private businesses,' the blonde woman snapped, her blue eyes cold. 'Next.'

'We might as well hear what they have to say, Valeria,' the older woman admonished.

The man with the handlebar moustache nodded. 'Quite right. What is it you'd like funding for?'

Gina took her folder from her bag and laid it on the table. She flipped open the cover and glanced down for a second. Then she began. 'Our application falls into two parts. Firstly, we'd like to apply for funding to refurbish the Palace Picture House on the promenade. Once the jewel in Polwhipple's crown, it's been falling further and further into disrepair with every passing year, but the good news is that with a little time, attention and money, I think it could soon be the heart of the community once more, drawing in audiences from much further afield and boosting our economy.'

She glanced sideways at Gorran, who, she was glad to see, looked a little less like he might vomit. 'It's a good little place,' he said quietly. 'I'd be the first to admit I haven't managed things as well as I might have done but now Gina is here and she's shown me how good the Palace could be. But to make it really shine, we need money – investment – and that's something I don't have. That's why we're here.'

Gina gave him an encouraging smile before continuing. 'Secondly, we'd like to ask for funding to finish the restoration work to Polwhipple's own train station, with a view to encouraging the Bodmin and Wenford Railway Preservation Society to extend the heritage line to Polwhipple from Boscarne Junction, where it currently terminates.'

Most of the committee were watching Gina, Gorran and Ben, their expressions curious and interested. The blonde woman called Valeria had her eyes fixed on her sheet of paper on the table. Every now and then, she made a small mark, making Gina wonder if she was doing the crossword or Sudoku. There was something almost familiar about her, although Gina couldn't work out where she might have seen her before. She wasn't going to let Valeria's rudeness deter her, though; straightening her shoulders, Gina raised her voice a little more and went on.

'We've brought detailed plans to accompany our application forms. The sums of money we're asking for aren't large but they will make all the difference to our proposed projects and to Polwhipple itself. Imagine the town thronging with visitors, waiting to see a film at the newly refurbished cinema. They might want something to eat, or to grab a coffee while they wait, which is extra income that Polwhipple's small businesses wouldn't have had otherwise.'

'Or maybe they've hopped on the steam train at Bodmin Parkway, looking for a day out,' Ben put in, as Gina handed out copies of their application forms. 'There's not much to see at Boscarne Junction, unless you want to walk the Camel Trail, so they go straight back to Bodmin. But what if they could stay on the train to Polwhipple and spend a few hours browsing in the shops?'

There was a brief silence as the committee skimmed through the forms. The man with the moustache eventually lowered his reading glasses to study Ben. 'It says here that you've already invested substantial amounts of your own money to renovate the station yourself. Why?'

'It was my dad's dream,' Ben replied simply. 'He was a driver on the line and wanted to bring the trains back to Polwhipple more than anything. Unfortunately, he died before he could do anything about it.'

Another of the male committee members lifted the application forms, his gaze suddenly sharp. 'You're Davey Pascoe's boy?'

Ben nodded. 'That's right.'

'I used to work with him,' the man said. 'Never met a man who loved trains as much as he did.'

A smile spread over Ben's face. 'That sounds like him.'

The older woman eyed Gina appraisingly. 'And what's your connection to Polwhipple, Miss Callaway? You'll forgive me for saying you don't sound like a local.'

'I'm not,' Gina said. 'I live in London now, although I was born in Truro. My grandfather runs Ferrelli's, the gelateria that sits inside the Palace. I'm working with him while he recovers from an accident.'

'I see,' the woman said. 'But that doesn't explain why you're here, asking for funding to refurbish the picture house.'

Gina fired a swift smile Gorran's way. 'No, it doesn't. I've been a fan of the Palace ever since I spent several summers in Polwhipple, with my grandparents. I have many happy memories of the films I used to watch there and I'm happy to give something back now. Gorran and I have been working together to run some film-centred events and they've been very popular. I think that proves that there's a demand in Polwhipple for a well-equipped, well-managed cinema.'

The man with the moustache looked over the top of his glasses. 'You were behind the *Brief Encounter* screening?'

She nodded. 'Yes. And we're showing *Singin' in the Rain* this Saturday, if you're interested? Ferrelli's is supplying an exclusive new gelato and the Scarlet Hotel has devised a cocktail especially for the evening.'

The woman called Valeria lowered the paper she'd been scanning. 'Do you have any experience of project management, Mr Dew? Miss Callaway has been quite disparaging of your abilities – it doesn't exactly inspire confidence.'

Gorran blushed. 'Not dreckly, but—'

Valeria fixed Gina with a humourless smile. 'How about you, Miss Callaway? Do you have any experience of project management on this scale?'

Gina tried not to bristle. 'No, but I run my own business and I'm well aware—'

'Running a party business is quite different to managing a major refurbishment,' the woman interrupted. 'I see that Mr Pascoe here has quoted to undertake the bulk of the restoration work – this is in addition to managing his own project of renovating the station.'

Heat began to crawl up Gina's cheeks. 'Ben is a master

craftsman who specialises in restoring old buildings. In point of fact, the renovation work at the station itself is almost finished and the funding will mostly be directed towards restoring the train tracks themselves.'

'But there's a clear conflict of interest here,' Valeria persisted. 'How do we know Mr Pascoe is as good as he says he is?'

Gina gritted her teeth and counted silently to five. 'There are three quotes in total, and you'll see that not only is Ben's the most competitive, he's also the only builder with direct experience of restoring historically important buildings. I've seen some of his work during a recent visit to Lanhydrock House – I can assure you, he's perfectly competent.'

The final committee member, a sandy-haired man who put Gina in mind of an accountant, glanced along the table at the others. 'I see. We'll read through your application in detail and come to a conclusion over the next seven days. You'll be notified of our decision. Thank you.'

And just like that, it was over. The older woman gave Gina an encouraging smile as they left, and the man who'd worked with Ben's father came around the table to shake their hands. Valeria did not look up and showed no sign she acknowledged they were leaving.

None of them spoke until they were outside in the fresh air. 'That was . . .' Gorran swallowed hard and shook his head ruefully. 'That was downright terrifying.'

'You can say that again,' Ben said, sounding as though he'd just run a marathon. 'Drink?'

Gorran backed away. 'Not for me. You go ahead, though.'

'Absolutely,' Gina said fervently. 'Maybe more than one.'

They bid Gorran a good night and started to walk in the direction of the Mermaid's Tail.

'I think that went as well as could be expected, under the circumstances,' Ben said, after a little while.

Gina shook her head. 'What circumstances? That shark-eyed Valeria woman, you mean?'

He tipped his head. 'Yeah. I wish I'd known she was going to be there.'

'How could you have known?' Gina shrugged. 'I don't know what her problem was – she seemed to have it in for all of us.'

'Mmm,' Ben agreed, and gave her a sidelong look. 'There's probably a reason for that. Well, you and me at least.'

Gina frowned. 'What?'

'That was Valeria Arundell. Rose's mother.'

Gina stopped walking and groaned. 'Bloody hell. Of all the bad luck . . .'

Ben let out a heartfelt sigh. 'There's more. That fair-haired bloke who only spoke up at the end? He's Valeria's brother – Rose's uncle.'

Gina swore softly and began to walk fast. 'Come on,' she said to Ben. 'I don't know about you but I think I'm going to need a double.'

# Chapter Seventeen

Max arrived at Bodmin Parkway late on Tuesday evening, crumpled and tired-looking from the journey. Gina had borrowed Nonna's car and driven over to meet him from the train and the moment he saw her waiting on the platform, he strode forwards to wrap her in a long embrace and bury his face in her neck. 'I've really missed you,' he murmured against her skin, holding her tight.

'I've missed you too,' she said, closing her eyes and breathing in the familiar scent of his aftershave. 'I'm so glad you're here.'

It wasn't a lie, Gina reflected, as she navigated the pitch-black roads back to Polwhipple; she had missed Max. She suspected that was what had made her so vulnerable to her flights of fancy about kissing Ben. But now that Max was here, those thoughts would vanish. It was Max she loved, after all.

'Sorry, what?' she said, suddenly aware he had asked her a question. 'I was concentrating on the road.'

'I said, how did the meeting with the town council go?' Max repeated. 'It was yesterday, right?'

Gina frowned. She didn't remember mentioning the meeting to Max but she supposed she must have done. 'Hard to say,' she said cautiously, not sure how to explain what her worries were without raising unnecessary suspicions about her relationship with Ben. 'They were a tough crowd. We won't know their decision until next week, anyway.'

She and Ben had spent an hour and a half in the pub after the meeting, analysing every aspect of the committee's response over a bottle of very nice red wine. Afterwards, Ben had insisted on walking her to her grandparents', where she'd arranged to stay over, and Gina had felt like she'd gone back in time and was a teenager again. Except that she'd never reached up to kiss his cheek when she was fifteen, and she'd never secretly wished she could invite him inside for another drink.

Max was speaking again. Gina forced herself to concentrate on his voice. '—and they're notoriously corrupt. I think you should prepare yourself for the worst and think about other options.'

'What other options?' Gina said, glancing over at him. 'The Palace belongs to Gorran, not me. It's up to him what he does with it – maybe he'll be able to follow my example and put on screenings that pull in a decent crowd.'

'He might,' Max said. 'You've certainly done more than anyone could reasonably expect. I'm sure he knows you can't go on propping him up like this.'

'I'm not *propping him up*,' Gina said in a cool voice. 'I enjoy organising the events and people seem to like coming to them. I've made friends here.'

Max was quiet for a moment, then rubbed his face. 'You know what, I'm being an arse. Of course you enjoy it – it's what you do best, you help people to have a good time. And it's one of the reasons people like you, because somehow you make everything seem fun.' He paused, then reached across to squeeze her arm. 'I'm just worried this Gorran is taking advantage of your good nature, that's all. He's not paying you to manage these events, is he?'

'No, he's not,' Gina said. 'But money isn't everything, Max.'

He sighed. 'I know, I know. You can take the man out of property development . . .'

Neither of them spoke for a few minutes. Gina was filled with a growing sense of guilt; she wasn't being fair to Max. Of course he was primarily concerned with money – it was his job, and the truth was she would never have considered working for free in London. But down here it was different – she wasn't being paid by Nonno either, because he was her family. She couldn't continue to work for free indefinitely, however; sooner or later, she'd have to get back to her real life.

'I'm sorry,' she said aloud. 'I know you're only looking out for me.'

'I am. And I don't want to argue with you, especially not over something like this. Why don't we start again?'

A gentle, apologetic smile was curving his mouth and she was filled with a sudden rush of happiness that he'd made the time and effort to be with her. 'Okay, you've got a deal. Why don't you tell me what's new with you?'

Gina awoke early on Wednesday morning.

She lay still for a few moments, listening to the now unfamiliar sound of Max's breathing beside her and watching the sun's rays creep through the gaps around the blind at the window. Slipping stealthily out of bed, she went to the kitchen to make coffee. In London, Max would have been up and at the gym by now, but they'd been awake long into the early hours, reacquainting themselves with each other's bodies and she wasn't surprised he was still sleeping. Gina stretched and yawned; maybe she'd go back to bed for an hour too.

She took Max to Nonno and Nonna's for lunch and she was pleased to see how much of an effort he made to charm them both. In the afternoon, they went to the Palace and Gina introduced him to Gorran, who insisted on giving him an access-all-areas tour while she went through ticket sales and confirmed that her VIP attendees could still come, including the local press, Polwhipple's mayor and the Director of the Cornwall Film Festival.

Max had a slightly glazed look about him when Gorran returned him to Gina. She hid a smile and made an excuse so that they could leave. Outside on the promenade, well out of earshot of Manda in the window of Ferrelli's, Max puffed out his cheeks and sent an admiring look Gina's way. 'He's a bit—'

'Disorganised?' Gina suggested, with a smile. 'Eccentric? Scatter-brained?'

'All of the above,' he said, shaking his head. 'How do you work with him?'

'Gorran's not all bad. He's also enthusiastic, open to new ideas and kind-hearted.'

Max appeared unconvinced. 'Not character traits that get you very far as a businessman.' He aimed a critical gaze at the careworn exterior of the Palace. 'I can see why you want to refurbish it. With the right kind of attention, it could be fabulous. And the view is stunning.'

He turned to study the Polwhipple beach. The tide was out, so golden sand stretched almost as far as the eye could see and azure blue water twinkled in the distance. There wasn't a cloud in the sky. 'I understand why you love it here,' Max said, turning to take Gina's hand. 'But don't forget London has its good points too.'

She squeezed his fingers. 'Of course I won't forget. London is my home, after all.'

His hazel eyes searched hers for a moment, as though he wasn't sure he believed her. 'Good,' he said at last. 'I'm happy to hear that. Nothing is the same without you.'

He pulled her into his arms and kissed her. And once again, Gina told herself that she hadn't really lied, but she hadn't entirely told the truth either.

*

Their table at the Scarlet Hotel was booked for eight o'clock, but Gina had arranged to meet the head bartender beforehand so that he could give them a sneak preview of his Moses Supposes cocktail. She almost laughed out loud in delight when he presented the drink; not only was it the most perfect shade of raincoat yellow, each cocktail was also topped with a red or black paper umbrella, exactly like the film poster.

'Amazing,' Gina said, pulling out her phone to snap a photograph for social media. 'You've really outdone yourself, Miquel.'

'Tastes good, too,' Max said, taking a sip. 'You should think about upgrading, Miquel – with mixology skills like these, you'd take the London bar scene by storm.'

The bartender smiled politely and shook his head. 'I'm happy here.'

Gina felt a shiver of embarrassment. 'Not everyone wants to move to London, Max.'

He shrugged. 'Sooner or later, that's where all the real talent goes.'

Focusing on Miquel, Gina smiled. 'I think the Moses Supposes is going to be a big hit on Saturday. Thanks for all your creativity and hard work.'

The bartender looked delighted. 'I can't take all the credit – it's a twist on a Harvey Wallbanger. But I'm glad you like it.'

Just before eight o'clock, the maître d' ushered Gina and Max through to the restaurant. They had just begun to study the menu when Gina heard a voice that made her blood run cold. She looked up to see Rose Arundell weaving her way through the tables, wearing the silky Grace Kelly dress she'd bought from Carrie's boutique. And walking right behind her was Ben.

Gina almost dropped her menu. She stared at Ben, who looked uncomfortable and ill at ease, unable to believe what she was seeing.

'What?' Max asked, noticing her frozen expression. He turned in his seat at the exact moment Rose spotted Gina. Gaze glittering, Rose switched direction and headed their way. Behind her, Ben blinked and frowned. Then his eyes followed Rose's intended path and a look of horror crossed his face.

Rose came to a halt beside Max and she fired a loaded smile Gina's way. But it was Max she spoke to. 'How lovely to see you again, Max.'

Gina felt as though she'd been punched in the stomach. Rose knew Max? How? It wasn't possible. And yet Max was getting to his feet and planting air kisses on Rose's flawless cheeks. 'This is an unexpected pleasure. How are your parents?'

Ben looked as confused as Gina felt. His eyes sought hers and she saw a mixture of bewilderment and embarrassment there, as though she'd caught him doing something he shouldn't, and couldn't understand how it had happened.

'They're very well,' Rose replied. 'Mummy will be delighted to hear you're in the area, although I'm sure she'll insist you come over for drinks.'

Her cool gaze flickered briefly to Gina, making it clear that the invitation would only apply to Max. But the slight barely registered with Gina; she was too busy trying to work out how Rose and Max could possibly know each other. Not only that but Max also seemed to be on more than nodding acquaintance with Valeria Arundell. How on earth had their paths crossed? Gina wondered. Had they met in London, on some business deal that involved the Arundells? It had to be a coincidence, she told herself. What else could it be?

'I'm afraid it's a flying visit,' Max said, sounding apologetic. 'You know how busy I am – I can't afford to be away from the real world for long.' He looked over Rose's shoulder at Ben and thrust out a hand. 'I don't think we've met. I'm Max Hardy.'

Gina wondered whether she might be having an out-of-body experience, so unreal did everything feel. Forcing herself to breathe, she watched as the two of them shook hands. 'Ben Pascoe. Pleased to meet you.'

Max's eyes widened. 'You're Gina's old surfer friend. She's told me a lot about you.'

The words were innocent enough but something about the way Max said them made Gina wary. Quite apart from anything else, it wasn't true; she'd barely mentioned Ben to Max, partly because her emotions lately had been so conflicted.

Ben glanced briefly at her. 'All good things, I hope?'

'Ben and I have just started seeing each other,' Rose purred, linking her arm possessively through his. 'We're rekindling an old love affair.'

Ben avoided Gina's astonished stare. And then, just when she thought things couldn't get any worse, Max waved a hand at the adjoining table. 'Why don't you join us?'

'Oh, I don't think—' Gina began.

'No, that's not—' Ben said, at exactly the same time but Rose spoke over both of them.

'That would be wonderful,' she said, beaming at Max. 'We'd love to.'

Max attracted the attention of the maître d' and explained. Moments later, the waiters had pushed the tables together and Gina found herself sitting next to Ben.

'Hi,' she said, without smiling.

He nodded. 'Hi.'

Gina fixed her gaze on the menu but found herself unable to concentrate long enough to read anything. Ben and Rose were seeing each other? When had that happened? *How* had it happened? When she'd seen Ben on Sunday, he'd been adamant that he had no romantic interest in Rose. What the hell was going on?

She became aware that the waiter was hovering next to the table. Rose was ordering the wild rabbit starter and the fallow deer main course. The waiter looked expectantly Gina's way but Max spoke first. 'We'll have the monkfish to start, followed by the Chateaubriand, please. What are your recommendations for wine?'

The waiter began to reel off suggestions. Cheeks burning, Gina cut across him. 'Max, since when do you order for me?'

He glanced over at her in surprise. 'But you love Chateaubriand. And monkfish, for that matter.'

Gina pressed her lips together hard and tried to keep a lid on her temper. 'I love having a choice more,' she ground out. Taking a deep breath, she turned to the waiter. 'I'll have the pumpkin soup, followed by the cheese soufflé. Sorry, Max, I'm not in the mood for beef tonight.'

There was an awkward silence. 'I don't mind sharing the Chateaubriand with you, Max,' Rose said, smoothly. 'Cancel my fallow deer, will you?'

Ben placed his order but Gina barely heard what it was. She stared down at the tablecloth, trying her hardest to blink back the tears that were threatening to fall on the pristine white material. Max had never tried to order for her before – what was he playing at? And worst of all, she'd somehow managed to make Rose Arundell seem reasonable and measured. It was like a nightmare she couldn't wake up from.

She said very little during the meal, meeting direct questions with monosyllabic answers even though she knew it made her come across like a sulky teenager. She was sure the food was delicious but it all tasted like ash and she left most of it. Once, Ben tried to take her hand under the table and she shook him off with such vehemence that she was sure Max and Rose must have noticed. Eventually, she excused herself to go to the ladies', claiming to have a headache, and when she came back, Max was settling the bill and the maître d' was holding her coat.

She went straight to bed as soon as they reached the

apartment, ignoring the frantic vibrations of her phone and Max's concerned enquiries about what was wrong. She removed her make-up and climbed into bed, turned her back so that she wouldn't have to see Max when he came in. Then she closed her eyes and allowed the hot tears that were burning her eyelids to leak slowly onto the pillow.

She was subdued the next morning at the dairy. Elena had clucked in alarm over her puffy eyes and pale cheeks but hadn't pressed her for the reason once it became clear Gina didn't want to talk. Ferdie was less gruff than usual, even when she spoiled a whole batch of custard by adding the hot milk to the eggs so fast that they curdled in the bowl. Eventually, he got up from the stool he was leaning on and took her hands.

'Gina, *mia bella*, tell Nonno what's wrong,' he said, and his tone was so kind that she couldn't prevent a fresh torrent of tears from coursing down her cheeks.

Ferdie handed her a crisp white handkerchief and waited patiently for the flood to slow.

'H-have you ever thought you knew someone and then realised you don't k-know them at all?' she stammered eventually, dabbing at her face with the cool cloth.

'Once or twice,' Ferdie admitted. 'This is Max, yes?'

'Yes,' Gina said, sniffing uncertainly. 'No. Oh, I don't know – it's both of them.'

Ferdie studied her, his eyebrows beetling into a fierce frown. 'Who else has been upsetting you? Shall I go and knock their heads together?'

The thought made her lips quirk; a small, wavering movement that barely counted as a smile. 'I don't think it would help. I think the problem must be me.'

Ferdie grunted. 'I don't pretend to understand what this is about, Gina, but I can see that it is making you very unhappy. And that makes me unhappy – it makes me want to step in and sort out all your problems so that you are smiling again and brightening up my days.' He shook his head. 'See? I am nothing but a selfish old man who wants his contented granddaughter back – I bet you didn't know that about me.'

Gina sniffed again, nodding; she thought she could see where he was going with this.

'My point is that sometimes the people we love hurt and disappoint us. And because we are hurt, the temptation is to react by lashing out or running away. But what if instead of doing either of those things, we saw it as an opportunity to fix something that had been broken?'

His eyes met hers and she saw that they were filled with regret. 'If I had taken the opportunity I was given when your mother and I fell out, who knows how different our lives might have been? But instead, I lashed out and she ran away. And now I think that the damage is too great to fix.'

Gina stared at her fingers, fidgeting with the handkerchief as she tried to make sense of his words. What was she more upset about – Max's heavy-handed presumption in the restaurant last night, or the knowledge that Ben and Rose were an item? She didn't know, and everything felt too confused to unravel. 'Maybe I just need some time,' she whispered.

Ferdie tipped his head. 'Time is good, in moderation. But leave it too long and fixing things becomes much harder. Take it from one who knows.'

He sounded so sad that Gina reached out to give him a hug. They stood unmoving for a little while, then Gina stepped back and wiped the last of the tears from her cheeks. 'Thank you, Nonno. I feel a bit better now.'

'Good,' Ferdie said, looking fierce once more. 'And remember, I am always available to knock heads together if you need me.'

# Chapter Eighteen

Gina arrived home later that afternoon to an apartment filled with red roses. They adorned every available surface, from the coffee table to the kitchen worktop and even the shelf around the bathroom sink. Max sat among them, perched on the edge of the sofa with a contrite expression.

'I'm sorry,' he said, the moment she stepped into the living room. 'I am a jealous, ridiculous moron and I acted like a total prick.'

Gina eyed him coldly, although her heart was thudding uncomfortably. 'Go on.'

Max ran a hand through his hair. 'I don't know why I did it. I mean, I suppose I do, if I'm honest – it was meeting Ben.' He gave her a level stare. 'You didn't tell me he looked like a swimwear model.'

Her face grew warm. 'He's one of my oldest friends, Max. We've known each other since we were kids.'

'I know,' Max said, sounding wretched. 'That's part of the

problem. You're down here, discovering friends you had before we even met and taking the whole bloody town by storm. It makes me feel a bit shut out, to be honest, like I'm not a big part of your life these days. So, when I realised who Ben was and he was all *He Man, Master of the Universe* – well, I think I might have lost the plot a bit.'

Gina couldn't help it – she laughed. 'Max, there isn't anyone in the world less *He Man* than Ben. He watches musicals and lives in a converted railway carriage, for God's sake!'

His shoulders slumped. 'I know – it's ridiculous. But that's how it felt. And so I tried to show him that I was in charge. With the benefit of hindsight, I couldn't have done anything worse. I'm sorry.'

He hung his head and the last of Gina's anger drained away. 'Max—'

'Just tell me you're not in love with him,' he cut in, so quietly that she wasn't sure she'd heard correctly.

'What?'

'Tell me you're not in love with Ben,' he said, meeting her gaze. 'That way I can go back to London with my tail between my legs and spend the next however many years trying to make this up to you.'

Gina's heart started to race. Did she love Ben, or was it merely the distance from Max and everything she knew that was making her feelings seem more than they were? She was definitely jealous of Rose; she'd known that when she'd seen her in the doorway of the railway carriage on Sunday morning, and again when she'd seen them together at the Scarlet. But did she love Ben?

'He's with Rose Arundell,' she told Max, breathing deeply to calm her thumping heart. 'And we only have to get through the next six weeks, then I'll be home. In London, with you. Where I want to be.'

Max nodded, as though he'd heard what he'd needed to hear. 'So,' he said, drawing in a long, deep breath. 'Can you forgive me?'

His eyes were suspiciously bright, as though he was on the verge of tears. Gina almost gasped; she'd never known anything to affect him like this. Hurriedly, she closed the distance between them and fell into his arms. 'Of course I forgive you,' she said, feeling her own eyes moisten. 'I love you, Max Hardy.'

Gina waved Max off on Friday morning, promising to come to see him in London soon. She was surprised at how sad she was to see him go; they'd stayed up late into the night, talking about everything from their feelings to their future, but she had plenty to take her mind off the sudden hole his absence would leave. And she had an apartment filled with the heady scent of roses to remind her of his love.

By the time Saturday evening came around, Gina had reconciled herself to the idea of Rose and Ben as a couple. It had come completely out of the blue, and Rose was the last person she would have chosen for him, but presumably Ben knew what he was doing and saw something in Rose

Arundell that Gina was blind to. Even so, she had to steel herself when they walked into the foyer of the Palace together.

Carrie spotted them at the same moment Gina did and sidled over to whisper, 'Isn't Rose the perfect Lina Lamont? But I bet she's furious over Ben's choice of outfit.'

Gina frowned. She couldn't argue with Carrie; Rose's silver flapper dress and diamond-studded head-dress looked great. Ben looked picture perfect too, as Don Lockwood, Lina's on-screen lover. 'What's wrong with it?'

'Isn't it obvious?' Carrie said, her eyes sparkling beneath her cute cloche hat. 'He's not Don Lockwood at all – he's Cosmo Brown, Don's comedy sidekick.'

Now that Gina looked closely, she saw exactly what Carrie had seen; the shirt and braces were less dashing and more slapstick, and his blond hair was slicked back in a style that definitely suggested Cosmo instead of Don. He chose that moment to glance over at her and she saw his eyes widen a fraction as he took in her figure-hugging, emerald-green dancer's dress. Then his attention snapped back to Rose, as though he hadn't noticed Gina at all.

Remembering Nonno's advice, Gina plastered a welcoming smile on her face and crossed the foyer to greet the new arrivals. 'Rose, Ben, how lovely to see you again.'

If the other woman was taken aback to be greeted so cordially, she hid it well. 'Hello, Gina. That's an interesting choice of costume.'

'It's a great choice of costume,' Ben said, although his eyes were fixed on Gina's, as though he was trying to work out whether they were still friends.

'Yours too,' she said, and this time her smile didn't need to be forced. 'Cosmo is one of my favourite characters – his *Make 'Em Laugh* routine is amazing.'

Rose's head whipped around and she stared suspiciously at Ben.

'Enjoy the film,' Gina said swiftly, because Nonno and Nonna had just appeared in the doorway, wearing matching yellow raincoats and causing a ripple of delighted applause. 'Don't forget to try the ice-cream.'

Before long, the foyer was packed with cinema-goers, all dressed in costumes to match the film. Ferdie and Elena were getting a lot of attention and Gina wasn't in the least bit surprised; underneath their raincoats, they'd mirrored Don and Kathy in the song *You Were Meant for Me*. Elena's lilac crepe dress hung in elegant folds and Gina suspected Ferdie's wide-collared white shirt and black-and-white spats might have been hiding in his wardrobe for a very long time. Gina shook her head and laughed; her grandparents had created an adorable impression of how the movie's stars might have looked after a lifetime together. It was perfect.

After making sure they each had a Moses Supposes cocktail, Gina slipped through the door that led to the business end of the Palace. She wanted to check Tash had everything she needed in the projection room, including the required number of reels to screen the film. After the near-disaster last time, she wasn't taking any chances.

She'd only taken a few of the steps that led to the projection room when she heard the door behind her open again. She turned around and was both surprised and yet unsurprised to see Ben standing there.

'Can we talk?' he said. 'Clear the air? I feel like I owe you an explanation.'

Gina began to turn away. 'I've told you before, Ben, you don't owe me anything. I'm happy for you and Rose.'

'Really?' he called. 'Because you don't look it. You look like you hate me, Gina. And I only did it for you. For *us*.'

Gina froze. 'What do you mean?' she said, slowly turning back.

Ben shrugged, his expression helpless. 'I know how much the refurbishment project means to you – the station renovation is important to me too. So I thought that maybe if I took Rose out on a date, wined her and dined her a bit, she might persuade her mother to put in a good word with the rest of the funding committee.'

'Ben!' Gina gasped, her hand flying to her face. 'You didn't!'

He nodded wretchedly. 'You weren't supposed to find out. I couldn't believe it when I saw you in the restaurant – I wanted the ground to swallow me up.'

'I can't believe you've done this,' Gina said, still reeling. 'Bloody hell, Ben, how do you think Rose is going to react when she finds out the truth?'

'She won't find out,' he said, his tone grim. 'I'm not going to tell her. Are you?'

Gina didn't know what was worse – the knowledge that

Ben was capable of something so sneaky and underhanded and wrong, or the tiny bubble of happiness she felt at knowing he and Rose weren't really together. 'You'll have to tell her something,' she said slowly. 'Or are you planning on playing a long game here?'

'God, no,' he said. 'I'll let her down gently once we've got the go ahead from the committee. She's already told me it's as good as agreed.'

'Even so ...' Gina shook her head. 'I don't know whether to kiss you or slap you.'

He was silent for several long seconds. 'I know which I'd prefer.'

The look he sent her way was so intense that it almost took her breath away. She took a single step towards him and then the door to the projection room swung open and Tash stuck her head out. 'Oh, hello,' she said, raising one pierced eyebrow. 'I just wanted to say that I'm all set in here. Thundercats are go!'

Gina avoided Ben's eyes as she nodded. 'Okay, I'll let Gorran know.'

Ben didn't try to stop her as she passed him and it wasn't until she'd reached the door to the foyer that he spoke. 'By the way, Gina, Rose was just jealous. That dress is hot.'

Fighting the urge to turn around, Gina glanced over her shoulder. 'Thank you. Now, come and help me round up the audience.'

The film itself was a triumph. Everywhere Gina looked, she saw people laughing and enjoying themselves. Feet were tapping during the dance numbers and the entire audience cheered when Lina Lamont was revealed as a fraud. Gina didn't dare look at Ben, sitting with Rose just a few seats behind; it was too close to the truth.

Afterwards, she stood beside Gorran in the foyer and thanked everyone for coming. He was dressed as the studio boss R. F. Simpson but he refused to take any credit for the success of the night. 'Really, all I do is provide the movie,' he told anyone who tried to congratulate him. 'Gina is the one who makes the magic happen.'

Ferdie was soaking up the praise too, and not just for his outfit; his Good Morning gelato was so popular that Manda ran out of stock and Ferdie had to promise to offer it for sale at Ferrelli's for a few more days at least. And judging by the look on Elena's face, she'd spotted a golden opportunity to talk Ferdie into introducing their Afternoon Tea ice-cream sooner rather than later.

Carrie caught up with Gina as the last few stragglers were finishing their drinks and leaving. 'You know, I'm not sure Rose has ever watched *Singin' in the Rain* all the way through before.'

'What makes you say that?' Gina asked.

Carrie grinned. 'Because she had a face like a cat's bum when she left with Ben just now – I don't think she realised that Lina is the villain of the film.'

'Oh dear,' Gina said, trying not to laugh. 'Well, I think she's perfect for the role. In fact, I can't think of anyone better suited to play Lina Lamont, can you?'

'Nope,' Carrie said. 'But I think she'll choose her costume a little more carefully next time. Speaking of which, any idea what your next choice might be? I wouldn't mind getting a head-start in sourcing outfits.'

Gina shook her head. 'There might not be a next film – not for a while, anyway. If we get our funding, the Palace will be closed for refurbishments for at least a few weeks.'

'But knowing you, you'll have big plans for a grand re-opening,' Carrie said, giving Gina a sidelong look. 'Let me know what I can do to help.'

Gina finally fell into bed at just after midnight, exhausted but happy. Her last thoughts before she drifted off were of Ben, and how much better she felt to be back on friendly terms with him again. She didn't approve of what he'd done but there was no going back now. And he'd liked her dress, she thought, smiling sleepily. She was glad he'd liked her dress.

An envelope was waiting for Gina when she got home on Tuesday evening. Recognising the Polwhipple council post-mark, Gina dropped her bag to the floor of the hallway and tore back the paper flap. Hardly daring to breathe, she scanned the letter inside, then let out a whoop so loud she thought Ben might have heard it.

Her fingers shook as she dialled his number. 'Have you seen it?' she said, as soon as he answered.

'I haven't had the chance to check the mail yet,' he replied, his voice tight with anticipation. 'What does it say?'

Grinning, Gina held up the letter. 'Dear Miss Callaway, Messrs Dew and Pascoe,' she read, 'I am pleased to advise you that your application for funding has been accepted. The amount requested will be split fifty-fifty between the two projects outlined in your application, with the proviso that the written agreement of the Bodmin and Wenford Railway Preservation Society is obtained within seven days of the date on this letter to extend the train line to incorporate the newly renovated station in Polwhipple. If this condition is not met, all funding will be withdrawn.'

Ben exhaled loudly. 'So, it all hangs on the Preservation Society?'

Gina frowned. 'Well, yes, but that's all right, isn't it? They're bound to say yes now that they know there's funding.'

'I suppose so,' he said, but he didn't sound sure. 'I'll have to set up a meeting, try and talk them round.'

Gina thought for a moment. 'How much work have you got left to do at the station?'

'Hardly anything,' Ben replied. 'There's a bit of snagging to do here and there, and some paintwork to touch up. Why?'

'I've got an idea,' she said. 'But we're going to need help to pull it off . . .'

# Chapter Nineteen

Ben tugged at the brim of his station master's hat and frowned at Gina.

'Are you sure this is necessary?'

Lowering her empty suitcase to the ticket hall floor, Gina reached up and straightened the collar of his liver-coloured uniform. 'Of course it is. Trust me, they're going to love it.'

'Target acquired,' Carrie called from the door that led to the front of the station. 'They're at the gates.'

'Okay,' Gina said, glancing into the ticket office and giving a smartly dressed Nonno the thumbs up. 'Places, everyone.'

Ben was at the door when the members of the Preservation Society arrived. 'Welcome to Polwhipple station, gentlemen,' he said smartly. 'If you'd like to follow me, I'll give you the grand tour.'

Gina glanced across from her position at the ticket office, where she'd been asking for a ticket to London. The men, who were all well over sixty if they were a day, gaped in confusion and Gina held her breath as she watched them taking in the original station clock that hung on the wall to their left, the immaculate mosaic tiles on the floor, the perfectly matched Great Western railway colour scheme that Ben had so painstakingly sourced. Would they get what she and the other Polwhipple residents were trying to do? Would they see the potential of extending the line to this jewel of a station?

Carrie appeared from the waiting room directly opposite the ticket office. 'Excuse me,' she said to Ben. 'What time is the next train to Bodmin, please?'

Ben consulted the pocket watch that was tucked into his jacket pocket. 'The next train leaves in fifteen minutes, Miss. Platform Two.'

Carrie nodded and headed through the door that led to the platforms. Gazing at one another in obvious confusion, the men followed Ben in the same direction as Carrie.

Gina couldn't resist going too. She watched as they took in the scene. Manda was presiding over a Ferrelli's branded cart that was stocked with their full range of ice-cream. Vintage-style posters adorned the walls, advertising the delights of Polwhipple.

Ben led them in and out of each area of the station, pointing out all the original features he'd worked so hard to preserve and lingering in the signal box so that they could admire the gleaming dials, levers and cogs. In the ticket office, Nonno stood back to let them examine the reels of authentic tickets and to study the ticket punching machine.

And everywhere the Preservation Society members looked, they saw happy smiling passengers, all apparently waiting to catch a train.

They finished up in the tea rooms, where Nonna was serving up a mouth-watering array of homemade cakes and biscuits.

'As you can see, we've got plenty of local support here, from volunteers to funding,' Ben said, as the men sipped their drinks. 'I think we've got everything we need to make Polwhipple station a great addition to the Bodmin and Wenford Railway.'

Gina stepped forwards. 'In fact, the only thing that's missing is the train.'

'So, what do you think?' Ben said, his tone steady. 'Do you think Polwhipple station is worth extending the line for?'

The men looked at one another. One of them took a large bite of the lemon drizzle cake Nonna had insisted he take and chewed slowly. Another nibbled on a biscotti. Gina held her breath; surely they couldn't say no?

'I think you've got yourself a deal, Ben,' Lemon Drizzle man said, and the others nodded. 'How soon can we start work?'

Two weeks later, Gina stood with Ben outside the Palace on a bright Monday morning, the key to the silver double doors in her hand. Gorran had removed the essentials from his cluttered office and would spend the next few weeks working from home. The projector had been draped with protective dust cloths and the projection room itself was locked. It was business as usual for Ferrelli's, however, although Ben had sealed the window that faced into the foyer to minimise the dust that would inevitably be flying around.

Hefting his toolbox in one hand, Ben looked at Gina. 'Ready?'

She nodded. 'As ready as I'll ever be. I really hope we haven't made the biggest mistake of our lives here.'

'Nah,' Ben said. 'This is the beginning of a beautiful refurbishment. You'll see.'

Gina sighed and squared her shoulders. 'Okay. Let's go and see what we've let ourselves in for.'

Turning the key in the lock, she pushed open the doors. With one final look at Ben, the pair of them vanished inside the picture house by the sea.

# PART THREE

## Dirty Dancing

# Chapter Twenty

'You look like you need a drink.'

Gina Callaway lowered the sanding block she'd been using on the fresh plaster of the Palace foyer wall and turned to face Manda Vickery, who was holding out a steaming mug of tea. Lowering her dust mask, Gina dredged up a grateful smile.

'Thanks,' she said, passing a weary hand across her forehead. 'Although to be honest, I could do with something stronger.'

She glanced around as she spoke, taking in the protective sheets that spilled across the floor and shrouded everything from the ticket desk to the bar in snowy whiteness. Beams of sunlight snuck around the edges of the paper-covered glass front doors, revealing a million dancing dust motes and reminding Gina all over again just how much there was left to do before the grand re-opening in the middle of June. Despite the reassurances of master builder and renovation expert Ben Pascoe, she couldn't see how they'd be ready; not in four weeks' time. Perhaps if the ceiling hadn't collapsed in the men's toilets just as the new light fittings were going in, and perhaps if the floor in the ladies' hadn't turned out to be riddled with woodworm . . . but they were just a few of the unexpected hiccups that meant the restoration project was already falling behind schedule. Maybe she ought to talk to the owner, Gorran Dew, about postponing the re-opening to the end of June.

Manda gave Gina a sympathetic look. 'The best I can offer you is one of your grandfather's gelatos,' she said, glancing over at the Ferrelli's ice-cream concession where she worked. Usually, the interior window was open, to allow cinema-goers to treat themselves during a screening, but it had been sealed off for the duration of the refurbishment, leaving only the outside window open for business. 'Maybe you could whip up a gin and tonic flavour next time you're in the dairy,' she suggested.

Gina couldn't imagine Nonno going for that idea. Ferdie Ferrelli was fiercely protective of the time-honoured gelato recipes he sold through the concession stand at the Palace. Gina knew better than to suggest anything too experimental to Ferdie. Nonna, on the other hand, would be very much in favour of a gin and tonic gelato . . .

'I think I'll stick to drinking one later,' she told Manda wryly. 'Safest all round.'

'I made a cuppa for Ben too,' Manda said. 'Do you know where he is?'

'I think I saw him heading into the screening room,' Gina replied. 'He plans to start ripping down the plasterboard in there today.'

Manda's eyes widened and Gina knew she was hoping they would find all the original Art Deco gilt decoration preserved behind the ugly woodchip-covered fake walls. But there was just as much chance that all they would find was damp and depressingly bare plaster.

'He's probably in need of something stronger as well, then,' Manda observed, offering the second mug to Gina. She glanced over her shoulder as though she expected the cinema owner, Gorran Dew, to be eavesdropping, and lowered her voice. 'I don't suppose you carry a hip flask, do you? It's past midday.'

Gina laughed. 'Unfortunately not. But I'm sure tea will do.'

Dropping the sanding block onto a nearby work table, she took the tea from Manda and went in search of Ben. She found him exactly where she'd expected, standing beside one of the side walls of the vast screening room that was at the heart of the picture house, surveying the scaffolding, with a crowbar in one hand. The radio was babbling in the background but Ben was deep in conversation with one of the contractors he'd hired to help with the restoration project.

Both men looked up as Gina approached and she was amused to see that Ben's blond hair, usually sun-kissed from hours spent surfing the Cornish waves, was almost white with dust. It contrasted with his golden tan and lent him an almost distinguished air, giving Gina a sudden glimpse of how he might look in twenty years' time. Then she realised that her own black hair was probably streaked with dust too. She doubted she wore it as well as Ben.

'Tea,' she said, offering the second mug to Ben. 'Sorry, Davey, I don't have one for you. Give me a minute and I'll find a cup for you.'

'Don't go yet,' Ben said, taking a swig of tea and swallowing it fast. He drained the mug in two gulps and handed it back to Gina with a swift smile of thanks. 'We were just about to make a start on removing the plasterboard, if you fancy watching? It can be quite dramatic, although the woodchip will make things harder – it's had a few coats of paint over the years, which will give it staying power.'

Gina gazed past the scaffolding to the tired-looking walls beyond, noticing several holes already; they must have been exploring what lay behind the glossy woodchip. Dust floated in the air, just as it had in the foyer, making Gina wonder where to stand to avoid yet another coating. She glanced around. The velvet curtains that had previously draped the edges of the projection screen were long gone, as were the aged tiers of seats that had seen much better days. The room felt cavernous and Gina's voice echoed when she spoke. 'Sure. I'll keep out of the way.'

Ben handed her a dust mask. 'Good idea. Who knows what's going to fall out when we pull this down.'

'As long as it isn't a skeleton,' she said, mock-shuddering.

He grinned. 'You've been watching too many movies.

Besides, a skeleton is too obvious – my money is on a basilisk.'

Gina backed away. 'Whatever. I'll stand over here, just in case.'

She half-listened as Ben and Davey discussed the best place to begin prying the plasterboard away, momentarily distracted when she heard the radio was playing *The Time of My Life*. Gina swayed slightly as she waited, smiling as she remembered one of her favourite scenes in *Crazy, Stupid Love* where Ryan Gosling used the song to seduce Emma Stone. And the original scene in *Dirty Dancing* had been pretty memorable too.

Clearly reaching an agreement with Davey, Ben walked to a hole at the farthest end of the wall, the one nearest to where the projection screen had previously hung, and ducked his head under the scaffolding to dig his crowbar into the woodchip. A low creak sounded as he applied pressure and Gina saw the paint start to crack as the woodchip splintered and the plasterboard underneath buckled. Ben pressed harder, frowning in concentration, and Gina was suddenly glad she was some distance away. Ben was a keen surfer in his spare time, so between that and his work as a builder, his muscles were in good shape. It had been all Gina could do not to stare the last time she'd seen him with his shirt off – like Emma Stone in the film, she'd wondered briefly whether the abs before her had been Photoshopped – and although Ben was appropriately dressed now, she could see his biceps working under the thin material. A bit of distance was undoubtedly a very good thing when Gina was trying hard to remember that he was an old friend and business partner, nothing more.

'It's starting to give,' Ben called to Davey, who came and placed his own crowbar a little higher up the wall. Together they heaved, and with a crack that sounded like a starting pistol, the plasterboard came away. The painted woodchip fractured, revealing a thin wooden support strut underneath as the large chunk fell from the wall, hitting the floor in a cloud of dust.

Once the first breach had been made, more soon followed. Ben climbed to the top of the scaffolding and began work near the ceiling; Davey mirrored him at the other end of the wall. Gina almost held her breath as he pried the plaster away: this was where the majority of the gilt-work would be, if it was still there. Had it survived the previous refurbishment? she wondered. The object of the plasterboard seemed to have been to remove all the character and original features from the picture house, something she'd never understood. It would be a terrible shame if all they found beneath it were bare walls . . .

Ben and Davey worked as fast as the woodchip allowed, dropping clumps of discarded plasterboard to the floor. More and more of the wooden battens were revealed and the air grew thick with dust. Gina pulled on the mask Ben had given her and tried not to imagine how she must look. Then Ben lowered his crowbar and peered more closely at the wall.

'What is it?' Gina called, anxiety creeping through the pit of her stomach. Please don't let it be bones, she thought.

Ben reached into the tool pouch fastened around his waist and pulled out a torch. He shone it behind the plasterboard for several long seconds, then turned around and pulled the mask from his face. 'Bingo,' he called, with a grin.

'Really?' Gina felt her own mouth curve into an answering smile. 'It's still there?'

He nodded. 'This bit is.'

'Over here too,' Davey said over one shoulder. 'Looks to be in pretty mint condition. Maybe the plasterboard has done us a favour.'

'Wonders will never cease,' Ben said with an incredulous laugh. 'I think this is the first time I've ever been grateful for a shoddy building job.'

Gina's smile widened into a deep grin. It was exactly what they'd hoped for. 'Gorran is going to be so pleased,' she said, removing her own mask. 'Any idea how long it will be before we can see it all in its original glory?'

The two men exchanged a thoughtful look. 'Another couple of days at least,' Ben ventured. 'Or maybe longer.'

'And that's just the start,' Davey added. 'Once all the plasterboard is off, we'll be able to see how those wooden battens have been attached – that could cause us some problems. And then there's the clean-up operation – the gypsum dust from the plasterboard is always a right pain to shift.'

Ben nodded. 'True,' he said, aiming a rueful glance at the debris that covered the floor. 'And I'll tell you something else – we're going to need a bigger skip.'

*

By the end of the day, Gina ached all over. She wanted nothing more than to lower herself into a hot bath and soak away the hard work of the day, but she and Ben were due to meet Gorran at six o'clock in the Mermaid's Tail Inn for a catch-up. A glance in the mirror of the newly refurbished ladies' confirmed her worst suspicions: she looked like Miss Havisham. Shaking plaster dust from her long hair, Gina splashed water over her arms and face and pulled on a clean T-shirt. Gorran wasn't exactly a snappy dresser and Ben would be even dustier than Gina; she doubted either of them would judge her, and the customers of the pub would barely bat an eyelid either. It wouldn't be the first time they'd seen her like this and it probably wouldn't be the last.

'Ready?' Ben called, as Gina made her way back into the picture house foyer.

'I suppose,' she replied. 'I think I ate some plaster dust, though.'

He smiled. 'I can imagine. But you can't restore an Art Deco cinema without sanding some walls so . . .'

Gina sighed. When she'd come up with the idea to apply for funding to return the Palace to its glory days, she hadn't envisaged being quite so hands-on with the actual building work. It was different for Ben – he liked nothing better than getting his hands dirty in a job that seemed too big to handle. Even so, she could totally see why he had the bug for restoring old buildings; there was still a long way to go but underneath the mess, the Palace was slowly starting to take shape. And Gina had a feeling that it was going to shine even more brightly than it had in its heyday.

'Come on,' she said to Ben. 'I don't know about you, but I need gin.'

The evening was warm and the sun sparkled on the tide as it ebbed and flowed against the golden sand of the beach. An auburn-haired mermaid gazed benevolently down from the pub sign as Gina and Ben cut through the seafront beer garden and ducked inside. The bar was fairly quiet – hardly surprising this early on a Thursday evening – but one or two regulars nodded in greeting as Gina and Ben entered the low-ceilinged snug. The owner, Jory, had two glasses in his hands long before they reached the dark wood bar. 'The usual?'

Gina gave Ben a wry look; clearly they were spending too much time in the pub if Jory knew exactly what they would order. She nodded at Jory, saying, 'Bombay Sapphire and tonic for me, please.'

'And I'll have a pint of Spotty Dog, please,' Ben said, his eyes resting on the cider pump. 'Is Gorran here yet?'

'Over by the window,' Jory said, as he turned to the bottles that lined the mirrored wall behind him. 'Got a face like a teasy tacker an' all. Best go easy there, I reckon.'

For the most part, Gina could work out Jory's frequent use of Cornish slang but this time she was defeated. *Teasy* meant bad-tempered, she knew, but *tacker*? A horse, maybe? She peered across to the window, where Gorran was staring morosely down at a half-empty pint glass; he certainly seemed long-faced.

'He means a grumpy toddler,' Ben whispered, seeing Gina studying the cinema owner. 'Which isn't like Gorran at all.'

He was right, Gina thought. Gorran was disorganised and flighty, and often drove her mad with his teetering piles of paperwork and his unfounded optimism that the cinema-goers of Polwhipple would grow to love obscure foreign language films in time, but he was generally affable and never moody. Something must have happened.

'All right, Gorran?' Ben said, as they approached the table.

The older man looked up, blinking owlishly, and Gina noticed that above the crumpled collar of his checked shirt, his shock of white hair was even wilder than usual. 'Oh,' he said in a subdued tone. 'Hello. How are things?'

'Not at all bad,' Gina said, as she and Ben sat down. 'In fact, we've got some great news – the original gilt-work is still in place behind the plasterboard in the theatre.'

She waited for Gorran's enthusiastic response but instead of a warm smile, he simply gave a preoccupied nod. 'That is good news.'

Ben leaned forwards. 'And there doesn't seem to be much damage so far – nothing that a touch up here and there won't fix.'

Again, Gorran nodded. 'Good, good.'

Gina felt a small frown crease her forehead as her own enthusiasm began to fade. 'You don't seem very excited. Is everything okay?'

The older man stared into his glass. 'No, it's all fine,' he mumbled. 'It's just . . . I mean, there's nothing for you to worry about, anyway.'

'Gorran?' Ben said. 'What's going on?'

For a moment, Gina thought he would ignore the question. But then he sighed and met their curious gazes. 'I've got a few financial issues, that's all. The Palace has been closed for a good few weeks now and that means it's not bringing in much money, apart from the rent Ferdie pays for Ferrelli's. But I've still got the same overheads – I still have to pay Tash and Bruno, even though they're not working, and the concession income isn't enough.' He paused. 'Like I said, nothing for you to worry about. I'm sure something will turn up.'

Gina and Ben exchanged alarmed glances. This was the first time Gorran had hinted that there could be a problem behind the scenes at the picture house.

'Well, we're still quite a way from completion of the project,' Ben said. 'But I know Gina has been thinking about some kind of grand re-opening event – would that help with cash-flow?'

'Maybe, if we show a film and ask people to buy tickets instead of inviting them as guests,' Gorran said, his tone subdued. 'It's a shame we can't squeeze in a screening around the refurbishment but I know that would be difficult.'

It wasn't just difficult, Gina thought: it was impossible. Quite apart from the dust and the lack of seating, the place was practically a building site; she could think of around twenty health and safety concerns without really trying.

There was no way they could let people inside as things stood . . .

'Maybe they don't have to come inside,' she said out loud, causing both men to eye her quizzically. 'What if we held a screening elsewhere? An outdoor screening, somewhere big enough to hold a decent-sized crowd, like the rooftop cinema clubs they have in London?'

'I can't think of any rooftops big enough round here but it's not unheard of for National Trust properties to host screenings in their grounds,' Ben pointed out. 'Lanhydrock House might be up for it, if we asked.'

Gina shook her head. 'But they've got overheads and want to keep most of the takings. What we really need is somewhere big, close to Polwhipple, that won't cost a fortune.'

The three of them lapsed into thoughtful silence. Finding an appealing venue was key, Gina thought, but the film choice mattered too; an outdoor screening suggested summer and warmth and fun. It would be no good showing something like *Dr Zhivago*.

'What about the beach?' Ben suggested, glancing through the window at the sun-drenched sands beyond. 'The tide only comes halfway up, it's close enough to run power cables from the Palace, and there's plenty of room for people to sit.'

Gina stared at the old-fashioned glass panels, her mind whirring. It wasn't a bad idea. 'You know, that could just about work. We could use deckchairs for seats and bring in some pop-up food stalls to give it a real party vibe.'

They glanced at Gorran, who seemed to have perked up

a little. 'Maybe we could show a watery classic, like *The Poseidon Adventure*? Or how about *Jaws*?'

'I'm not sure a disaster movie is quite the right way to go,' Gina said doubtfully. 'We want people to dress up and have fun, remember, not relive their worst nightmares.'

She gazed around the bar, searching for inspiration, and her eyes came to rest on a poster advertising salsa lessons in nearby Mawgan Porth. How long had it been since she'd been dancing? She'd suggested taking some classes once, back when she and her boyfriend, Max, had just started dating, but they'd never managed to find the time. A dance movie might work, she thought; people would love to kick off their shoes and let their hair down on the sand. But what film perfectly encapsulated dance-along summer fun?

'*Dirty Dancing*!' she burst out, remembering the song she'd heard in the cinema earlier. 'It's definitely a classic – everyone loves Johnny and Baby's story and it's perfect for an outdoor screening. We could even have some dancing lessons on the beach beforehand.'

Ben nodded, frowning at Gina. 'Didn't we watch that together once at the Palace? Or was it *Grease*?'

She snapped her fingers. 'You're right, we did!' A sudden memory of being embarrassed during the romantic scenes almost made Gina blush. 'And neither of us understood what was wrong with Penny – we thought she had food poisoning.'

'It took me years to work out the truth,' Ben admitted, laughing. His eyes were warm as they rested on Gina's face.

'I think it's the perfect film to show. What do you say, Gorran?'

'Gina's the expert at this kind of thing,' the cinema owner said, holding up his hands in surrender. 'If she thinks people will want to come and see *Dirty Dancing* then who am I to argue? As long as you don't expect me to strut my stuff.'

Gina grinned. 'Strutting will be entirely optional,' she said. 'But who knows – the right partner might bring out your inner Johnny Castle.'

Gorran shook his head. 'Trust me, it's better if I sit the dancing out.' He hesitated, looking embarrassed. 'So, I hate to ask, but how soon do you think you can pull all this together?'

It was a good question, Gina mused, tapping the table thoughtfully. They'd need to approach the town council for permission to hold a commercial event and to use the beach, which probably meant risk assessments and a lot of paperwork, and then they'd have to make enquiries about the technicalities of screening a film outdoors. It wasn't going to be anywhere near as simple as showing a film at the Palace and it was undoubtedly going to cost more but, if they got everything right, Gina was confident they'd be able to attract a bigger audience. She cast a reluctant look at Ben. 'Have you finished things with Rose yet?'

Was it Gina's imagination, or did Ben wince?

'We – uh – still haven't had that conversation yet,' he said. 'Every time I've tried to cool things off, she somehow manages to change the subject.'

That sounded right, Gina thought; manipulative Rose made Machiavelli look like an amateur. But she was also a useful ally, even though it felt a lot like going over to the dark side, and desperate times required desperate measures. 'Maybe you should wait a few more days,' Gina said, hating herself for suggesting it.

Resigned understanding flashed over Ben's face. 'Oh. Yes, I suppose I could manage another date.'

Gina felt her stomach writhe as she pictured him sitting in a restaurant with Rose, making small talk and forcing himself to laugh at her sneering jokes about anyone who wasn't rich and influential. 'I wish it didn't work this way but we both know that we need Valeria Arundell on side. And we'll never get permission for an outdoor screening if you've just dumped her daughter.'

She shifted uneasily, aware that what she was suggesting wasn't very fair. But it helped to remember that Rose was cold and calculating too. Besides, as Gina's boyfriend, Max, was always saying, business was built on relationships; wining and dining clients encouraged them to put work his way. Was what Ben was doing with Rose really that different? Except . . . Rose was used to getting whatever she wanted, and Gina couldn't help wondering how much longer she'd be content with small talk and a peck on the cheek at the end of the night. Or had she taken what she wanted already? She and Ben had been a couple before, after all; surely it wouldn't take much to rekindle the flames . . . It was a thought that made Gina's stomach churn.

Beside her, Ben puffed out his cheeks. 'Okay. I'll mention the screening to Rose – maybe she can have a word with Valeria and find out the best way to approach things.'

Gina pulled her frazzled thoughts together. 'And the moment everything is sorted, we'll start selling tickets.' She gave Gorran what she hoped was an encouraging look. 'I'm sure it will be a smash hit.'

'Thank you,' he said quietly, his cheeks growing even rosier than normal. 'I can't tell you how much I appreciate everything you're doing to help. It's above and beyond the call of duty.'

'No problem, Gorran,' Gina said, and the gratitude in his voice made her certain they were doing the right thing. 'That's what friends are for.'

# Chapter Twenty-One

'I've got good news and bad news.'

Ben's voice crackled with static as Gina pressed the phone to her ear on Sunday morning, twisting slightly to shelter it from the wind cutting down from the cliffs of Mawgan Porth beach. 'Okay,' she said. 'Give me the good stuff first.'

'Rose says getting permission for the screening should be a formality, as long as Gorran has all the necessary insurance. He'll need a temporary event licence from the council, too, but apparently they don't cost much and the application is pretty straightforward.'

'Excellent,' Gina said cautiously, watching the clouds part in the breeze and trying not to wonder what Ben and Rose had been doing when they'd had the conversation. She cleared her throat. 'What's the bad news?'

There was a brief silence on the other end of the phone. 'Rose wants to get involved with the screening.'

Gina's heart plummeted. 'Why?' she said, her tone flat. 'What does it have to do with her?'

'Nothing, really. She says she's curious about what you do.'

Recalling the thinly veiled insults Rose had let fly the last few times they'd met, Gina let out an unladylike snort. 'I bet she didn't phrase it quite like that.'

'She did, actually,' Ben replied in a mild voice. 'It made me wonder if she's thinking of turning her hand to events planning. There'll be a gap in the market once you go back to London, after all – maybe she wants to pick your brains.'

Gina narrowed her eyes; Rose had shown scant regard for her professional abilities before. Ben was much more generous than she was. 'And if I say no?'

'I'm not sure that's an option, to be honest,' Ben said carefully. 'I got the impression that it was a bit non-negotiable, in exchange for a straightforward licence application.'

I wonder what else is non-negotiable? Gina thought, feeling irritated at the thought of first Ben and now Gorran and herself dancing to Rose's tune. Would she be able to swallow her dislike long enough to work with her? She supposed she'd have to, for the sake of Gorran and the picture house, but it wasn't going to be easy. She'd need a crash course in holding her tongue, for a start ...

'Fine,' she said, forcing herself to sound as though the idea didn't bother her in the slightest. 'Although she'll need to understand a few ground rules. Gorran is in charge – he has the final say.'

'I'll make sure she knows,' Ben promised. 'Listen, I was

thinking about your dance lessons on the beach idea, before the screening. Do you want to go and check out some classes together, before you book anyone?'

Gina blinked. 'You want to go dancing?'

He laughed. 'Why not? I'm no Patrick Swayze, but it sounds like fun.'

It would be a lot of fun, Gina thought, gnawing at her lip. And that was half the problem; dancing with Ben was unlikely to help her remember they were strictly friends. 'I don't think Rose will like that.'

'We won't tell her,' he answered cheerfully.

'This is Polwhipple,' she reminded him. 'The Arundells have spies everywhere.'

'Then we'll wait until after the licence application has been approved and they can't cause any problems.'

Gina shook her head; Ben clearly had no idea of the real reason she was reluctant to go dancing with him. 'If she wasn't so awful, I might feel sorry for Rose.'

'Don't,' he said. 'She's like a cat stalking a mouse – the moment she thinks she's caught me, she'll lose interest and move on.'

'Then maybe it's you I feel sorry for,' she countered, nettled in spite of herself.

'No need for that either. I can look after myself.' There was a pause. 'Just make sure Gorran puts the licence application in first thing tomorrow.'

Gina felt herself soften. 'I will,' she promised. 'Thanks, Ben.'

She rang off and spent a few pensive moments watching the waves crash against the sandy shore. On one hand, what they were doing made her uncomfortable for lots of reasons; this was the second time Ben had used Rose and her connections to the town council, and the stakes got higher each time. But on the other hand, the council shouldn't be controlled by the whims of the Arundell family – if it was fair and impartial, then Ben dating Rose wouldn't make the slightest difference to the outcome of their application.

Letting out a long sigh, Gina turned from the sea to trudge back towards the cliff steps that led to her apartment building. It wasn't life or death – in practical terms, Rose might have her feelings hurt when Ben ended things, but she'd get over it. The sooner he was free from her clutches, the happier Gina would be.

'You're quiet,' Gina's grandmother observed over Sunday lunch, passing her the gravy with a concerned look. 'Everything all right?'

The question caused Ferdie Ferrelli to study her too, prompting Gina to summon up a reassuring smile. 'Of course,' she said, glancing back and forth between them. 'A little tired, but that's no surprise.'

Her nonna sniffed. 'Between the cinema and the dairy, you are working too hard. Look at how thin you are.'

Gina hid a smile. Nonna never missed an opportunity to offer her food.

'Honestly, I'm fine,' Gina said. 'Never better.'

Elena seemed unconvinced. 'What you need is a break,' she went on, as though she hadn't heard, adding another roast potato to Gina's plate. 'Why don't you go to London for a weekend and see Max? Let your hair down for a change, instead of working all the time.'

Gina concentrated on chewing her mouthful of beef, trying not to eye Elena with suspicion. Nonna had never been Max's champion before – why was she trying to push them together now? Although given that it had been weeks since Gina had seen her boyfriend, she supposed Elena could hardly be accused of that. And the truth was that Gina did miss Max. They were both so busy that even catching each other on the phone was difficult; if Gina went to London then Max would automatically make time for her.

'Maybe I will,' she said. 'Once the refurbishment work is more under control. But I've got a new project to work on now.'

She explained about the screening on the beach, taking care to leave out the reason behind it: Gorran's financial situation was his own business.

'It sounds wonderful,' Elena said, her eyes gleaming. 'And of course you will need to invent a new ice-cream flavour for the event.'

Ferdie's salt and pepper eyebrows beetled together. 'Another one? Gelato recipes are not like your London buses, you know – they don't come along every ten minutes.'

Elena ignored her husband. 'I can just imagine sitting

beneath the stars, watching a wonderful movie with the sea lapping gently at the shore. Will there be dancing?'

'I hope so. Ben and I are going to check out some classes to see if we can find someone to run a group lesson on the beach.'

'How romantic,' Elena said, and Gina wasn't sure whether she meant the beach lesson or the classes with Ben. Then her grandmother winked. 'There's nothing like dancing with a handsome man to put a spring in your step.'

*Ah.* Gina turned hurriedly to Ferdie, anxious to change the subject. 'So what do you think, Nonno? Is there any chance you might whisk up a *Dirty Dancing* Ferrelli's exclusive?'

He grunted. 'I'm not sure I have ever seen the film. It doesn't sound like my kind of thing.'

'I thought you might say that,' Gina said, reaching down to the handbag next to her feet. She pulled out a DVD. 'So I brought a copy with me – we can watch it after lunch and you can make your mind up then.'

Ferdie gave her a look that suggested he'd rather poke needles in his eyes but he didn't argue. After they'd cleared the table, they settled into the soft leather sofas in the living room and started to watch the film. Elena's toes tapped throughout every song and Gina thought she spotted her grandfather swaying along to the music once or twice, although she was sure he would deny it if she asked.

'All this wonderful music brings back memories,' Elena said, glancing fondly across at Ferdie. 'Do you remember the dances we used to go to?'

'I remember how terrifying it was to ask a girl to dance,' he grumbled. 'You never knew if they would laugh in your face.'

Elena arched a dark eyebrow. 'So it's a very good thing I took the initiative and asked you. Otherwise I might still be waiting for you to pluck up the nerve.'

Ferdie shook his head. 'Never. You would have been worth the risk.'

They shared a smile then and Gina felt a rush of love for her grandparents; they really were soulmates. If she and Max were half as happy in forty years' time they'd be doing well.

As the end credits rolled, she glanced over at Ferdie. 'So? What do you think?'

'Not bad,' he said. 'It's no *Casablanca*, of course.'

Elena let out an impatient sigh. 'Nothing is as good as *Casablanca*, according to you.'

'But did you have any thoughts about an ice-cream flavour?' Gina pressed her grandfather, crossing her fingers that the film had inspired him.

Ferdie was silent for a moment. 'Watermelon is the obvious choice,' he said eventually. 'But it's too liquid for gelato and the flavour is too subtle – it would be lost amongst the sugar. A sorbet would work better but you know how I feel about those.'

Gina did. She'd made the mistake of suggesting an orange-flavoured sorbet for the *Singin' in the Rain* event she'd organised a few weeks earlier and Ferdie had made it clear that Ferrelli's was above such things. 'What about a dance-themed gelato? A Passionfruit Pachanga, maybe?'

His eyebrows lifted. 'Not bad, except that good-quality passionfruit would need to be imported.'

'I'm sure the Scarlet would help us out again,' Gina said, thinking of the way the hotel had sourced the Seville oranges Ferdie had needed for his Good Morning gelato for the last event.

'Cherries would work well and they should just be coming into season,' Elena suggested. 'How about a Cherry Cha-Cha?'

'Perhaps,' Ferdie said diffidently. 'I'll think about it.'

Elena and Gina exchanged a covert look; they both knew that the best way to get Ferdie to do anything was to allow him the time to feel as though the whole thing had been his idea in the first place. By tomorrow, he'd have come round completely and would amaze them both.

'Enjoy your dance classes,' Elena said as Gina kissed her goodbye on the doorstep. 'If I was thirty years younger, I'd be joining you.'

Gina glanced over her grandmother's shoulder to where she could just see the edge of Ferdie's plaster-encased leg propped up in the living room. 'You'd have to find a new partner.'

Elena's eyes twinkled. 'If I was thirty years younger, I'd make a beeline for Ben Pascoe – young, muscular and good with his hands. What more could you ask for?'

'I think Rose Arundell might have something to say about that,' Gina said, laughing.

'I think you might have something to say about it too,'

Elena said with a knowing look as she slid the door closed. '*Ciao, bella.* See you in the morning.'

Gina spent most of Monday morning working through the council's Temporary Event Notice paperwork with Gorran, and drafting a request for permission to screen *Dirty Dancing* on the beach. They'd settled on the second Saturday in June as the best date; as long as the council didn't drag their feet, they'd have just enough time to build up some interest and make the event a smash-hit.

'Jory says we can use the toilets here, so that makes life easier,' Gina said, tapping her pen against the edge of the table in the beer garden of the Mermaid's Tail. 'In return, I've said he can look after the beer and cider drinkers and the Scarlet would love to run a pop-up cocktail bar on the night.'

'I suppose we're going to need some kind of perimeter,' Gorran said. 'Be hard to check tickets otherwise.'

Gina nodded. 'It's all going to be a bit harder to manage outdoors.' She took a deep breath. 'Are you sure you want to do this? We could wait a few more weeks and do it after the grand re-opening.'

Gorran looked as though he wanted the ground to swallow him up. 'Except that I need to pay my employees. I can't afford to wait.'

She felt a wave of sympathy for him; it couldn't be easy to admit he was struggling. 'Then we'll make it work,' Gina said briskly. 'Ticket sales can go live as soon as we get the go ahead from the council. You'll drop the forms off this afternoon?'

He gathered up the paperwork. 'I'll head over there now.'

'Good,' Gina said, checking the time. 'And I need to go and see a man about some cherries.'

The crate of glistening crimson fruit that Gina collected from the farm looked so tempting that she couldn't resist testing a few on her way back to her grandparents' house. Ferdie gave her a knowing look when she lowered the crate onto the stainless steel work top in the dairy and he saw her red-stained fingertips.

'Tasty, are they?' he asked, plucking one and rinsing it briefly underneath the tap.

'Very,' Gina admitted. 'They'll make an amazing gelato.'

Ferdie popped the fruit into his mouth and chewed for a moment. '*Eccellente*. So, *mia bella*, how do you think we should do this?'

Gina blinked in surprise. She wasn't used to Ferdie asking for her opinion where ice-cream was concerned; he was more usually barking instructions and frowning when she failed to follow them to the letter. 'Uh, stew them with some sugar? Then remove the stones and add them to a traditional vanilla gelato base.'

Her grandfather tilted his head. 'We could do it that way – it would create a perfectly acceptable flavour.' He paused and fixed her with a stern stare. 'But we do not settle for *acceptable* where Ferrelli's gelato is concerned. We want intensity – an explosion of flavour in the mouth to give a tiny moment of ecstasy.'

She thought hard. When Nonna was making a tomato base for her own hand-made pizza, she roasted the tomatoes to give them more flavour. Could that be the answer here?

'Exactly!' Ferdie cried, when she suggested it. He held up a bottle of clear liquid with a bright red cherry on the front. 'And we'll add a splash of kirsch for richness – the alcohol will evaporate in the oven, leaving us with a flavour that is pure heaven.'

So he wasn't averse to using alcohol in his recipes, Gina observed, thinking of Manda's gin and tonic flavour idea. Making a mental note to try an experiment or two when she had time, Gina concentrated on washing and destalking the fruit, while Ferdie hobbled over to the oven set in one of the walls and switched it on to warm up. His mobility was much better than it had been when she'd first arrived in Polwhipple, although he continued to need crutches and still burned with a sullen fury at the restrictions his injury placed on him. Thankfully, however, his attitude to Gina's presence had softened and he even seemed to appreciate the way she'd quietly reorganised the stock-management and ordering systems. It was a far cry from the mulish resentment he'd displayed when she'd appeared out of the blue, at Nonna's request, to save him from his own stubborn refusal to admit he needed help.

The cherries were roasted for around fifteen minutes, during which time Gina whipped up a batch of the vanilla custard they used as a base for most of the gelato Ferrelli's sold, to replace the already chilled mix they were about to use. Once the cherries had cooled, Gina removed the stones and chopped the fruit.

'Keep the juice,' Ferdie instructed, from his perch at the end of the work top. 'We'll add that into the gelato mix for flavour.'

At last, the cherries were cool enough to go into the ice-cream machine. The dairy had two industrial-sized machines – one to pasteurise the mix and the other to turn it into ice-cream, but for sample batches, they used a much smaller machine. Gina left it churning while she cleaned up and put together a fresh batch of salted caramel gelato to go out to one of their restaurant clients.

By the time she'd finished, the cherry mix was ready. Tentatively, she scooped it out into two bowls and held one out to Ferdie. Then she dipped her spoon into the pale pink ice-cream and put it into her mouth.

The sweet taste of the ice-cream mingled with the tartness of the cherries to produce a mouth-watering flavour that was so good Gina almost groaned. She let the frozen goodness melt across her taste-buds and reluctantly swallowed. Beside her, she saw Ferdie dig his spoon in for another mouthful.

'I can't believe how good this is,' she said, after a few more spoonfuls. 'I think it might be our best yet.'

Ferdie pursed his lips, frowning thoughtfully. 'A touch less kirsch and perhaps a hint of salt next time,' he said, once his mouth was empty. 'But I agree that it is good. You see how roasting the fruit brings out the intensity?'

Gina nodded. 'Absolutely. So what do you think? Does it get the Ferrelli seal of approval? Have we found our Cha-Cha Cherry recipe?'

Ferdie took another mouthful of gelato and nodded. 'I think you'd better get on to the fruit farm. We're going to need a lot more cherries.'

# Chapter Twenty-Two

Rose was late.

Gina fiddled with the napkin under her glass of wine, resisting the urge to turn around and peer at the door again. They'd arranged to meet on neutral ground, at a wine bar in Newquay, and the longer Gina waited, the more she became certain she was making a horrible mistake. It was Wednesday evening, three days since Ben had dropped the bombshell that Rose wanted in on the *Dirty Dancing* screening, and Gorran had heard nothing back from the council. That in itself wasn't unusual – local government often worked at speeds that made glaciers look fast. Then Ben had told Gina that Rose wanted to meet her and the penny had dropped; the council's permission depended upon how the meeting went. Maybe this was Rose's way of showing Gina who was in charge, she thought. Maybe she was going to stand her up.

Pulling out her phone, Gina tapped out a message to Ben: *Are you sure it was 7.30 p.m.?*

*That's what she said. But punctuality isn't one of Rose's strong points.*

'Now he tells me,' Gina muttered under her breath, checking the time again. She'd give it ten more minutes and then she'd leave.

Eight minutes later, Gina felt a gust of wind wash over her as the door of the wine bar opened. She glanced over her shoulder and was simultaneously pleased and disappointed to see Rose in the doorway, looking as effortlessly elegant as ever. Plastering what she hoped was a conciliatory expression on her face, Gina waited for the blonde-haired woman to remove her jacket and deign to notice her.

Gina's jaw was starting to clench by the time Rose glanced around and spotted her. She gave a cool smile and threaded her way towards the bar.

'Gina,' Rose said, air-kissing both of Gina's cheeks in a way that reminded her of *The Godfather.* 'How nice to see you. I'm so glad you didn't go to the trouble of dressing up.'

Clamping her lips together, Gina counted to five; it had taken her almost an hour to decide what to wear. 'It's nice to see you too,' she managed after a long few seconds, praying the words didn't sound as false out loud as they did in her head. 'Can I get you a drink?'

Rose ordered a gin and tonic. There was no sign of an apology for keeping Gina waiting – no sign that Rose even realised one might be necessary. Saying sorry was something that other people did, Gina thought. Swallowing a sigh, she eyed the half-drunk wine glass in front of her. Would it be enough to get her through the meeting? she wondered. Was there enough wine in the whole of Newquay for that?

'So,' she said, once Rose had her drink and was seated on one of the nearby bar stools. 'What can I do for you?'

Rose smiled, with no trace of humour. 'It's really quite straightforward. As I imagine Ben told you, my family has been an important part of the local community for centuries. That's why my mother and my uncle do so much for the town council – we like to feel as though we're giving something back.'

Gina took a deep swig of wine; Rose's Lady Bountiful tone was grating on her nerves already.

'And of course, the Palace is one of Ben's pet projects, which makes me even keener to help out,' Rose went on, her peach-coloured lips curving into a faint smile. 'I'm not one of those women who try to undermine their partners.'

What was that supposed to mean? Gina wondered, battling to keep her face impassive. 'What did you have in mind?'

'I'd like to help out with the next screening,' Rose replied. '*Dirty Dancing* has always been one of my favourite movies so it seems like the perfect time to jump on board. And I hope you don't mind me saying this, but I think you've been a little unambitious with your efforts so far.'

Gina couldn't help it; she bristled. 'Oh?'

'Now I've made you cross,' Rose said, looking very much as though that had been her intention. 'I mean, obviously you've done a good enough job. I'm just not sure you have the contacts to take things to the next level. Have you thought about sponsorship, for example?'

'Yes, but—'

'You could approach a drinks brand or an upmarket holiday company,' Rose continued, ignoring Gina. 'I'm sure there'd be plenty of takers, if the right person was asking, and all they'd need in return is some product placement and advertising space.'

'I know how sponsorship works,' Gina managed to grind out. 'It's part of my job back in London.'

Rose smiled. 'Of course it is. But my family happens to have excellent links with the drinks and hospitality industries – why don't you let me see what I can rustle up?'

Gina hesitated. On the one hand, sponsorship seemed like a great way to reduce Gorran's overheads and bring in some much-needed cash. But it meant giving Rose the satisfaction of being right, and Gina wasn't sure she could bear it.

'Of course, all of this depends on whether the town council is able to grant the temporary event notice and give permission to use the beach,' Rose said. 'My mother says they're meeting tomorrow to discuss it.'

The implication was obvious. Gina pictured Gorran's worried expression whenever the subject of money came up and squashed her rising irritation. 'Of course. But providing the council gives us the go ahead, I'd be happy for you to chase up some sponsorship leads.' She managed a strained smile. 'Thank you.'

Rose's forehead crinkled. 'Oh, but we're getting ahead of

ourselves. Don't you need to check with Gorran first?' she asked innocently. 'Ben told me he runs the show – you're just a volunteer.'

Silently counting to ten, Gina drained the last of her wine and set the glass down carefully. 'You're absolutely right,' she said, standing up and reaching for her bag. 'I'll speak to him tomorrow morning. Sorry I can't stay for another – I'm expecting a call from Max soon.'

Rose tipped her head graciously. 'I understand. Do say hello from me, won't you?'

Gina felt her carefully constructed smile start to slip. 'Good night, Rose.'

It took her most of the cab ride home to calm down. The first thing she did when she walked through the door was to head to the fridge to pour a large glass of Pinot Grigio, which she carried out to the balcony that overlooked the cliffs. The sun had vanished below the horizon and the sky was a mixture of navy blue and mauve, streaked with velvet grey and dotted with early stars. Gina sipped her drink, allowing the rhythmic crash of the waves below to soothe her jangling temper. On the surface, Rose hadn't said or done anything especially terrible; she was far too clever for that. Even so, Gina still felt unsettled, mostly by things that hadn't been said. Her parting shot, asking Gina to say hello to Max, had been designed to ruffle feathers, and Gina was irritated to note that it had worked. She still wasn't entirely sure how Rose knew Max, other than some vague reference to Arundell family business interests, but at least that was something Gina could address. Lifting up her phone, she stabbed in Max's name and hit call.

It rang for a long time before he answered and Gina could tell right away that he was in a bar. 'Hi,' he shouted, causing her to wince and hold the phone away from her ear. 'Can you hear me okay?'

'Yes, I can hear you. Is this a bad time?'

'No, not especially. Hang on, let me just –' His voice trailed off, leaving her with a confused impression of loud conversations and thumping music. Then there was the thud of what sounded like a door and the music faded away. 'Is that better?'

'Much,' she said, relieved both that he was no longer bellowing and that he hadn't made an excuse to hang up. 'How are you?'

'Not bad. How are things in the shire?'

Gina pulled a face. 'Challenging. The refurbishment is going well, but Gorran has cash-flow issues so we're staging an outdoor screening to bring in some money.'

Max sighed. 'Why doesn't that surprise me? Honestly, it's just one disaster after another with him, isn't it?'

'That's not exactly fair—' Gina began.

'It's true, though,' Max interrupted. 'That business would have collapsed months ago if it wasn't for you. And I bet he's not paying you for any of this, is he?'

Gina thought guiltily of her bank balance, which was starting to dwindle at an alarming rate while she worked for free. 'No, but—'

'He's taking you for a ride, Gina,' Max cut in again. 'Does he have any idea how much you normally charge for managing events like this?'

'No,' Gina said quietly.

'And Ferdie,' Max went on. 'Has he offered you anything for your time? He does know you've put your career on hold to ride to his rescue, right?'

'That's different – it's family,' Gina replied, trying her hardest not to sound defensive. 'Look, Max, we've talked about this already – not everything boils down to money. And I didn't ring you to have an argument, I rang because –' She swallowed hard. 'Because I miss you and I wanted to hear your voice.'

Max was silent for a moment. 'I'm sorry,' he said at last, his tone much softer. 'I miss you too. Let's start again, shall we? How are you?'

Gina took a deep breath, tasting the faint tang of salt in the air, and let it out again slowly. 'I'm fine. Getting by. What's new with you?'

She listened as he described the usual jumble of meetings, dinners and drinks, interrupting here and there with a question or a comment. Max was always busy; his business and personal life swirled together into a complicated tangle that Gina had once accepted as completely normal. But things had changed since she'd been in Polwhipple and now the merry-go-round of social engagements and business lunches made her head spin, making her wonder how she used to manage.

'Jamie and Violet were asking after you,' Max said. He paused. 'Actually, they asked if we were still together. I put them straight.'

'Good,' Gina said, aware that her stomach had suddenly swooped into freefall. Her grandmother's words echoed in her ears. 'I was thinking I might come up to London for a few days, actually. Once everything is under control with the refurbishment.'

Max was instantly enthusiastic. 'That would be fantastic. There's a great new exhibition on at Tate Modern that I think you'd love, and I've got around a million party invitations with your name on them, stretching right up to Christmas.'

Christmas, Gina thought with a jolt. She hadn't thought that far ahead; in fact, she hadn't thought much past August, when she was due to return to London permanently. The festive period was always the most frenetic time of the year in the city, but what would December in Polwhipple be like? Quieter and more thoughtful, she decided, with a twinkling Christmas tree on the high street and fairy lights looping back and forth between the shops. Maybe Gorran would arrange a sing-along screening of *White Christmas* and everyone could dress up in red and white . . .

'Gina?' Max's voice crackled down the phone. 'Are you still there?'

She gave herself a mental shake. 'Yes, I'm still here. Listen, I'd better let you go back inside. I just wanted to say hello, that's all.'

'I'm glad you did,' Max said, his tone warm. 'And I love the idea of you coming up here. Make it soon, okay?'

'I will,' Gina promised. 'Oh, by the way, Rose says hello.'

She waited, willing him to say, 'Rose who?' but he didn't. 'Great, thanks – give her my love, will you?'

The phone hissed in her ear. Frowning, she held it away for a second then pulled it near to speak again. 'Of course. I've been meaning to ask – how do you two know each other again?'

'What was that?' Max said, the words distorted by static. 'You're breaking up.'

'I said, how do you and Rose—' Another burst of crackling filled her ear and Gina gave up. 'Never mind. Speak to you soon, okay?'

A jumble of noise tumbled out of the phone that sounded a lot like Max had suddenly been plunged under water. Gina rang off and sat cradling her wine glass, staring at the inky sky. Had Max really told her to give Rose Arundell his *love*? Surely that was a bit much for casual acquaintances. Then again, Gina had no real idea how well they knew each other; they'd certainly got on well during their disastrous impromptu double date at the Scarlet hotel. Perhaps it was a subject she could tackle when she went to London. When she could see the expression on Max's face.

# Chapter Twenty-Three

Gina thought Gorran might cry when he told her the council had approved his application and granted permission to use the beach.

'That's great news,' she said, smiling warmly into his suspiciously damp eyes as they stood in the foyer of the Palace on Friday morning. 'So we're all systems go?'

He nodded. 'Valeria and Rose stopped by to give me the news personally. I'll get on and book the film licence, then speak to a mate in Truro about borrowing some equipment.'

'And I'll get the deckchairs sorted and make a start on the publicity materials,' Gina replied, trying to ignore a stab of unease at the thought of Rose insinuating herself into the Palace already. 'We haven't got long to drum up interest.'

She found Ben at the top of the scaffolding in the screening room, a tub of gilt paint in one hand and a paintbrush in the other. His expression was one of intense concentration as he called down to her. 'Just give me a minute. You can't rush the detail on these things.'

Davey was hard at work on the wall opposite Ben. He waved at Gina as she took the opportunity to glance around her; already she could see there'd been a vast improvement. The walls were no longer pebbled with ugly stiff woodchip but were smooth and creamy. There was no sign of the wooden struts that had supported the plasterboard. Instead, fresh plaster flowed into the ornate swirls of the gilt that swarmed up the edge of each wall and snaked along the ceiling; some of the designs had clearly benefited from Ben's expert skills and others still needed some TLC, but enough had been done that Gina could see how amazing the finished effect would be.

Moments later, Ben lowered his paintbrush and fixed a critical gaze on his work. Apparently satisfied with what he saw, he lowered both the paint and the brush to the planks that made up the scaffolding floor and gazed down at Gina. 'It's not looking too bad, is it?'

'It looks amazing,' she said. 'Even better than I remember.'

Ben climbed down and stood beside her. 'Imagine row after row of plush velvet seats,' he said, pointing to where the bank of tired old seating had previously been. 'With all mod cons, like drinks holders and springs that don't try to disembowel you. And dotted about in front of those will be fifteen little round tables with chairs that swivel round to face the screen, for those who prefer their cinema experience to be more Parisian.'

She laughed. 'It sounds fabulous – I can't wait to see it. Do you think you'll have finished restoring the gilt by this time next week?'

Ben narrowed his gaze thoughtfully. 'The gilt will be done, but the floor needs to be resealed, and that can only be done once the scaffolding is out of the way. Then the seats and tables can go in. While that's happening, Davey and I will finish building the remodelled bar and box office booth.'

'And then the new carpet will be laid, right?' Gina asked, picturing the schedule she had spread across her kitchen table. 'Leaving us the best part of a week for dealing with any snags that come up before we re-open.'

'Hopefully,' Ben said. 'The snagging should only take a day or two so there's a bit of wiggle room there if we need it.' He threw her a sideways glance. 'Speaking of wiggle room, I looked into a few dance classes. There's one tomorrow night in Padstow, if you're up for it?'

Gina stared at him, trying to ignore the sudden sinking feeling in her stomach. 'What kind of dancing?'

'Ballroom,' he said, shrugging. 'The woman said tomorrow night was salsa but it doesn't matter if you've never danced before.'

'But we're just going to get a feel for whether it might work to incorporate a dance lesson into the *Dirty Dancing* screening,' Gina said. 'We're not actually going to be dancing. Are we?'

He grinned. 'Where's the fun in just watching?'

Gina pictured the glitz and glamour of *Strictly Come*

*Dancing* and tried to imagine herself twisting and twirling to a pulsing Latin beat. It wasn't an attractive image, until she pictured Ben doing it too. 'Uh –'

'Come on, what have you got to lose?' Ben asked, his grin softening. 'Apart from your dignity, and you lost that when you fell off my surfboard at the age of fifteen.'

He had a point, Gina supposed, especially as she hadn't simply fallen off; she'd belly-flopped into the waves with a loud shriek, in front of a packed summer beach. Unsurprisingly, it had been her one and only attempt at surfing. She did her best to glare at him. 'You're not helping.'

'Look at it this way,' he went on. 'How can you tell whether the instructor is any good if you're not actively following their instructions?'

'By watching everyone else,' she said. 'And seeing whether they seem to be having fun.'

Ben shook his head. 'I don't agree. But I can't force you to join in so let's agree to go and take a look, and see how the mood grabs us.'

That seemed safe enough, Gina thought; the mood definitely wouldn't be grabbing her. But Ben had been much too easy to convince. She eyed him suspiciously. 'And you won't shame me into dancing if I don't want to?'

'Nope,' he said, shrugging. 'I'll pick you up at six-thirty – deal?'

She gazed into his wide blue eyes, trying to decide whether she could trust him. 'Okay,' she said at last. 'It's a deal.'

*

Gina caught Carrie just as she was unlocking the door of Carrie's Attic, the vintage boutique she owned just along the promenade from the picture house, early on Saturday morning.

'Hello, stranger,' Carrie said, her green eyes dancing beneath her dark-brown fringe. 'I thought you'd been abducted by aliens.'

'Sorry,' Gina replied, pulling a face. 'Between the refurbishment and Ferrelli's I've been run ragged – in fact, alien abduction sounds restful by comparison, as long as they're not the kind that burst out of your stomach. How are things with you?'

Carrie held open the pink and grey shop door and invited Gina to go inside. 'Can't complain. Business is booming, which is always a relief.' She made her way through rails of silky fabrics towards the counter. 'How's the refurbishment going?'

Gina described the transformation. By the time she'd finished, Carrie's expression was full of delighted anticipation. 'I can't wait to see it,' she said. Then she paused. 'Who's the guy I've seen Ben hanging around with?'

'Davey?' Gina said, frowning. 'Ben's worked with him before, on other restoration projects. He seems nice. Definitely knows what he's doing.'

Carrie nodded. 'Single?' she asked in an idle tone, concentrating a fraction too hard on the computer screen on the counter.

A smile curved at Gina's lips. 'You fancy him.'

'I do not!' Carrie's cheeks turned red. 'Well, maybe a bit.'

Gina waited, eyebrows raised.

'Okay, a lot,' Carrie admitted. 'But you have to admit he's cute.'

Gina's forehead crinkled as she summoned up a mental image of Davey Bevan. He was dark-haired, with chocolate-brown eyes and laughter lines when he smiled. He was muscular too, although shorter than Ben and nowhere near as well-defined. He wasn't bad-looking, she concluded, but not what she'd describe as cute. 'I can't say I've noticed.'

Carrie gave her an enigmatic look. 'No, I don't suppose you have. Anyway, do you know if he's single, or do I have to look him up on Tinder to find out?'

'I don't know,' Gina began, mentally sifting through the few conversations she'd had with Davey. 'Oh, I think he is! Ben was telling me he broke up with someone and had to find somewhere new to live.'

Carrie's face fell. 'So he's nursing a broken heart?'

Gina racked her memory. 'No, I think it was at the end of last year. I can find out, if you like?'

'No!' Carrie yelped in alarm. 'I don't want him to know I'm interested yet.'

Gina couldn't help laughing. 'I wasn't going to launch into a "my mate fancies you" routine, Carrie. I do know the meaning of the word *discretion*.'

The other woman gnawed at her lip. 'Well . . . I suppose if you don't make it obvious . . .'

'Consider it done,' Gina said, still amused. 'So, apart from your undying passion for Davey, what else is new?'

'Not much,' Carrie said, gazing around the shop. She frowned. 'Except that I had a visit from Rose Arundell yesterday. She says she's organising a *Dirty Dancing* screening on the beach in a few weeks, with Gorran. Is that right?'

Gina felt her jaw tighten. 'What?'

Carrie shrugged. 'That's what I said. And she told me that you're busy with the refurbishment, so Gorran has asked her to take over the event management. She wants me to source a hundred blow-up watermelons and a Penny outfit for her.'

She shouldn't really be surprised, Gina thought, sidelining the competition was a move straight out of the megalomaniac playbook. Even so, she hadn't expected Rose to be quite so blatant about it. 'She's meant to be helping to organise it,' Gina told her friend. 'Not taking over.'

'But it is happening?' Carrie said, looking earnest. 'Because I have got the perfect pair of tiny denim shorts for you.'

'It's happening,' Gina said. 'There'll be cocktails, gelato and maybe some ballroom dancing lessons – Ben and I are going to check out a teacher tonight.'

Carrie's face lit up. 'Excellent! I love ballroom dancing. I had lessons a few years ago – it was so much fun.'

A thought occurred to Gina, one that might solve a number of problems in one easy hit. 'Why don't you come with us?' she said. 'Ben has this crackpot idea that we're going to actually take part in the class – if you come, you can dance with him.'

And save me from making a fool of myself, she added silently. In more ways than one.

Carrie pursed her lips thoughtfully. 'I don't mind tagging along. But are you sure I won't be in the way?'

'Trust me, the more the merrier,' Gina said firmly. 'There's safety in numbers.'

Gina waited until Davey had gone for lunch to pump Ben for more information.

'He seems nice,' she said, sitting cross-legged on the floor and watching Ben layer more gilt onto a tired-looking curl. 'Have you known him a long time?'

'Davey? About four years, I think. He's reliable and very good – one of the best, in fact.' He glanced over at her. 'Why?'

'No reason,' she said easily. 'I had the impression you always worked alone, so I was curious when I realised it wasn't actually the case, that's all.'

Dipping his brush into the paint once more, Ben continued to paint. 'I renovated the station building all by myself but that's because no one else was daft enough to do it without getting paid. Usually, I'm more of a team-player.'

Gina cleared her throat, wondering how to introduce the subject of Davey's love life. 'He looks a bit younger than you. How old is he?'

'I'm not sure I know, to be honest. Late twenties, I think.'

Carrie was thirty, Gina thought, mentally ticking age compatibility off her list. Not that an age gap mattered that much these days. 'And no kids, right?'

This time, Ben lowered his brush and stared at her. 'Not as far as I know. And I assume he's got all his own teeth and no criminal convictions, before you ask. What's going on?'

Gina felt her cheeks grow warm. 'Nothing.'

'Right, I forgot,' Ben said, his lips quirking in amusement. 'You're just curious.'

'If you must know, I'm asking for a friend,' she replied, lifting her chin. 'It's not against the law, is it?'

Ben smiled and continued with his work. 'No, it's not.'

There was a small silence, during which Gina worried that she'd said too much. It wasn't that much of a leap for him to work out who she was asking for.

'I could invite Davey along tonight,' Ben went on. 'If you want to interrogate him in person.'

'That won't be necess—' Gina began and stopped. What better way for Carrie and Davey to break the ice than by dancing together? 'Actually, that's not a bad idea. Do you think he'll be free?'

'No idea,' he replied. 'I'll ask him when he gets back. How long has Carrie been interested, anyway?'

Gina groaned. Clearly she hadn't been as subtle as she'd thought, or maybe Ben just knew her too well. 'She'd be mortified if she knew you know. Don't tell her I told you.'

'Your secret is safe with me,' Ben said, smiling. 'Do you really want me to invite Davey?'

She decided to come clean. 'Well, Carrie has already said she'd like to come along. If you invite Davey then they might actually talk to each other.'

'And then, at the wedding, we can remind everyone of how we brought them together,' Ben went on solemnly. 'Although I can't give everyone a lift – there's not enough room in my van.'

'I suppose it's better if they come on their own, anyway,' Gina said. 'Just in case they don't get on and want to bail out early.'

'First rule of date club: always have an escape plan,' Ben agreed dryly. 'Okay, let me find out what Davey is up to this evening. I'm sure I can persuade him to join us.'

Gina grinned at him: she felt like Cher from *Clueless*. 'This match-making business is fun, isn't it? Have you got any more single friends?'

He threw her an amused glance. 'A few. Maybe you could organise a singles' night once the Palace is open again.'

Gina considered the idea; it wasn't half bad. 'You know, I might just do that,' she said. 'Who knows – we might even find a date for Gorran.'

'Steady on now,' Ben advised her, grinning. 'Let's take things one miracle at a time.'

# Chapter Twenty-Four

The journey to Padstow took much longer than Gina expected. The roads around the tiny village of Porthcothan were especially clogged, much more than usual for May. As well as blocking the roads, many cars seemed to have been abandoned on grass verges or parked haphazardly on the street and it was baffling.

'What's going on?' Gina asked, peering into the empty vehicles as they passed them. Despite the number of cars, there didn't seem to be many people around. 'Why is it so busy?'

Ben nodded towards the road that led to the bay. 'Haven't you heard? They're shooting the latest series of *Smugglers' Inn* down there. I suppose these cars belong to the die-hard fans, wanting to get a glimpse of the stars.'

'Of course,' Gina breathed, picturing the show's deliciously dark-haired star, Nick Borrowdale. 'I didn't realise it was filmed around here.'

'They move between locations quite a bit – you can usually tell where they are from the contingent of adoring women swooning in the streets,' Ben said with a wry look. 'But the film crew make the scenery look amazing so I can't complain. I read that loads more people are visiting Cornwall because of the show.'

Gina was sure he was right; *Smugglers' Inn* was required Sunday night viewing for most of her friends. 'I wonder if there's any way we could get someone from the cast on board with the Palace grand re-opening – you know, cut the ribbon or something.'

'You could ask,' Ben replied, concentrating on squeezing his van between parked cars on an already narrow lane. 'What's the worst that could happen?'

Nick Borrowdale, the brooding star of the show, would probably say no, Gina thought, but imagine if he said yes. People would flock from far and wide to catch a glimpse of him, especially if he agreed to say a few words. But she had no idea how to even contact him, much less convince him to open a cinema in a little seaside town he'd almost certainly never heard of. And then a memory stirred, of a party Gina had attended back in London where she'd met the PR girl who handled all Nick Borrowdale's public appearances . . . what had been her name now?

Gina racked her brain for several long minutes, then reluctantly gave up. She'd have to ask Max the next time they spoke – he never forgot a name, especially not when the owner had been as attractive as Gina remembered the PR girl being. And with a bit of luck, Max might have a contact he could use to put Gina in touch with her. Who better to cut the Palace ribbon than the heartthrob star of *Smugglers' Inn*?

The dance class was being held in a hall belonging to St Merlyn's church on the outskirts of Padstow. Carrie was already there, leaning against the bonnet of her red Mini and looking effortlessly cool in black cigarette pants and a gingham blouse. That must be the best thing about owning a vintage clothes shop, Gina thought as she waved to her friend; you'd never be short of an outfit to wear.

Ben spotted Davey walking towards the hall and beeped the horn. 'Just let me park up,' he called out of the window. 'Then we can go in together.'

Gina watched Carrie, waiting for her to notice Davey. When she did, it was like watching someone do a comedy double-take. She threw Gina a confused look but had pulled herself together by the time they all met at the entrance to the hall. 'Hi,' she said, smiling at Davey. 'I didn't know you were coming.'

'I didn't know you'd be here, either,' Davey replied, with a sideways look at Ben.

'It was a last-minute thing,' Ben lied blithely. 'Davey Bevan, meet Carrie Summers. Shall we go in?'

Gina wasn't surprised when Carrie gripped her arm as they headed through the door. 'Is this your idea of being discreet?' she hissed. 'A blind date? I might as well have a sign over my head that says "Carrie fancies Davey".'

'We didn't plan it this way,' Gina murmured. 'Well, not entirely. But it felt like too good an opportunity to miss. You don't have to dance with him.'

Her friend shook her head as she studied Davey's rear view. 'And let some other woman have all the fun? Not a chance.'

The hall was busy; clearly ballroom dancing had a bigger appeal than Gina had anticipated. There was a good variety of young and old, and a reasonable mixture of the sexes too – for some reason, she'd expected the balance to be skewed in favour of women but apparently there were plenty of twinkle-toed men in the Padstow area. The instructor was standing beside a table, checking names off a list. She looked up as Ben approached her.

'Hi, I rang earlier in the week,' he said. 'I'm Ben Pascoe and this is Gina Callaway.'

The lithe, blonde-haired woman smiled. 'Nice to meet you, I'm Mimi. And you're interested in booking a beach dance class, is that right?'

'Possibly,' Gina said. 'We're here today to get an idea about whether it might work, that's all.'

Mimi nodded. 'No problem. And you've brought a couple of friends, I see,' she said, glancing at Carrie and Davey. 'The regulars will be so pleased – they like a bit of fresh meat.'

Gina saw Davey's eyebrows shoot up and Carrie covered her mouth to hide a giggle.

'Just drop your things on one of the chairs and find a space,' Mimi went on. 'We'll be starting our warm-up exercises in a moment.'

Gina avoided eye contact with Ben. 'I'm not dancing. I'd like to observe, if that's okay?'

'I'm afraid it isn't,' Mimi said briskly. 'I encourage all dancers to throw themselves into the spirit of the dance, and having someone watching can often make them feel inhibited.' She gave Gina a no-nonsense smile. 'If you're not dancing, you'll have to wait outside.'

'But—' Gina began.

'No exceptions – sorry,' Mimi said, turning away and raising her voice. 'Okay, everyone, find yourself a space and let's get warmed up!'

Gina swallowed a heartfelt groan as Ben dropped her an encouraging wink. 'Looks like you'll be dancing after all.'

Mimi turned out to be an excellent teacher. She led her students slowly through the basics of the salsa then watched as they attempted the moves themselves, passing through the couples to correct posture and give advice. Gina lost track of Carrie and Davey almost immediately; she was too busy concentrating on getting the steps right and not treading on Ben's feet or bumping into his chest. They seemed to be holding hands a lot, something Gina found a little distracting – Mimi had explained at the start of the class that dancing the salsa involved two dancers side by side or opposite each other most of the time, often connected by their hands while their feet did all the hard work.

'The basic salsa steps are a lot like walking,' Mimi said,

demonstrating by stepping forwards and backwards. 'Move on the one, two, three. Pause on four, then move again on five, six, seven. Pause on eight.'

After another run through, she encouraged the class to try it. Emboldened by how easy it seemed, Gina risked a quick glance around and could immediately tell who the regulars were; they were the ones who looked at home on the dance floor, with good posture and confident smiles.

'See?' Ben said, smiling at Gina and causing a faint squiggle of something warm to work its way down to her toes. 'It's not so bad.'

'Now try it with a partner,' Mimi called and that was where things got complicated. Following the teacher's lead, Gina had practised moving her right foot forward but it turned out that only the men did that; ladies moved their left foot back first and it took several attempts for Gina to remember. Once she'd mastered that, Mimi introduced a turn and that caused Gina to stumble into Ben's chest more than once.

'Now do you see why I didn't want to do this?' she asked, feeling her face flood with warmth as she jolted backwards. 'I'm really not cut out to be a dancer.'

'Just relax,' Ben said. 'Everyone is too busy concentrating on their own steps to notice what we're doing.'

There was also the fact that Gina could feel Ben's fingers pressing lightly against her back, and she knew his attention was fixed on her, although all he would be able to see was the top of her head as she stared at her feet.

'That's easy for you to say,' Gina said, observing the ease with which Ben had mastered the dance so far. 'You're not the one with two left feet.'

'You're over-thinking it. Look up,' Ben said, waiting until she lifted her head and met his gaze. 'Now trust yourself – you do things that are ten times more difficult than this every day before breakfast. You can definitely do this.'

Doubtfully, Gina took a deep breath and gazed into his summer-blue eyes. Now that she wasn't staring downwards, her muscles seemed more relaxed and she could feel a gentle push or pull from Ben's hands as he guided her through the steps. Looking at him helped too; he was patient and encouraging, and seemed to be genuinely enjoying dancing with her. Gina tried her hardest to loosen up; by the end of the class, she was amazed to realise they'd mastered a whole sequence of steps and danced them to a simple salsa rhythm.

'You're a good lead,' she said, beaming breathlessly at Ben. 'Have you done this before?'

He shrugged but looked pleased. 'No, although I suppose surfing helps with the posture and balance. And you're better than you think. All you need is confidence.'

She fanned her face. 'I wouldn't go that far, but I did enjoy myself more than I expected. Thanks for making me do it.'

Carrie hurried over, her eyes sparkling. 'That was a lot of fun. Davey almost broke one of my toes, but luckily I have nine more.'

Gina glanced over her friend's shoulder to see a rosy-cheeked Davey heading their way. She lowered her voice to a whisper. 'So? Any chemistry?'

'Maybe,' Carrie replied. 'We didn't stop laughing, if that means anything.'

Gina's gaze flickered back towards Ben; they'd laughed a lot too. 'That's a good sign. Are you seeing him again?'

Her friend nodded. 'We're meeting for a drink tomorrow evening.'

A wave of delight washed over Gina. She reached out and squeezed Carrie's arm. 'See? My work here is done.'

Leaving Carrie, Ben and Davey to compare notes, she went to catch up with Mimi. 'Thanks for a great lesson.'

The dance instructor nodded. 'You looked like you were getting the hang of it.' She glanced across at Ben. 'And the two of you look good together.'

Gina felt the start of a blush creep up her neck. 'Oh,' she exclaimed quickly. 'Oh, we're not a couple. We're old friends, that's all.'

'My mistake,' Mimi said, completely unruffled by Gina's embarrassment. 'Dancing together is such an intimate thing that I'm always seeing romance where there isn't any.'

'We really are just good friends,' Gina said. 'Now, what are you doing on the second Saturday in June? Please say you're free.'

'Is this for the beach dance class?' Mimi pulled out a diary and consulted it. 'Nothing that can't be moved. What have you got in mind?'

Gina explained her plans for the evening.

'Sounds brilliant,' Mimi said. 'And I expect a lot of my regulars would be interested in helping to demonstrate the moves, if you'd like a few more bodies on the beach?'

It was an excellent idea, Gina thought, picturing some of Polwhipple's residents getting into a tangle. Gorran would probably need one-to-one attention. 'It's a deal,' she told Mimi. 'If you let me know their names, I can organise complimentary tickets '

The instructor's eyes twinkled as she smiled. 'Excellent. All you need to decide now is how dirty you want the dancing to be.'

Rose drummed her fingers on the table in the Mermaid's Tail, her blood-red nails rattling like machine-gun fire.

'And you didn't think to consult me or Gorran before booking this dancing teacher?' she said, her pale blonde eyebrows drawn with severe displeasure. 'You just went ahead and did it?'

Gina glanced across at Gorran for support but his gaze was fixed uncomfortably upon his drink. 'Yes,' she said. 'Today is Tuesday, the screening is just over ten days away and I wanted to be able to include the classes on the flyers. The design of which you still haven't approved, by the way.'

'Because they look like they were done in the dark by a five-year-old,' Rose replied. 'I know several graphic designers who could do a much better job.'

'At twice the price,' Gina countered. She took a deep breath. 'Look, we don't have long to build up some buzz for this event. There's nothing wrong with the flyer design we have – let's just get them printed and start distributing them.'

For a moment, she thought Rose would dig her heels in. 'You don't leave me much choice,' she snapped. 'I just hope this teacher is as good as you say she is.'

'She is,' Gina said, almost adding, 'Just ask Ben.' But she held her tongue at the very last second. It wasn't a secret that she and Ben had gone dancing, but Gina doubted Rose would take kindly to the news, especially coming from her. 'How are you getting on with the press? The local paper has been very supportive of the last few events. Any chance of some advance coverage this time?'

'I'm working on it,' Rose drawled. 'But you'll be delighted to hear that my mother has managed to secure sponsorship from a major vodka company – they're going to be supplying us with fifty free bottles in return for product placement and branding before and after the screening.'

Gina blinked. What on earth were they supposed to do with fifty bottles of vodka?

'And the Proper Cornish Ice-cream company have enquired about being allowed to run a concession,' Rose went on. 'We're just working out terms with them.'

'What?' Gina said, thinking she must have misunderstood, and even Gorran looked up. 'Obviously, Ferrelli's will be supplying the ice-cream for the screening, Rose, like they do for every film shown at the Palace. Why would we need another vendor?'

The other woman fixed her with a cool stare. 'Because Proper Cornish Ice-cream are offering us a cut of their profits.' Her gaze flicked sideways to Gorran. 'And because the whole point of this exercise is to get you and the Palace out of a financial hole, none of which you disclosed during your application for funding.'

Gina felt her jaw drop. How did she know about Gorran's money troubles? Had he confided in her? It seemed very unlikely, given the expression of extreme embarrassment he was currently wearing. 'That's because it's a fairly recent development,' she said, when it became apparent Gorran wasn't going to defend himself. 'It's only temporary.'

Rose sniffed. 'It's still a fact, regardless of how *temporary* it is. Which means that if another ice-cream company is offering us money, we'd be foolish not to take it.' She paused and aimed a superior stare Gina's way. 'I don't expect you to agree – you're hardly impartial, after all.'

This time, Gorran did speak. 'Ferrelli's has supplied the ice-cream at the Palace for a long time,' he said, in a tone of quiet defiance that made Gina feel better. 'And I'd quite like them to continue to supply it – they're as much a part of the picture house as the films we show. So we'll say a polite "thanks but no thanks" to the Proper Cornish Ice-cream company, if you don't mind, Rose.'

There was a very heavy silence. Then Rose stood up sharply, her chair screeching against the wooden floor. 'Fine.

But don't blame me if profits are down. I tried to help.'

With a final pointed glare at Gina, she swept out of the pub. From the other side of the bar, Jory watched her go with mild amusement. 'Credit where it's due, they do a proper line in flouncing, the Arundells.'

Gina managed a weak smile before turning back to Gorran. 'Thanks for sticking up for Ferrelli's. I don't think Nonno would have reacted well to having direct competition, do you?'

Gorran grunted. 'He'd have been furious.' He glanced up at Gina, and something in his expression worried her. He looked as though he was caught between mortification and disappointment. Clearing his throat, he lowered his voice to a whisper. 'I wish you hadn't told Rose about my financial problems, Gina. I know she's helping out but I don't want the whole bleddy town to know my business.'

'Me?' Gina said, startled. 'I didn't tell her a thing, Gorran. I thought you must have said something.'

'No,' he said, shaking his head. 'Weren't me. Maybe Ben let something slip? You know, pillow talk, that kind of thing?'

Gina's mind was filled with a sudden image of Ben and Rose in bed together. Her chest tightened as she shook the thought away. 'It's very unlikely,' she replied, forcing her thudding heart to slow. 'I don't think Ben trusts Rose with his own secrets, let alone anyone else's.'

'Someone told her,' Gorran pointed out. 'And you were the only people who knew.'

If that was true then Ben must be the guilty party, Gina thought uneasily, whether by accident or on purpose. And that begged the question of what else he might have told Rose ... maybe the two of them were closer than he was letting on after all.

# Chapter Twenty-Five

Gina found it hard to concentrate on her work in the dairy that afternoon. Thankfully, Ferdie wasn't around or she felt sure he'd have had a few forceful words to say about her lack of focus. When at last she'd finished topping up the stock levels ready for the weekend orders, she turned down a cup of Nonna's excellent coffee and headed for home. But instead of taking the road that led to Mawgan Porth, Gina found herself driving towards Polwhipple station. The thought of Ben sharing Gorran's secret with Rose had been tormenting her all day; her stomach had lurched every time she'd thought of the two of them together. Exactly what else had they shared? She had to know.

Ben looked surprised to see her when she banged on the door of the railway carriage.

'Gina! This is a nice surprise. Come in.'

He stood back to let her in. As she climbed the steps, she saw he was barefoot in jeans and a faded Saltrock T-shirt and there was more than a hint of golden stubble on his chin. His welcoming smile as she passed him was so sincere that it caused her certainty that he'd been the one to let Gorran's secret slip to falter. This was Ben. How could she think he'd been gossiping behind Gorran's back? And yet, someone had . . .

'I can't stay,' she said, once he'd closed the door and offered her a drink.

'Okay,' he replied, frowning a little. 'Is everything all right?'

She glanced around the oval-ceilinged carriage, taking in warm lamplight, the half-drunk glass of wine and the battered paperback draped over the arm of the sofa. There was no sign of a female presence; no clue that he might even have a girlfriend and Gina found that soothing. Rose Arundell couldn't be easy to keep at arm's length – if there was more to their relationship than Ben was letting on, surely Gina would see evidence of it here, in Ben's home?

'Everything's fine,' she said, swallowing a sigh. 'Well, no, it isn't, but I don't know how to phrase this nicely, so I'm just going to come right out with it. Did you tell Rose about Gorran's financial difficulties?'

He stared at her, shock written all over his face. 'No, of course not. Why?'

'Because somehow she knows and Gorran says he only trusted you and me,' she said, searching his eyes. 'And I know I haven't told anyone so . . .'

Ben ran a hand through his hair. 'So the only person left is me.'

Gina nodded. 'And Gorran thought you might have—'

'Gorran thought I might have *what*?' Ben asked, his expression suddenly stony.

Now that she had to say it, Gina found she couldn't. 'He thought that maybe you and Rose had – you know – that you were closer than you'd suggested.'

'Closer?' he repeated, his gaze incredulous. 'So, let me get this straight: Rose Arundell, a member of the most manipulative, power-hungry family this side of the River Tamar, knows something she shouldn't and you decide that not only am I the one to have told her, but that I've also been leading some kind of double life for the last month, telling you how much I dislike her when, actually, I am sleeping with her. Is that what you're suggesting?'

Gina wanted to groan. Now that Ben had spelled it out, the whole idea seemed ridiculous. 'No, I—'

'That's what it sounds like to me, Gina,' Ben went on, his cheeks growing pink. 'It sounds like you're calling me a liar, when all I've ever tried to do is help.'

'I know,' Gina said, wishing she could crawl under the sofa.

'Do you think it's easy for me to sit opposite Rose in restaurants, listening to her boast about her insufferable family?' Ben glowered at Gina. 'Do you think I enjoy pretending to be happy when she phones and messages and tries to control me all the time? Because believe me, I don't. But I put up with it for the greater good. For you and the picture house and even for Gorran bloody Dew.'

Guilt washed over Gina; she pushed it away. Ben had chosen to do this; he wasn't entirely the victim. 'So don't put up with it,' she fired back. 'Be honest and tell Rose it's over.'

Ben stared at her for a moment, his lips pressed together in a thin line. 'It's not that simple,' he said eventually. 'And since we're being blunt, Gina, I don't think you've got any right to lecture me about honesty.'

'What's that supposed to mean?'

He opened his mouth to speak and then seemed to think better of it. After a few seconds, he shook his head. 'Nothing. Forget it.'

He must mean the kiss they'd shared, Gina decided, feeling heat start to rise in her cheeks. Was that kiss what this was really about? she wondered suddenly. Could it be jealousy that was making her react so badly to the thought that Ben had confided in Rose?

'Ben—' she began but he waved her away.

'I think you should go.'

'Go?' she echoed.

He gave her a bleak-eyed look. 'Yeah. Go and phone Max or something.'

She stared at him, her heart thudding uncomfortably in her chest. 'If that's what you want.'

'Yeah.' His shoulders slumped. 'Of course that's what I want.'

Unable to think of anything to say that wouldn't make the situation worse, Gina turned to leave. She was almost at the bottom of the stairs when she heard him call after her.

'I didn't tell Rose about Gorran. However she found out, it wasn't from me.'

The door of the carriage swung shut, leaving Gina standing in a little puddle of light from the window. Swallowing a sudden wave of misery, she hurried for the safety of her car.

# Chapter Twenty-Six

Paddington station was sparkling in the midday sunshine. Gina took a deep breath and looked around, noticing the pigeons hopping under the rows of metal seats, the queues at the coffee stalls, the hustle and bustle of a busy London station. She'd been there less than five minutes and already it felt as though she'd never been away.

'Gina!' Max's voice rang out across the concourse. Moments later, he'd swept her into his arms. 'I wanted to be here to meet you off the train but the traffic was awful,' he said into her hair. 'How was the journey?'

'Fine,' she said, breathing in his aftershave and casting her mind over the four-hour journey that she'd barely even noticed slipping by. 'The usual.'

He smiled and reached for her overnight case. 'It's so good to see you.'

It was good to see him too, she decided, observing his sharp pin-striped suit, handsome profile and perfectly styled brown hair. But before she could tell him so, he was speaking again. 'So what brought this on? One minute you're telling me you can't possibly get away for ages, the next I'm reading a message to say you're on the train.'

Gina avoided his eyes. She didn't want to explain about her argument with Ben the night before. 'Can't a girl drop everything to see her boyfriend when she wants to?'

Max smiled, evidently pleased by her words. 'Of course she can.' He glanced up at the time on the digital boards. 'I don't have long before my next meeting. I hate to do this but can I get you settled at the flat and meet you for drinks later?'

'Of course,' Gina said. 'I might have dropped everything but I don't expect you to. I imagine it'll take me a few hours to adjust to being back in London, anyway. And if the loneliness gets too much, I'll call Sarah or Tori.'

'Good girl,' Max said, looking relieved. 'I knew you'd understand. So, how long can you stay for? Is a week too much to hope for?'

'I wish I could stay that long,' she said as they approached the taxi rank, raising her voice to be heard over the hustle and bustle of the street. 'But I can probably stay until Sunday.'

He reached out with his free hand and took hers. 'Then we'll just have to make the most of the time we have.'

'You're where?' Elena's voice sounded confused in Gina's ear. 'What on earth are you doing in London?'

'I needed a bit of time to myself,' she told her grandmother, gazing out at the Thames and wishing she didn't feel as though she'd abandoned her responsibilities and run away. 'It was kind of a last-minute decision – there wasn't time to tell you before I left.'

Gina heard a low murmuring in the background: Ferdie. 'Tell Nonno that everything is under control. There's more than enough stock in the dairy freezers to fulfil our weekend orders and I'll be back by Sunday at the latest to see what's needed for the week after.'

Elena relayed the message and Gina heard more mumbling. 'We'll get started on the Cha-Cha Cherry supplies as soon as I'm back,' she said, anticipating his next question.

'He's not asking about the ice-cream,' Elena said impatiently. 'He wants to know how you are. It's not like you to just vanish like this – has something happened?'

Gina hesitated. She wanted nothing more than to spill the whole sorry tale to her grandmother, and hear the brilliant advice Elena would undoubtedly give. But she couldn't go into detail without revealing Gorran's financial embarrassment, and it seemed as though too many people knew about that already. 'No, everything is fine. I just fancied a break, that's all. Weren't you telling me that I should go and see Max?' She gave a small self-conscious laugh as she looked around her boyfriend's empty apartment. 'Well, here I am.'

Nonna sniffed. 'Make sure he looks after you, then. And come back to us on Sunday – who knows what kind of a mess Gorran Dew will get himself into if you don't.'

They talked for a few more minutes before Gina hung up. She checked her screen again, the way she had a million times during the train ride from Bodmin Parkway; there were still no messages from Ben. Although that was hardly a surprise, since she hadn't messaged him either. She had contacted Gorran, though, to let him know she wouldn't be around in person for a few days, and she assumed he would let Ben know, if Ben thought to ask him. And of course she'd told Carrie, who had immediately rung her. Carrie was the only person Gina confessed to about the argument with Ben.

'He said what?' Carrie had said, when Gina relayed the conversation with Ben. 'That doesn't sound like him.'

'I had just accused him of sleeping with Rose Arundell,' Gina pointed out, with an embarrassed laugh. 'Maybe he had the right to be a bit touchy.'

Carrie was silent for a moment. 'You don't really think he has been, though? I mean, obviously you know Ben much better than I do but he doesn't seem like the type of guy to go there unless there are feelings involved.'

Once again, Gina considered the possibility. Putting her own messy emotions to one side, it didn't really matter what Ben and Rose did together; they were both single, consenting adults, after all. But if things had progressed, then the fact that Ben was only using Rose – worse, that he actively disliked her – changed everything. It turned Ben from someone Gina thought she knew and liked into a man she recognised only too well from her life in London; the kind of man who saw women as disposable and had little regard for them as human beings. Unless Ben was exaggerating his dislike of Rose to appease Gina, which wasn't a much better option. She closed her eyes and sighed; it was all such a tangled mess.

'He says he hasn't,' she said to Carrie. 'And if you'd asked me a week ago, I would have believed him. But to be honest, I don't know what to think. That's why I'm getting away for a few days. Maybe being in London will help to clear my head.'

'Good luck,' Carrie said, her voice warm with sympathy. 'I'll keep an eye on things here, make sure Rose doesn't do anything too outrageous at the Palace while your back is turned.'

Gina gave a hollow laugh. 'It's not me who needs luck, it's you.' Her voice softened. 'Listen, I need to go and catch my train. Keep an eye on Ben as well, okay?'

'Consider it done. I'll rope Davey in too. Speak soon.'

Gina felt bad as she hung up; she hadn't thought to ask how her friend's date had gone. But her mind was full of her argument with Ben – she was sure Carrie would understand. And it sounded as though things were going well, which made Gina feel a tiny bit better. Once the worst of her argument with Ben had passed, she'd get all the details from Carrie. And until then, she had London to distract her.

The restaurant was stuffy and packed. Gina found herself sandwiched in between Max, who was discussing a new skyscraper that was being planned near Canary Wharf, and an ample, sweaty business associate of his who kept calling her Tina. Her head ached and her shoulders hurt from the effort of keeping her arms tucked into her sides.

She forced herself to smile as the man regaled her with yet another story about his 'bitch of an ex-wife' and tried to resist checking the time. Of course she hadn't really expected Max to cancel everything the moment she arrived but she had hoped they might be able to spend her first evening back together. As it stood, they'd hardly exchanged more than a few words.

The waiter gave her a sympathetic smile as he topped up her empty glass. Gina thought longingly of her quiet clifftop apartment and wished she was there, listening to the Atlantic crashing onto the beach. And what would Ben be doing now? Was he thinking about her as often as she was thinking about him? Her fingers twitched and she almost reached for her phone but Max turned around to put his hand on her knee.

'Is Archie boring you?' he whispered.

'Very much so,' she replied. 'Do you think we can get out of here soon? It's been a really long day.'

Max smiled. 'Of course. Let me just close this deal and we can head off.' He leaned past her and frowned at the sweaty man. 'Archie, stop talking about your divorce. You're sending Gina to sleep.'

The man's piggy eyes widened and his jowls quivered. 'Sorry, Max.' He glanced at Gina. 'Have I really been that bad?'

Embarrassed, Gina shook her head. 'No.'

He sighed. 'I have, haven't I? You can be honest.'

'Well,' Gina said, feeling sorry for him. 'Maybe a bit.'

'None of the guys listen any more,' he went on, his face settling back into the same morose lines as before. 'And it has been very difficult. Did I tell you she took custody of my Porsche?'

'You did,' Gina said, reaching for her glass.

By the time Max had finished wrapping up whatever business deal he'd been negotiating, it was after eleven o'clock and Gina was dead on her feet. She leaned into him in the taxi on the way home, allowing her eyes to close as they made their way to his apartment overlooking the Thames.

'It's good to have you home,' Max said, pulling her close. 'Sorry this evening was such a drag. I promise you'll have my undivided attention tomorrow.'

'Mmmm,' she murmured, snuggling against his shoulder. 'Can we have a night in?'

'I think that can be arranged, although I'll get lynched if I keep you all to myself for the entire time you're here. People are desperate to see you.'

Gina nodded sleepily. 'I'm grabbing lunch with Sarah and Tori tomorrow. But other than that, I don't have any plans.'

Max kissed her forehead. 'Good. I reckon you and me and a bottle of something cold should all make plans together.'

By the time they reached the apartment, Gina couldn't fight her exhaustion any longer. She fell into bed beside Max, barely doing more than wishing him goodnight before her eyes closed and she was asleep.

# Chapter Twenty-Seven

'So what's new with you?' Gina's friend Sarah asked on Thursday, leaning forwards in her seat. 'Tell us all the gossip.'

She and Tori studied Gina expectantly across their starters, their expressions avid. Gina gave a self-conscious laugh. 'I don't know what you're expecting me to say. You're the ones with the exciting London lives.'

Tori waved a hand at her baby daughter, Ava, who was snoring in her top-of-the-range pram. 'Listen, the highlight of my week was whether this one slept for five hours without waking up. Literally anything you've done will top that and if all else fails, you can just talk to us about ice-cream.'

'You wouldn't say that if you'd spent the last two weeks sanding down the walls of your local cinema,' Gina said, pulling a face. She tried to consider the past week objectively. 'We're planning an on-the-beach screening of *Dirty Dancing*, complete with I Carried A Watermelon Daiquiris and dancing lessons, if that sounds exciting enough?'

Sarah leaned forwards. 'See? That's exactly what we mean. *Dirty Dancing* and daiquiris sounds good to me – are there any eligible men in this Polwhipple place?'

Unbidden, an image of Ben appeared in Gina's head. 'One or two.'

Tori gave Sarah a scandalised look. 'She's hardly going to be paying attention to anyone else – she's got Max, remember?'

But Sarah, who had always been the more perceptive of Gina's friends, even before Tori had become wrapped up in motherhood, frowned. 'There's nothing wrong with window shopping.'

'But why window shop when you already own the outfit?' Tori argued.

Sarah folded her arms. 'I don't know – maybe because it doesn't fit you any more,' she fired back.

'Sarah!' Gina objected, just as Tori's mouth dropped into an O of understanding.

She turned a wide-eyed stare upon Gina. 'Have you met someone else?'

'No,' Gina said, willing herself not to blush. 'I'm very happy with Max.'

Sarah gave her a shrewd look. 'Really? Because you don't seem to be.' She raised her hands to quell Gina's indignant reply. 'Hear me out. You used to love socialising with Max, right? All the parties and dinners with clients, all the schmoozing and boozing. But I heard from a mutual friend who was there last night that you spent most of your time with your back to Max, staring at your phone.'

'That's not fair,' Gina said, and this time she felt the blood rush to her face. 'I wasn't on my phone all night; I was listening to some boring divorcee drone on about his ex-wife. And Max turned his back on me, if you must know.'

Sarah nodded. 'Right. And what happened when you got back to his flat after the meal?'

'We went to bed,' Gina said, giving her friend a level stare. 'What's your point?'

'To sleep?'

'Of course to sleep,' Gina said, exasperated. 'What else would we be – oh.'

Now Tori was shaking her head. 'That's not good, Gina. Unless you made up for it this morning.'

Gina thought back to earlier in the day: Max had kissed her on the cheek and rolled out of bed to hit the gym before his breakfast meeting. Sex had been the last thing on either of their minds. 'Not as such, no,' she admitted.

'It's been how long – over a month? – since you saw each other,' Sarah reminded her. 'I'm not saying you should be all over him or vice versa but surely there should be some flicker of interest? He's a good-looking guy.'

Gina said nothing. What could she say when Sarah was right? The truth was, she should have been all over Max.

'And when I talk to you back in Cornwall, you sound so different,' her friend pressed on gently. 'Happy and fulfilled, like you've won the lottery or something. I can't put my finger on exactly what it is but I think maybe you've changed,

Gee. And although you don't want to hear it, maybe that means it's time to change your outfit too.'

'No,' Gina said and she was surprised by how steady her voice was. 'Max and I might have lost our way a bit since I've been down in Cornwall but it's just a temporary blip. We'll be fine once I move back to London and everything gets back to normal.'

Sarah studied her for a long moment, then sat back and dug her fork into her ham terrine. 'Okay – you know how you feel better than I do. I'm only telling you what I see.'

An awkward silence stretched between them. Tori cleared her throat. 'So tell us more about this screening – it sounds amazing.'

Gina did as she asked and the three of them spent the rest of the meal avoiding any touchy subjects. As they were hugging goodbye, Sarah took Gina's hand and squeezed it. 'I hope you don't think I was speaking out of turn earlier,' she said. 'You're one of my oldest friends – I only want what's best for you.'

'I know,' Gina said, returning the squeeze. 'And I love you for it. But what's best for me is Max.'

Sarah looked deep into her eyes. 'Okay. Then we'll say no more about it.'

But Gina couldn't help thinking about it as she took the Tube back to Max's apartment. Was Sarah right? Had she and Max outgrown each other? Was it really time for a new outfit?

*

Keen to remind herself of all the things she loved about London, Gina spent some time wandering along the South Bank, trying to untangle the jumble of thoughts in her head. She was almost tempted to stop by Tate Modern, until she remembered that Max had said there was an exhibition there that he thought they might enjoy together. So she turned away and crossed the Millennium Bridge, admiring the sparkle of the late-May sunshine on the river and the white dome of St Paul's Cathedral silhouetted against the blue sky. London really was a beautiful city; she'd missed its majesty.

Unexpectedly, Max was already home by the time she arrived back at the apartment. She opened the front door to be greeted by the mouth-watering aroma of roasted chicken. Max appeared in the hallway, a flute of champagne in each hand, and smiled.

'This is what we should have done yesterday,' he said, coming towards her. 'Welcome home, Gina.'

She took the drink he held out and sniffed the air. 'You cooked?'

Max nodded. 'I did. In around fifteen minutes, we'll be eating butter-roasted chicken with new potatoes and asparagus tips.' He leaned closer to plant a soft kiss on her lips. 'Unless we get distracted.'

He led her through to the living room, where Spotify was playing her favourite album. Refusing her offer of help, Max ushered her onto the sofa and insisted she stay there. The dining table at the far end of the room had been laid for two, with a tall vase of deep red roses in the centre and ruby petals scattered all over the pristine white tablecloth. It was practically perfect in every way.

Max himself was on good form. He asked about her day and, when she mentioned Tate Modern, reached into the jacket that was hanging on the back of a chair and pulled out two tickets for Saturday. 'And I've booked dinner at the Savoy,' he said. 'Just us. No business talk allowed.'

Gina tried hard not to narrow her eyes. 'Okay, who are you and what have you done with the real Max Hardy?'

He spread his hands in a gesture of mock hurt. 'What? Can't a man take care of the woman he loves every once in a while?'

She raised her eyebrows. 'In almost two and a half years, I have never known you to cook anything more challenging than toast.'

'Maybe I've changed,' he said simply. 'Maybe I've decided it's time I grew up a bit and started to think about settling down.'

Gina thought back to Sarah's comment earlier that she was different too. Could it be that she and Max were both evolving into new versions of themselves at the same time? 'Well, whatever the reason, I like it,' she said. 'Thank you.'

'You're welcome,' he said gravely, topping up her glass. 'And if all of this reminds you of everything you love about being here, then I'll be even happier.'

The food was delicious: the chicken was cooked to perfection and the potatoes and asparagus melted in the mouth. For dessert, he'd managed to get his hands on some Ferrelli's

Good Morning gelato, which left Gina almost speechless; the only cartons in existence were in her grandfather's dairy so Max must have done some serious sweet-talking to get his hands on it. But he refused to explain how he'd done it, leaving Gina mystified and intrigued. She'd have to ask Nonna when she got back to Polwhipple.

Once they'd eaten, they took their glasses out onto the balcony and watched the sun set over the city. And then they took turns spotting the stars that appeared in the darkening sky, stars that were nowhere near as bright as in Polwhipple, until Max took Gina by the hand and led her inside to the bedroom.

By the time Saturday came around, Gina's argument with Ben had faded to the back of her mind and she was beginning to feel as though she'd never been away from London. Getting together with a huge group of friends for drinks on Friday night had been a particular throwback to the way things used to be and Max had been the perfect boyfriend, rarely leaving her side. They'd spent Saturday afternoon together too, exploring the new sculpture exhibition and sharing observations about the work on display.

'Are you missing Cornwall?' Max asked, as they jumped in a black cab to whisk them to the Savoy.

Gina considered the question. She missed Nonna and Nonno, of course, and she was worried about how they would be coping without her. And she missed her apartment, and her own space more than she would have thought possible. But she didn't miss the feeling of anxiety she'd had every time she'd thought about Ben recently. And she didn't miss Rose Arundell.

'A bit,' she said carefully.

'But not enough that you think you'll want to stay there long-term,' Max said, searching her face. 'What I'm asking is – do you see yourself coming back to London permanently once your grandfather's leg is totally healed?'

She gazed out of the window, watching the streets whizz by. It wasn't that long ago that she'd wondered whether her future lay in Polwhipple; now she was wondering how she could ever have considered leaving London for good. 'Perhaps not right away,' she said, hedging her bets. 'But yes – I feel like there's more for me here so I'll definitely be coming back.'

Max nodded, evidently satisfied. 'I'm very glad to hear that.'

The food at the Savoy was excellent, although Max didn't eat much and was less talkative than usual. Gina put it down to tiredness and made more of an effort to fill the silences. By the time their after-dinner coffees arrived, Max looked pale and clammy.

'Are you okay?' Gina asked in concern, as the waiter placed a plate of chocolates in front of her.

Max cleared his throat. 'I'm fine.'

Gina peered at him more closely, her sense of disquiet only growing. 'Are you sure? You look very pale.'

'Honestly, I'm perfectly okay,' he said, nodding at her plate. 'Eat your chocolates.'

She gave the dish a cursory glance; chocolate was the last thing on her mind. But something shiny caught her eye; whatever it was, it glistened among the delicate milky-brown arrangement. Frowning, Gina pushed the chocolates aside and then let out a tiny gasp. Nestled among the caramels, pralines and noisettes was a diamond ring.

Max took her hand and when he spoke, his voice only shook a little bit. 'I didn't think you'd want me to go down on one knee. Gina Callaway, will you marry me?'

Sunday train journeys always seemed to take longer than those taken on other days of the week, but for once, Gina didn't care. She kept replaying over and over in her mind the moment when Max had proposed: her own stunned reaction and his anxious, hopeful expression as he'd waited for her to answer. And her own unexpected wave of happiness when the word 'Yes!' popped out of her mouth before she'd even really worked out how she felt.

The waiters had applauded and the Michelin-starred head chef had left his kitchen to come and congratulate them. The sommelier had presented them with champagne and then had left them alone to gaze at each other and get used to the feeling that everything had suddenly shifted underneath them. Even now, a sense of newness seemed to pervade everything; the unfamiliar weight on her ring finger, the sparkle that caught her by surprise each time she moved her hand. She wasn't sure how long it would take her to get used to the idea that she was going to spend the rest of her life being married to Max but for now, she hugged the knowledge to herself like the best kind of secret.

They hadn't made any plans, beyond how they would tell their families. Gina suspected Nonna would notice something was different almost immediately, even if Gina removed the ring, and it made sense for her to share the news with them sooner rather than later. But Max wanted them to see his parents together and that would have to wait until they both had a clear weekend, so they'd agreed to keep things under wraps with their London friends, too. It was quite a nice feeling, Gina decided as she watched the Devonshire sea roll past the train window, having something that only she and Max knew.

She toyed with the idea of going to see Nonna and Nonno that evening but decided she had more chance of fooling Elena in the morning. So she was at home, watching *Working Girl*, when the bell of her apartment buzzed.

Frowning, she got to her feet. Who could be bothering her at nine o'clock on a Sunday evening? No one even knew she was back in Polwhipple.

'Hello?' she said, into the intercom. 'Who is this?'

There was a loud, static-filled crackle and a low mumbling escaped the speaker. 'Sorry, I didn't quite catch that,' Gina said, her frown deepening. 'Who is it?'

This time the mumbling was clearer and she recognised the name *Ben.* Pressing the button to open the communal door, she gave the speaker an experimental tap. Was it broken? And what on earth was Ben playing at, coming round uninvited at this time of night?

Moments later, she had her answer: Ben was drunk. She realised the moment she opened her door and he almost fell through it, but if that hadn't been a big enough clue, the smell would have given him away. Nose wrinkling, Gina stared at him as he leaned against the door frame. This was exactly what she didn't need.

'You're back, then?' he said, the words slurring slightly.

Gina folded her arms, unsure whether to be furious or amused. 'Obviously.'

Ben's eyes slipped out of focus for a second, then he gave her a lopsided smile. 'Good. Because I bleddy missed you.'

His Cornish accent, usually soft enough that Gina barely even noticed it any more, had grown more pronounced; he sounded more like Jory than the Ben she knew. He leaned towards her and hiccoughed. She stepped back, waving away the strong scent of apples.

'We need to talk. Can I –' he paused and hiccoughed again. 'Can I come in?'

She thought about telling him to come back in the morning, sending him away to sleep it off. But she wasn't sure how she'd manage it – he couldn't have driven over to Mawgan Porth, not in this state, so he must have taken a taxi. And she'd be lucky to get another that would take him as he was. No, what she ought to do was try to sober him up.

'I suppose you'd better,' she said, holding open the door and beckoning him inside. 'Shall I make you a cup of coffee?'

He blinked like an owl that had just woken up. 'Yeah, that would be lovely.'

She was amazed when he made it to the sofa without knocking anything over. He slumped down with a gratified sigh and peered blearily at the television. 'That's Sigourney We –Weaver. What is this – *Ghostbusters*?'

'*Working Girl*,' she called from the open-plan kitchen. 'Classic eighties stuff.'

She left him watching the screen, hiccoughing gently, while she made an extra strong cup of coffee and placed it on the coffee table. 'So, what do you want?'

He took a mouthful of too-hot coffee and grimaced. 'Don't want nothing, really,' he said, swallowing hard and making Gina wince in sympathy for his throat. 'Except to say sorry.'

'I'm listening,' she said, taking a deep breath.

Ben transferred his unsteady gaze from the TV and focused on Gina. 'So, I'm sorry. I've been a proper idiot and you were right about everything.'

Gina froze. What exactly did he mean when he said she was right about *everything*? That he had been sleeping with Rose? 'In what way?' she asked carefully.

He waved one hand wildly, making Gina grateful he wasn't holding his coffee. 'In every way! Rose, the screening – the whole shebang. You called it all.' He paused and fired an imaginary gun at the ceiling. 'Shebang.'

'Why don't we take this one step at a time,' she suggested, trying to stay patient. 'In what way was I right about Rose?'

'I needed to be honest with her,' he said, holding up a finger. 'I shouldn't be using her to get – to get – what am I using her to get?'

Gina almost smiled. It was the first time she'd seen Ben drunk since they'd been teenagers and back then, she'd been equally drunk and couldn't remember what he'd been like. He was actually quite endearing and, drunk or not, she was suddenly glad to see him. 'Permission to show a *Dirty Dancing* screening on the beach,' she said, trying to be helpful.

'Which,' Ben burst out, suddenly louder than he'd been before, 'is one of the best ideas we have ever had.' His eyes slid vaguely out of focus as he looked at Gina. 'Nobody's going to put you in a corner, baby.'

Gina's mouth twisted again. 'So near and yet so far,' she said, shaking her head in amusement. 'Okay, that's one thing. What else are you sorry for?'

Ben blinked hard. 'I'm sorry for telling you to go away. I only meant for you to go home – I didn't think you'd go *away* away.'

'But you didn't try to get in touch with me to say so,' Gina pointed out. 'Not even one single message.'

Ben shrugged. The movement made him almost slide off the sofa. 'That's true. I'm sorry for that too. But you didn't mess – mess'ge me either.'

'No,' Gina conceded. 'And you're right, I probably should have.'

His eyes widened suddenly. 'No, *you're* right. About everything. About Rose and being honest and – and –' He tailed off to stare morosely at Melanie Griffiths and Harrison Ford. 'She didn't take it well.'

Mentally spooling back through the conversation, Gina gave him a confused look. 'Who didn't? Rose?'

'No,' he said, nodding hard. 'She said I'd never do better than her. She said –' He pulled himself upright and adopted a snooty expression. '"I'm the catch of the county!"'

This time Gina couldn't help laughing, because his impression of Rose was actually very good, if a little blurry around the edges. 'Really? She said that?'

'Yeah,' Ben said. 'And she told me I'd be sorry, which I am, but I'm not sorry for what she thought I'd be sorry for.'

He stared at her, wobbling a little, and Gina felt the last of her anger at him slip away. It was impossible to stay cross at someone this drunk, she decided. She might as well be angry at a puppy.

'So anyway,' he went on. 'I just wanted to say I'm sorry.'

She smiled. 'Okay. And I'm sorry too. I shouldn't have flown off the handle at you.'

The coffee cup in his hand lurched a bit and Gina reached out to steady it. The movement caused Ben to look down. 'What's that?' he said, pointing to the ring on her finger.

'Oh,' Gina said, cursing herself for not taking it off the moment Ben arrived. 'It's just a ring.'

His head bobbled as he peered at her hand more closely. 'S'an engagement ring. Did you get engaged?'

Gina hesitated. His voice had become noticeably quieter. 'Why don't we talk about that another time?'

Ben studied her for a few seconds, then slumped back against the sofa with his eyes closed. 'You did. You got engaged to Max.'

'Yes,' Gina admitted. 'I did.'

'Shouldn't have done that,' Ben mumbled, his eyes still shut. 'Max can't be trusted.'

Gina held her breath. This wasn't a conversation she wanted to have right now, although she knew she couldn't put it off forever.

Opening his eyes, Ben fixed her with a beady look. 'I know things about Max. Bad things. You shouldn't be 'gaged to him, Gina. He's a wrong 'un.'

'Let's talk about this tomorrow,' Gina said, not unkindly. 'You seem a bit . . . tired right now.'

'I am tired,' Ben said, closing his eyes once more. 'I'm very tired. It's not right.'

'Maybe it's time to go home,' she went on. 'And tomorrow, when you're not tired any more, we can talk.'

Ben said nothing. Gina waited. 'Ben?'

He let out a long riffling sigh.

'Ben!' Gina said more sharply, poking him in the ribs. 'Wake up. You need to go home.'

Breathing deeply, Ben angled his body away and nestled into the sofa. Gina shook his shoulder. 'Ben – wake up!'

Nothing she did made a difference. Exasperated, she considered getting a saucepan of water from the kitchen but she'd get more on the sofa than she would on Ben. Muttering under her breath, she settled down on the sofa next to him to watch what was left of the movie. Maybe he'd wake up when the credits rolled.

By ten-thirty, Ben was snoring and Gina had given up hope that he'd wake up in time to take himself home. Wishing she'd left him on the doorstep, she removed his shoes and grabbed a spare blanket from the cupboard. Satisfied that he was as comfortable as she could make him, Gina went to bed. She'd deal with her unexpected house-guest and his hangover in the morning.

# Chapter Twenty-Eight

Gina didn't think she'd ever seen anyone look as embarrassed as Ben did on Monday morning. His face was crimson as she walked into the living room and his eyes were mortified. She opened her mouth to speak, but Ben held up a hand.

'Whatever I said or did last night, I apologise.'

If she'd been the sadistic type, she might have strung him along. But judging from his pained expression, he was suffering enough. 'That's pretty much what you said last night,' she told him, smiling. 'You were extremely apologetic, about everything.'

Ben threw her a cautious look. 'I was?'

'Yep. And you also said you'd finished with Rose.'

He nodded gingerly. 'I remember that – I did it last night. She didn't take the news well.'

'What else do you remember?' Gina asked. She'd taken her ring off and hidden it at the bottom of her jewellery box. 'Do you remember telling me that Max can't be trusted?'

Ben let out a heartfelt groan and passed a hand across his eyes. 'I didn't, did I?'

'You did, although you fell asleep before you could explain why.'

'Sorry,' he said, and Gina knew he meant it. 'I must have been pretty wasted.'

She nodded. 'How did it happen?'

Ben explained that he'd met Rose to let her down as gently as he could. After things had taken a turn for the worse, he'd called Davey to commiserate with him. Davey had brought his two brothers, both rugby players, and everything had started to get hazy after the fifth pint. The next thing Ben remembered was waking up on Gina's sofa, with a mouth that tasted as though something had died in it.

'Is it safe to assume Rose won't be interfering with the *Dirty Dancing* screening any more?' Gina asked hopefully.

Ben sighed. 'I don't think it's safe to assume anything where Rose is concerned. But I'd be surprised if she shows her face, unless it's to cause trouble.'

'She can try,' Gina said, her expression grim. 'But the gloves are coming off. From now on, no more Miss Nice Girl!'

The next few days rolled by in a whirlwind. Gina's grandparents were cautiously happy to hear the news of her engagement to Max, although Ferdie felt he should have come to talk to him first.

'Ignore him,' Elena said, with a dismissive glare at her husband. 'He thinks it is the Dark Ages still.'

Ferdie and Gina devoted some of their time to perfecting the Cha-Cha Cherry recipe and making sure they had plenty of stock for Saturday's screening; Gina didn't want a repeat of last time, when Ferrelli's had sold out of the Good Morning gelato they'd invented to go with *Singin' in the Rain*. And Gina called into the Scarlet hotel to see Miquel, the head bartender, and taste the Watermelon Daiquiri he'd created.

'Perfect!' she declared, taking another long sip through her straw. 'I hope you've cornered the watermelon market because these are going to fly.'

Rose was *very* conspicuous by her absence. Gina tried not to get her hopes up as the days went by; she wasn't foolish enough to think she'd seen the last of the Arundells. But with a bit of luck, they might leave her alone long enough to get the screening done and dusted. After that – who knew?

Work at the Palace was coming along too; the carpets had been laid and Ben was satisfied that everything would be in place for the grand re-opening a week after *Dirty Dancing* on the beach. And Max had come up trumps with the name of the PR who handled the star of *Smugglers' Inn* – she was called Sam Chapman. Apparently, she'd moved out of public relations and was now running a pub in Shropshire but she remembered meeting Gina and was happy to contact Nick Borrowdale on her behalf.

'Be warned, he's mega busy,' Sam told Gina over the

phone. 'But this sounds like exactly the kind of thing he likes to get involved with, so fingers crossed.'

Carrie delivered Gina's outfit on Friday morning. 'The weather forecast says June looks hot so you should be good to wear these,' she said, holding up a pair of cut-off denim shorts. 'And I brought you a peachy-pink top like the one Baby wears when she's dancing on the steps outside Johnny's room.'

'Amazing,' Gina said, grinning at her friend. 'But who are you coming as?'

Carrie smiled. 'I'm going to be Lisa, Baby's sister, and Davey is going to be Robbie the waiter.'

Gina's eyes widened. 'That sounds promising. Are you official yet?'

Her friend batted her arm with the shorts. 'Stop it. We're just having fun and enjoying each other's company at the moment.' She smiled. 'Speaking of fun, I've really enjoyed sourcing everyone's *Dirty Dancing* costumes – so many people are going to be there. How are the ticket sales coming along?'

'Pretty well,' Gina said. 'Last time I checked, we only had twenty more to go before we've sold out.'

'Ooh, a sold-out event – that would be awesome. Maybe we should do more screenings on the beach.'

It was a nice idea, but Gina doubted very much whether Gorran would get the go-ahead from the town council again, not when Rose was so clearly nursing hurt feelings. Gina had tried to contact her several times to ask about the sponsorship arrangements but each time the call had gone to voicemail and Rose had ignored all Gina's messages. She wasn't even sure whether Rose would come to the screening, although Carrie confirmed she had collected her costume. 'Maybe,' she said, in a non-committal tone. 'We'll have to see what happens.'

She suspected Hell might freeze over first.

Saturday dawned bright and sunny. Gina spent the morning with Tash, the Palace's projectionist, making sure the projection and sound equipment was all working as it should.

'Relax, Gina, it's going to be fine,' Tash said, after they'd tested everything for the third time. 'Trust me, I've got this.'

Gina had left Ben in charge of laying out the green and white striped deckchairs inside the makeshift perimeter, according to the seating plan she'd drawn up, and Davey had constructed a platform for Mimi the dance instructor to stand on so that she could demonstrate the moves for the audience. By mid-afternoon, Gina was starting to believe they were as ready as they could be. All they needed now was an audience.

The crowds started to arrive dead on time. As always, Gina was blown away by the effort everyone had put in; the outfits were amazing – due in no small part to Carrie's Attic. She couldn't help laughing when she saw Nonna and Nonno; they'd come as the Schumachers – the wily pair of elderly thieves – complete with a handbag full of stolen wallets and purses. She led them over to the pop-up bar and grabbed a couple of Watermelon Daiquiris for them, promising to bring them cones of Cha-Cha Cherry from Ferrelli's as soon as she got the chance.

She couldn't find Ben anywhere. And then, just as Mimi took to her platform to lead the dance lesson, Gina saw him, strutting his way along the promenade with his hair slicked back into a quiff and a battered leather jacket slung over one shoulder. Several heads turned to watch him pass and Gina could understand why; he looked incredible.

As he came nearer, he lowered his sunglasses to look at her. 'Ready to salsa?'

She nodded, trying to ignore the fizzing feeling in her stomach that was either pre-event nerves or Ben's appearance. 'If I can remember the steps.'

'Don't worry, you'll be fine.' He smiled. 'You look great, by the way.'

Gina touched her hair. 'Thanks – you look good too. Scarily like Johnny Castle, actually.'

'Shame I can't dance like him,' Ben said. He draped his jacket over a nearby chair and held out a hand to her. 'Ready?'

Gina straightened her shoulders. 'As ready as I'll ever be.'

The dance lesson was a roaring success, helped along by Miquel's generous measures of rum in the Watermelon Daiquiris. Everywhere Gina looked, she saw people laughing and having fun. It was all going better than she could have hoped. And then she saw Rose.

The other woman was in costume, wearing a pink dress that Gina remembered the Rockette, Penny Johnson, wearing in the film. She was dancing with a man Gina didn't recognise and every now and then, she fired venomous looks at Ben and Gina.

'I don't know why she bothered to come,' Gina said to Ben as they danced. 'She's clearly not enjoying herself.'

'Ignore her,' Ben said firmly. 'She'll hate that most of all.'

And then it was time for the film to begin and Gina forgot all about Rose in the scramble to make sure all the guests found the seats they'd paid for. There was space at the front for picnic blankets and cushions, and row after row of deck-chairs behind for those who preferred a little more comfort. As the sun began to dip below the horizon, the opening bars of the film started to roll across the beach.

'Happy?' Gina whispered to Gorran, who'd come as resort owner Max Kellerman.

He nodded. 'Very. Thanks, Gina. I owe you. Again.'

She smiled. 'I'm just glad I could help.'

Settling into her seat beside Ben, Gina allowed herself to spend the next two hours getting lost in the romance. It wasn't until the end, when the audience broke into whoops and cheers, that she remembered where she was and realised she and Ben were holding hands.

'I'd better get moving,' she said, shaking her fingers free and climbing to her feet without looking him in the eye. 'I'm part of the exit team, making sure everyone leaves when they're meant to.'

Getting everyone out was a slow process. Some were keen to stick around to dance and Gina had to politely move them on. She'd just started to make progress when she heard a raised voice. Her heart sank – the last thing they needed was a scene. It was sure to be all anyone remembered the next day. But she soon realised this was no ordinary disgruntled customer: the person doing the shouting was Rose. She was standing on the sand, in the middle of a small crowd, and the person on the receiving end of her fury was Ben.

'You might as well own up,' Rose was shouting, her pale complexion suffused with furious red blotches. 'I know it was you – you were caught on camera!'

Ben shook his head. 'I've got no idea what you're talking about.'

'My car!' Rose bellowed. 'You scratched my car.'

Ben's mouth fell open as the crowd around them began to whisper and mutter. 'I promise you I didn't.'

'You did. Last Sunday evening, in the car park here. It's taken me this long to get the footage from the management company.'

'Look, Rose,' Ben replied in a measured tone, 'I'm sorry to hear that your car has been damaged but whatever you think you saw, I can categorically tell you it was not me.'

'Prove it!' Rose snapped, brandishing blown-up copies of CCTV images. 'Tell me where you were at 11 p.m. last Sunday.'

Gina felt the beginnings of a blush start to creep up her cheeks, because she knew just where Ben had been – fast asleep and snoring on her sofa. But she wasn't sure she wanted to say so – there were bound to be some people who didn't see how innocent it had been . . .

Ben didn't look at Gina. 'All I can tell you is that I was fast asleep then. Sorry, Rose, you've got the wrong man.'

'Hang on a minute,' Gina said, as Rose launched into yet another accusation and the muttering of the crowd grew louder. 'Just supposing it was Ben. What possible motivation could he have for doing something like this?'

Rose fired a withering look her way. 'Obviously, it was revenge for me dumping him.'

'Revenge?' Gina repeated.

'Revenge?' Ben said. 'For you dumping me? Are you being serious?'

'Of course I am,' Rose snapped. 'I told you last Sunday that our relationship was over and the first opportunity you got, you scratched my car to teach me a lesson.'

Now some members of the crowd were firing suspicious looks Ben's way. Others were muttering behind their hands as they watched the argument develop. But Gina had heard enough; she wouldn't let Rose drag Ben's good name through the mud like this. Taking a deep breath, she said, 'I'm sorry to disappoint you, Rose, but Ben couldn't have scratched your car.'

'Oh, how predictable,' Rose sneered, looking down her nose at Gina. 'It's Little Miss Ice-Cream, riding to the rescue. And how could you possibly know it wasn't him?'

Gina squared her shoulders and met Rose's derisive gaze head on. 'He couldn't have been in the car park at 11 p.m.

last Sunday, because he was with me.' She glanced over at Ben. 'And he stayed with me all night.'

Immediately, the crowd broke into gasps and mutters. Gina stood firm, trying not to blush too much. None of what she had said was untrue but she could hear the sound of two and two being put together all across the beach. There was no going back from this; from now on, she'd be inextricably linked to Ben.

'Prove it!' Rose demanded again.

'There's CCTV in my building,' Gina said, fighting to keep her voice calm and level. 'It will show Ben arriving around nine o'clock that night. He didn't leave again until the following morning.'

It looked as though Rose would try to argue but at the very last second, she gave Gina one last derisive, almost triumphant look and stormed off.

Ben walked over to Gina. 'You didn't need to do that.'

'Yes, I did,' Gina said, shrugging. 'She was trying to set you up for something you didn't do.'

He gazed after Rose. 'You know she'll make sure Max hears about this, don't you?'

Nodding, Gina swallowed hard. 'Not if I tell him first. Don't worry, he trusts me.'

Ben smiled. 'As he should. I hope he knows how lucky he is.'

Gina touched the empty space on her ring finger. 'Me too,' she said.

*

Max was silent for a long time after Gina stopped talking into the phone on Sunday morning. In fact, he was so quiet that she half-suspected they'd been cut off.

'Max? Are you still there?'

He sighed. 'I'm still here.'

'So I just wanted you to hear it from me, rather than second-hand gossip,' Gina said, hoping her voice was steadier than she felt. 'Absolutely nothing happened – he snored on the sofa all night – but I suppose it's easy to read something into it, if you don't know better.'

Again, Max was silent.

'Come on, Max, surely you can see it's all perfectly innocent?'

'Here's my problem,' he said slowly. 'If this is all so innocent, why didn't you tell me straight away? We talked on the phone on Monday evening – you told me what your grandparents had said about our engagement. Why not tell me that Ben slept on the sofa then?'

Gina stared at the carpet of her apartment. It was a fair question: why hadn't she told him? 'Because I suppose I knew it didn't look good,' she said, after a while. 'Because it was Ben.'

'I see,' Max said, his voice cold. 'And that leads to my next question, which is, if Rose hadn't accused Ben of damaging her car, would you have told me about this at all?'

'Of course I would,' Gina said, stung by the accusation she heard behind the words. 'I might have picked my moment and told you the next time I saw you but I definitely would've told you.'

'I don't believe you.'

The words felt like a slap. 'You don't believe I would have told you?' she asked. 'Or you don't believe that nothing happened?'

Max sighed. 'You know I've had issues with Ben before. I've seen the way he looks at you, Gina. Maybe this was all innocent on your part but I don't believe the same can be said of Ben. And I think—' He paused and took a deep breath. 'I think that for me to be able to trust you when you're so far away – I think you're going to have to break off your friendship with him.'

'What?' Gina stared at her phone, aghast. 'You can't mean that.'

'But I do,' Max said grimly. 'Think about it – we're hundreds of miles apart and we only see each other once every other month. I don't want to be sitting here tormenting myself, thinking about what you're getting up to with Ben.'

'But – but we have work to do,' Gina argued. 'Joint projects to oversee. I can't just cut him dead.'

'You have to,' Max insisted, his voice tight. 'Look at it this way, how would you feel if the situation was reversed? Would you be happy for me to continue seeing someone you suspected had feelings for me?'

Gina closed her eyes, feeling sick. 'Probably not.'

'Then you know what you have to do.'

'And –' She hesitated, then blundered on. 'And if I refuse?'

The last vestiges of warmth dropped from Max's voice. 'Then you can consider our engagement off.'

He hung up, leaving Gina staring at her feet in shock. Slowly, she lowered the phone to her lap. And then she burst into tears.

# Chapter Twenty-Nine

It seemed to Gina as though the next few days passed in a grey fog, even though the Atlantic sparkled in the June sunshine and the temperature soared. She spent most of Sunday moping around her flat, trying to resist the temptation to get on the next train to London. Right now, Max was angry and hurt, and Gina supposed she understood why; as he'd pointed out, if the situation had been reversed, she'd have been unhappy with him. But it felt very unfair all the same; she hadn't done anything wrong.

She arrived at the dairy on Monday morning with her smile fixed firmly in place. She didn't intend to tell Nonna and Nonno what had happened; with luck, she and Max would be able to repair the damage to their relationship before anyone had to know there was a problem. But she'd underestimated Elena's emotional superpowers; it took less than ten minutes for her to sniff out that something was wrong and only a few minutes more to winkle the whole story out of Gina. And then the tears had come; Ferdie had threatened to go to London himself to talk some sense into Max.

'Please don't, Nonno,' Gina had said, once she'd dried her face. 'He'll calm down on his own, and when he does, then maybe we'll be able to talk and sort everything out.'

Ferdie had looked even more furious then. 'Never mind talking some sense into him, maybe I should knock some sense into his blockheaded brain. *Idiota*!'

'Sssshhh!' Elena glared at him, waving at him to sit down. 'The last thing she needs is you breaking another limb by hitting her boyfriend.'

Gina sighed and straightened up with determination. 'At least I have the Palace re-opening to keep me busy. But as soon as it's over, I'm catching a train to London. Max can't ignore me if I'm standing in front of him.'

By Thursday, Gina was beginning to wonder if the Palace would ever re-open its doors. Whatever could go wrong did go wrong; they seemed to be cursed.

'It's that Rose Arundell,' Manda said darkly, when the lights blew for the third time that morning. 'She's sticking pins into a great big doll of the Palace and twisting 'em.'

Even the seat fittings hadn't been straightforward. The tiered rows had been fine; both Gina and Ben declared they were a huge improvement in comfort. And the round tables looked good too, but there was a problem with the seats that went with them. They didn't swivel.

'I don't believe this,' Ben said, staring at the static seat with an incredulous expression. 'What use is a swivel seat that doesn't swivel?'

The delivery man shrugged. 'Must be a faulty batch. You can order some more online.'

Ben stared at him. 'And risk the same thing happening again? No, thanks. Besides, these need to be in place for Saturday – we haven't got time to re-order.'

Gina gave the seat an experimental prod. It didn't move. 'What we need is an expert in mechanical engineering,' she said with a sigh. 'How about your mates at the Bodmin Railway Preservation trust? They seem to know a lot about this kind of thing.'

'Steam mechanics, yes,' Ben replied, doubtfully. 'But swivel seats might be a different kettle of fish entirely.'

'Ask, please,' Gina suggested and passed a weary hand over her eyes. 'They might be our only hope before Saturday.'

She left him working his way through his contacts and went to find Gorran. He was in his newly redecorated office, gazing at the plain white walls and bank of filing cabinets with a bemused expression. 'You look like a character from one of your arthouse flicks, Gorran,' Gina said, when he failed to turn around as she opened the door. 'Is everything okay?'

'Hmmm?' he said, twitching at the sound of her voice. 'Sorry, Gina, what can I do for you?'

'Stop staring at the wall and start sorting out all these papers,' Gina said, waving a hand at the boxes of papers that

Gorran needed to put away. 'If this place catches fire after all this hard work, I will not be happy.'

After lunch, she and Gorran and Ben went on a tour of the building, looking for issues. And they found plenty, from faulty toilet door locks to a sticky curtain mechanism that meant only half the screen could be seen. There were still a few finishing touches to be made to the gilt-work, although Ben and Davey both assured Gina it would be finished by the end of the day, to allow time for it to dry and the paint fumes to dissipate.

'This is the list of things that need attention,' Gina said, holding up a page of an A4 notepad that was almost filled with items to be fixed. 'We've got a lot to do.'

'Top of the list are the seats,' Ben said, glancing towards the screening room. 'I've got some friends on their way who might be able to help.'

'And if they can't?' Gorran looked alarmed.

'Then we can't re-open this Saturday,' Ben said, with a sigh. 'We'll have to postpone.'

'Let's hope it doesn't come to that,' Gina said. 'I'm not sure I can cope with another week of this.'

Ben caught her arm as she was about to go back into the screening room. 'Hey, is everything okay? You've been very quiet.'

Gina tried her hardest to smile. 'It's nothing. Stress, mostly. You know it's bad when you dream about snagging.'

'Welcome to my world,' Ben said, pulling a face. 'I have

those dreams all the time, although I'm usually naked too. But I'm sorry you're stressed – is there anything I can do to help?'

For a heartbeat or two, Gina wondered about asking Ben to talk to Max, to make him understand that he had no reason to be intimidated or threatened, and to explain that Gina's version of events was the right one. But she knew it wouldn't help; her problems with Max were for the two of them to work through. And Ben had enough on his plate here at the Palace. 'Honestly, I'm fine,' she told him, doing her best to smile. 'Just get the seats sorted by Saturday and I'll be even better.'

He touched her arm and lowered his voice so that Gorran wouldn't hear. 'It's okay if you don't want to tell me what's wrong right now. But I will always be there if you want to talk.' He paused and sighed with what sounded like extreme embarrassment. 'Except for when I fall asleep on your sofa.'

'Gina, *mia bella*, how are you?'

Elena slipped a sympathetic arm around Gina's shoulders and squeezed as they stood outside the Palace.

Gina did her best to smile. 'I'm fine, Nonna. Don't worry.'

'You are not fine,' Elena clucked. 'You are brave but you are not fine.'

It was Saturday afternoon and the stage was finally set for the Palace grand re-opening in just over an hour's time. The paint was dry, the seats finally swivelled where they were meant to, thanks to Ben's colleagues at the Bodmin Railway

Preservation Society who'd identified and fixed the problem on thirty chairs, and the gremlins in the electrical system seemed to have finally been evicted. The building wasn't quite snag-free but Gina knew when to quit; it was as close to perfect as it was going to get.

The mayor of Polwhipple was due to attend the re-opening ceremony, along with half the town, and Nick Borrowdale had agreed to cut the ribbon. It was the moment Gina had been working towards for the best part of two months and she wished she could enjoy it. But she still hadn't heard from Max and was now see-sawing between inconsolable misery and rage that Max could put her in such an impossible position. There wasn't even any way she could talk it through with him; he was still ignoring her messages and refusing to take her calls. Nonna was right – she wasn't fine. But at the same time, she didn't have the luxury of being able to wallow in misery. She had too much to do for that.

'Is everything ready over at Ferrelli's?' she asked.

Elena nodded and for the first time in Gina's life, she thought her grandmother looked nervous. 'I think so. Today is a big day for me too.'

Gina nodded. After decades of refusing to allow his wife to have any input into the gelato recipes he served at Ferrelli's, Ferdie had finally relented and allowed her to make a Tiramisu flavour. Today was its debut and both Gina and Elena hoped it would prove popular with Polwhipple's residents. 'It's going to be fine,' she assured Elena. 'Just wait and see.'

Ben appeared around the corner, smartly dressed in a crisp white shirt and dark jeans. 'Everything is set,' he said, once he was close enough to Gina. 'Tash has the film all ready to run, just as soon as everyone is settled into their seats.'

'And Nick?' Gina asked, certain that they were going to lose their guest of honour before he could cut the ribbon and open the cinema.

'In the Mermaid's Tail, discussing cider with Jory and most of the women in the county, I think,' Ben said, grinning.

Gina wanted to smile too but her face felt permanently frozen into a frown these days. 'What about Gorran? Where's he?'

'Last time I saw him, he was inside with Tash.' Ben aimed a concerned look her way. 'Relax, Gina, it's all going to be fine. Look, here comes Nick and his fan club now.'

Sure enough, there was the star of *Smugglers' Inn*, surrounded by a large crowd of adoring fans. 'I'd better go and rescue him,' Ben said, hurrying towards the actor.

Elena leaned closer to Gina. 'Ben doesn't know about you and Max?'

Gina shook her head. 'No. It seems simpler this way. Besides, what can he do? Max and I need to work through this on our own.'

Her grandmother pursed her lips, as though there was something she wanted to say, but Ben was on his way back, with Nick in tow, and there was no time.

Gina dredged up a friendly smile. 'This shouldn't take too

long, Nick. All you need to do is cut the ribbon, using the scissors Gorran passes you, and say something along the lines of "I now declare this cinema open" and then there'll be a few pictures for the local paper.'

Nick smiled. 'Got it.'

'After that, you're free to hang about for the screening we've got planned, or you can head off, if you'd rather,' Gina said.

'What film are you showing?' Nick asked, looking interested.

'We've gone totally old school,' Gina replied. 'It's *Casablanca*, which was actually the first film the Palace ever showed, back when it first opened.'

'Perfect,' Nick said, and he raised one perfectly arched eyebrow. 'Play it again, Sam.'

Gina was sure she heard Elena let out a tiny sigh beside her. 'The crowds are starting to build up,' she said, nodding at the tape they'd strung between poles to create a perimeter. She checked the time – less than half an hour to go. 'Okay, let's get everyone into place.'

'Good luck,' Elena whispered.

'Thanks,' Gina muttered in reply. She'd planned almost every detail of the re-opening and gone over it in her mind a hundred times; she might not be able to control her personal life but she was determined to keep her work running smoothly. Nothing could go wrong today – she wouldn't allow it . . .

*

'Anyone who knew me growing up knows that I spent every spare moment in a cinema like this one,' Nick said to the enormous crowd gathered outside the Palace. There were so many people there that they spilled along the promenade and the car park, and even down onto the beach. 'I can honestly say that without that cinema, I wouldn't be the actor I am now. So I'm especially delighted to be helping this building to re-open and inspire even more cinema-goers.'

Gorran passed the actor a large pair of silver scissors and he cut the ribbon that was placed between the Art Deco panels of the cinema's silver and glass double doors. 'I now declare the Palace open all over again!'

The crowd burst into applause as Gorran heaved the doors back and began to usher people inside. 'Those of you lucky enough to have tickets, please don't forget to visit our world-famous ice-cream concession, Ferrelli's, to try their delicious new flavour,' he said jovially. 'Do help yourselves to complimentary cocktails from the bar. And finally, when you're ready, please take your seats for *Casablanca* at the picture house by the sea.'

Gina hung back, watching the ticket-holders file into the refurbished cinema, while Nick chatted to those who didn't have tickets. Ben watched her watching him. 'Can you believe it? We did it – we actually pulled this crazy job off.'

Gina laughed. 'I must admit, there were times when I really thought we'd bitten off more than we could chew.'

'Honestly?' he asked. 'I had plenty of moments when I thought we were doomed. But we got through them.'

'We did. I've told you before, we make a good team. I knew we'd get there in the end.'

Ben smiled. 'But it was mostly down to your skill and determination. Has anyone ever told you you're a remarkable person, Gina Callaway?'

To Gina's horror, her eyes started to fill with tears. 'Not recently.'

'Well, you are. And I'm not quite as suave as Nick but –' He reached down and took her hand. 'Here's to a wonderful friendship.'

Gina blinked as hard as she dared and did her best to smile. 'Thanks, Ben. You have no idea how much that means right now.'

'You're welcome,' he said. And, hand in hand, they walked in through the double doors to watch *Casablanca*.

# PART FOUR

## Some Like it Hot

# Chapter Thirty

'How do you feel about murder?'

Gina Callaway lowered her crab-laden fork and stared at Ben Pascoe across the table, unsure whether she'd misheard. It wasn't a question she'd been asked in a packed seafood restaurant. In fact, it wasn't a question she'd *ever* been asked. 'Sorry?'

Ben grinned, his blue eyes twinkling beneath his thatch of golden-blond hair. 'I said, how do you feel about murder?'

Was it Gina's imagination or did the passing waiter give the two of them a slightly suspicious look? 'That's what I thought you said,' she said, raising both eyebrows. 'I've been tempted once or twice but so far I've resisted. Why?'

He slid a flyer across the gingham tablecloth.

'The Bodmin and Wenford Railway Preservation Society presents *Murder on the Cornish Express*,' Gina read, then looked up. 'Oh, it's a murder mystery evening?'

Ben nodded. 'On board the train. In between the welcome

cocktails and a five-course dinner, news will spread of a terrible murder and it'll be up to the passengers to work out whodunnit. Up for it?'

'Dress code: Gatsby Chic,' Gina said, with a little surge of anticipation at the thought of the costume possibilities. 'Are you kidding – of course I'm up for it. It sounds amazing.'

'Great,' he said, then paused. 'It's a Friday evening – do you think Max might want to come?'

Gina chewed a mouthful of crab as she gazed out at the sparkling seas of Padstow harbour and considered the question. If Ben had asked a few weeks earlier then she might not have hesitated; after Max's proposal, she'd spent a few days walking on air. But then everything had gone wrong and the diamond ring Max had given her was now in the bottom of her jewellery box. Ben had no idea of the damage his night on the sofa had caused.

She took a sip of perfectly chilled Pouilly-Fumé, savouring its dryness after the sweetness of the crab. 'I'll ask him,' she said, finally. 'It's not really his kind of thing.'

'Okay,' he said, picking up the leaflet. 'Let me know as soon as you can. It's not until the end of July, so we've got a few weeks but tickets are selling fast.'

Where had the time gone, Gina wondered in mild bewilderment. She'd originally planned to return to London after three months in Cornwall and yet she was still there, more than four months later. It was something else Max was unhappy about . . .

'Carrie and Davey might be interested,' Gina said, forcing

Max out of her mind. She pictured her friend's excitement when she heard about the Roaring Twenties theme. 'Well, Carrie will be. I'm not so sure about Davey.'

Ben grinned. Davey was one of his workmates, a fellow builder who'd recently helped to him to pull off a triumphant renovation of the Palace, Polwhipple's Art Deco picture house. 'I can just imagine him in a flapper dress and pearls, can't you?'

She laughed. 'He'd make a perfect gangster. Except that I don't imagine they had many of those in 1920s Cornwall.'

'Who cares?' Ben replied. 'The dress code is just for guidance – there won't be any costume police checking for authenticity.'

'Fair point,' Gina conceded. 'I wonder if Nonna and Nonno will want to come.'

Her grandparents had surprised everyone by raising their cosplay game for every event that she organised at the Palace; she couldn't wait to see what they might put together for a murder mystery evening aboard a steam train.

'Well, like I said, let me know fast,' Ben said. 'The Preservation Society has held a few fundraising events like this before and they're always popular. And this time, there's an added bonus – part of the money raised will go towards the opening day celebrations of Polwhipple station.'

'That's great,' Gina said warmly. Ben had spent months restoring the station in his spare time, at his own cost, to encourage the Preservation Society to re-open the heritage line from its current final station to Polwhipple; it was only right that they should invest in the project too and an opening day celebration had a lot of PR potential. 'Let me know if you want any advice.'

Ben flashed her a grateful look. 'I was hoping you'd say that – the Preservation Society are handling most of the planning but they've invited me to a few committee meetings and I've realised I know even less about this stuff than Gorran.'

Gina smiled. What Gorran knew about events management could be written on the back of a ticket stub. 'Just let me know what you need.'

'Thanks,' he said. 'You can be Yoda to my Skywalker.'

She shook her head in amusement; Ben was probably the only person in the world who knew her well enough to fire a *Star Wars* joke at her. 'Flattered I am,' she said gravely. 'Although obviously from a looks point of view I'd rather be Princess Leia.' She raised her wine. 'Here's to working together, anyway, and saving the universe.'

Ben's eyes crinkled as he tapped his glass against hers. 'I'll definitely drink to that – cheers!'

Gina was surprised to see the window of Ferrelli's was very firmly closed when she crossed the car park to the Palace early on Saturday morning. Manda Vickery was standing outside the cinema, her usually cheerful face looking thunderous in the already fierce mid-July sunshine.

'Manda? What's going on?' Gina asked, as soon as she was near enough for the other woman to hear her.

'I'll tell you what's going on,' Manda burst out, her Cornish lilt growing stronger with each furious word. 'That bleddy Gorran Dew hasn't shown up yet.'

Gina glanced sideways; sure enough, the ornate silver and glass double doors that led into the Palace were uncompromisingly shut.

'I can't get into the kiosk,' Manda went on, waving at the blind-covered window of Ferrelli's. 'And we're supposed to open in three minutes. I need to get the freezers on before the rush starts.'

Polwhipple might be sleepier than a lot of other Cornish seaside towns but Ferrelli's was always popular, especially when the sun was bouncing off the waves and it promised to be a gloriously hot day. The beach already had its first families laying out deckchairs and blankets.

'Have you spoken to Ferdie?' Gina asked, dreading to think how her grandfather might react. He didn't suffer fools gladly at the best of times and Gina knew he'd have plenty of choice things to say about Gorran if he cost him business.

Manda nodded. 'Of course. But he said he'd give Gorran a ring and I've already done that. The dozy lump's not answering his phone.'

An uneasy thought sprang into Gina's mind. 'You don't think something's happened, do you? An accident, I mean.'

Manda considered this. 'Nah,' she said after a few seconds had passed. 'I reckon he overdid it at the Mermaid's Tail last night and is sleeping it off.'

As she finished speaking, Gorran hurried around the corner from the promenade, his Einstein-esque hair in even more disarray than usual. 'Sorry,' he puffed. 'Got a bit held up at home.'

'By his hangover,' Manda muttered to Gina under her breath.

He rummaged in the pocket of his crumpled trousers and pulled out a bunch of keys. Avoiding their gaze, he wrestled a key into the lock and pulled open the door. 'Sorry,' he said again, standing back as Manda swept past, and Gina saw that he was sweating. Maybe he is hungover, she thought, although there was no tell-tale smell of stale alcohol.

'Are you still okay for our meeting?' she asked him. 'There's something I need to talk to Carrie about – I can pop along to her shop now and come back here later if you'd rather.'

Gorran mopped his brow with a large white handkerchief. 'No, I'm fine. Just need to catch my breath and sit down for a minute or two.'

Gina studied him more closely. His normally florid cheeks were much less ruddy than normal and there was something behind his eyes that she couldn't pin down. He looked slightly shell-shocked. 'Let's reschedule,' she said, deciding to give him time to pull himself together. 'How about nine-thirty?'

'Perfect,' Gorran replied, and Gina thought she saw his shoulders sag in relief. With a sheepish wave, he turned and escaped into the Palace, just as Manda opened the blind of Ferrelli's and slid the window back.

'He looks like death warmed up,' she observed to Gina. 'I hope you haven't got anything important to sort out with him today.'

'Just the next screening event,' Gina assured her. 'Although I think *Dirty Dancing* will be hard to beat.'

'You'll think of something,' Manda said confidently. 'I'm starting to wonder how we ever managed without you.'

'You got along just fine,' Gina said, laughing. She checked the time and looked hopefully at the other woman. 'Is it too early for a Strawberry Sensation skinny shake?'

The door of Carrie's Attic was propped open as Gina approached five minutes later, two ice-cold milkshakes in her hands. She glanced into the window as she passed, pausing for a second to admire the polka-dot swing dress at the heart of the display, and then ducked inside the already warm shop.

Carrie was halfway up a stepladder, hanging a wide-brimmed *My Fair Lady* hat from fishing wire from the ceiling. Her assistant, Tegan, was standing underneath with a box of safety pins and a pair of scissors. Both were concentrating hard on the task at hand and had their backs to the door.

'Morning,' Gina called.

Carrie turned sharply, causing the stepladder to wobble and the hat to slip. Tegan clutched at the metal steps, steadying them as Carrie smiled. 'Hello. This is a nice surprise.'

Gina held up one of the milkshakes. 'I brought you this.' She fired an apologetic look at Tegan. 'But I didn't know you were working today so I'm afraid I only have one.'

'She can have mine,' Carrie said, reaching up to finish attaching the enormous black and white hat to the ceiling. 'Give me a minute and we can walk back to Ferrelli's for another. Unless you're here to shop?'

Gina shook her head with a regretful sigh. 'No, as gorgeous as your stock is, it's you I'm here to see.'

Once the hat was secured, Carrie climbed down and folded the steps away. Tegan took the milkshake with shy thanks and retreated behind the counter.

'You'll be okay to mind the shop for a little while, won't you?' Carrie asked her assistant.

The twenty-year-old smiled. 'Of course.'

Outside on the promenade, Carrie blew her brown fringe from her forehead. 'It's going to be a scorcher today. Ferrelli's is going to do a roaring trade.'

Gina nodded. 'And it's only going to get hotter, according to the weather forecast. I'm going over to Nonno's later, to build up our gelato stocks. Something tells me we're going to need a lot of ice-cream.'

Manda was only too pleased to whip up another milkshake. Carrie took a long sip and sighed. 'Heaven.'

They began to stroll back to the shop. Gina raised one hand to shade her eyes as she gazed at the sea, azure blue as it lapped against the golden beach at the base of the promenade wall. She fired a questioning look Gina's way. 'Fancy a quick paddle?'

Kicking off her flip-flops, Gina smiled. 'Always.'

They picked their way through the early sun-seekers to

the shore. The water was deliciously cold against Gina's hot feet. The sea was one of the things she'd miss most when she went back to London the following month, she thought, splashing through the shallows and sipping her drink. In fact, there was a lot she'd miss about Polwhipple: her family and friends, the less frantic pace of life, her work at her grandfather's dairy. There was plenty waiting for her in London, of course, but leaving Cornwall was going to be more of a wrench than she anticipated when she'd first arrived back in March. But then, she'd always found it hard to leave; the summers she'd spent as a teenager with Nonna and Nonno had been idyllic. She'd never wanted to go back to her real life then, either.

'So what did you want to see me about?' Carrie asked as they walked slowly along the shore.

Gina explained about the murder mystery evening. Carrie interrupted her as soon as she mentioned the dress code. 'Okay, I'm in. I bet I can find us some killer costumes.' She stopped and grinned. 'See what I did there?'

'Nice work,' Gina replied, laughing. 'Do you think Davey might be interested?'

Carrie walked along in silence for a moment. 'I don't know. He's been working in Chester – we haven't spoken for a few weeks.'

Her voice sounded unruffled but Gina wasn't fooled. 'But I thought everything was going so well,' she said, nonplussed. 'I thought you really liked each other.'

'So did I,' Carrie said, with a sigh. 'But we both must have read too much into it because he's gone all quiet on me. I suppose it's just because he's busy, but it doesn't take much to fire off a message, does it? I'm not expecting *War and Peace*.' She kicked at the water and sighed again. 'Men.'

Gina frowned. She didn't know Davey very well but he hadn't seemed like the type to play games. 'It's probably just work. Ben says there's more info on the Railway Preservation Society website – why don't you send Davey a link?'

And then Ben can follow up and see what the problem is, she added mentally.

'Okay,' Carrie said. She looked pensive for a moment, then her expression brightened. 'I do love the 1920s fashions. You should persuade Gorran to show *The Great Gatsby* at the Palace – the Baz Luhrmann version, obviously – then we could turn the whole place into a speakeasy.'

'It's too recent to be a classic,' Gina replied. 'Although it is a gorgeous-looking film and I love the speakeasy idea. There are loads of other famous films set during Prohibition – *Bugsy Malone*, *The Untouchables*, *Midnight in Paris*.'

Carrie pursed her lips. 'What's that old black-and-white movie – the one where the two musicians dress up as women and join a band?'

Gina thought for a heartbeat, casting her mind back to her teenage years when she'd spent many a rainy Sunday afternoon on Nonna's sofa, watching classic movies. '*Some Like It Hot*?' She took a slow sip of her milkshake. 'That definitely qualifies and it's full of cosplay opportunities – there's plenty of overlap with the murder mystery theme.'

'Plenty of cross-dressing opportunities too,' Carrie said, sliding Gina an amused sideways look. 'I'd pay good money to see the men of Polwhipple in high heels and dresses.'

'Some of them, anyway,' Gina replied, trying and failing to imagine Gorran in drag. She considered the film; from what she remembered, it was brilliantly funny. Marilyn Monroe lit up the screen as the unlucky-in-love singer, Sugar Kane, but it was the male stars, Jack Lemmon and Tony Curtis, who really stole the show. Part of the action was set aboard a steam train, which dovetailed neatly with the opening of Polwhipple's station – they'd be able to cross-promote both events. It was perfect, Gina decided with a fizzle of satisfaction. All she needed to do now was convince Gorran.

She glanced across at Carrie. 'You'd better start sourcing large ladies' shoes and gangster spats.'

The other woman pulled out her phone. 'Consider it done.' Her mouth quirked into a grin. 'I think Ben would make a marvellous Daphne.'

The thought of Ben's muscular frame squeezed into a dress almost made Gina snort. 'Don't buy anything yet – I still have to persuade Gorran it's a good idea.'

'Are you kidding?' Carrie said, scrolling through images. 'A black-and-white classic film starring actors who are all dead? He's going to love it!'

Carrie was right: Gorran loved the thought of screening *Some Like it Hot.*

'It's a masterpiece,' he said when Gina suggested it. 'Way

ahead of its time. Did you know that the director, Billy Wilder, insisted on shooting it in black and white instead of Technicolor because Jack Lemmon and Tony Curtis looked too ugly in colour?'

Gina laughed. 'I didn't know that. So you're happy to go ahead?'

'Of course,' Gorran said, rubbing his hands together. 'I think I might have a copy of it in the archives. Want to pick a date?'

They compared diaries.

'How about here?' Gina said, pointing to the second Saturday in August. 'That gives us four weeks to pull everything together and should allow us time to spread the word at the murder mystery evening too. I'll ask Ben to speak to the Preservation Society.'

Gorran threw her a grateful look. 'Thanks. I don't know how I'm going to manage when you go back to London. I might have to lock you in the projection room so you can't leave!'

He was smiling as he spoke but Gina picked up more than a little panic behind the words. 'You're going to be fine,' she reassured him. 'And I'm not falling off the face of the planet – I'll still be able to give you advice.'

Doubt shadowed his eyes as he nodded. 'Of course. It's just –'

Gina leaned forwards. 'You've been running this place for years, Gorran. You do know what you're doing – all I've brought is a pinch of inspiration.'

'You've done a lot more than that – thanks to you, the Palace has a bright future ahead of her.' He rubbed at his forehead, looking tired. 'I'm just not sure I'm the best person to manage it, that's all.'

'Of course you are,' Gina said, frowning. 'You and the Palace are inseparable. You're like Bogart and Bacall.'

Gorran let out a reluctant-sounding laugh. 'You're very kind, but we both know I've lurched from one almost-disaster to another. And when I think about what you've achieved in just a few months . . .' He shook his head. 'It makes me wonder whether I'm too old, that's all.'

Gina studied him in alarm. She'd never seen him so defeated. 'Rubbish,' she said briskly, casting around for more famous cinematic partnerships. 'You're Thelma and Louise.'

He gave her a grim look. 'That's exactly what I'm afraid of.'

# Chapter Thirty-One

The beach at Mawgan Porth was one of Gina's favourite places, especially early in the morning. She'd come to recognise most of the surfers she saw and, thanks to Ben, she was on first name terms with the regulars; he'd introduced her to some of his friends whenever they bumped into each other on the sand. Today, however, the surfers were outnumbered by the bodies on the beach, despite it being seven-thirty on a Monday morning.

Gina waited beside Nonna's mat, her feet sinking into the already warm sand, and tried not to panic as her seventy-something grandmother rolled her body into a perfect headstand. Elena did yoga several times a week and Gina knew there was no reason to worry but folding an elderly body into a downward dog was one thing – lifting her legs into a headstand was something else.

'You really don't need to hover,' Elena murmured. 'I've been doing this since before you were born.'

Gina glanced around. There were eighteen other students on the beach – some were balancing independently; Gina assumed these were the hard-core regular attendees. Others were working in pairs, helping their partner to balance. And that was something else to worry about, because Gina was under no illusions about her own yoga abilities – what if she accidentally kicked Nonna in the face while trying to get into position when it was her turn? She'd carry the guilt for the rest of her life. Not to mention what her grandfather would say . . .

Doing her best to relax, Gina stepped back a fraction. 'I know,' she told Nonna. 'I have no idea how you manage it.'

Elena closed her eyes. 'Practice, core stability and a good centre of gravity.'

She took a long, deep breath. Then, as the teacher called out more instructions, she lowered her legs and stretched into the child pose. Around them, Gina saw the others do the same. After a few more moments, Nonna sat up. 'Your turn.'

Gina smothered a groan and bent her head to rest it on the sand. Feeling her muscles protest, she pulled her knees into her chest and lifted them into a wobbling headstand that was nowhere near as graceful as her grandmother's.

'Steady,' Nonna said. 'Find your balance. Now lift.'

Gina knew she'd fall long before she actually toppled. For one amazing moment, she managed to straighten her legs and point her toes but then Elena started to cough. The sound broke Gina's concentration and she felt herself start to slide. She fought to balance but it was a lost cause; she was going down. With an involuntary squeak, she leaned left to avoid Nonna and allowed herself to crumple into an undignified heap in the sand beside her other neighbour.

Blushing, she got to her feet. 'I don't think I'm cut out for yoga.'

'Nonsense,' Elena said, patting her chest as though trying to clear it. 'You just need to work on your balance, that's all. Again.'

'Are you okay?' Gina asked, frowning slightly. 'That cough sounds painful.'

Nonna waved away her concern. 'I'm fine. It's just the tail end of that cold Nonno and I both had a few weeks ago.' Her eyes narrowed. 'Don't think you can distract me, Gina Callaway. Try the headstand again.'

It took Gina three more attempts but she finally mastered the pose. Elena gave her arm a warm squeeze at the end of the lesson. 'See? I knew you could do it.'

They were making their way across the steps that led to the top of the cliff when Gina heard someone shout her name. She looked up to see Ben jogging towards them, his surfboard tucked under one arm. Like all the serious surfers at the beach, he was wearing a wetsuit, in spite of the hot sun, and Gina knew it was for protection; the sea floor could cause some nasty grazes.

'Hi,' she said, shielding her eyes from the sun. 'Fancy seeing you here.'

He grinned. 'I know – total shock, right?' Still smiling, he turned to Gina's grandmother. 'Good morning, Mrs Ferrelli.'

'Oh please, call me Elena,' she said, returning his smile. 'We are all friends now.'

Ben nodded. 'Okay – good morning, Elena. Enjoyable session?'

Gina felt her cheeks begin to grow warm; she hoped he hadn't seen her humiliating tumbles into the sand. But there was nothing in his expression except interest – no hidden spark of amusement.

'Of course,' Elena replied. 'Yoga is good for the mind as well as the body.'

'You'll get no argument from me,' Ben said easily. 'Most of the surfers I know practise yoga – balance is something you need plenty of when you're surfing. In fact, they even do yoga on stand-up paddle boards over at Newquay harbour – me and the guys sometimes go.' He glanced at Gina. 'You should come along next time.'

She laughed. 'Not a chance – remember what happened the last time I let you talk me into getting on a surfboard?'

She'd belly-flopped into the sea, aged fifteen, in front of what felt like every surfer on the Cornish scene and had vowed never to set foot on a board again. 'Come on, Gina, that was sixteen years ago,' Ben said, his lips quirking. 'We were just kids. You'll be much better now.'

'Don't count on it,' Gina muttered under her breath.

Elena's eyes gleamed. 'You should go. It will be good for you.'

There was a mischievous twinkle behind her smile and Gina couldn't tell whether her grandmother was picturing her falling into the sea or trying to force her into spending more time with Ben; either was possible.

'No,' she said firmly.

'I could give you a surf lesson or two beforehand,' Ben suggested.

'If you don't think Max would mind,' Elena cut in.

If only you knew, Gina thought ruefully. It wasn't as though she wanted to go surfing, and yet Nonna's comment had riled her a little; Max didn't tell her what she could and couldn't do and she didn't like the implication that he did. 'It's got nothing to do with him.'

Elena raised her eyebrows. 'Then you are afraid.'

'I'm not afraid,' Gina said, staring in exasperation. 'I don't want to, that's all. Surfing isn't my thing.'

'If you are too scared to fail then you will never grow,' Elena said with a faintly dismissive sniff.

'I'm not afraid to fail,' Gina said, stung. She turned to Ben. 'All right, you're on. Tell me where and when and I'll be there.'

He looked back and forth between her and Elena, then shrugged. 'Okay. I know a little bay not far from here – the waves don't get very high so it's not popular with other surfers. How about seven o'clock tomorrow morning?'

Aware of her grandmother's doubting gaze, Gina raised her chin. 'Fine. You'll need to lend me a board, though. And a wetsuit.'

'Leave it with me,' he said. 'I'll pick you up just before seven, if that's okay?'

'Perfect,' Gina said. 'See you then.'

As she turned to walk away, she saw Ben and Elena exchange a conspiratorial look. Was it her imagination or did her grandmother actually wink? What had she let herself in for?

Ferdie seemed unsurprised when Gina described her suspected entrapment at the beach. He leaned back against a stool in the dairy, crutches resting against the stainless-steel work top, and shook his head.

'Your grandmother is a wonderful woman but I often think she missed her true calling,' he said. 'Still, MI5's loss is our gain and it's not as though you won't enjoy the lesson.'

The idea of Elena as a spy caused the last vestiges of Gina's irritation to melt away; she could picture her petite, raven-haired grandmother telling all the other operatives what to do and feeding them biscotti. She stirred the vast saucepan of vanilla custard and sighed. 'I suppose you're right.'

'Speaking of enjoyment, what are you doing next Monday afternoon?'

Gina summoned up a mental image of her diary. 'Nothing much. Why?'

Ferdie fixed her with a thoughtful look. 'There's a shop to let on the harbour in Newquay. I thought we could take a look together.'

'A shop?' Gina said, almost dropping her spoon. Nonno was famously resistant to any kind of change – why did he want to look at a shop? 'Okay – who are you and what have you done with my grandfather?'

'Ferrelli's is doing well so it seems like good business sense to think about expanding,' he said, shrugging. 'But it's just an idea.'

It was an excellent idea, Gina thought, and one Nonna had been encouraging for years. But no one had ever expected Ferdie to agree, let alone take steps to make it happen. 'I'd love to come,' she said. 'As long as I survive the surf lesson tomorrow.'

He smiled. 'You'd better. We have a large order of Triple Chocolate Delight to deliver by the end of this week.'

Gina started to stir the custard again and gave a wry shake of her head. 'I'm glad you've got your priorities straight, Nonno.'

Corlyn Cove was less than a twenty-minute drive from Mawgan Porth. The sun was still low in the sky when Ben and Gina arrived, bathing the tops of the surrounding cliffs in a golden glow and causing the ocean to twinkle as though it was spread with a million tiny lights.

The bay itself was half-shadowed as Gina waded into the shallows in her borrowed wetsuit.

'The trick is to start small,' Ben said once the water was over their knees. He laid his surfboard flat on the gently lapping waves. 'Hop on and get used to paddling around.'

Gina did as she was told. She lay flat on the board, feeling it rise and fall with the tide, and tried not to remember the last time she'd attempted surfing. She'd been too impatient to bother with this stage back then; she'd wanted to stand up and ride the waves like Ben did and she'd refused to listen when he'd told her to take things slowly. It wasn't a mistake she intended to make again.

'Now use your hands to move further out,' he instructed. 'The tide will try to push you back to the shore so you'll need to be stronger.'

Gina quelled a sudden flutter of anxiety. Cupping her hands, she dipped them into the sea and paddled. The tip of the board rose as she crested each small wave and it felt as though she was going backwards faster than she could push forwards. Gritting her teeth, she paddled harder.

'I'm not going to need a gym session after this,' she said, as her arm muscles started to burn.

'No,' Ben replied. 'It's a surprisingly good workout. Okay, that's far enough. Now turn the board around and let the tide carry you back to the shore.'

Using one hand, she turned and was gratified to see how much distance she'd covered; the shore was a good twenty metres away. But the next moment, the board was caught by a wave that carried her back to the shallows. She slid to a graceful halt as it ground smoothly against the sand.

'Good work,' Ben said, splashing back to her. 'Let's try that again.'

They repeated the same actions several times, and Gina realised with a jolt that she'd forgotten to feel anxious; in fact, she was enjoying herself. Ben was a good teacher – patient and calming. She was in safe hands with him.

'Ready to take things up a notch?' he asked, looking pleased with her progress.

'What do you mean?' she said warily.

He grinned. 'Don't look so panicky – I'm not going to make you flip a 180 just yet. But you could try kneeling on the board if you want to.'

Gina scanned the beach – it was empty. There was no one there to watch her fall off. She swallowed. 'Okay.'

Ben showed her what to do. Instead of staying flat on her stomach as she rode the board back to shore, she needed to kneel up as soon as she'd turned it around. Her fingers turned white with the effort of clinging to the board but she managed it and the rush of satisfaction when she stayed on was immense.

'All right!' Ben said, wading through the shallows to join her. 'That was great. How are you feeling?'

'Good!' she said, beaming at him. 'I can see why you love this so much.'

His eyes sparkled. 'Wait until you grab your first air. Then you'll really be hooked.'

'Let's not get carried away,' Gina said, laughing. 'I can't even stand up at the moment.'

She practised kneeling on the board until she felt steady enough to leave her hands flat against the board's surface instead of gripping the sides. She was almost disappointed when Ben told her it was time to call it a day. 'The wind is getting up,' he said, pointing to the white-tipped waves rolling in from further out to sea. 'You don't want to get out of your depth.'

'But I haven't even stood up on the board,' she objected.

He smiled. 'Well, I'm hoping we can save that for another day. If you're up for another lesson, that is?'

Pushing her disappointment away, Gina nodded. She wasn't sure whether it was Ben's expert guidance or the adrenaline rush from riding the waves, however modestly, but she was really starting to understand the appeal of surfing. 'This has been fun. I'm in.'

Ben looked pleased. 'Good. And well done – you're a much better student than you used to be.'

She slid from the board and stood beside him in the shallows. 'Or maybe you're a better teacher,' she teased, smiling up at him.

His eyes flickered with something unreadable. 'Maybe we've both changed.'

They stood gazing at each other for a moment, then a wave buffeted their legs, causing them both to sway. 'Time to go and dry off,' Ben said, reaching past Gina to lift his board from the water.

She hadn't taken more than a few steps when she felt something rough underfoot. An agonising pain shot through the sole of her foot. She staggered on until she reached shallower waters and then sank to the sand to examine it. Red blossomed from an inch-long graze.

'What's wrong?' Ben asked, frowning. His eyes widened when he saw the blood. 'You're hurt.'

Gina winced as she prodded the injury. 'I think I trod on a rock.'

He dropped his surfboard on the sand and knelt to

examine her foot. 'Ouch, that's a nasty laceration.' He cupped his hand into the sea and trickled water over the wound. 'But it looks fairly clean – I can't see any sand or grit caught underneath.'

She tried not to blanch at the strips of shredded skin dangling from the rest of her foot. 'It bloody well hurts.'

Ben looked up, sympathy etched on his face. 'Believe me, I know. Most surfers have feet like leather but I've still had plenty of cuts and grazes in the past. We should get you some painkillers and bandage this up – the salt water will be numbing some of the pain but it's no substitute for ibuprofen.'

Nodding, Gina forced herself to stand up.

'Here, let me help,' Ben said, holding out his arm for her to grip. She took it and balanced on one leg, the toes of her hurt foot resting on the ground. 'Ready?'

'Ready,' Gina replied, grimacing as she took a step and her weight shifted onto the injured leg. Fresh blood oozed onto the sand. 'Ow. Ow ow ow.'

They stopped. Ben scanned the beach ahead of them, as though judging the distance to his van. 'This isn't going to work – it's too far.' He hesitated then glanced sideways at her. 'I could carry you.'

It was such a ridiculous suggestion that Gina let out a short, incredulous bark of laughter. 'No, you really couldn't. Not unless you want to put your back out.'

Ben tilted his head, assessing her. 'You're tiny, Gina. I don't think my back is in any danger.'

'You only think I'm thin,' she said. 'I've been eating Nonna's cooking for four months – trust me, I am not tiny.'

He bent down to examine her foot once more. Blood dripped from her toes. 'I don't think we've got much choice. I don't have a first-aid kit in the van so I can't bandage it here and you can't walk.' His mouth twisted into a wry smile. 'You're also polluting the beach a bit.'

He had a point, Gina thought, a cold dose of reality washing over her; there wasn't much choice. She almost groaned at the idea of being lugged like a sack of potatoes up the beach. It was going to be even more embarrassing than the last time she'd tried surfing. 'But your board –' she began, launching one final protest.

'I'll come back for it,' Ben said reasonably. 'And I promise not to drop you.'

Gina stared at him, wishing a giant wave would come and swallow her up. Eventually, she managed a reluctant nod. 'Okay.'

Bending, he slid one arm beneath her arms and slipped the other around the back of her legs. 'You'll – uh – need to put your arms around my neck.'

*Oh God, he was right.* Hoping her cheeks weren't burning as much as she thought they were, Gina did as he suggested. Seconds later, he'd swept her easily off the ground. 'All right?' he asked, glancing down at her.

'Fine,' she said, dying a little at the squeak in her voice as he started to walk. It was a scene straight out of a romantic movie, she thought as her heart thudded in her chest at the thought – *An Officer and a Gentleman* or *From Here to Eternity*. Except that Ben was her oldest friend, not a romantic hero. And she most definitely was not a luminous leading lady.

It was the first time in her adult life that she'd been entirely lifted off her feet by someone else and she was surprised by how effortless Ben made it seem. She'd expected him to tire quickly but instead he strode easily up the beach, his arms encircling her, and she never felt even the tiniest wobble. If this was a film, she'd rest her head against his shoulder, she thought, and her muscles tensed at the thought.

'Everything okay?' Ben asked, picking up on her tension. 'Am I hurting you?'

She looked up. His summer-blue eyes were filled with concern. 'No,' she said, her heart beating faster. 'Not at all.'

He smiled. She waited until he'd looked away to close her eyes. Being in Ben's arms was awakening all kinds of feelings she'd fought hard to suppress since returning to Polwhipple. If she lifted her hands, she could stroke the fine blond hair at the base of his neck. If she reached up higher, she could pull his head to meet hers in a kiss. Her eyes snapped open as she struggled to banish the idea. He'd almost certainly drop her if she did that. And all of Max's suspicions would have been proved right.

She was both relieved and sorry when they reached the van and he lowered her carefully to the ground. Wincing, she tried not to put any weight on her foot; the throbbing pain seemed to have doubled now that she was standing up again.

'Here, sit down,' Ben said, pulling the van door open and spreading a towel over the seat. 'There's not much room for you to keep your leg elevated but at least you don't live miles away. Unless you'd rather we went to the Minor Injuries clinic in Newquay?'

Gina shook her head; she didn't want to waste anyone's time, least of all Ben's. 'It looks worse than it is,' she said, lifting her legs carefully into the passenger seat foot-well. 'A plaster and some painkillers will sort me out.'

Ben glanced at the wounded foot, which she'd lifted so that it rested on top of her other knee. 'I think it's going to need more than a plaster. Have you got a first-aid kit at home?'

She nodded, easing the hand-towel she'd brought under her foot. 'I think so.'

'First order of business is to get you home,' he said, reaching for the door to close it. 'We'll worry about everything else afterwards.'

# Chapter Thirty-Two

It wasn't until they pulled up outside Gina's apartment block that she started to consider how she was going to get to her second-floor flat. There was no lift, just four flights of stairs to be negotiated.

Ben saw her worried expression and followed her gaze to the door. 'I could always carry you again,' he offered.

Wrapping the hand-towel firmly around the injury, Gina shook her head. 'The stairs are too narrow.'

He grinned. 'Piggy-back?'

'I'll walk, thanks,' she replied, laughing. 'Or take it one step at a time on my bum if I have to.'

She'd almost forgotten they were both still in their wet-suits; when Ben appeared to open the van door she got an eyeful of well-defined ab muscles sculpted in black neoprene. She blinked and looked hurriedly down, which reminded her that she hadn't changed either. She knew none of her neighbours would bat an eyelid – the block was filled with holiday lets and she'd seen plenty of surfers come and go, tempted by the proximity to Mawgan Porth beach. Most of them had put their wetsuits on before leaving their apartments; it saved them leaving clothes on the beach where they might go missing.

'Take it slowly,' Ben said once he'd pulled back the passenger side door. He offered her an arm. 'Lean on me.'

They made their way into the block. Gina clenched her teeth and tried not to grip Ben's arm as she hobbled along; who knew a graze could hurt so much? By the time they'd reached the stairs, more blood had started to seep through the hand-towel.

'Piggy-back,' Ben instructed. 'No arguments. The more you walk on that foot, the more damage you're going to do.'

Gina folded her arms. 'I'm not five. You are not giving me a piggy-back.'

'Climb up a couple of steps,' he said, pointing at the staircase. 'It'll be easier for you to get on.'

'I'm not getting on,' she insisted. 'Like I said, I'll go up on my bottom.'

She sat down and started to push her way up the stairs but stopped when the pain made her cry out.

Ben fixed her with a sympathetic gaze. 'Look, I know it's not glamorous, but we need to get you upstairs somehow and no one ever needs to know.' He made a cross over his heart. 'I promise I'll take the secret to my grave – surfers' honour.'

She glared at him. 'That's not a thing! You just made it up.'

'Surfers are very honourable,' Ben said, trying his hardest to look wounded. 'I really won't tell anyone.'

Gina stared at her foot for a moment and then sighed. 'I'll know if you do,' she warned. 'Come on, let's get it over with.'

In the end, the journey was surprisingly smooth; only Gina's dignity was bruised and that was soothed the moment Ben set her down inside her own apartment.

'First-aid kit?' he asked.

'In the bathroom, under the sink,' she replied.

Ben worked with practised efficiency, cleansing and then dressing Gina's foot with a skill that would have put a nurse to shame. 'You've done this before,' Gina said, watching him wrap cool white bandages over the pristine dressing.

He pulled a face. 'Once or twice. Like I said, cuts and grazes are all part of being a surfer. I've seen friends lose teeth when they've collided with their own boards – it's not a sport for the faint-hearted.'

Helping her up, he offered her his arm once again. 'Why don't you get changed while I find you some painkillers?'

It felt good to be out of the wetsuit. Gina did her best to wash the worst of the sand and salt away – she needed a shower or a bath to do the job properly but she knew both were a bad idea while her injury was still bleeding; the heat would only make things worse. Once he'd settled her onto the sofa, with her leg elevated, Ben handed her a glass of water with two ibuprofen.

'Mind if I get changed too?' he asked. 'I've got some clean clothes in the car.'

Gina lay back against the sofa and closed her eyes. 'No problem. I'll be here when you've finished.'

When she woke an hour later, she found Ben had been busy. Not only had he called Nonno to explain what had happened and let him know Gina would be off her feet for a few days but he'd cleared away the cereal bowl from her hurried breakfast before she'd left that morning and made them both steaming mugs of tea.

'You really are amazing,' she said, smiling as he passed her one.

'I'm not – I'm being a friend,' Ben said, then paused. 'So, since I can't very well abandon you here on your own all day, what movie do you want to watch?'

She frowned. 'Don't you need to go to work?'

'Not today,' he replied. 'Since it's practically my fault you're injured, it's only right that I spend the day looking after you.'

The warm look he gave her made her own cheeks feel rosy and she felt a rush of affection. She couldn't imagine Max taking a day off to nurse her through anything, even before they'd hit crisis point.

'It was an accident,' she reminded him.

'One you wouldn't have had if I hadn't dragged you to the beach,' he said. 'So I'm afraid you're stuck with me.'

'Well in that case, I've got a treat for you,' she said, reaching for the TV remote control. 'Have you ever seen a movie called *Some Like it Hot*?'

*

'That was excellent,' Ben announced as the end credits rolled. 'Jack Lemmon was incredible – so funny.'

Gina smiled. 'We're going to be showing it at the Palace next month,' she told him. 'Cross-dressing is optional, of course.'

'That sounds a lot like a gauntlet being slammed down,' he replied, his gaze enthusiastic. 'One I don't think I'm going to be able to resist.'

'I was hoping you'd say that,' Gina said, delighted. 'I have high hopes for this screening – it could be the best one yet.'

'Count me in,' he said. 'I don't know what Polwhipple is going to do for fun when you go back to London, Gina.'

'You'll manage,' she said, glancing away.

Ben cleared his throat. 'Actually, I might not have to. I've – erm – been offered a job somewhere else. In London, to be exact.'

Gina felt her forehead crease. 'What kind of a job? Where in London?'

'Putney,' he said. 'An Elizabethan manor house that's been taken over by the National Trust. They say it's almost derelict and they're assembling a team of experts to help restore it, starting in September.'

Her frown deepened. It would be very strange knowing Ben was living and working in London; he was part of her Polwhipple life. She wasn't at all sure where – or if – he'd fit into her other life. 'That's great,' she said, doing her best to sound encouraging.

Ben raised his shoulders in a shrug. 'I haven't said I'll do it yet.' He glanced across but didn't quite meet her eyes. 'It sort of depends on what you plan to do.'

'Me?' Gina repeated, even though she suspected she knew what his answer would be. 'What's it got to do with me?'

'I know things have gone pretty well at the dairy,' Ben began. 'And obviously, you've revitalised the Palace – the screenings you've held have been a huge success. In fact, it wouldn't be a total surprise if you stuck around.'

An image of Ferdie in his dairy popped into Gina's head. If he went ahead and expanded the business to include the shop in Newquay, he'd need her help even more than he had when she'd first arrived. And then she thought of Max; unhappy Max who said he missed her and wanted her to come home. She sighed. 'I don't think I can stay, Ben. I've already stayed longer than I planned and my life is in London.'

He nodded. 'That's what I thought you'd say. So do you think Max would mind you showing me around the city, if I took this job?'

Max would blow a fuse, Gina thought, but she would find it much easier to leave Cornwall behind if she knew Ben was going to be living in London too. 'No,' she said, crossing her fingers where he couldn't see. 'That wouldn't be a problem. But what about Polwhipple station? Don't you want to enjoy it once the line re-opens?'

'Of course,' he said. 'But I've finished restoring it now and the National Trust place is a great opportunity. I'm always up for a new challenge.'

Gina smiled. 'It sounds amazing – of course you should

do it. And on a purely selfish note, it means I get to hang out with you more, which can only be a good thing.'

She didn't think Max would see it like that, but the only way she could make him happy would be to promise never to see Ben again. And that wasn't something Gina was prepared to do.

She called Max that evening, telling herself it wasn't a guilty conscience that made her pick up the phone. Usually when she rang in the evening, she caught him out for drinks or dinner with business associates so she was slightly taken aback when he answered with no background noise to muffle his voice.

'Don't tell me you're at home,' she said, once they'd said hello. 'Wonders will never cease.'

He didn't laugh. 'I know you think my life is one long party but there is more to me than that,' he said and Gina cringed at the coldness of his tone. 'Like I told you last time you were here, I'm growing up.'

He had told her that, she recalled, and a few days later, he'd proposed. She still remembered the sense of unreality that had settled over her when she'd found the diamond ring nestled among the after-dinner chocolates. She glanced towards her bedroom, where the ring now lay in her jewellery box. Would they ever get back to how things had been that night? Did she want to?

'It's nice to be able to hear you properly for once,' she said and instantly regretted the final two words.

There was a brief pause. 'You too,' Max said gruffly.

'So, how are things with you?' she asked and listened as he talked about business deals and clients whose names were unfamiliar. Had she ever been interested in this stuff, she wondered, or was it the distance that made it all seem so samey?

Forcing herself to tune back in, she took a deep breath. 'But what have you been up to apart from work?' she cut in, midway through a story about a property deal that had fallen through. 'What have you done for fun?'

Max fell silent. 'I played squash with James Wendover yesterday,' he said after a moment's thought.

Gina raised her eyebrows. 'Isn't he one of your financiers?'

'That's right.'

'And did you let him win, to keep him sweet?'

Max didn't reply.

'Then it doesn't count as fun,' Gina said firmly. 'It's still work. What else?'

'I visited my parents at the weekend,' he said. 'They send their love.'

Gina hesitated. Was that meant to be a dig? She and Max had been meant to go and visit his parents together, to tell them about the engagement. That was unlikely to ever happen now.

'Did you – you didn't tell them about the engagement, did you?'

Max let out a heavy sigh. 'No, of course not. What's the

point in getting their hopes up? Let's be honest, there's more chance of hell freezing over than there is of us setting a date.'

Now it was Gina's turn to stay silent. He sounded so angry.

Max sighed again. 'I'm sorry, that was out of order. It's just hard to sort all this out when you're so far away, Gina.'

She closed her eyes. 'I know.'

'Tell me what you've been doing,' Max said, and she could tell he was making an effort.

She thought carefully before answering. She couldn't talk about her injured foot, because he would want to know how it had happened and that would mean mentioning Ben, which would cause him to explode. She didn't dare tell him that Ferdie was considering expanding Ferrelli's – that might make Max question her commitment to leaving Polwhipple. But she could talk about the *Some Like it Hot* screening, she mused – nothing to land her in hot water there.

'Sounds great,' Max said, once she'd finished describing her plans. 'I might see if I can sneak away and come along. If you want me to.'

'Please do,' Gina said. 'I'll save you a VIP slot at one of the speakeasy tables. You haven't seen the place since we finished the refurbishment – I think you're going to love it.'

'I wouldn't say love it,' Max said in a dry voice. 'You know how I feel about the cinema.'

She did; Max hated the cinema and had never taken her on a date to see a film, something her friends found hard to believe. It hadn't bothered Gina for a long time but now his aversion to films was something else to trouble her, another warning sign. Polwhipple's cinema had become such a big part of her life in recent months and Max had always stayed on the periphery.

'But the Palace was a magnificent building before the refurbishment,' Max went on. 'I bet it's even more impressive now.'

Gina smiled, grateful he was making an effort to appreciate the hard work that had gone into the project. 'I think it is,' she said, picturing the Art Deco swirls Ben had carefully restored in the screening room and the new seats they'd sourced together. 'A lot of love has gone into bringing the Palace back to glory.'

'I know,' Max said. Silence grew, making Gina wonder if he resented how much care she'd lavished on the cinema. He cleared his throat. 'And how's Gorran doing? Are his finances less tumultuous now?'

Gina shifted uncomfortably; the cinema owner had asked her not to discuss his money worries with anyone else. But this was Max, she told herself; who among his social and business circles was he going to tell? Who would care?

'I hope so,' she said, keeping her tone as natural as she could. 'But with Gorran it's hard to tell. He always looks like—'

'He's down to his last slice of bread?' Max interrupted in a sardonic voice.

'He's lost a fight with a hairbrush, I was going to say,' Gina finished. She tried to ignore the little spark of annoyance growing inside of her; did he always have to be so disparaging about anything to do with Polwhipple? 'But Gorran knows a lot more than any of us about keeping the Palace going.'

'You're right,' Max said, almost immediately. 'He's not a complete buffoon. Just incompetent where money is involved, which isn't the best trait in an employer.'

Something about his tone caught Gina's attention. A few weeks earlier, Gorran had berated her for telling Rose Arundell about his personal financial affairs. Gina hadn't told Rose, and Ben swore he hadn't breathed a word. It was a mystery Gina hadn't managed to get to the bottom of and now another suspicion had occurred to her. Max had known exactly why they'd had to arrange an emergency screening; Gina had confided in him about Gorran's money troubles. Could it have been Max who shared Gorran's secret with Rose? They did know each other, after all . . .

Gina shook the thought away. I've been watching too many Jason Bourne movies, she decided. 'It was just a one-off, Max,' she said, fighting her sense of unease. 'He's doing much better now the Palace has re-opened.'

The conversation started to dry up but it was Max who took the initiative and ended the call. Gina sat gazing at her phone for a few long moments after they'd finished talking, then struggled to her feet and hobbled across the room, using the furniture as impromptu crutches. Ben was right; surfing was a good workout. What she needed was a bath to soak away the ache of her muscles and nothing, not even a heavily bandaged foot, was going to stop her.

# Chapter Thirty-Three

On the following Monday afternoon, Gina and Ferdie headed over to Newquay. The empty shop Ferdie had heard about was in prime position, right on the harbour-front. It had clearly been a hairdresser's in its previous life: Gina could see the sinks on one side and long mirrors that lined the other wall. The décor was dingy and a little tired but even so, it had potential and its most important attribute was its location; the busy harbour was thronging with tourists. Only Fistral Beach would be more perfect and Gina knew there was at least one ice-cream shop there already.

'What do you think?' she asked Ferdie as they explored the inside of the shop.

He grunted. 'There's not enough room to swing a cat in that kitchen – we couldn't make gelato here. We'd have to increase production in the main dairy and transport it across.'

'But it's full of possibilities,' she said. 'Imagine a long counter over there, filled with Napoli pans of the famous

Ferrelli's flavours, and a service window like the one at the Palace so not all the customers have to come inside. There'd be room for some booths along this wall, with a few tables and chairs just here and some more on the pavement.' She turned to Nonno, her enthusiasm bubbling over. 'We could serve coffee with Nonna's biscotti, and milkshakes and sundaes. It could be amazing.'

Ferdie turned on his crutches and gazed around, as though seeing through her eyes. 'Perhaps. It sounds like a lot of work.'

'Initially, yes,' Gina agreed. 'But you could bring in a project manager to handle the shop fitting. And you could promote Manda – I bet she'd jump at the chance to run this place for you.'

'We'd need more flavours,' he said.

Gina spread her hands wide, thinking of her grandmother's thick book of handwritten recipes. 'Nonna has plenty of ideas – she'd be happy to share them with you if you ask her. You could design a whole new range, especially for this shop.' She waved a hand at the window, at the crowds of tourists milling around the harbour. 'They'd lap it up.'

Now Ferdie fixed her with a direct look, his salt-and-pepper eyebrows bristling together. 'I can't do it alone, Gina. Will you help?'

She gazed at him, some of her enthusiasm fading. She'd half-suspected this was coming. 'You know I'd love to, Nonno.' She took a deep breath and ploughed on. 'But I can't keep working for free – I need to earn a living. And then there's Max—'

'So become part of the business,' he interrupted. 'Not an employee – a partner, with a proper salary. You've done so much to help that it's only right you are rewarded.'

Gina gazed at him, torn between delight that he valued her contribution so much and anxiety over her relationship. 'But what about Max? Being in Polwhipple has put a real strain on us.'

Ferdie frowned. 'No one is saying you have to be here every day. Go back to London if you need to, and manage things from there.'

Her head began to whirl. Could it work? Could she help to expand the Ferrelli's empire at a distance? 'I can't make gelato in London,' she pointed out. 'And you're going to need a lot more of that – how will you cope with the increased demand?'

'I'll employ someone else,' he suggested. 'Train them up. Maybe I could get one of those apprentices I've heard so much about at the Rotary Club.'

'I don't know,' Gina said. 'I mean, of course you can train some new staff and even take on an apprentice. I just don't know whether I can give you what you need.'

Ferdie came towards her. 'Don't decide now – just think about it. And if you decide you can't do it, there'll be no hard feelings.'

His smile was so kind that Gina felt tears prickle at the back of her eyes. He was doing this for her, to give her a reason to stay in Polwhipple if she wanted to and while she didn't suppose that was his only motivation, it was still a generous thing for him to offer. And he was right; he couldn't do it on his own.

'Okay, I'll think about it,' she said, returning his smile. 'I'm sure we can work something out.'

'That's my girl,' Ferdie said, patting her hand. 'Now, why don't we take a walk over to the beach while we're here? It can't hurt to check out the competition, no?'

Gina laughed, grateful the cut on her foot was so much better. 'And you say Nonna is ruthless . . .'

'I'm not sure I'm cut out to be a flapper.'

Carrie stepped out from behind the curtain of the changing room in Carrie's Attic and gestured at the tassel-covered black dress she wore. 'Did these women even have hips?'

Gina smiled. It was seven o'clock on Wednesday evening and they were trying on their outfits for Friday's murder mystery evening. 'I think it looks great.'

'No, yours looks great,' Carrie said gloomily, eyeing Gina's sequined, drop-waisted dress with envy. 'Mine looks like two hippos got tangled up in a lampshade factory.'

'It really doesn't,' Gina said. She handed Carrie a plastic cigarette holder. 'You look like a *femme fatale*, totally capable of murder.'

Carrie's expression lifted. 'And you look like you've just stepped off the set of *The Great Gatsby*. That fascinator is so perfectly Daisy Buchanan.'

Gina raised a hand to touch the silver headband Carrie had

found for her on Etsy. 'It's amazing. I'm looking forward to Friday.'

'Me too,' Carrie said, jiggling around to make her tassels dance. 'It's a shame Davey can't make it – I hope you don't mind me tagging along with you and Ben.'

'Mind?' Gina repeated. 'Why would I mind?'

Carrie avoided her gaze. 'Oh, you know – obviously, he's going to be all Leonardo DiCaprio to your Carey Mulligan. I'm going to feel like a gooseberry.'

Feeling the beginnings of a blush creep up her neck, Gina shook her head. 'We're just three friends hanging on a steam train and investigating a murder,' she said firmly. 'No gooseberries in sight.'

The other woman sighed. 'I suppose so. You know Rose is going, don't you? She and her mother came in last weekend, asking me to find costumes for them.'

'It's a free country,' Gina replied, fighting to keep her voice even; Ben's ex never missed an opportunity to put her down. Rose's presence at the murder mystery evening would lessen Gina's enjoyment of the event considerably.

'I – er – might have refused to source costumes for them,' Carrie went on, sending a small conspiratorial grin Gina's way. 'Good 1920s outfits are so hard to find at the moment.'

'Really?' Gina's heart lifted. 'You shouldn't be turning customers away, though. Especially since I'll be back in London soon and they'll still be here.'

Carrie shrugged. 'I can afford not to do business with the Arundells,' she said. 'Your events at the Palace are bringing me more customers than I can handle, anyway. The *Some Like it Hot* tickets must be selling like gold dust, judging from the costume requests I've had.'

A quiet sense of pride settled over Gina as she thought about the screening – over seventy-five per cent of the seats had sold already, with more than two weeks left to go. And this time, all she'd had to do was send an email to the Palace's mailing list – word-of-mouth buzz had done the rest. 'They're flying out of the door,' she told Gina. 'Gorran might have to think about putting on more than one screening in the future.'

Her friend gave her a strange look. 'You don't seriously think he's going to attempt to put on events like this once you've left, do you? I mean, I love Gorran to bits but the man couldn't organise a picnic in a pasty factory.'

'I hope he will,' Gina said, suppressing a sigh. 'It would be a shame to throw away everything we've worked for. And I've already told him I'll only be a phone call away.'

Carrie seemed unconvinced. 'I think he's getting twitchy already – I ran into him outside the cinema this morning and I had to call his name three times before he heard me. And Manda reckons there's something going on too – she says his drinking is really getting out of hand.'

Gina shifted uneasily, thinking back to her meeting with Gorran earlier in the week. He had seemed distracted and she'd noticed his eyes were bleary and bloodshot.

'Just a touch of hay fever,' he'd explained, when she'd asked if he was okay. 'I suffer every year.'

But now she was wondering whether Manda was right and Gorran's drinking was getting worse. Maybe she'd have a quiet word with Jory, the landlord of the Mermaid's Tail, and see if she could find out just how much time Gorran was spending in the pub.

'You could be right,' Gina said to Carrie. 'I'll try to reassure him next time I speak to him.'

'Do,' Carrie urged. She reached for a decadent feather boa and wrapped it around her neck. 'Because all of this is too much fun to give up. Polwhipple needs cosplay!'

Gorran wasn't there when Gina called in the next morning. Manda had insisted on her own set of keys and was busy setting out her wares for the day's trade. She waved at Gina and pulled a face. 'No sign of his lordship yet.'

'That's fine,' Gina called back. 'I've got some paperwork to go through – I'll wait in his office.'

She couldn't have been in the cluttered room for more than fifteen minutes when Manda's head appeared around the door. 'Gina? There's a man downstairs insisting on speaking to Gorran. I've told him he's not here but he won't leave.'

Frowning, Gina got to her feet. 'Did he say what he wants?'

'Nope. He refuses to say.'

'Okay, I'm coming.'

Gina's misgivings increased when she saw the man. He was big, with an ill-fitting suit and the air of a boxer who'd gone to seed. His nose looked as though it had been broken more than once; Gina thought he wouldn't have looked out of place standing outside a club, managing the queue.

'Can I help you?' she called, allowing the door that led to the non-public areas of the cinema to close behind her.

The man looked her up and down. 'Not unless you're Mr Gorran Dew.'

'He's not here,' she replied, moving nearer. 'What's this about?'

'I need to speak to Mr Dew,' the man repeated, eyeing the door Gina had come through as though he didn't believe Gorran wasn't somewhere behind it. 'What time are you expecting him?'

'Honestly?' Gina said, raising her hands. 'I have no idea. He should be here by now.'

The man looked slowly around, taking in the bar, the ticket office and the chandelier over their heads. He reached into his pocket and pulled out a card. 'When he does turn up, tell him to contact me. I've tried to catch him at home but he never seems to be there, either.'

Gina took the card without looking at it. 'I'll be sure to pass the message on.'

'Do,' the man said, and turned on his heel. 'And tell him it's his last chance.'

'That doesn't sound good,' Manda said, from her vantage point in the doorway of Ferrelli's. 'What sort of mess has that idiot Gorran got himself into this time?'

Curling her fingers around the card, Gina shook her head. 'I don't know. But I think it's high time I found out.'

She waited until she was safely inside Gorran's office before she examined the card. *Pendower Collection Services*, it read, and Gina's heart sank. She pulled out her phone and tapped the name into Google; a second later, her worst suspicions were confirmed. The man had been a debt collector.

She sat there seething for several long minutes. How had Gorran got himself into this situation? And how bad was it? Was this just the tip of the iceberg? She glanced around at the untidy piles of paperwork; Gorran was so disorganised that it was just about possible this was simply a case of an unpaid invoice. But then she thought about his erratic behaviour over the last few weeks, and Manda's insistence that he was drinking more. They were classic symptoms of a man who was buckling under pressure.

Reaching a decision, Gina picked up the nearest pile of letters and started to sift through them. One way or another, she was going to get to the bottom of this.

She was sitting amid a sea of letters, ashen-faced and shaking, when Gorran arrived almost an hour later. He froze guiltily in the doorway when he saw her and for a moment she thought he might bolt.

Instead, he hung his head. 'So now you know.'

Gina flashed him a look of furious disbelief. 'Now I know? Bloody hell, Gorran, I should have known months ago, long before the town council invested so much money in refurbishing this place. You owe thousands and thousands of pounds – I'm amazed you haven't been declared bankrupt and the Palace seized.'

'I thought I could fix it, especially now that takings are up. Maybe sort out some repayment schedules before it was too late.' He stepped into the office and closed the door. 'No one else knows.'

'They will soon,' Gina fired back. 'You had a visit from a debt collector this morning and he didn't look like the type to discuss repayment schedules. He looked like the type to break fingers.'

Gorran sank onto the small sofa and put his head into his hands. 'I know – I've been dodging him at home for weeks – that's why I've been late a few times. But you're right, I should have been honest with you.' He looked up, his eyes damp with tears. 'But I really did think I could sort everything out. I – I suppose I just stuck my head in the sand so that I wouldn't have to see how bad things had got.'

He looked so miserable and scared that Gina felt a tiny glimmer of sympathy for him. 'You stuck your head in a bottle from what I'm hearing.' She flicked through the sheaf of letters in her hand. 'Okay, as far as I can tell, these are the most urgent. You need to ring every single one and offer to pay a little bit of each. And then you need to agree a monthly repayment that you have to stick to. How much money have you got in the bank?'

He told her. It was a pitifully low figure.

'And have you covered Tash and Bruno's wages for this month?' she asked. The last thing they needed was for the Palace's projectionist or box office manager to walk out.

Gorran nodded, looking as though he wanted to dive beneath the sea of paper.

'Good,' Gina said. 'I'll transfer some money over to you from my own account, to help cover some of the repayments – you can pay me back out of the takings for the next screening, okay?'

Again, he nodded and this time Gina thought he would actually cry. 'Thank you,' he said. 'I don't know where I'd be without you.'

'Out on the street,' Gina said, with a severe shake of her head. She held up the Pendower Collection Services business card. 'Sort this one out first. I don't want to see his ugly mug hanging around here again, unless he wants to buy a ticket for *Some Like it Hot.* He'd make an especially convincing gangster.'

'I will. Thanks.'

'Stop thanking me and get on with it,' she said, passing him the phone. 'The sooner you start, the happier we'll both feel.'

# Chapter Thirty-Four

'Seriously?' Ben hissed when Gina told him what she'd uncovered in Gorran's office.

They were standing outside the café at Bodmin Parkway station, both in their Roaring Twenties finery. Ben looked every inch the dapper millionaire in his cream suit and wing-tip shoes and Gina felt like a perfect society darling in her dusty pink dress. Inside the café, the murder mystery guests were assembled, sipping champagne and chatting as they waited for the event to begin. It looked like a cross between *Poirot* and *The Great Gatsby*.

'Seriously,' Gina replied, her tone grim. 'Max said a few weeks ago that we should start looking around for investors to bail Gorran out but I'd be embarrassed to approach anyone the way things are.'

Ben looked thoughtful. 'It's not the worst idea I've ever heard. And having someone to answer to might help to keep

Gorran on the straight and narrow. He's obviously no good at managing on his own.'

Gina sighed. 'I don't understand why he didn't tell us what was going on. I mean, we knew something was wrong before the *Dirty Dancing* event but I thought that was an isolated incident, brought on by the drop of income when the cinema closed for the refurbishment.'

'This must have been going on for ages,' Ben agreed. 'What a mess.'

Carrie appeared in the doorway, her cigarette holder held aloft. 'There you are! What are you two whispering about out here? Things are about to kick off inside.'

'Sorry, just coming,' Gina called. She glanced at Ben. 'Don't breathe a word about this to anyone, okay? If the town council find out there'll be hell to pay.'

'My lips are sealed,' Ben promised. 'The funding they gave us for the refurbishment was also tied into the steam train restoration, remember? And we haven't been paid the money for that yet.'

Even more reason to help Gorran to find a way out of his situation, Gina thought as she followed Ben into the café. If Gorran lost the Palace, they would all lose out.

She touched his arm. 'One last thing – did you manage to speak to Davey? About Carrie, I mean.'

'Nope,' Ben said, sighing. 'But I suppose that's a good thing – it means it's not Carrie that's the problem. I'll try again next week.'

Inside the café, Gina spotted Rose Arundell and her

mother, Valeria, immediately. This was the first time she'd seen them together and she was struck by how alike they were, especially dressed as upper-class ladies of the 1920s. If she didn't know better, she might think they were sisters; they shared the same cool English beauty. It was a shame they were so unpleasant underneath, she thought just as Rose noticed her. She whispered to Valeria, who turned to stare at Gina and Ben before raising her champagne flute in a mocking toast.

'Ugh,' Carrie murmured as Gina returned the toast. 'I suppose it's too much to hope that one of those two might be the victim, right?'

Gina laughed. 'Probably. Let's hope we're not on the same table for dinner or it's going to be a very long evening indeed.'

Suddenly, there was a blood-curdling scream. Gina was gratified to see Valeria almost spill her champagne as a woman dressed as a maid appeared in the doorway that led to the kitchen. 'Murder! Gawd bless my 'eart, there's been a murder!'

One of the other guests hurried over to her, gripping her shoulders tightly. 'What are you babbling about, woman? Who's been murdered?'

The maid turned a horrified face towards the crowd. 'It's Lord Finch – 'e's lying in the parlour with a carving knife in 'is back!'

A glamorous, forty-something woman wearing an extravagant fur coat beside Gina dropped her glass with a gasp. 'No! It can't be true. Not Arthur?'

'Well, well, well,' a male voice drawled. 'It looks as though Great-uncle Arthur finally met his match.'

Every head whipped around to see who had spoken. A devilishly good-looking young man, dressed in plus fours and a tweed jacket, was pushing his way through the crowd. He stopped in front of the woman in the fur coat. 'You can stop pretending to be upset, Grace. We all know you only married him for the money.'

Grace slapped him hard across the cheek. 'How dare you? I love my husband very much.' Her face crumpled and she spun around to bury her face in an astonished Ben's chest. 'Loved. Oh, I can't believe he's dead!'

'There, there,' Ben said, patting her awkwardly on the back and causing Carrie to break out into giggles. 'It'll all be okay.'

A portly man dressed in chef whites pushed past the maid to point a quivering finger at Lord Finch's great-nephew. 'You did this, Basil! I saw you running along the servants' corridor only moments ago.'

Basil gave a cool smile. 'My dear Claude, you must be mistaken.' He slipped his arm through Gina's. 'I've been chatting to my charming friend here the whole time. Isn't that right, darling?'

'Uh—' Gina said, unsure how to answer.

'Put the poor girl down, Basil,' Grace said, her voice dripping with derision as she leaned into Ben. 'I doubt very much whether she has a fortune large enough to pay off your gambling debts.'

Titters broke out among the guests as Basil instantly dropped Gina's arm with a growl of disappointment.

'Enough of this!' A red-faced vicar stepped forwards, mopping at his face with a large white handkerchief. 'A man is dead, by fair means or foul. Shouldn't we call the police?'

The door of the café opened and a smartly dressed man in a trilby came in, followed by two uniformed officers. 'No need for that, Reverend Cooper. We're already here.'

Carrie leaned towards Gina. 'If this was any hammier, it would oink.'

Gina grinned. 'Oh, shush. It's all good fun.'

'Ben seems to have made a friend,' Carrie went on, glancing back to where Grace was clinging onto Ben as though he was her knight in shining armour. 'Although I wouldn't turn my back on her if I was him, especially not if there's a knife nearby – there's more to her than meets the eye.'

'My name is Inspector Barnet, of the Cornwall County Constabulary, and I'm afraid I shall have to detain everyone in this room on suspicion of murder. I know you must all be hungry so my colleagues will escort you to a place where you can have a bite to eat while you wait to be questioned.' He stared beadily around the room, making eye contact with as many guests as he could. 'For your own safety, please do not try to leave. And try not to be alone at any time. One of you is a murderer – who knows who the next victim might be?'

One of the uniformed policemen stepped back and held

open the door. 'This way, ladies and gentlemen. All aboard the Cornish Express, if you don't mind.'

'Form an orderly queue,' the other officer intoned. 'Keep your hands where I can see them – no sudden movements.'

Grace reached up to touch Ben's cheek. 'I hope to see you later, sweetie,' she breathed, before heading towards the door.

Ben met Gina's quizzical look with wide-eyed innocence. 'What? I hope you don't think I had anything to do with Lord Finch's murder.'

Gina narrowed her eyes theatrically as she peered around the room. 'At this point, I'm not ruling anyone out. Not even myself.'

The train carriages were very different to the ones Gina had travelled in before on the Bodmin line. Gone were the faded seats and sooty smell, replaced by dining carriages with pristine white tablecloths and shining silver cutlery. They found their seats quickly; much to Gina's relief, they weren't in the same carriage as Rose and Valeria.

'We've got an empty seat,' Carrie noted, nodding at the fourth place that had been laid on their table. 'Do you think anyone will sit there?'

Her question was answered almost as soon as the whistle blew and the train jolted into movement. The Reverend Cooper appeared in the doorway, mopping his forehead and looking even more florid than before, and swayed his way between the tables until he reached the empty seat.

'So charming to meet you all,' he said, shaking Ben's hand. 'It's a shame it's in such terrible circumstances.'

He chatted away as their starters were served, taking great care to establish his own alibi while confiding that Lord Finch was Grace's third husband. Her third Lord, in fact.

'To lose one peer is unfortunate,' he intoned, glancing around the carriage. 'But to lose two looks like carelessness and a third –' He paused and made the sign of the cross. 'Well, I'm sure I don't need to spell it out. Lady Finch seems to be making a career out of losing her husbands.'

Ben smiled. 'I thought she was quite nice.'

Reverend Cooper fixed him with a severe look. 'Then you need to take care, young man. Although you look rather too *American* to be in possession of a peerage so perhaps you're safe.'

Carrie snorted into her prawns, causing Reverend Cooper to enquire after her health and offer up his handkerchief. He made his excuses as the plates were being cleared, and vanished into the next carriage. Basil Hunterton-Smythe swaggered in and took great care to kiss the hand of every woman there, lingering particularly over Gina. He slid into the empty seat and let out a long-suffering sigh.

'This is a total bore, isn't it? Trust my insufferable old fart of a great-uncle to ruin a perfectly lovely dinner.'

Basil was at great pains to establish his alibi too, claiming he was resting in his room before dinner when the murder had been committed. He also had a secret to share; he'd seen

Lord Finch and Nancy the maid together in the birdwatching hide near the marshes at the farthest end of the estate.

He raised one rakish eyebrow and winked at Ben. 'Great tits all over the place, if you know what I mean. And rumour has it there's an egg in her nest.'

One of the guests at the next table asked him about his gambling debts. 'Oh, they're hardly worth mentioning,' Basil said dismissively. 'Certainly nothing like as much as Grace owes.'

Basil was followed by Nancy, who confessed that Claude was not really a chef, but a conman intent on swindling Lord Finch out of his fortune. When questioned, she tearfully admitted she was pregnant with her employer's child, then dropped the bombshell that Basil and Grace had been having an illicit affair and she suspected they'd plotted together to kill Lord Finch before his heir was born to solve their respective money problems.

'That's a thought,' Ben whispered to Gina. 'Does Gorran have any rich relatives we can bump off?'

Gina whacked him on the arm. 'Sssshh! And no, I don't suppose he does.'

Grace herself denied the affair with Basil and claimed he was trying to blackmail her into paying off his debts. She also suggested that Reverend Cooper was secretly in love with Basil and would do anything for him.

'And I mean *anything*,' she said, arching a delicate eyebrow.

Claude the chef arrived just as coffee was being served. He

was outraged by the diners' suggestion that he was anything but a talented chef who had worked for the finest restaurants in the land.

'If you had tasted my filet mignon, you would know that,' he declared. 'But I will tell you who is not all that she seems – Nancy. If she is so innocent, why did I see her sneaking out of that scoundrel Basil's room in the early hours of this morning?'

'Well,' Carrie said once he'd gone, peering at the sheet they were supposed to write the name of the murderer and the motive on. 'I haven't got the foggiest idea who did it. Have you?'

Ben shrugged. 'Everyone seems to be sleeping with everyone else, except Claude and Reverend Cooper. They all have alibis except for Nancy and Basil, who both claim they were alone at the time of the murder. But I still don't know who the killer is.'

A shadow fell across the table. Gina looked up to see Rose standing there, a faintly superior expression on her face. 'Obviously, it's Nancy,' she drawled. 'Mummy and I had worked it out by the end of the entrees.'

Gina summoned up her sunniest smile. 'Maybe you watch more *Midsomer Murders* than we do.'

Rose didn't smile back. 'I had dinner with Max last time I was in London – I can't tell you how sorry I was to hear that he's broken off your engagement.' She sent a malicious glance Ben's way. 'How does it feel to be a relationship-wrecker?'

But Ben was staring at Gina. 'You were engaged to Max? When did that happen?'

Gina cleared her throat. 'Briefly. He proposed when I went up to London to see him last month. After you and I had that argument.'

Rose let out a delighted little laugh. 'I didn't realise it was a secret. Didn't she tell you, Ben? Max broke it off after he found out she'd spent the night with you.'

Gina stood up abruptly. 'There's no need to make it sound so grubby, Rose. Ben slept on the sofa. Nothing happened and Max knows that.'

'Of course he does,' Rose replied. 'That's why he gave you that ultimatum, right? To choose him or Ben? It looks like you've made your choice – I'll be sure to let Max know.'

She swept away before Gina could say another word.

'Is that true?' Ben asked, as she sank back into her seat. 'Did Max really ask you to choose between us?'

Gina ran a hand over her face and sighed. 'Yes. Obviously, I refused.'

Carrie glanced down at Gina's left hand. 'And the engagement is definitely off?'

'Right now, I don't think either of us is sure whether we'll make it to the end of the month, let alone spend the rest of our lives together. So yes, the engagement is definitely off.' Taking a deep breath, Gina pointed at the sheet in front of Carrie. 'So are we going to write our answers down or not?'

They began to discuss their suspicions once more, although Rose's appearance had dampened their enthusiasm.

'I'm confused,' the man at the next table said, staring at Gina and Ben. 'Was that part of the murder enquiry or not?'

His wife threw them an embarrassed look. 'Shut up, Malcolm. Of course it wasn't. Now why do you think that strumpet Nancy did it, eh?'

# Chapter Thirty-Five

'Is that cough still bothering you?'

Elena waited until she'd caught her breath to answer Gina's question. 'A bit. The doctor thinks it's some kind of virus.'

Gina frowned across her grandmother's kitchen table. It was Sunday morning, almost two weeks since the yoga class on the beach when she'd first noticed Nonna's cough, and it showed no signs of improvement. 'But you've had it for ages – surely it would have cleared up by now if it was a virus?'

'Don't fuss, *mia bella*,' Elena admonished her. 'I'll be fine in a day or two, you'll see. Now, have you thought any more about your grandfather's offer?'

Gina bit back a sigh; she had and she'd come to the conclusion that to do the job properly, she'd need to stay in Cornwall, which would almost certainly be the final nail in the coffin for her relationship with Max. And if Ben took the job he'd been offered with the National Trust, she might end up staying in Polwhipple while he was in London, and she'd have lost her best friend as well as her boyfriend. She just couldn't win; no matter which way she looked at it, she was going to disappoint someone.

'I don't know what to do, Nonna,' she said at last. 'Of course I'm tempted to stay and join the family business – I know it would make Mum and Dad happy too. But I can't see how I can – it would be the end of me and Max.'

Elena said nothing.

'And if I leave Polwhipple, it feels like I'm turning my back on everything I've achieved here,' Gina went on. 'Gorran needs me more than ever, it feels like I've only just got the Ferrelli's stock control system working the way I want it to and Nonno has finally accepted the idea that adding more gelato flavours to our menu won't cause the apocalypse. If I leave now, what will happen here?'

Her grandmother shrugged. 'The world will still turn. We will get by, the way we did before you came. We'll miss you, of course, but don't feel you have to stay here for our benefit. Even that fool Gorran will survive without you.'

Gina thought of the pile of threatening letters she'd unearthed in his office and cringed. Gorran might survive but she wasn't at all sure the Palace would. And if the Palace went down, it would take Ben's station with it. 'Maybe,' she said.

'And as for what your parents want,' Elena continued with a sniff, 'if the family business mattered so much to them they would have some part in it, instead of hiding away in California.'

'Come on, you know it's not as easy as that,' Gina said, feeling obliged to defend her mother and father. 'Mum and Nonno are both so stubborn – neither of them will ever admit they were wrong long enough to resolve their differences. I bet they don't even remember what they fought over now, it was so long ago, and still they won't talk to each other.'

'Nonno remembers,' Elena said softly. 'But he's too proud to make the first move.'

Gina shook her head. 'Mum's like that too – they're so similar it's not funny.'

Elena gave her a sideways look. 'What we need is a reason for them to come back here,' she said. 'A good reason they can't refuse. Like a wedding.'

The loaded suggestion made Gina even more conflicted. 'I don't think you should rely on me and Max getting married to bring the family back together,' she said gloomily.

'Max?' Elena said, lifting her eyebrows. 'Who said anything about Max? My money is on Ben Pascoe.'

'Not you too?' Gina cried, giving her grandmother an incredulous look. 'You're as bad as Rose. For the last time, Nonna, there is nothing going on between me and Ben. We are friends, that's all.'

Her grandmother looked unconvinced. 'I know there is a lot to think about, but look into your heart and decide what you truly want before you go rushing back to London next month. Max might have been right for you in the past but is he right for your future?'

Gina thought about those words later that night, as she listened to Max's phone ring and ring. Was he avoiding her because Rose had got to him after their conversation on Friday night? Or was she simply being paranoid? It was possible that Max hadn't been able to take her call on the three separate occasions she'd tried to ring him. Possible, she told herself dully, but not likely. And it was very unlike him not to ring her back after a missed call. In fact, it was unheard of.

By Tuesday night, she was starting to worry that something had happened to him. She rang her friend, Sarah, who told her Max had been fine when she'd seen him on Saturday night.

'And he didn't mention going away anywhere?' Gina pressed her.

'Actually, I think he did,' Sarah said, after a few seconds of thought. 'I didn't talk to him much – you know what these nights out are like – but I'm sure I overheard him say he was going on a business trip at the start of this week. What's this about, Gina? Is everything okay?'

'Everything is fine,' Gina said as breezily as she could, hoping Sarah wouldn't pick up on the lie. 'We just keep missing each other's calls, that's all. Sorry, I've got to go – there's someone at the door.'

It wasn't a lie; the doorbell had buzzed.

'Ben,' Gina said in surprise when the visitor announced himself over the intercom. 'Come on up.'

'I won't stay long,' he said, once she'd settled down beside him on the sofa. 'I just thought we should have a quick chat about the *Some Like it Hot* screening. Gorran mentioned something about you wanting to turn the place into a speakeasy?'

'I do,' Gina said, feeling her spirits rise for the first time that day. 'I want to serve cocktails in cups and saucers, just like in the film, and maybe even for the foyer to be set up like a funeral parlour.'

Ben shook his head in amusement. 'You get more and more ambitious every single time.'

'That's what brings people back in,' Gina said. 'It would be no fun if every event was the same.'

He tilted his head. 'True. Speaking of events, I heard from the Preservation Society today. They've completed work on the track between Boscarne Junction and Polwhipple and should be in a position to run some test trains later this week.'

Gina beamed at him. 'That's brilliant news, Ben. You must be so pleased.'

'I am. I thought it would never happen and, to be honest, it probably wouldn't have if you hadn't come to Polwhipple and helped me to show the town council what a good idea it could be.' He ran a hand through his hair and gave her a nervous look. 'So I know being here has caused you problems – I know *I've* caused you problems – but I just wanted to say that I'm really glad you came. You have no idea just how glad I am.'

She met his intense blue-eyed gaze full on and an all-too-familiar stab of desire cut through her. 'Thank you,' she said in a low voice. 'You're right, it hasn't been easy but right now, I'm really happy I came too.'

He studied her in silence for a moment, then reached across to brush a strand of hair from her cheek. The gesture was so intimate that it made Gina shiver.

'We've come a long way from that moment on Platform 2, haven't we?' he asked.

She smiled, remembering how he'd stopped to help when she'd got some coal dust caught in her eye. 'We have. I didn't expect to ever see you again.'

'But here we are,' he replied, returning her smile.

'Here we are,' she agreed, her heart speeding up. He was close enough to kiss – all she had to do was lean forwards and she knew he'd meet her halfway. But he was leaving it up to her; if she wanted him, she'd have to make the first move.

She lowered her gaze from his eyes to his mouth, remembering how it had felt to kiss him before the *Brief Encounter* screening. What would have happened if Gorran hadn't appeared and forced them to spring apart? Gina wondered. Would she have chosen Ben then instead of persevering with Max? She had no idea; what she did know was that she was tired of fighting her attraction to Ben. He was kind and generous and he made her laugh. More than that, he soothed her, as though he was a favourite book she returned to again and again when she needed to feel comforted. All she had to do was lean forwards . . .

Their lips were almost touching when Gina's phone rang.

She jerked back, wide-eyed and confused. 'Who could that be?' she muttered, picking up the handset and praying it wasn't Max's name on the screen. It wasn't. It was Sarah's.

'You got me wondering about Max,' her friend said, the moment Gina had said hello. 'So I asked around a bit to see if I could find out where he'd gone.'

'And?' Gina said, glancing guiltily at Ben.

'And he's gone to Cornwall,' Sarah said, her voice flat. 'Max is in Polwhipple, Gina.'

# Chapter Thirty-Six

It was a strange feeling, knowing Max was in Polwhipple but not knowing exactly where, Gina thought as she crossed the car park next door to the Palace on Wednesday morning. She'd called him again as soon as she'd got off the phone with Sarah the night before; this time it hadn't even rung.

'Maybe he wants to surprise you,' Ben had said, when she'd explained the reason for Sarah's call.

Gina had let out a little laugh. 'He's certainly managed that.'

Ben had eyed her uneasily. 'Do you think he's come to sort things out between you?'

Gina considered the possibility; grand romantic gestures weren't beyond Max. 'I don't know. Maybe.'

'And how would that make you feel?' Ben asked, in a tone that seemed carefully neutral.

'Honestly?' Gina had let out a long, unhappy sigh. 'I don't have the faintest idea.'

The last place she expected to see Max was outside the doors of the Palace. She stopped dead in her tracks and gasped. 'What are you doing here?'

For a heartbeat, he looked almost pleased to see her, making her wonder if Ben had been right; Max had come to win her back. But then his expression clanged shut and he gave a stiff nod. 'Hello, Gina. How are you?'

Her heart sank. 'How am I?' she echoed. 'Surprised to see you here, especially since you seem to be ignoring my calls. What's going on, Max? Why are you in Polwhipple? You're obviously not here for me.'

'No, it's business,' he said. He hesitated and his expression softened. 'But it is good to see you.'

She stared at him as though he was a stranger; there was something about his manner that made her wary. 'Don't try to distract me. What business could you possibly have all the way down here?' she demanded. 'There are no riverside skyscrapers to buy and sell in Polwhipple. Or do you know something I don't?'

Max said nothing.

Gina's eyes narrowed as she detected a trace of guilt in his eyes. 'What are you doing coming out of the Palace?'

'Like I said, it's business. Ask Gorran – I'm sure he'll tell you.'

A cold, unpleasant feeling settled in the pit of Gina's stomach. 'I'm asking you, Max. What's going on?'

This time, he sighed. 'The Palace is drowning under the weight of Gorran's debts. I've made him a very generous offer to buy the building, with a view to turning it into luxury sea-view apartments.'

Gina felt as though her head might explode. 'What?'

'Don't worry about Ferrelli's,' Max went on, glancing sideways at the concession window. 'That can stay. Your grandfather will simply lease it from the management company instead of Gorran. I'm sure we can come to some agreement over a fair rent.'

'You – you utter snake!' Gina cried in disbelief, her hands balling into furious fists. 'You planned this all along, didn't you? I could practically see the pound signs in your eyes the first time I showed you the Palace, and now you can see a way to get your grubby little hands on it. Well, it won't work, Max. Gorran won't be selling the building to you.'

Max put a hand on her arm. 'You're angry and I suppose I can see why. I should have told you what I was planning. But I knew you'd try to talk me out of it.'

She shook him off. 'Angry? Of course I bloody am – I'm furious. You took all the information I shared with you in confidence and turned it into a business opportunity. How am I supposed to feel?'

'You'll calm down,' he said quietly. 'And when you do, you'll see that this is the best course of action all round. Gorran gets rid of his debts, the townspeople get the opportunity to invest in some lovely new apartments and I get to make a nice little profit. Everybody wins.'

'Not everybody,' Gina ground out.

Max's mouth thinned. 'I don't see why this matters so

much – have you forgotten you're supposed to be moving back to London next month?'

Gina raised her chin. 'Am I?'

Max stared at her. Then he shrugged. 'I thought you were. But clearly I'm wrong – I don't seem to know much about you any more.' He paused, gazing at the distant horizon. 'I'm staying at the Scarlet when you're ready to talk. Room 124. Take care, Gina.'

He walked quickly towards the car park and climbed into a red Audi TT. And that was when Gina's world really imploded. Because there was only one person who owned a car like that in Polwhipple: Rose Arundell.

Gorran actually jumped when Gina slammed back the door to the office.

'H-hello,' he said, taking in her obvious agitation with an anxious grimace. 'Have I forgotten a meeting or something?'

'I know what you've done, Gorran,' she said, surprised by how level her voice was. 'What I don't understand is why.'

With a sideways glance at an expensive-looking bottle of single malt whisky that Gina suspected hadn't been there before Max's visit, Gorran caved in. 'He made it sound so good,' he moaned, his head in his hands. 'No debts and a nice little nest egg for my retirement. What would you have done?'

He looked so wretched that Gina couldn't help feeling sorry for him. 'Just tell me you haven't signed anything yet.'

'No, not yet,' Gorran said. 'But we made a gentleman's agreement – he's gone away to get the paperwork drawn up. I can't back out now.'

Gina shook her head. 'A verbal agreement isn't legally binding, even if you shook on it. I'm going to need all the details, Gorran. Don't leave anything out.'

He opened his mouth to speak but Gina held up a hand. 'Wait. I need to make some phone calls first. Quite a few people have something at stake here and it's only fair to include them all.'

She grabbed her phone and called up the first number in her contacts list. 'Ben? We've got a major problem at the Palace. How soon can you get here?' She covered the handset and pointed to the bottle of single malt. 'I suggest you put that out of sight, in case someone decides to brain you with it.'

There was a lot of shouting when Gina broke the news. Ferdie let out a volley of ferocious Italian, in amongst which Gina picked out several unflattering descriptive terms, and Manda was equally enraged. Tash the projectionist declared she wanted to rip Gorran's arms off and Ben looked as though someone had just pounded him over the head with a gigantic rock. And at the far end of the office, Gorran cowered, looking as though he was living his worst nightmare.

'All right, everyone, that's enough,' Gina bellowed. 'We're all angry but this isn't helping. What we need is to work out an alternative plan of action – preferably one that doesn't involve turning the Palace into a block of holiday homes.'

Ferdie glared at Gorran. '*Idiota*. What were you thinking?'

'Nonno!' Gina said sharply. 'That's not going to help, either. Gorran has his reasons for listening to Max's offer.'

Manda pursed her lips, as though there was plenty she wanted to say, but she kept her mouth shut.

'These are the facts,' Gina said, once she was satisfied that everyone was listening. 'Max has offered £300,000 to buy the building.' She took a deep breath and tried to ignore the ache of betrayal in her heart. 'He's not stupid, he knows Gorran needs the money so I have no doubt that's way below the market value of the property.'

'*Che palle*,' Ferdie announced in disgust. 'What kind of lowlife is this man of yours?'

Gina swallowed hard and didn't dare look at Ben. 'It's just business, Nonno. It's how they all operate in London. And please don't call him *my man*.' She glanced across at Gorran. 'Do you honestly want out of the Palace? The truth, please – yes or no.'

He sighed. 'But the answer is yes *and* no. I see everything you touch turn to gold here, Gina, and it makes me feel so inadequate. And before I know it, I've got a little voice in my head telling me that I'm too old, that I should give it all up before it's too late. Then I wonder what I would do with myself if I didn't come here every day and I can't imagine what Polwhipple would be like without the Palace.'

'What about me?' Tash asked. 'What about Bruno? This place is our livelihood – didn't you stop to think about how we'd feel when you sold our jobs out from underneath us?'

Gorran hung his head. 'I didn't. I'm sorry.'

Gina held up one hand. 'I know you're hurt and angry – I am too. But we really need to focus.' She gazed round at them one by one. 'I've got an idea but it all depends on you, Gorran. Do you want the Palace to close down?'

'No,' Gorran said. 'I don't.'

'Not even if it solves all your problems?' she pressed on, determined to make sure he understood what was at stake.

He met Tash's sullen stare and hesitated. 'Not even then.'

Gina let out the breath she hadn't realised she'd been holding. 'Okay. So, this comes out of something Max once said to me – he suggested that what the Palace needed was investors. Silent partners who invest money in the business, for reasons best known to themselves and their accountants, and in return we give them a percentage of the profits and a VIP invitation to attend whenever they like.'

Manda looked sceptical. 'But who do we know who's got a spare £300,000 lying around? Because I certainly don't.'

'We won't need that much,' Gina pointed out. 'That was the amount Max offered Gorran to buy the building outright. We only need enough to settle Gorran's debts with a bit of extra cash left over to plough back into the business.'

'Again, who do we know who might do that?' Manda repeated.

Gina looked at Ben. 'I might know some people. I'm hoping you might too.'

He nodded. 'Maybe. The trouble is that we'll have to move fast – Max will want to get a deal drawn up and signed quickly, before Gorran can change his mind.'

'I'll make some phone calls,' Gina said. 'Gorran, you'll have to stall Max when he starts pressuring you to sign. Tell him you need your lawyer to check the paperwork over.'

'I don't have one,' Gorran replied.

'He doesn't know that,' Gina said patiently. 'Max moves in circles where everyone has a lawyer, remember? Besides, you're probably going to need one before too long.'

'What about the *Some Like it Hot* screening?' Manda asked. 'Should we cancel?'

'No,' Gina said. 'We carry on as though it's business as usual. We're going to need all the goodwill we can get if we're going to make this work out long-term.'

Ben caught up with Gina as they were leaving. He drew her to one side of the foyer. 'What are we going to do about the town council?' he asked in a low voice. 'If Rose is involved then Valeria probably already knows what's going on. They could demand that we return the money they gave us for the refurbishment.'

'And refuse to release the payment for the train track renovations,' Gina added with a groan. 'I need to talk to Max, find out what ròle Rose has played in all this. And then I suppose we factor it into our plea for investment.'

Ben reached out to take her hand and she felt a thrill of excitement at his touch, in spite of her jumbled emotions. 'Are you okay? About Max, I mean.'

Gina prodded the hurt and bewilderment she felt. 'Not really. But I will be.'

'You're amazing, you know that?' he said gently, squeezing her fingers. 'This is all going to work out fine and we're all going to owe you big time.'

She squeezed back. 'You don't owe me anything, Ben. And we're a team, remember? Whatever happens from now on, we tackle it together. Agreed?'

Ben smiled at her and Gina hoped she hadn't imagined the flare of something more than friendship behind his eyes. 'Agreed.'

The lobby of the Scarlet Hotel was quiet, so quiet that the click-clack of Gina's heels on the tiled floor sounded like bullets being fired from a rifle.

She took a deep steadying breath when she reached the receptionist and did her best to smile. 'Hello, Shelley. Could you ring up to room 124 and let Mr Hardy know that I'm here to see him, please? Tell him I'll wait for him in the bar.'

'Of course, Gina,' the receptionist said. 'Miquel will be pleased to see you – he's been working on a cocktail for your next event.'

'I can't wait to try it,' Gina said warmly.

In the bar, the head bartender's eyes lit up when he saw her. 'Wait,' he said, when her gaze slid to the cocktail menu. 'I have a surprise for you.'

Gina took a seat at the bar. 'I really hope it's a drink, Miquel. I think I'm going to need one.'

Five minutes later, Gina was admiring a tall red and orange cocktail with a lollipop balanced across the top. 'I call it Sweet Sue's Syncopated Sling. Or maybe a Sweet Sue for short.'

Gina laughed. 'No one will be complaining about getting the fuzzy end of the lollipop when we serve this beauty. It's fabulous.'

'A bit like you,' Max's voice said from behind her.

Instantly, Gina's happiness evaporated. 'Hello, Max. What do you want to drink?'

'Whisky, please. On the rocks.'

Miquel inclined his head to show that he'd heard.

'Why don't we take a seat over there?' Max suggested. 'Bring my drink over, will you?'

Taking a bolstering sip of her cocktail, Gina followed Max to the table he'd indicated, tucked away in a dimly lit corner of the bar. She'd barely sat down before Max started to speak.

'Look, I know you're angry, but I want you to understand that I did this for you – for us. The Palace is going under, Gee – you know it, I know it, half of Polwhipple knows it. At least this way your grandfather gets to keep his business – that's something, right?'

Gina stared at him in astonishment; he couldn't seriously have convinced himself he was doing a good thing, could he? She gazed into his eyes and almost laughed as she realised the truth; as far as Max was concerned, he really had done nothing wrong.

'Tell me what Rose Arundell has to do with all this,' she

said, leaning back in her seat as Miquel discreetly delivered Max's drink.

'What?' Max asked warily.

'I saw you getting into her car earlier,' Gina went on. 'And suddenly quite a few things fell into place. How Rose knew things that Gorran had only shared with Ben and me – things I'd then discussed with you: who had recommended this hotel to you when you came down to stay; how she knew that I hadn't told you about Ben staying over that night. So I'll ask you again – what has Rose got to do with your offer to Gorran?'

Max sighed. 'She said this might happen. There's no need to be jealous of Rose – we've been friends for years. A bit like you and Ben.'

Gina fought the urge to blush then because she'd had, and continued to have, some distinctly non-platonic thoughts about Ben over the past few months. 'I'm not jealous of Rose. It's completely the opposite – she's jealous of me.'

'Because you turned Ben against her?' Max asked, sipping his drink. 'She told me a while ago that you couldn't bear for him to be happy with anyone except you.'

This time Gina couldn't stop the heat from rising in her cheeks. 'I don't want to talk about Ben and Rose, or me and Rose, or me and Ben,' she ground out. 'What I want to know is how involved Rose is with your offer to Gorran.'

Max sat forwards. 'Fine, I'll tell you. She rang me up last weekend, to tell me about your cosy murder mystery night with Ben.' Gina went still. Max threw her an amused glance.

'Did you think I wouldn't find out about it? That was what tipped the balance and made me realise I had to do something.'

A roaring started in Gina's ears. 'You did this because of me and Ben?'

'Don't flatter yourself,' Max said, scowling. 'It just so happened that I thought I could kill two birds with one stone. When I mentioned Gorran's financial black hole to Rose, she agreed that the time was right to put in a bid for the Palace. She even agreed it would help you and me get back on track, because it was one less thing to keep you down here.'

Gina felt tears prick her eyelids. How could things have come to this? It was her fault they were in this mess; she was the one who'd introduced Max to Polwhipple, and the Palace. And whether Rose admitted it or not, she was jealous of Gina's friendship with Ben, which had prompted her to toss a grenade into the heart of Gina's world. But Max wasn't innocent; he'd been happy to exploit the situation for financial and personal gain.

'She was wrong,' Gina said, swallowing the ache in her throat. 'You both were. It hasn't helped our relationship. In fact, it's killed it.'

'What?' Max said, narrowing his eyes. 'You can't mean that.'

Gina got to her feet. 'I'm sorry, Max, but I do.'

He jumped up, sullen irritation all over his face. 'Bloody hell, Gina, just think about what you're saying. I know you're angry, but think about what you're throwing away.'

Blinking hard against the tears that threatened to spill down her cheeks, Gina shook her head. 'That's just it – I'm not angry. Not any more. I'm sad and disappointed and hurt but that's all. And one day you'll thank me for this. One day you'll wake up and realise that it was the right thing to do.' She took a long shaky breath and let it out slowly. 'It's over.'

He stared at her as though the seriousness of what she was saying was just starting to sink in. 'If you walk away now, there's no going back.'

'There's no going back anyway,' she said, her voice thick with emotion. 'Goodbye, Max.'

She walked away, concentrating on putting one foot in front of the other until she reached the safety of her car. And then she cried until there were no more tears to fall.

# Chapter Thirty-Seven

The next few days passed in a blur. Max tried to ring her several times but she ignored every call and eventually he gave up. She'd have to speak to him at some point – a two-year relationship didn't dissolve overnight – but it would have to wait until the battle for the Palace was over. When it hurt less.

Gina was unsurprised to hear he'd tried to pressurise Gorran into a quick signature. The cinema owner had stood his ground, insisting that the contracts needed to be read by his lawyers first. And then, on Gina's instructions, he'd put the paperwork into the bottom drawer of the filing cabinet and done his best to forget about it.

Gina and Ben had been busy contacting anyone they thought might invest in the Palace. Ideally, what they wanted was a silent partner, but they were resigned to taking whatever they could get. Gina was also trying to tread carefully so that she didn't alert Max to her plan; there were plenty of investors in London who might innocently mention a new project and then Max would issue Gorran with an ultimatum: sign or lose the deal for ever. And faced with losing his dream of financial security, Gorran would almost certainly sign.

By the middle of the following week, both Gina and Ben had a couple of promising meetings lined up but Gina was run ragged between the dairy and the *Some Like it Hot* screening. She was beginning to wonder whether she'd bitten off more than she could chew by deciding to transform the cinema into a speakeasy; she felt as though she'd bought every mismatched cup and saucer from every charity shop within a fifty-mile radius. It would all be worth it when she looked around on the night and saw all the delighted faces but for now, it felt like a task that even Wonder Woman would struggle with.

'How are you doing?' Carrie asked on Saturday morning, when Gina stopped by the shop to collect a few last-minute costume accessories for her grandparents. 'All set for tonight?'

'I think so,' Gina said. 'Gorran is convinced Max is going to burst through the doors mid-film and demand that he signs on the dotted line, but apart from that I think everything is in hand.'

Carrie paused to run the purchase of a rainbow-coloured kaftan through the till for a customer. 'Have you heard from him recently?' she asked, once the shop was empty again.

Gina shook her head. 'I know he's back in London, and he hasn't made it obvious that we've split up, which makes me wonder if he thinks there's hope that we'll get back together . . . But no, he hasn't tried to speak to me.'

Her friend busied herself with wiping some dust from the monitor screen in front of her. 'And is there hope? I mean, you were together a long time – do you think that maybe when all of this blows over, you might remember the things about him you loved?'

'I . . .' Gina paused and tried to marshal her thoughts. There were plenty of things she'd loved about Max – his drive and determination, his attention to detail that meant he'd never forgotten a date or an event that mattered to her, his passion for what he did – all of those things were what had drawn her to him in the first place and she'd allowed them to blind her to the aspects of his personality she didn't like. Besides, Gina herself was no longer the woman she'd been when they'd first met. She was beginning to suspect she was no longer the woman she'd been before leaving for Polwhipple.

'No,' she told Carrie, squaring her shoulders. 'It's definitely over.'

Carrie studied her in silence. 'So where does that leave you?' she said, after a few moments. 'Will you go back to London?'

'I have no idea,' Gina admitted. 'Nonno wants me to stay and run his new Ferrelli's shop but I can't tell if it's the right thing to do. I think maybe I need to get tonight's screening out of the way, and see what happens with the Palace before I make any decisions.'

'And Ben?' Carrie asked with a direct look. 'What if he wants you to stay?'

'He's been offered a great job in London,' Gina said, refusing to allow herself to dwell on her own feelings where Ben was concerned. 'The last thing he needs is me clouding the waters and making him feel as though he needs to stay in Polwhipple.'

Carrie gave her a level look. 'I seriously doubt he'll see it that way.'

'Even so . . .' She trailed off, then took a deep breath. 'I'm not going to stand in the way of a good opportunity for him just because my circumstances have changed.'

Her friend raised her eyebrows. 'It's your call – if that's the way you want to play things then who am I to argue?' She sent a brisk smile Gina's way and glanced thoughtfully around the shop. 'Now, where did I put that violin case?'

Gina's nerves were jangling by six-thirty. The screening had sold out, everything was in place – including Ferdie's new Sugar Kane peppermint gelato flavour – and her costume still fitted, in spite of the monstrous amount of comfort food she'd put away since her break-up with Max. But even so, Gina felt an odd sense of disquiet, as though something was wrong, and she couldn't put her finger on what it was.

The foyer of the Palace looked incredible. Ben had outdone himself, recreating the Mozarella funeral parlour from the film perfectly. Sombre organ music played over the speaker system and Gorran was dressed as the funeral director, Mr Mozarella. Beyond the doors that led to the screen room, the speakeasy awaited; Ben had set up a temporary bar and Miquel was ready to serve up his Sweet Sue cocktails to a swinging jazz soundtrack. All they needed now were some mourners.

Carrie was the first to arrive.

'I've come to Grandma's funeral,' she said to Gorran.

'Right this way,' he intoned, pointing her towards Bruno, who was checking tickets.

'Nice wig,' Gina said, admiring the blonde Marilyn-style hairpiece Carrie was wearing.

Carrie winked. 'I figured I might as well go all out.'

'Might as well,' Gina agreed. 'Let me show you to your table – I bet you're desperate for a cup of coffee, right?'

As the speakeasy started to fill up, Gina kept her eyes peeled for Ben, keen to thank him for turning the Palace into everything she'd hoped it would be. Trying not to check the time, she chatted to Nonno and Nonna, who'd come as violin-toting gangsters, and gritted her teeth when she saw Rose. But the clock grew nearer and nearer to eight o'clock and there was no sign of Ben. Something must have happened, she thought. Maybe he wasn't coming.

She was just about to go to find Gorran to tell him to announce the start of the film when she became aware of laughter echoing over the hubbub of music and chatter. She looked up and immediately understood why: Ben and Davey were wiggling their way through the speakeasy in dresses, high heels and full make-up. An enormous grin spread over

Gina's face as she caught Carrie's astonished eye. No wonder they were late, she thought with a delighted laugh. It must have taken them ages to put their outfits together.

'Did you know?' she mouthed to Carrie.

Her friend shook her head. 'No idea!'

'Look at you,' Gina exclaimed, when Ben stopped in front of her.

'My name is Josephine,' he said, in a squeaky falsetto voice.

'And I'm Daphne,' Davey added, fluttering his mascara-coated eyelashes.

'We're the new girls,' they said together, causing everyone who overheard to erupt into laughter.

'You certainly are,' Gina said, smirking. 'Well, ladies, if you'd like to take your seats, the performance is about to begin.'

Her eyes met Ben's and lingered there for a moment. Then, with another amused shake of her head, Gina went to find Gorran.

'Gina, *mia bella*, you have outdone yourself this time.'

Elena gripped Gina's hands tightly, her eyes bright and glittering.

'Thank you, Nonna,' Gina replied, squeezing her grand-mother's fingers. 'It was mostly Ben, actually. He'd exceeded even my expectations.'

Elena clutched one hand to her chest as she looked around the speakeasy. 'He could get a job as a set designer at a theatre, you know. It really is marvellous. Or as a drag queen.'

Gina frowned. Was it her imagination or was her grandmother's breathing a little bit laboured? 'Is everything all right?' She looked at the older woman more closely, noticing the beads of sweat on her upper lip for the first time. 'You're sweating.'

Elena waved her concern away. 'Being a gangster is hot work,' she said, lifting up her black Homburg hat and fanning her face with it. 'I think I just need some air.'

She tried to smile but her eyes rolled back into her head. A second later, she had toppled backwards and landed in a heap on the floor.

'Nonna!' Gina cried in horror, kneeling beside her inert body. She placed a hand against her grandmother's forehead and gasped. 'She's so hot.'

She began unbuttoning the jacket of Elena's suit just as Ferdie pushed through the crowd and reached her.

'What happened?' he asked, bewildered. 'What's wrong?'

Gina looked up. 'She's burning up. How long has she been running a temperature?'

Her grandfather rubbed his ashen face. 'I – I don't know. She's had this cough, I suppose, but you know what Nonna is like. She doesn't complain.'

Gina patted Elena's cheek. 'Nonna. Nonna, wake up.'

Their family doctor appeared and Gina tried not to notice that he was dressed like Osgood Fielding III. He felt for Elena's pulse, then glanced across at Gina. 'You'd better call an ambulance.'

Everything moved fast after that. Gina left Gorran and

Carrie to reassure the worried film-goers as she left with her grandfather in the ambulance. When they arrived at Newquay Hospital, Nonna was whisked away and they were left to anxiously await news. It felt like an eternity had passed before a doctor came to speak to them, just after two o'clock in the morning.

'Hello, Mr Ferrelli, my name is Dr Perrett,' she said. 'I've been looking after your wife.'

'How is she?' Ferdie asked, his voice filled with quiet desperation.

Dr Perrett gave him a reassuring smile. 'I'd say she's comfortable. We've managed to bring her temperature down but her oxygen levels are still much lower than we'd like.'

'But what's wrong with her?' Gina asked. 'She just collapsed, there was no real warning—'

'We suspect pneumonia,' Dr Perrett said. 'X-rays show fluid on her left lung but otherwise, she's quite dehydrated, probably from the fever. She's resting now and we've started her on antibiotics and fluids, plus oxygen to help with her breathing.'

A sense of unreality settled over Gina. 'But she seemed fine. How could she have been so ill without either of us noticing?'

'Don't blame yourselves,' Dr Perrett said. 'Pneumonia can develop very quickly, often as the result of another infection. It's quite treatable but I'm sure I don't need to tell you that this could be very serious, particularly at her age. The next forty-eight hours will be critical.'

Her words caused a stab of panic to Gina's insides. 'But she'll be okay, right?'

Dr Perrett nodded. 'I hope so. She's very healthy for a woman of her age – as long as there are no complications, then I'm hopeful she'll pull through.'

Ferdie let out a shaky sigh. 'Can we see her?'

She nodded. 'Of course. Come this way.'

Gina let out an involuntary gasp when she saw her grandmother in the hospital bed. She was in a room on her own and looked much smaller than normal, surrounded by a number of machines and drips. Her face was almost entirely covered by an oxygen mask. Beside her, Gina felt Ferdie fumble for her hand. He squeezed her fingers tight, as though drawing strength from her.

'*Mio dio*,' he muttered under his breath.

'I know it looks frightening but she's getting the best treatment,' Dr Perrett said. 'Would you like a few moments alone?'

Dazed, Ferdie nodded.

'Thank you,' Gina said to the doctor as she left the room.

'How could I have missed this?' Ferdie asked, turning in confusion to Gina. 'One minute she is laughing and joking with me, the next she is in hospital.'

She rubbed his arm. 'You heard Dr Perrett – pneumonia can take hold very quickly. I don't think even Nonna knew how ill she was.'

His expression settled into a determined frown. 'I am not leaving her side until she is better.'

'I'll stay too,' Gina began but her grandfather interrupted her.

'No. You should go home and get some rest. And –' he hesitated then ploughed on. 'You need to contact your mother. She needs to get on a plane, now, and fly over. In case – in case –'

He swallowed, blinking hard. Gina felt her own eyes swim with tears as she rested her head on his shoulder. 'It's okay, I understand.'

They stood like that for a moment, then Gina stepped back. 'You're sure this is what you want?'

Ferdie nodded.

'And you'll call me if there's any change?'

He settled into the chair beside the bed. 'Of course.'

She watched as he took Elena's hand in his and her heart ached. 'Okay. I'll be back first thing in the morning.'

She bent to kiss his cheek and touched the back of Elena's hand. 'Get well soon, Nonna.'

She was almost at the door when Ferdie called her name. 'Yes?' she said, turning back.

'Bring me a change of clothes, will you, please?' he said, tugging at his black and white gangster suit. 'I'm not sure this is especially appropriate.'

In spite of herself, Gina smiled. 'I will. See you soon, Spats.'

# Chapter Thirty-Eight

Gina met her parents at Newquay airport.

Her mother looked the way she always did, like a younger, more tanned version of Nonna. Her father had put on some weight but was basically the same tall, brown-haired bear of a man who'd swung her round as a child until she was sick.

'How is she?' Sophia asked, after greeting Gina with a fierce hug.

'She's not out of the woods yet,' Gina said cautiously. 'But the doctors are optimistic that the antibiotics are doing their job.'

Her father, Paul, pulled Gina into his arms. 'It's so good to see you, even if the circumstances aren't the best.'

Gina managed a smile. He was right, it *was* good to see them. She never realised how much she missed her parents until she was standing right in front of them. 'Come on, I'll take you to the hotel so you can drop off your bags. Then we'll go and see Nonna.'

They'd checked into the Headland Hotel in Newquay, a grand old red-bricked building that overlooked Fistral Beach. But there was no time to admire the blue skies and golden sands; no sooner had they left their suitcases in their room than they were heading for the hospital.

Gina's nerves began to screech as they approached her grandmother's room. Sophia Callaway hadn't spoken to or seen her father for sixteen years. At best, the next few minutes were going to be awkward beyond belief. At worst, they were going to be explosive.

The atmosphere was thick as Gina opened the door. Ferdie got to his feet, a look of mulish defiance on his face, and Gina knew without looking that her mother's expression would be almost exactly the same. That was part of the reason they'd clashed so hard when Sophia was growing up, and it had a lot to do with why Gina's parents had upped sticks and moved to California when Gina was fifteen. The other reason had been Gina herself; things had come to a head when Gina had been arrested, aged fifteen, for shoplifting make-up from Boots while her mother was working in Paris. The ensuing argument when Ferdie found out had been so vitriolic that Sophia hadn't spoken to her father since. But surely they wouldn't continue to fight at Nonna's bedside?

'Sophia,' Ferdie said, his tone clipped and wary.

'*Papà*,' Sophia replied, but her voice was not tight or angry as Gina expected. It sounded instead as though it was thick with tears.

Gina glanced sideways and saw that her mother's cheeks

were wet. Stomach tensing, her head whipped back to Nonno. How would he react? Whatever he said next would set the tone for the rest of Gina's parents' visit.

The silence stretched as father and daughter looked at each other. Then Ferdie let out a sigh, as though he was letting go of something he'd been holding tight for a long time, and opened his arms. 'Come here.'

With a half-strangled sob, Sophia rushed towards her father. He wrapped her in a hug and they stood like that for a long time. 'I'm sorry,' Sophia said.

'Ssshhh,' Ferdie soothed and Gina noticed his cheeks were wet too. 'There is nothing to be sorry for. It is me who should be apologising to you.'

Sophia shook her head. 'No. You were right and it took the shock of our argument to make me see that.'

'It is all water under the bridge now, *mia bella*,' Ferdie replied. He drew back a little and smiled sadly. 'Thank you for coming.'

Gina's father put an arm around her shoulders. 'Finally,' he said, with a rueful smile of his own. 'It's only taken them sixteen years to get over themselves.'

She sighed, gazing at Nonna unmoving on the bed. 'It's a shame it took something so serious to make it happen.'

Sophia turned her attention to her mother. 'Has there been any improvement?'

'Not much,' Ferdie admitted, stifling a yawn. 'They say the fever is under control and her oxygen levels are better but she hasn't woken up yet.'

'*Ciao, Mamma,*' Sophia said, taking her mother's hand. 'I'm here.'

Gina held her breath as they all stared at Elena's face. If this was a movie, Nonna would open her eyes and everyone would know things were going to be okay. But this was real life. Elena didn't move.

Glancing up at her father, Sophia managed the ghost of a smile. 'You must be exhausted, Papà. Why don't you get some rest? We'll look after Mamma.'

'No, no. I am fine.'

There was more than a hint of determination about Ferdie's expression and Gina could sense an argument on the horizon. 'Nonno, listen to her,' she said gently. 'There's no point in making yourself sick too. What would Nonna have to say about that?'

'I would tell him to stop being such a foolish old goat,' a weak, croaky voice said from the bed.

Four heads whipped around as one. 'Nonna!' Gina exclaimed, her heart leaping with joy.

'Mamma!' Sophia said, at exactly the same moment.

Elena's lips twisted into a faint smile, although her eyes remained shut. 'I must be dreaming. It can't really be Sophia's voice I hear, can it?'

Hurriedly, Sophia sat in the chair and pulled it close to the bed. 'It is me,' she said, gripping her mother's hand. 'I'm here.'

Elena's eyes flickered. She peered at her daughter in wonder. 'So you are.' Her gaze wandered blearily around the room, taking in the machines and drips beside her, Paul and Gina next to the door, and coming to rest last of all on Ferdie. 'And has anyone knocked some sense into you yet or do I have to get off my sick bed to do it?'

Ferdie placed a hand on Sophia's shoulder and squeezed. 'No need for that. We both seem to have grown up since we last met.'

'Good,' Elena said, her eyes drifting shut once more. 'That's . . . good . . .'

The sound of gentle snoring filled the room. 'She's sleeping,' Sophia said, smiling. 'We should probably tell the nurses that she woke up.'

'I'll go,' Gina volunteered.

'And I'll come too,' her father said. He stretched his neck and sighed. 'I don't know about anyone else but I could really do with a caffeine hit. Is there anywhere good for coffee around here?'

'Unlikely,' Gina said cheerfully, linking her arm through his. 'Not with Nonna out of action, anyway. But why don't we go and see what we can find?'

'Of course,' Ben said into his phone, gazing up at the rounded ceiling of his living room with a look of pure frustration. 'No, I completely understand. Thanks for your time.'

Gina watched him from her chair at the small table at the other end of the long narrow carriage, observing his defeated expression as he ended the call. 'That sounded disappointing.'

He slumped back against the sofa. 'For what it's worth, they said it was a close run thing.' He sighed, and tossed his phone onto the cushion beside him. 'That's it. I'm all out of options. I can't think of anyone else who might be in a position to invest in the Palace.'

It was Tuesday afternoon, three days after Nonna's collapse, and Gina had finally felt as though she had the headspace to think about something other than her grandmother's health. Unfortunately, the outlook for the Palace was bleak.

'I'm waiting to hear from a few people in the City,' she told him. 'But none of the investors I hoped for have bitten. It's almost as though they've been warned off.'

Ben threw her a searching glance. 'Is that likely?'

'It wouldn't surprise me,' Gina admitted. 'My ex-boyfriend can be very single-minded when it comes to getting what he wants.'

'Can you chase anyone up?' Ben asked. 'Gorran says Max is really piling on the pressure. I think he's close to breaking point.'

Gina picked up her mobile. 'I can try.'

The station doorbell chimed, causing both of them to look up.

'Expecting anyone?' Gina asked.

'No,' Ben replied, getting to his feet. 'I suppose I'd better go and see who it is.'

He vanished through the door and Gina heard him crunching across the gravel to Platform 1 of Polwhipple station. His home sat in a railway siding, out of the way, and for the first time, Gina thought to wonder what would happen to it when the station opened for business. The converted carriage wasn't in the way and was clearly marked as off-limits but she wasn't sure Ben would enjoy being surrounded by people after being used to such peace and quiet.

A few minutes later, he was back, wearing a thunderous expression.

'What?' Gina asked, as he stepped from the tiny metal staircase and into the room.

He didn't answer, merely moved aside to reveal Valeria Arundell.

'Oh,' Gina said, a dull flame of fury igniting in the pit of her stomach. 'It's you. If you've come to say I told you so then the door is behind you.'

Valeria pursed her lips. 'There's no need to be rude. I come in peace.'

Gina let out an unladylike snort. 'Of course you do. You were opposed to giving us funding to refurbish the Palace all along. And now I suppose you've come to gloat, haven't you?'

'You will no doubt find this hard to comprehend, Miss Callaway, but I haven't,' Valeria said. 'In actual fact, I've come to offer you a lifeline.'

'What kind of lifeline?' Ben asked, his forehead wrinkling in deep suspicion.

She crossed the room and perched on the edge of the sofa. 'A one-hundred-and-fifty-thousand-pounds lifeline. Exactly the amount that you need to stave off Max Hardy's bid to buy the Palace.'

Gina almost fell off her chair. 'You can't be serious,' she said, gripping the table for support. 'Why would you even consider doing that? In case you're not aware, it's your daughter who encouraged Max to launch his bid in the first place.'

Valeria fired a haughty look Gina's way. 'I'm perfectly aware of what Rose has been up to,' she said. 'And believe me, there will be consequences for her behaviour. As I'm sure you are aware, my family has links with Polwhipple that go back centuries, but it may surprise you to know that I feel that connection to the town very strongly.'

Ben muttered under his breath and Valeria turned sharply towards him. 'I mean it. Polwhipple is my home and it holds a special place in my heart. That's why I serve on the town council and do my best to ensure that everything we do has the community's best interest firmly at its centre.' She took a deep breath. 'The Palace is an integral part of Polwhipple history and I will not stand by and let it be carved up into vulgar apartments that nobody from the town can afford so that some jumped-up little *businessman* can make a fast profit.'

Gina blinked; the other woman's normally frozen face was alive with passion. 'So what are you suggesting?' she asked Valeria slowly.

'You're looking for a sleeping partner, am I right? Someone who will invest in the business but not interfere with the day-to-day running of the cinema.'

Both Ben and Gina nodded.

'Very well, then,' Valeria said. 'I am prepared to be that partner, on the strict understanding that the Palace continues to operate as a cinema that serves the local community as it has done these past few months. The building may not be sold or modified without my permission and, should the business fail, I will have first option on buying it outright. Is that clear?'

Ban ran a hand across his golden stubble. 'Let me get this straight – you're offering to bail us out with £150k, and all you want in return is for things to carry on the way they are?'

'Essentially, yes.'

'But why?' Gina burst out. 'You looked at us as though we were a bad smell when we put forward our funding application.'

Valeria inclined her head. 'I admit that I had my doubts at first. But now that I've seen what you've done with the money, I am of the opinion that the council's faith in you was justified.' A faint smile pulled at her mouth. 'You've done a good job, Miss Callaway. You too, Mr Pascoe.'

Gina sat back in her seat, staring at Ben in disbelief. 'I think under the circumstances, you'd better start using our first names.'

The older woman got to her feet. 'As you wish. Does this mean we have a deal?'

Gina gazed at Ben and she saw her own confusion mirrored on his face. It was like encountering a cobra and expecting to be bitten, only to have it lick you instead. 'What choice do we have?' she said, simply, and he nodded. 'Okay, Valeria, you've got yourself a deal.'

A look of satisfaction crossed Valeria's face. 'Excellent. I'll have my lawyers draw up the paperwork immediately. They can respond to Mr Hardy's bid, too, if you'd like to make sure he gets the message?'

Gina almost laughed; she'd love to be a fly on the wall when Max received that particular communication. 'That would be very helpful, thanks.'

'And of course you will want your own lawyers to go through our agreement before you sign – to whom should I have the papers sent?'

Ben cleared his throat. 'I'm not sure we –'

'I hear Coleman and Cohen in Truro are good,' Valeria suggested. 'But of course it is up to you.'

'We'll let you know,' Gina said. 'Thanks for this, Valeria. You don't know how much it means.'

'Actually, I rather think I do,' the other woman said. 'I was also young once, you know, and I spent many a happy afternoon watching films at the Palace. I had my first kiss with my late husband there too.'

Gina didn't dare glance over at Ben. 'I suppose the old girl has looked after us all at one point or another.'

'Yes, I suppose it has,' Valeria said. 'Thank you both for your time. I am very much looking forward to being in business with you.'

She shook each of them by the hand and moved towards the door. As Ben opened it, she paused and glanced back at

Gina. 'There is one more thing, Miss Callaway, and I'm sorry if this causes a problem, but my offer is dependent on you continuing to work at the Palace.'

Gina gasped. 'What?'

'You'll be paid a handsome salary, of course, in recognition of your particular talents and it won't preclude you from also working for your grandfather's ice-cream business. I rather imagine the two of them will go hand in hand, actually.' She fixed Gina with a piercing stare. 'Is that going to be a problem?'

Gina waited for the shockwave that had just hit her to pass before she replied. 'No,' she said in a faint voice she hardly recognised as her own. 'That won't be a problem at all.'

'Good,' the older woman said and she swept out of the door. 'Then I'll be in touch again very soon. Good day.'

Ben said nothing as he closed the door.

'Did that really just happen?' Gina said, after a few seconds of stunned silence.

'I think so,' Ben said. 'Unless we're both having the same weird hallucination.'

'Unlikely,' Gina said. She gave an incredulous laugh. 'I think it did happen – the Palace is saved! And I'm staying in Polwhipple!'

'Yeah,' Ben said. 'Amazing.'

She felt her smile start to slip at the lack of enthusiasm in his voice. 'What – don't you trust her?'

He shook his head. 'No, it's not that. It's just – ah, nothing. Forget it.'

'Ben?' Gina said, crossing the room to stand in front of him. 'What is it?'

'It doesn't matter, in the general scheme of things,' he said, shrugging. 'But I kind of assumed you'd be leaving Polwhipple at the end of this month. So I accepted that job in London.'

Gina felt her mouth drop open in dismay. 'Oh no!'

'Oh yes,' he said with a grim little laugh. 'I start on the first of September.'

# Chapter Thirty-Nine

The day of the Polwhipple station opening ceremony dawned hot and clear.

'Can you believe this weather?' Gina asked Ben, shading her eyes as she peered along the platform to where the newly refurbished train track stretched into the distance towards Boscarne Junction. 'It couldn't be better.'

He smiled. 'I'm sure Valeria organised it. She's certainly determined enough.'

They'd both got to know the Palace's new business partner fairly well over the weeks since she'd appeared at Ben's door with an offer they couldn't refuse, mostly because Gorran was too terrified to speak to her. And they'd grown to like and respect her, although Gina felt that her definition of 'sleeping partner' didn't quite match the dictionary's. But on the whole, things were going well. Gorran no longer seemed to be spending all his nights drowning his sorrows at the

Mermaid's Tail, for a start, and Max had been banished with his tail firmly between his legs.

Gina glanced at the steam train that stood gently chuffing beside Platform 1, waiting for its first official journey. A cream and chocolate ribbon, in the colours of the Bodmin and Wenford Railway, stretched across the track; in just over an hour, Polwhipple's mayor would cut it and declare the station open. And the joint restoration project Gina and Ben had launched together would be complete.

'I suppose we ought to check everything over one last time,' she said, glancing around. 'People are going to start arriving soon.'

'You mean the public are going to start arriving soon,' he said, as an elderly man in a train guard's uniform appeared in the doorway that led to the ticket hall. 'The volunteers have been here for hours.'

All the stations along the Bodmin and Wenford Railway were staffed by volunteers. In fact, almost everything the Preservation Society undertook was run by volunteers and railway enthusiasts, from the maintenance of the engines and carriages to the Heritage Line café at Bodmin Parkway.

Gina tipped her head. 'Sorry – yes, I mean the public. The paying punters.'

They walked side by side, checking that the station looked exactly as it should. 'I feel like a proud parent, watching their baby take its first few steps,' Gina said, once they were both satisfied.

He gazed at her for a long moment. 'It's been fun, parenting with you.'

A small hard lump lodged itself in Gina's throat. 'Yes. But it's not like we'll never see each other again.' She waved a hand at the pristine station building. 'If I know you, you'll be back from London every weekend to make sure they're not wrecking all your hard work.'

Ben shifted his weight. 'About that—'

A shout rang out across the platform. 'Gina!'

She looked up and let out a squeal of delight when she saw Nonno and Nonna making their way towards them. 'Look at you,' she said, hurrying forwards to kiss them both. 'You're out of the house!'

Elena's recovery, while steady, had been slower than the medical staff had expected. Gina's parents had stayed to help out for as long as they could but they'd had to fly back to Los Angeles earlier that week, leaving Gina and Ferdie to manage her care. And since Ferdie had only just had his plaster cast removed, most of the hard work had fallen to Gina. She didn't mind, though; having Nonna at home after her illness was something she wasn't about to take for granted. Today was the first time Elena had left the house.

'Here,' Ben said, carrying over a chair. 'Why don't you have a seat? You won't miss a minute of the action here.'

'Don't make a fuss,' Elena grumbled but Gina thought she looked glad to sit down. The road to recovery was going to be long, making Gina even more grateful that her future lay in Polwhipple.

'And here's one for you, Ferdie,' Ben said, bringing another seat. 'If you give me half a minute, I'll grab a table and bring you out some coffee.'

It was such a thoughtful gesture, Gina thought, smiling at his retreating back. But that was Ben all over; she was going to miss him so much when he left.

The crowds started to arrive in earnest not long after Elena and Ferdie had appeared. Gina spotted Carrie and Davey, hand in hand, and nudged Ben. 'I'm so glad they made up.'

'Davey can get a bit too tied up with work,' Ben said. 'It's what cost him his last relationship. Luckily for him, Carrie is more forgiving than his ex. But I don't think it's a mistake he'll make again.'

Gina smiled. 'I hope not. I'm not just saying this because she's my friend but Carrie is one in a million. I want her to be happy.'

'Davey deserves a happy ever after too,' Ben said. 'With a bit of luck, they'll be happy together.'

It was a sentiment Gina entirely agreed with. Allowing her gaze to travel around, Gina saw Valeria chatting animatedly to Gorran, who looked a tiny bit intoxicated by her. Manda was nearby, too, with Tash and Jory and Bruno. Through the door that led to the platform, Gina was delighted to see that the ticket office was doing a brisk trade – demand for the inaugural journey along the new line was high. Everywhere she looked, she saw familiar smiling faces. The people of Polwhipple had turned out in force, as they should; the opening of this station would mean more visitors to the town and increased trade. There was no downside to it and Gina was proud to have played her part in making it happen.

Just before midday, the station guards ushered all those with tickets to take their seats in the carriages. Gina caught Ben's arm as he passed her, intent on reaching the engine. 'Good luck,' she said, grinning. 'Drive safely.'

He flashed her an answering grin and swung himself into the cab at the front of the engine with one of the other volunteers. At midday precisely, the mayor took his place at the front of the train, while anyone who wasn't travelling on the train assembled on the platform, waving chocolate and cream flags.

'This is a very momentous day,' Elena said, smiling at Gina. 'You and Ben should be delighted with what you have achieved.'

'We are, Nonna,' Gina said. 'Thank you.'

'I look forward to seeing what you achieve next,' Elena said, with a sly wink. 'You know, you would make beautiful children together.'

'Nonna!' Gina said, feeling her cheeks become suddenly roasting hot.

'What?' Her grandmother shrugged. 'If I was thirty years younger I'd go there myself.'

Ferdie lifted his bushy eyebrows. 'And if I was thirty years younger I might go there too. Ben made a very attractive woman, I thought.'

Gina was caught halfway between a cough and a laugh.

She took a gulp of water, glancing affectionately down at her grandparents. 'We're all going to be disappointed – Ben leaves for London at the start of September, remember?'

The mayor cleared his throat self-importantly. 'Ladies and gentlemen, boys and girls, it is my very great honour to be here today. This train line is more than just steel – it's a hand extended in friendship.'

Gina felt her own hand being tugged. She glanced down to see Nonna gripping her fingers. 'Tell him,' she whispered, loud enough that Gina could hear over the droning voice of the mayor. 'Tell Ben how you feel, before it's too late.'

Gina felt herself blush again. 'I don't know what you mean.'

'Don't give me that rubbish,' Elena growled. 'Any fool can see that you love him. Any fool except Ben, that is.'

'I can't,' Gina replied. 'He's going to live in London.'

'So?' her grandmother demanded. 'Haven't you ever heard of long-distance relationships? Tell him today, while you both bask in the glory of what you have achieved here, or you never will.'

Gina glanced over the heads of the crowd towards the engine and gnawed at her lip. Should she tell Ben how she felt? Or was it too late?

'Do it,' Elena urged. 'Don't wait for the perfect moment; it will never come. Do it *now*.'

The last word hit Gina like a jolt of electricity. She stepped forward and stared at the window of the cab. Ben stood silhouetted there, gazing down at the train controls, ready to go.

She pushed her way past the onlookers, silently urging Ben to look her way. He didn't.

At the front of the engine, the mayor raised the scissors he'd been given to do the job. 'And so, without further ado, I now declare Polwhipple station open!'

The cut ribbon fluttered to the ground and the train whistle shrieked. Steam burst from the chimney.

'Ben!' Gina shouted, waving her arms in the direction of the cab. 'Ben!'

The crowd in front of her parted and she ran along the platform, just as the train started to move. 'Ben!'

He stuck his head out of the window. 'Gina! What's wrong?'

'Nothing,' she called, panting a little. 'It's just – I wanted to tell you that I love you.'

Frowning, Ben cupped a hand to his ear. 'What?'

Gina took a deep breath and swallowed what was left of her pride. 'I love you!' she shouted, as loud as she could. 'I love you!'

The train started to pick up speed. Gina watched anxiously as Ben's head ducked back inside. A second later he reappeared, jumping lightly from the moving train to land on the platform. He walked towards Gina, his eyes never leaving her face. 'Say that again.'

She glanced past him at the departing train. 'But—'

'Never mind that,' he said, stopping in front of her. Steam billowed around them. 'Tell me again what you just said.'

Now that he was standing right in front of her, Gina felt

her nerve slipping away. She glanced at Elena, who nodded. Gina took a deep breath. 'I love you. I think I've always loved you, even back when we were kids. And it's okay if you don't love me because—'

And then his lips were on hers and nothing else mattered. It should have been a passionate kiss, Gina thought afterwards, the kind that stripped the breath from her lungs and left both participants bruised but exhilarated, but it wasn't. It was gentle and passionate and full of love. And it seemed to go on for a very long time.

When they finally broke apart, it was only the tiniest distance so that Ben could gaze deep into her eyes. 'You have no idea how long I have been waiting for you to say that.'

She smiled up at him. 'About sixteen years?'

He shook his head. 'No, around eighteen. Because I think I fell in love with you the first moment I saw you, queuing up at your grandfather's ice-cream stand. And I was only thirteen, too young to know what it was I felt, but it never left me. You never left me, even when your parents took you away and I had no idea where you'd gone.'

He kissed her again then and this time she felt all the yearning and longing he'd nurtured throughout the years that they'd known each other. This was what love was, she thought, sinking deeper into the kiss. Whatever happened next, she knew she could never love anyone the way she loved Ben.

The sound of applause and whooping reminded them that they were not alone. Embarrassed, they sprang apart, but

Gina could only see approval and friendliness on the faces around them. 'About bloody time!' Carrie called and everyone laughed.

'I know you're going away,' Gina said, glancing up at Ben. 'But we'll find a way to make it work.'

He shook his head, ruefully. 'Except that I'm not. I've been trying to tell you, I rang my new boss and told them something had come up, that I couldn't take the job.' He wrapped his arms around her. 'I'm staying right here in Polwhipple, with you.'

It was too much for Gina; tears of happiness began to spill down her cheeks.

'You're crying,' he said in alarm, reaching into his pocket and pulling out a white handkerchief. 'Have I said the wrong thing?'

'No,' she replied, smiling at him through her tears. 'You said exactly the right thing. I've just got a little something in my eye, that's all.'

Acknowledgements

My everlasting thanks to Jo Williamson, of Antony Harwood Ltd, for keeping me going and propping me up. Enormous teary hugs to superstars Emma Capron, SJ Virtue and everyone at Simon & Schuster UK – the journey was bumpy but we got there in the end: THANK YOU. Cocktails are on the house for Kate Harrison, Miranda Dickinson, Rowan Coleman, Julie Cohen and Cally Taylor – you're my life support system. Thanks to lovely author, Lisa Glass, for sharing her surfing expertise. So much love to T and E – thanks for being amazing every single day. And lastly, thank you to all the fabulous readers, reviewers and cheerleaders who've visited The Picture House by the Sea – your continuing support and enthusiasm is so appreciated. Of all the books in all the world, I'm glad you walked into mine.

# Coming Home to Brightwater Bay

****The BRAND NEW series from Holly Hepburn****

Merina Wilde has it all: a successful writing career, a perfect carousel of parties to keep her social life buzzing, and a childhood sweetheart who thinks she's a goddess. But Merry has a secret: she can no longer summon up the sparkle that makes her stories shine. And as her deadline whooshes by, her personal life falls apart too, and Merry finds herself single for the first time since – well, ever.

Desperate to get her life back on track, Merry escapes to the windswept Orkney Islands, locking herself away in a secluded clifftop cottage. But can the beauty of the islands and the kindness of strangers help Merry to fool herself into believing in love again, if only long enough to finish her book? Or is it time for her to give up the career she's always adored and find something new to set her soul alight?

COMING JANUARY 2021.
AVAILABLE NOW TO PRE-ORDER.

**Can't wait for the paperback? Parts one to four are available in ebook now:**

*BROKEN HEARTS AT BRIGHTWATER BAY*
*SEA BREEZES AT BRIGHTWATER BAY*
*DANGEROUS TIDES AT BRIGHTWATER BAY*
*SUNSET OVER BRIGHTWATER BAY*

SIMON & SCHUSTER